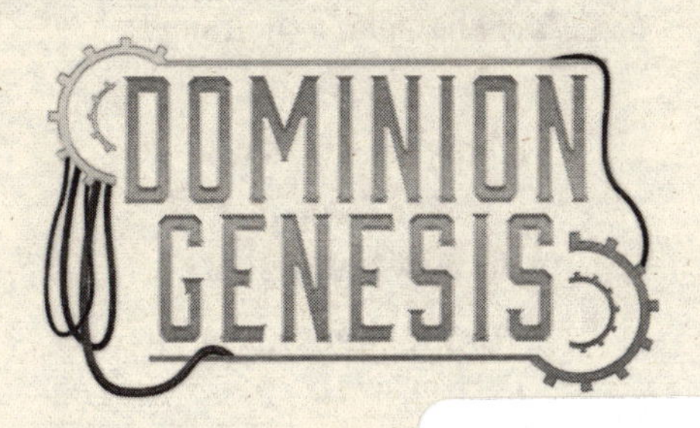
DOMINION
GENESIS

T0408660

More great Warhammer 40,000 fiction from Black Library

BELISARIUS CAWL: THE GREAT WORK
A novel by Guy Haley

FORGES OF MARS
An anthology by Graham McNeill
(Contains the novels *Priests of Mars, Lords of Mars* and *Gods of Mars*, plus a short story)

GENEFATHER
A novel by Guy Haley

LEVIATHAN
A novel by Darius Hinks

• DARK IMPERIUM •
by Guy Haley

Book 1: DARK IMPERIUM
Book 2: PLAGUE WAR
Book 3: GODBLIGHT

• DAWN OF FIRE •
Book 1: AVENGING SON
by Guy Haley

Book 2: THE GATE OF BONES
by Andy Clark

Book 3: THE WOLFTIME
by Gav Thorpe

Book 4: THRONE OF LIGHT
by Guy Haley

Book 5: THE IRON KINGDOM
by Nick Kyme

Book 6: THE MARTYR'S TOMB
by Marc Collins

Book 7: SEA OF SOULS
by Chris Wraight

Book 8: HAND OF ABADDON
by Nick Kyme

Book 9: THE SILENT KING
by Guy Haley

WARHAMMER 40,000

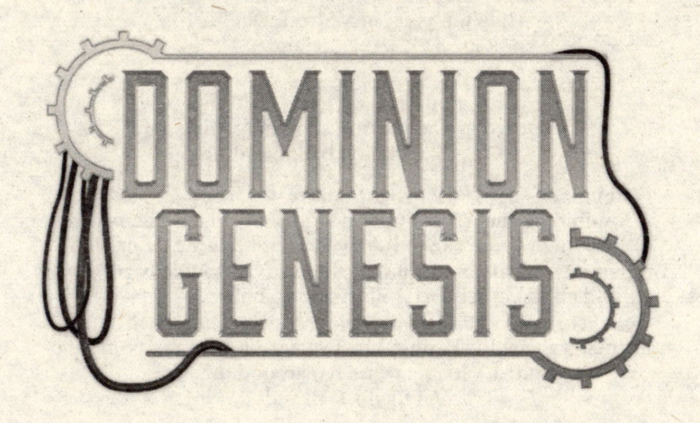

JONATHAN D BEER

A BLACK LIBRARY PUBLICATION

First published in 2024.
This edition published in Great Britain in 2025 by
Black Library, Games Workshop Ltd., Willow Road,
Nottingham, NG7 2WS, UK.

Represented by: Games Workshop Limited – Irish branch,
Unit 3, Lower Liffey Street, Dublin 1,
D01 K199, Ireland.

10 9 8 7 6 5 4 3 2 1

Produced by Games Workshop in Nottingham.
Cover illustration by Jodie Muir.

A CIP record for this book is available from the British Library.

ISBN 13: 978-1-83609-149-3

Printed and bound in the UK.

For Will, for getting me to the starting line,
and Paul, for dragging me across the finish.

For more than a hundred centuries the Emperor has sat immobile on the Golden Throne of Earth. He is the Master of Mankind. By the might of his inexhaustible armies a million worlds stand against the dark.

Yet, he is a rotting carcass, the Carrion Lord of the Imperium held in life by marvels from the Dark Age of Technology and the thousand souls sacrificed each day so his may continue to burn.

To be a man in such times is to be one amongst untold billions. It is to live in the cruelest and most bloody regime imaginable. It is to suffer an eternity of carnage and slaughter. It is to have cries of anguish and sorrow drowned by the thirsting laughter of dark gods.

This is a dark and terrible era where you will find little comfort or hope. Forget the power of technology and science. Forget the promise of progress and advancement. Forget any notion of common humanity or compassion.

There is no peace amongst the stars, for in the grim darkness of the far future, there is only war.

GRYPHONNE IV

ONE

I am not wholly human.

If I were, I would be equipped to express the emotion – cruel, logic-corrupting emotion – that pours from what is left of my amygdalae as my ship bursts from the empyrean's grasp, and I behold the apocalypse that bears down upon my home.

Tears might spring from lacrimal glands, but they, along with the rest of my organic eyes, were excised on the thirty-eighth anniversary of my induction into the Most Holy Cult Mechanicus.

Anguished cries might erupt from my lips, had my skull not been artfully reshaped in steel and bronze. My lips are immobile, subtly sculpted to permit the function of the vox-grille that has replaced my teeth.

I could tear my hair, or rend my clothes. But my scalp bears a dense weave of monofilament mechadendrites that permit coupling with my ship, and my robe is marked with the griffon-and-cog of my home world. Even in the depths of despair, I will not damage my connection to the Peregrinus*, nor besmirch the icon of my forge and home.*

I am not denied an outlet for my anguish solely by the incompatibility of my physical form. My rank requires that I prevent any trace of the torment that dominates my thoughts from spilling into the communion, the noospheric connection I share with my crew. I am Talin Sherax, ductrix and explorator superior of the Peregrinus. *It falls to me to set an example for my adjutants, my acolytes and thralls.*

There have been few times over the course of my long life when I have wished to be free of the gifts of the Omnissiah, unburdened by the demands of rank, that I might indulge the remnants of my humanity and give voice to the heartbreak that grips my animus.

But seeing a tide of xenos horrors approaching my home world, I dearly wish for it now.

TWO

<The home world!>

<Omnissiah be with us in the hour of our need.>

<Attempting spatial reckoning – Error – Error – Aggregated hostile entities defy spatial reckoning!>

<Cease.>

I allow the more expressive members of my command crew two point six seconds of impeded efficiency before my order cuts across the communion. In testament to their adherence to doctrine, the blurts of panicked binharic vanish instantly. The noosphere is still polluted by snippets of unfiltered emotion-signifiers, wafting around their bearers like noxious emissions, but I can forgive these lapses. They are witnessing a crisis without equal in the annals of their home.

<All stations, report readiness condition.>

The command is redundant. My cranial dendrites permit an interface with the Peregrinus' *machine spirit comparable to that of a* Collegia Titanica *princeps; I know my ship as I know my physical form. But the order gives my subordinates an action upon which*

to focus their attentions. The communion calms as each officer and adept attends to their function and that of their thralls, diverting their awareness from the atrocity unfolding across the planet of their birth.

There is no such respite for me. There cannot be. I am forced to stare, through every one of my ship's many eyes, at the apocalypse that bears down upon the fourth planet of the Gryphonne System.

Tyranid bio-ships, living organisms adapted to endure the rigours of the void, crowd the orbital space around the rust-red world. Millions of creatures, billions of tons of claws and tentacles and malignant, alien flesh, form a vast fist poised to crash down into the planet's gravity well, drawn like locusts to the mass of humanity that labours across the world's surface.

The same panicked awe that grips my crew churns within me. The scale of the hive fleet defies attempts at computation. Thermal scans show only a great smear of colour thousands of miles across, close-packed bodies bleeding heat into the void. Optical imaging displays a concentration of creatures so dense they occlude the light of the stars that lie beyond them. The light of a galaxy ravaged by ceaseless war, and now blighted by a tireless, hungering leviathan.

<Friend/foe interrogative received from the forge-cradle, ductrix,> Kalida Isocrates, the Peregrinus' magistrix of transmission, sends from her casket. The silver-chased shell that holds Isocrates' mortal form is suspended twenty yards above the epicentre of the deck, a host of input-output cables connecting her to the ship's vox-arrays. The magistrix is one of several members of my command cadre who are semi-permanently installed within their posts, sacrificing independence of motion for a deeper connection with the machine and their role aboard the ship.

<Response authorised.> I cling to the lifeline of protocol, an anchor against the twin buffets of calamitous data and unfamiliar emotions. <Has the Kurzgesagt completed translation?>

<Nothing yet, explorator superior.> Krishnan-Psi, my magister of augury, is at their station beside the primary sensoria displays, coiled spine moving sinuously as they pore over data-feeds.

I open my awareness to the host of signifier codes that present themselves for the Peregrinus' attention. Hundreds of vessels, each emblazoned with the ident-flag of their home, crowd Gryphonne IV's orbit. The sight and sensation of so many ships brings a small measure of calm to my animus. I draw strength from the gathered might of my people.

The forge world is prepared for the storm that falls upon it.

The precursor signs of tyranid invasion had been identified months before this day – primarily geological instability caused by the xenos' strange form of interstellar travel, which drew upon the gravity of the Gryphonne star itself to pull them towards their goal. More subtle, but no less disruptive, were the waves of sabotage, assassination, and ambush that erupted within every forge-city and population centre. Reports reached the Peregrinus telling of genomic perversion among the serf class and running battles with xenos-worshipping sects that had burst from their slums. The forge world was gripped by war before the first bio-ship caught sight of the Gryphonne star.

These signs were heeded. The strength of Gryphonne IV's arms is famed across the length and breadth of humanity's realm, and the dominars of the forge-synod have not been idle in preparing its defences. The call went out to the forge world's allies and vassals, to its tributary worlds and its far-flung fleets. It is that call that has brought the Peregrinus back, racing through the immaterium's tides so its crew can stand with their home in its hour of need.

The vagaries of the empyrean have caused the Peregrinus to be the first vessel of our flotilla to force apart reality's membrane and translate back to the true void. It was a harsh and difficult passage, most acutely for Zubin Kian, the ship's Navigator. For the past seventy-one hours, the abhuman has filled the vox-link connecting his armoured *chamber with the command deck with low moans and whispered prayers, begging humanity's God-Emperor for respite from his task.*

His has been a battle I comprehend, but do not truly understand. Over the previous two and a half centuries, the archives of the Adeptus Mechanicus have become replete with studies documenting the stages of tyranid predation, recorded by doomed magi who learnt even as the worlds around them were devoured. All analyses report a disruptive influence in the warp, whose effect on individuals with a connection to the empyrean is debilitating, to say the least. Reports that I have inloaded speak of astropaths breaking their skulls against bulkheads in order to silence the sibilant chittering that fills their minds, and blinded Navigators who drive their ships onto the warp's treacherous tides.

That Kian's outbursts have been restricted to impassioned pleas to the Omnissiah is a testament to his resilience, not his weakness.

The shudder of the Peregrinus*' void engines lighting travels through its superstructure, demanding my attention. My vessel has just completed translation from the empyrean, and while the disconcerting spectacle of the xenos host drags at my focus, duty requires more of me than a self-indulgent fear response.*

I expurgate my active cognition of unrequired inputs, and plunge my mind into the ship's data stream. The Peregrinus *responds immediately, its machine spirit and my animus conjoining in holy synthesis.*

Immediately, my psyche is struck by a gale of unfamiliar sensations. I momentarily struggle against the current, overwhelmed by all that the Peregrinus *perceives from second to second. My cardiovascular pump lurches towards hypertension, matching the racing tempo of the ship's reactor-heart.*

It takes me a moment to grasp the problem. My vessel is afraid.

The fears of its crew – and its ductrix – are bleeding into the Peregrinus*' soul, conveyed by every panicked runeboard strike, unguarded vox-burst, and elevated heart rate. Every fearful action is absorbed*

and aggregated by the millions of sensory inputs around and within my ship, infecting its animus with thoughts of ruin and loss.

I was appointed to the command of the explorator ship Peregrinus *twenty-seven Martian years ago. Though a brief period in the lifespan of a void-going vessel, in that time I have learnt much about my ship's nature, and my own.*

The human cerebrum's instinctual response to overstimulation is to withdraw, to curl back on itself in self-preservation. I master that impulse, routing my cognition through formidable logic-baffles of my own design that conquer my cerebellum's fearful reaction. Instead, I diffuse my essence through the tempest of sensation and information, the storm of data rendered as clusters of binharic and other, more esoteric code. I make myself a filter, rather than a dam. With deft commands I compartmentalise the Peregrinus' *sensory feeds, isolating those that are impeding efficiency, diverting the ship's mighty cognition towards familiar actions and processes. I skim the data stream, drawing out what insights I require, shaping the ship's demands and urges to my design.*

Such an approach is not without risk – more belligerent machine spirits require domination, rather than partnership. But my trust in my vessel is absolute.

Krishnan-Psi's sending rises from the rushing river of data. <Ductrix, empyric emanations detected.>

I shift my focus to the readings of the primary auspex array in time to watch, through the comforting abstraction of hexamantic code, a tear begin to form in the skin of reality.

The remaining ships of the explorator flotilla break free of the immaterium's grip minutes after the Peregrinus, *having retained remarkable cohesion in spite of the shadow in the warp. I speak a brief catechism of thanks as each vessel emerges. Cloying streamers of ectoplasmic residue cling to their hulls, as though the empyrean itself is attempting to claw them back into its embrace. Such sentience* is an impossibility, but I nevertheless feel a shiver of relief through the organic portions of my brain as the wounds from which my companion vessels burst clench shut.

Protocol requires immediate vox-contact between each vessel of the flotilla following a warp translation, but as the seconds stretch on, nothing is forthcoming. No doubt the same spasm of shock that impeded our functions is hindering theirs.

Finally, I feel an incoming vox-link, interpreted as a prickling against my cochlear augmetic.

<All vessels, report your condition.> The brief code-string betrays nothing of the sender's emotional condition, the order relayed in perfect, unclouded binharic. If Satavic Yuel, lord explorator and praefector of Explorator Fleet Rhi-Alpha-2, is affected by the vision of doom before him, he does not show it.

<Nominal, lord,> I return immediately, bypassing Kalida Isocrates and taking direct control of the Peregrinus' vox-array in my haste.

<Steady yourself, Talin. Trust in the Omnissiah.>

I pulse a clipped acknowledgement. Yuel's use of my familiar identifier is revealing; he is disturbed after all.

<Recall the challenges our world has overcome,> Yuel continues, now on an open frequency to every ductor and ductrix under his command. <The trials it has endured. This will be the latest chapter in our proud history.> The vox-link closes abruptly.

Yuel is right.

Yielding to an impulse that arises not from the authority precepts I inloaded upon my ascension to command of the Peregrinus, but from somewhere far more human, I open the ship-wide communications net.

'Servants of the Omnissiah, heed me.'

My words rasp from the vox-grille mouths of gargoyles and grotesques, hum from noospheric interlinks, and wink into being across jade-green consoles. They are transliterated into binharic, *lingua technis, skit-code, and the dozen other dialects used by the tech-priests, skitarii, and serfs aboard the* Peregrinus. *They will be recorded, naturally, by all who hear them, either in the grey matter of their memories or else the more robust implanted data cores of those honoured to possess them.*

'Xenos fall upon our home. The forge-cradle of us all. It is possible, in this moment, that you experience doubt, even dread. Be on guard, for these concerns are unfounded. A corruption of your duty and purpose.

'Gryphonne IV must not fall. Our foundries have burned for ten thousand years and more. We are the redoubt, the bastion of the Deus Mechanicus. While we endure, the Omnissiah endures. Our quest for knowledge, for the purity of comprehension, goes on.

'Gryphonne IV cannot fall. Our walls have stood against every threat to arise since the dark ages of myth and legend. The god-machines of the Legio Gryphonicus walk, against whom no foe can stand. The maniples of our skitarii are without peer, resolute and unyielding. The war-algorithms of Arch-Dominus Zane and the forge-synod are infallible, promising annihilation with the surety of mathematic precision.

'Gryphonne IV will not fall. The xenos will break against our birthworld, and afflict humanity's galaxy no more. We, the honoured defenders of the Most Holy Cult Mechanicus, will ensure their destruction.

'Praise to the Omnissiah. May He honour and guide our labours.'

I close the vox-net with a crisp crackle of static.

My words are met with silence, as is appropriate. Not for the Mechanicus the gross and raucous cheers of Imperial soldiery, nor the solemn oaths of moment of the Astartes. Expressions of emotion are symptoms of organic frailty, reminders of the distance each acolyte of the Cult Mechanicus stands from the purity of the Machine God. They are to be comprehended, even tolerated when necessary, but resisted at all times.

I remain as I was when my vessel first crashed from the immaterium's embrace, rigid in my command throne, augmetic eyes locked on the forward viewportal.

<Prime weapons arrays. Begin sequential testing of void shield emitters. Bring secondary and tertiary generatoria online.>

I release my orders into the communion with my bridge officers, speaking as much with the ship itself as with its crew. Both respond immediately, the Peregrinus' *eager machine spirit reacting to the streams of subsidiary commands from my officers and to its ductrix's bellicose humour.*

<Void engines to maximum output. Take us home.>

THREE

Mechanicus vessels are not built to run, to charge headlong through the void with solar winds sheeting from their flanks. And yet the nine ships of Explorator Fleet Rhi-Alpha-2 race in-system, the Peregrinus *at the fore, its engines burning at the threshold of their tolerance. It is the will of every soul on board, the will of the ship itself. The* Peregrinus' *machine spirit remembers well the long decades of its construction in the crowded void-yards above Gryphonne IV. It beholds the threat to its birth-world, feels the fears that bleed from its tens of thousands of crew-worshippers, and stokes its reactors to an inferno's blaze.*

We have been in flight for ninety-six hours when I finally relent, and allow the insistent pleas from the ship's enginarium to penetrate my focus.

<Ductrix, I implore you. The primary magnetic containment couplings are showing signs of severe degradation. To maintain this pace risks permanent injury to the ship's motive function.>

Haphos Akoni, the Peregrinus' *magister of locomotion, is not given*

to exaggeration. What is more, I know the truth of his warning; within the furnace of the ship's reactor-heart there is the sharp, insistent pain of material deterioration. The Peregrinus *is a beautifully swift vessel, but it is unused to the demands of such reckless haste.*

<The ship will endure, magister.>

I am not deaf to Akoni's concerns, nor am I indifferent to damage to my vessel. But before me lies a vision of encroaching destruction, and I strive to reach it with every fibre of my being.

First, the forge world's orbital defences fall silent. Some are literally swallowed by the largest of the tyranid bio-ships. The colossal web of void-yards, whose wharfs have sent forth vessels to ply the void for ten millennia, is rendered into scrap by devouring maws and crushing claws, its fragments overrun by broods of gaunt-genus beasts.

The seething mass of the leviathan consumes the Dioscuri, Gryphonne IV's twin fortress-moons, on the third day of the invasion. The two orbs emerge barren, entirely swept clean of life. The scars of radiological detonations are carved across the surface of Dioscuri-Alpha, and hundreds of bio-ship corpses tumble in the planetoid's wake.

Few static defences remain above Gryphonne IV, but the void-war is far from abandoned. Absent any action I can take to influence events, I drink in every data packet and missive, devoting much of my active cognition to tracking the evolution of the battlesphere.

The space around the forge world is swamped with the electric blaze of weapons discharge, the constant churn of exotic energies and bio-plasma. Void shields stutter, chitinous armour shatters. Skeletons of both metal and bone break under the strain of the violence that dances around them.

At the centre of the Gryphonnen armada is the Logos, *the venerated Ark Mechanicus of Arch-Dominus Zane, encircled by its guardian battlefleet. The* Logos *is the headland, the breaker upon which the tyranids founder. Death streams from its flanks, arcane weaponry*

eviscerating whichever creature comes within their reach. No hive ship can approach the embodiment of Mechanicus dominion and live. An Ark Mechanicus is a forge world in miniature, suspended in space, armed and armoured accordingly. Gravitation, electromagnetism, the flow of time itself – the Logos harnesses the fundamental interactions of the physical universe and turns them into weapons.

But for all its might, the Ark Mechanicus and its lesser brethren cannot be everywhere. The Gryphonnen armada is like a weir on a river. The xenos tide simply flows over and around it.

Thousands of bio-ships hang in the planet's thermosphere. They spill forth millions of spores, each the size of a macrocannon shell, to rain down upon my home world. Within each fleshy capsule, charred black by the heat of atmospheric entry and shedding thick plates of ablative chitin, are xenos creatures of such varied physiology they defy taxonomic classification. Things with taloned forelimbs and razor teeth. Toxic bile and acidic ejecta. Hammer claws and parasitic sub-organisms.

When a spore strikes the bitter earth of Gryphonne IV, its occupants burst free from their confines, each a single voracious organism among tens of millions, whose only desire – whose only reason for existing – is the eradication and ingestion of all life upon the planet.

No, that is incorrect. Desire implies intelligence, the capacity for reason and decision-making. My expertise does not lie within the biologis arena, but all accepted doctrine agrees that the tyranid is not, by any scale employed by the Adeptus Mechanicus, sentient. It is driven by impulse, not intellect.

It is true that battlefield observations – and the few dangerously unsanctioned experiments conducted on captured beasts – make it clear that there is a hierarchy within the species. The psykana of the extragalactic predators is little understood, but the dominance-connection between certain rarer strains and the more common brood variants is well documented. The tactical value of this insight is obvious, and all Mechanicus battle codices identify these synaptic node-creatures for high-priority elimination.

I try to lose myself in these reflections, going so far as to access the Peregrinus' *archive manifolds and inload additional reports on tyranid physiology, swarm tactics, and biomechanical function. But each report only increases the frequency of superfluous code-spikes that interrupt my thought patterns. Distraction should be an impossibility for me, but my attention continually drifts to the* Peregrinus' *auspex feeds, and the violet tendrils that spread their grasp around my home.*

When we cross the orbit of Gryphonne V, the flotilla begins to slow. We rein in our breakneck flight to ensure that we will enter the orbit of our home in good order, able to manoeuvre to whatever element of the battlesphere the dominars of the forge-synod order us.

I wait with mounting impatience for that order to arrive. As the red orb of Gryphonne IV grows larger and more occluded by xenos bodies, the absence of commandments from the forge world's ruling council is a source of disquiet among the explorator fleet.

Other news reaches us, passed on from contingents of Mechanicus warships who have arrived from other points. The eight systems of the Gryphonnen Octad are similarly assailed by splinters of the greater host. The Octad are the forge world's closest stellar neighbours, tributary worlds by ancient treaty. Stripped of defenders to bolster their capital, the Octad are dying swiftly. Even if Gryphonne IV survives – I am unsure when the treachery of that variable first entered my thoughts – the forge world's power will be forever diminished.

Finally, with the fleet less than a day from entering the grip of the planet's gravity well, a tight-beam signal is received by the Kurzgesagt, *Lord Explorator Yuel's flagship.*

Long seconds pass while I wait for my lord and mentor to relay our instructions. Isocrates, suspended high within her cradle, is subjected to the full force of my attention, but this does nothing to hasten the news.

Finally, the vox-link blooms. <Vessels of Rhi-Alpha-2. Gryphonne IV has spoken, and we obey.>

Yuel's hesitation causes a fresh spike of concern to pierce my focus.

<It is the judgement of the synod that there is no viable scenario in which the xenos are defeated. Therefore, evacuation protocols have been enacted across all claves still answering the synod's communion. Our assigned task is to aid the exodus. Adjust your course to the enclosed heading, and ready all docking bays and flight decks for inbound traffic.>

Rationality deserts me. In the deepest recesses of my mind, something vital shatters.

<Repeat your last transmission, lord,> I say.

Yuel is merciless. <The defence has failed, Talin. Our world is lost.>

Impossibility steals me for several seconds. The lights of the command deck flicker as the Peregrinus *registers my distress, triggering power fluctuations and data-ghosts to race around the deck. Heads and sensing organs turn towards me as my anguish explodes across the communion, bypassing the layers of stoic reserve that are supposed to dampen such emotional exclamations.*

<What can we do?> The plea bursts from me.

Yuel's response is accompanied by a fragment of sharp-edged code, bitterness bleeding from his mind to mine.

<Prepare your decks for refugees.>

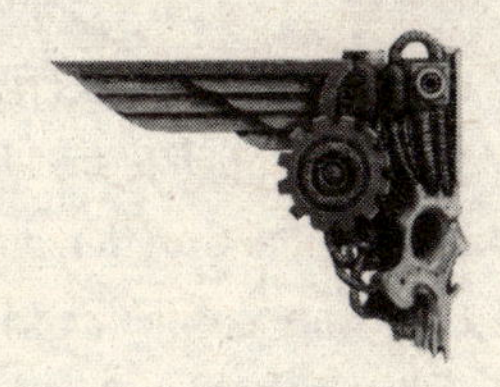

FOUR

The Peregrinus *is a tool for exploration. It was built to pursue the Quest for Knowledge, the most sacred duty of the Cult Mechanicus. Its sensor clusters have peered into the hearts of nebulae, and heard the song of quasars. Its hull has felt the heat of stars whose light would take a thousand mortal lifespans to reach Sacred Mars. It has carried genetors, technoarchaeologists, and datasmiths across the length and breadth of the galaxy for three millennia in pursuit of the lost knowledge of ages past.*

<Targeting solutions acquired, all arrays primed. We await your order, ductrix.>

The Peregrinus *is a ship of exploration and rediscovery. But Mars knows well the dangers that lie in the depths of the void, and so we also build our ships for war.*

<Fire.>

The void around the Peregrinus *erupts with prismatic shards of violence. Lances reave the closest bio-ships, carving thick slabs of chitinous armour from towering flanks. Macrocannons hurl shells*

the size of hab-blocks that punch through these fissures to detonate deep with alien flesh. Plasma batteries unleash the chained fury of star-fusion. Graviton pulsars shake the void with crushing thunder. Laser cannons whine with concentrated energy.

Two miles of iron and adamantine shake as the Peregrinus *speaks its rage with every weapon at its command.*

It is like spitting into an ocean. The tyranid craft-creatures are so tightly packed it is impossible to miss, but the undulating host of city-sized claws and tendrils and open, gaping maws seem to absorb every shot and blast. Organisms that mass in the millions of tons die by the moment, but for each swollen carapace burst open by Martian warcraft, a dozen more swim on through the void.

Most continue on their paths, drawn by whatever compulsion animates them, towards the billions of souls on the planet's surface. Others, the lesser beings that cling to the flanks of the gargantuan hive ships, peel away to strike back at their attackers.

Bio-plasma coughs from projecting limbs and maws, tumbling slowly through space to crash against the Peregrinus' *shields. Flocks of winged creatures spring from hooked perches, and globular spores are spat from grotesque, muscular cannons. They propel themselves through the void, seeking to choke my ship's guns with their bodies or burn through its sanctified iron with their corrosive innards. Behind them come swarms of fat-bellied worms, each pregnant with a host of the same spine-tipped monstrosities that are rampaging across the surface of my world.*

The Peregrinus' *point-defence turrets chatter, hundreds of macro-bolters expending thousands of shells that explode in a rippling curtain around its hull. Xenos die in droves, their screeches of inhuman agony lost in the vacuum. Those few that survive the firestorm fling themselves against the ship's hull, painting smears of bile across crimson steel and heavy armaglass.*

And then the flotilla is through.

The host of tyranids thins as the Peregrinus *and its peers fly beneath the greatest concentration, grazing the upper edges of Gryphonne IV's atmosphere. Hundreds of spores are flattened against her square-faced prow with every second. Their viscera scars the surface of its adamantine, but each mycetic cyst that bursts against the* Peregrinus *is one that will not add its cargo to the tidal wave of bodies that rampage across the red earth below.*

Unhindered by xenos bodies, I behold for the first time the true scale of the atrocity that unfolds across my home world.

The battle-front rages across the primary continent for hundreds of miles, visible by the devastated ground that lies in the wake of the tyranid advance. Reactor heat and vox-beacons denote the god-machines of the Legio Gryphonicus, walking where the tide is thickest, duelling with bent-backed xenos gargantuans. Whole macroclades of skitarii war in their shadows, holding back the press of brood-form bodies with ceaseless volleys of las, phosphor, and exotic particles. Packs of noble Knights bearing the loyal colours of House Cadmus hunt, lances and chainblades couched and dripping with gore. Machines of every possible configuration walk, roll, and fly through the spore-choked skies, the boundless genius of Gryphonnen tech-priests unchained by the demands of war.

And it is not enough. It is not nearly enough.

Titanic corpses stand where they died, iron monoliths to stalwart, futile resistance. Vast craters have been ripped in the earth by the Titans whose reactor-hearts have broken, annihilating any trace of the god-machines and their killers. Soldiers of the skitarii legions are robbed of the capacity for fear at the moment of their creation, and so they die atop ramparts that crack beneath the weight of the beasts overrunning them. Knights fall one by one, ursine masters of war laid low by packs of chitin-clawed killers that foul the machines with their dead.

Thousands of leagues of manufactoria and habitation units are already lost. Even as the Peregrinus reaches the perigee of its flight, a string of atomic detonations burst along the great ridge of Sevarista. The foundry-city's generatoria run wild, scourging ancient vaults and towering obelisks with unchained radiation and nuclear fire.

Sevarista holds a population of six hundred million souls. Its archives are respected throughout the sector for their assembled wisdom, its forges for their metallurgy. With the slow, relentless fury of atomic decay, all is rendered to ash.

The crew of the Peregrinus with the capacity to weep do so openly, saline or promethium distillate running over augmetic implants and grey-skinned cheeks alike. The communion between us is silent as a desert. Each stray emotion-signifier that bleeds from an adept is a soft whisper of code, lost in the howling desolation of our collective thoughts. Our outrage at the forge-synod's orders dies with the first auspex pass of the surface. Nothing can endure in the face of such boundless spite. Bastions of iron, cohorts of war robots, the greatest of the War Griffons' Battle-Titans. None of them can hold back the tide. All are overrun, pulled down by razored claws and hungering jaws.

I am immobile upon my throne, a passive witness to a billion tales of heroism as a world fights to save itself. It takes a concentrated effort to raise my consciousness from the vision of apocalypse and deliver my order.

<Flight decks, prepare to receive boarders.>

Out of the carnage comes every kind of craft capable of making orbit.

Inter-orbit lifters, cargo shuttles, Knightly drop-keeps, mass conveyors. The rarest are the coffin ships of the Legio Gryphonicus, bearing away the few precious Titans that can be extracted from the front line without risking its collapse. All light their engines and burn through the tortured sky, struggling through an atmosphere choked with the dust of dead cities.

The escaping craft are not burdened with bodies. The eight point five

billion labourers, serfs, and menials whose toil has fuelled the ceaseless output of a world are the least of the forge world's losses. Human life is the cheapest and most easily replenished of all the resources the Mechanicus requires, and thus is the first to be abandoned.

They flee with data. Precious data, the accumulated knowledge of an empire – the true legacy and source of Gryphonnen pride and strength. From the monumental – blueprints for battle tanks, instructions for feats of genomic manipulation, the most carefully guarded secrets of the Legio Gryphonicus – to the prosaic – minutes of conclave discussions, records of production quotas exceeded or missed, tithe and census data stretching back across the centuries. All that the forge world's magi have learnt across ten thousand years of labour is hurled into orbit, in the hope that it might survive beyond the planet's fall.

Every method of information storage known to the human species is present within the transports' holds. Towering columns of data-stacks accompanied by humming generatoria. Trays of crystalline shards encoded in long-dead dialects. Parchment scrolls pulled from environmentally inert archives, now time-locked within stasis fields.

Tucked amongst the data towers and memory coils are tech-priests, magi, genetors, logisticians, enginseers, fabricators, secutors. All whose rank or reputation elevate them above the vulgar commonality have hastened aboard whichever vessel could accommodate them. A few have brought their closest acolytes, fortunate that their masters' esteem outweighs the synod's commandment that only those of greatest worth be spared.

The transports close with whichever vessel is within their reach. Dozens of shuttles make for the Peregrinus*, boosting on exhausted thrusters to crash onto the salvation of its flight decks. It is only through the profound mercy of the Omnissiah that there are no collisions in the crowded hangars.*

The Peregrinus *soars above the dying world for three point six-two minutes. Its superstructure groans, fighting the covetous grip of* gravity that it was not made to endure. More craft find their refuge, and more, until the Peregrinus' course carries it beyond the reach of the remaining forge-bastions. Binharic pleas chase the ships of Rhi-Alpha-2 as we light our engines and climb.

Tyranids descend on us from above, and now it is our turn to suffer. Point-defence turrets hammer at the minor creatures that dive towards the flotilla, but most ships lack dorsal weapon arrays with the elevation to offer a meaningful reply to the bio-ships' punishment. The Peregrinus and its fellows burn up into the melee, void shields straining against alien spite.

The Decimus/AYX drives headlong into a hive ship as it stoops towards Gryphonne IV's atmosphere. Blessed adamantine meets xenos flesh, and both are rent asunder.

The Erudite is swarmed by tyranid parasites. Tearing claws and grasping tendrils all but engulf the explorator ship. Acidic drool eats at its hull, and xenos rampage through the fissures. The Erudite's internal sensors record and relay the horror that sweeps through its decks.

Bio-plasma ravages the Kurzgesagt. The flotilla's flagship lists as its shields give out in a promethium-sheen burst of collapsing energies, admitting an inferno of emerald fire that tears at its flank. Secondary explosions rip from the cruiser's gunnery decks, but Lord Yuel's ship flies on, true to its course even as it bleeds its innards into the void.

Finally, the remaining ships of Rhi-Alpha-2 burst free of the densest portion of the hive fleet, trailing fire and wreckage behind us. Other knots of Mechanicus vessels, similarly scarred and similarly burdened with rescued magi, fight their way free of the xenos mass.

As one, we turn our engines towards our dying home and run.

FIVE

The xenos let us go. In the only calculus of worth to the ravaging beasts, the meagre quantity of organic matter that escapes aboard the refugee fleet is nothing compared with the bounty we leave behind.

The Logos *forms the vanguard, along with all that is left of its guardians. It leads a caravan of ships thousands of miles long towards the system's secondary Mandeville point, and an uncertain future.*

To an outside observer, our assembled vessels are an armada, capable of subjugating a subsector and then rebuilding it to the Machine God's design. But every soul aboard every ship knows the truth. We are the paltry remnants of a fallen empire.

Gryphonne IV is no more. The iron and silica of its mantle remains, but any life that yet endures only delays its doom. Already, chimneys are sprouting to cough corrosive spores into the poisoned and rad-choked sky, rendering down every organism they touch to an acidic slurry. Vast columns, impossibly strong, are extruding themselves from the surface. In days they will reach the upper atmosphere,

and hungering bio-ships will descend and suckle at the devoured strength and vitality of a world that had endured for billions of years.

Gryphonne IV will be left lifeless, a barren husk. Not even the planet's atmosphere will survive; the xenos will drink the very molecules of its polluted air.

Even as we flee, our vessels dutifully turn their sensors towards our dying world. It is our nature. When again will we have an opportunity to gather such valuable data on the final stages of tyranid devastation?

SIX

No more. After six days of constant vigilance, unwavering in my duty to observe, to learn, to bear witness, I can endure no more. For the first time since the Peregrinus *broke free of the empyrean and I beheld my birth-world's peril, I look away.*

I lean forward, and the thousands of monofilament mechadendrites that are my bond with the ship come free, coiling themselves at the nape of my neck. Nutrient delivery and waste evacuation tubes similarly disconnect, snaking away into subtle recesses in my throne. I stand on limbs that are steady only through the aegis of internal gyroscopics.

I give no orders to my crew. None are needed; the ship has its place in the great train. They will remain at their stations, compensating for my absence. But my fortitude has been exhausted. I have no energy left for shame.

I can still sense glimpses of my world's destruction. The communion shows me snatches of the data the Peregrinus *dutifully provides its officers, which they pass between them. These fragments*

are maddening – intrusive bursts of unfolding horror, made worse by data points that engage my curiosity.

The global temperature is cooling rapidly as alien spores choke forges that have laboured for millennia. The alchemical mixture of the air, already toxic to an unaugmented human, has been altered by the waste gases of a billion xenos beasts. The vox-beacons of the few remaining bastions flicker and die.

I cannot bear it. I sever my connection with the ship's noosphere.

Several of my acolytes turn, physical expressions of surprise to match their requests for clarification from a ductrix who is no longer listening.

I leave the crew to their dismay. Each of them will grieve in their own way, as I must. Duty can sustain me no longer.

The silence of my thoughts swallows me as I walk to the rear of the command chamber, my foot-claws clanking softly against the deck plating. The folds of my robe – its outer face the cream of Gryphonnen livery, its inner the red of Sacred Mars – close about me, like the swaddling clothes some Imperial cultures wrap about their infants. There is no comfort in the sensation; my mode of reference to all stimuli renders such experiences to data points, shorn of cultural sentiment and unproductive emotion.

I pass the skitarii demi-maniple on guard at the rear of the chamber, their carbines and arc mauls unpowered and idle. Phocon Xal, my devoted lifeward, steps from his place at the head of their formation and makes to follow me. I still him with a blurt of skit-code.

I embrace my sudden solitude. I wallow in it. I set many of my passive internal processes to run themselves out, like flywheels releasing the last of their stored energy, until I am left with only the background tick of life-sustaining operations and the all-consuming depths of my sorrow.

At the far end of the command chamber, some fifty yards from my throne, a chapel waits for those who wish to pay obeisance to the Machine God with minimal interruption to their duties. I enter, and lock the hatch behind me.

It is a minor place of worship, compared with the Peregrinus' *Hall of Making and its galactic orrery. Small forges and anvils sit beside rows of ritual hammers. Cogitators and metriculating engines hum. Stations laden with reagents and genomic samples wait for those whose devotion to the Omnissiah is expressed through alchemical experimentation.*

No officiant waits for me – within the Cult Mechanicus, every magos is both priest and disciple, a guide and one guided through the mysteries of the universe.

The sanctuary is jarringly loud. Even now, the air shakes with the blessed echoes of hammer blows, funnelled up from the foundry decks by ingenious brass pipework. Vox-trumpets proclaim the findings of my peers, boasting of the veil drawn back inch by inch on the lost wonders of science and reason. Hololithic projections celebrate acts of creation and rediscovery, made in defiance of a spiteful galaxy, in praise of a god who promises comprehension of all things.

My clenched fist crashes against a control, silencing it all. Valves seal themselves within the pipework. The trumpets cease their fanfare. The projectors flicker and die.

I stare at the icon of the Deus Mechanicus mounted upon the far wall, thirty feet above me. A great skull, half-bone, half-augmetic – the divine union of humanity and machinery – sits within a cog of steel, sheened with unguents that are periodically misted over its surface by recessed pumps.

The plating around the icon is thick with acid-etched fragments of holy texts. Infrared projectors within the chapel's walls beam binharic catechisms and mantras that slowly circle the icon, visible to my augmented sight. These are controlled by a different circuit, impossible to still. They are exhortations to the strength and purity of metal. Litanies that recite the sacrosanct duties of the servants of the Omnissiah.

The honoured tenets of the Quest for Knowledge, the hallowed purpose to which every occupant of the ship has pledged themselves.

All hollow. All shorn of meaning, rendered inert by the rigours of war and loss.

I stand in the silence, metallic hands clenched in the sign of the cog across my torso. I wait – I pray, in the strange privacy of my thoughts – for succour. For a miracle. For deliverance from the broken reality in which I am trapped.

But none comes.

I access old memory spools, reviewing essays and treatises from the earliest years of my initiation into the Cult. I recite cantrips and mantras that have inspired me, that roused my passion and set me on the path of exploration. I try to force the fire of my belief into life, as if faith is simply a matter of brute will.

I stare at the symbol of my religion. For the first time in my life, it inspires nothing. No awe, no hope, no rousing spark of clarity or surety that cuts through the static of my conflicted cognition. In place of my faith there is only a void, a lacuna that swallows the entity that was Talin Sherax, explorator superior and devotee of the Omnissiah.

I stand alone amid the icons of my lost religion for a long time. The precise duration is unimportant, although my internal chronometer records it by the nature of its function.

Finally, my indulgent isolation is brought to an end when every vox in the chapel awakens as one, speaking the same plea.

'Ductrix, your input is required.'

I turn and leave. There is no solace to be found amongst the stilled trappings of a god that has abandoned its people.

MISERY'S DAUGHTER

ONE

An icon of the Imperial faith was embossed upon the hatch before Sherax. The spread wings of an accipitridae barred her progress, its two heads glaring from time-scuffed metal. The servos that should have raised the door had seized. The Motive Force that once drove them had not flowed through the cable-veins of the vessel for over four centuries.

'Cut it open.'

Sherax had not returned to the noospheric union with her brethren, not once in the long, hard years that had passed since the fall of Gryphonne IV. At first, she justified this as a necessary sacrifice, lest her despair infect her crew and colleagues. But over time, she had become used to the silence, the privacy, unclouded by the intrusions and judgements of others.

She had not returned to the union, and so she voxed her order to her companions as a sharp click of binharic.

'Ductrix, we can circumvent this obstacle. Or repower the

mechanism.' Thess Rahn-Bo, her chief datamancer, offered judicious advice.

'Desecration is unnecessary.' Erasmus Luren, the *Peregrinus*' master of techseers, was more critical, ascribing her order to a moral failing rather than mere expediency.

Her senior advisors were ahead of her, above her, around her. Gravity was mocked in their surroundings, and so Sherax and her companions proceeded under whatever motivation, and at whatever angle relative to the architecture of the service duct, best suited them.

Sherax was undeterred by their objections. 'No,' she replied. 'Our goal is near, and our period of opportunity limited.'

'This will be an insult to the animus of this vessel.' Pious Luren. His eyestalks twitched and revolved as he regarded her.

She met his gaze, and that of the cog set proudly upon his bronze brow. 'This will be the least of the insults it has endured. Cut it open.'

They relented.

One of Sherax's attendant servitors stepped forward, a plasma torch held ready. As the torch bit into the metal, illuminating the duct in the harsh glare of electric force, Sherax did not need the communion to know the doubts her officers exchanged. The three of them had served the Omnissiah together for over a century, peers and companions for long decades prior to Sherax's ascension to the command of the *Peregrinus*. She knew their minds, the actions that awoke their doubts. Their anxieties arose from rational concerns; Sherax was not so detached from who she had once been to be ignorant of her altered behaviour.

Her claws crunched on worn deck plating as she paced, a physical manifestation of impatience that had crept into her habits in recent months. Each step sent shivers of resonance radiating through the thin metal. They would have echoed along

the duct had it not been unpressurised and open to the desolate vacuum of the void. That was no impediment to Sherax and her colleagues; they were all familiar with the hazards found in the depths of a space hulk.

The agglomeration of shattered hulls and wrecked reactors had first been encountered in the three hundred and forty-third year of the 38th millennium, and received the florid designation *Misery's Daughter* from the chartered mercantilist who discovered it. Since that time it had been given many other names, most often spoken as curses spat at its unwieldy bulk from the decks of warships and orbital defence platforms.

Its violent emergence from the warp had preceded anarchy and death for a dozen planetary systems. Even weeks after the campaign against the orks that had inhabited it had been won, warships of the Changrit Subsector battlefleet still stood as sentinels over its malformed bulk, wary that yet more terrors might spill from its misshapen hangars and darkened holds. Sherax had been plagued by fears that Admiral Kroy would yet destroy the assemblage of ancient hulls, despite the crime against the Omnissiah's precepts that would represent.

The hulk could not be destroyed. Somewhere within its compacted wreckage of once-proud void-craft – somewhere that Sherax was sure was close at hand – lay the hope of her people.

It had been three years since she watched Gryphonne IV die beneath alien claws. A blink of an eye in the grand scale of the cosmos, but an eternity for one such as Sherax, whose cognitive processes parsed millions of calculations with each second. In that time, disorder and destruction had flourished. The Cicatrix Maledictum had riven the galaxy, spilling empyric energies and the warp-touched foulness humanity had named *daemon* into their reality. Xenos rampaged across the stars. Predators lurked at every shadowed corner, stealing a little more of mankind's strength with each passing day.

In its mythic past, humanity had harnessed miracles. The antecedents of the Adeptus Mechanicus unchained the boundless possibilities of technology to work wonders, bending the galaxy to their will. The duty of the Explorator order – Sherax's duty – was to seek out the knowledge and relics of that fabled time and restore them to human hands, for the benefit of the Martian Empire and the Imperium of Man.

Now, Sherax knew, the Adeptus Mechanicus required such a miracle.

Steel turned red beneath the servitor's torch, then white, then melted, evaporating into mineral-rich vapour. It took the slaved unit two point three minutes to breach the hatch. Curiously, it had ensured that the Imperial eagle remained whole, despite Sherax not proscribing that directive in her voxed order.

As the unit manoeuvred the slab of metal to one side, she peered through the glowing gap. The service duct stretched away. Her claws bit deep into the thin deck grating, the servo-bundles of her musculature denied an outlet for their restrained potential. She yearned to throw herself forward, to race the final steps in pursuit of what she hoped would be the salvation of her people.

The galaxy required a miracle, and Sherax would deliver it.

 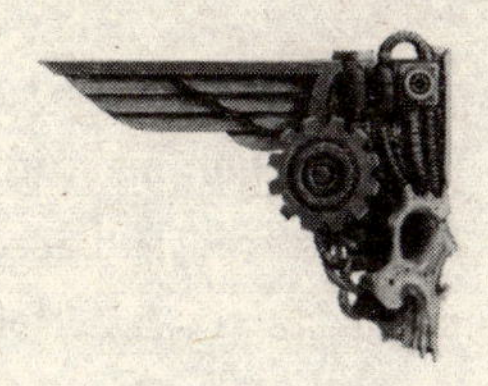

TWO

<It was an affront to the Omnissiah.>

<It was expedient.>

To the uninitiated, the noospheric union was a system for facilitating discussion between individuals, a more efficient form of exchange than verbal statements or binharic vox-bursts. While this description was accurate, it was also insufficient. The communion between the *Peregrinus'* upper echelon was a consensual joining of minds. It was all too easy for unconscious thoughts or emotions to slip past one's internal firebreaks, particularly in moments of high tension.

In this case, Techseer Erasmus Luren withheld nothing, purposefully interweaving his thoughts with sharp-edged snippets of indignance. <Does that justify doing injury to the animus of this vessel?>

<It is dead, Luren. Conserve your ire for a more worthwhile cause.> Cogitatrix Thess Rahn-Bo, as ever, rose to their ductrix's defence.

Phocon Xal observed the disagreement, but restrained his own thoughts behind sturdy partitions. As lifeward of the ductrix, Xal was accorded access to the communion, but he was not a part of it. His function was to guard Sherax, and by extension her colleagues. It was not to pass judgement or opine on matters beyond his understanding.

Nevertheless, Xal had to consciously purge his own flickers of disquiet as he stalked forward to assess the threat potential of the space beyond the excised hatch. The explorator's casual dismissal of her adepts' concerns was the latest example of the more direct behavioural template to which Sherax now adhered.

Xal was first through the disfigured hatch. In the absence of gravity's pull, the pneumatic actuators in his legs and talons worked in reciprocal action to propel Xal forward without launching him clear of the deck grating.

The service duct through which they proceeded was narrow, one of the many crawlspaces that threaded through the ship's inner hull, permitting access to its systems for maintenance and sanctification. Such spaces were havens for parasitic predators and the numerous xenos species that typically occupied macro-agglomerations, and so he advanced with arc pistol and transonic halberd extended in his three hands. His ocular scanner – a red-tinted visor that replaced the organic eyes he had no memory of using – interrogated the visible and infrared wavelengths of the electromagnetic spectrum hundreds of times a second, piercing the duct's stygian darkness. Ultrasonic pulses tested the deck's metal for micro-vibrations caused by creatures lurking in ambush.

No threats were evident. Nevertheless, he voxed a command to Rho-6-2, the skitarii alpha who functioned as the node for the demi-maniple of rangers accompanying Sherax's party. They trudged in single file through the mangled hatch and set off,

once more forming a vanguard for the expedition. Like Luren and Rahn-Bo, each of the skitarii and their servitor attendants were clad in full-body pressure suits, the Gryphonnen cream marked with Mechanicus red and indigo rank-stripes. Sherax and Xal himself were blessed to be augmented beyond the concerns of void exposure.

There were six other sub-expeditions roving through the *Matriovska Hesprilax,* a macro-conveyor whose identity had been gleaned from runes embossed on the ship's interior plating. All parties were pursuing the same goal – an unimpeded and defensible passage through the vessel, driving towards a promising power signature detected on its far side. Each clade's location was carefully tracked, continually confirming or noting deviations from the schemata of the transport's construction pattern retrieved from the *Peregrinus*' archives.

The *Peregrinus* had been lying at anchor in close proximity to the southern pole of the *Misery's Daughter* for four days. In that time, they had made much progress. Sherax had expressed frustrations with her crew's pace, and though it was not Xal's place to gainsay his ductrix, he was uncertain what additional actions might have been taken to hasten the exploration.

Hundreds of servo-skulls and tracked cyber-altered task units had been released immediately upon shipfall, swarming out from the explorator's chosen staging post to probe beyond the outer edges of the anomaly, past which the *Peregrinus*' sensors could perceive only the strongest of signals. Most hummed or trundled through the darkness in placid silence, steadily documenting the human and xenos vessels whose fate had been to fuse with other misfortunates over the millennia. Some encountered bellowing orks or other, stranger beasts. The surveyors' violent destruction identified the zones to which Sherax's bonded skitarii would be directed, once their primary duty was complete.

Dispatched at intervals, their first units raced along the widest thoroughfares in Skorpius hover transports towards any hint of active warp signatures detected by the scout-constructs. Space hulks – the common designation for these supermassive accretions of wrecked void-craft – were feared for their vastness and for the multifarious organisms and dangers they contained. But they were inconstant beasts, erupting into and out of realspace without warning on misfiring warp engines. Centuries went by between sightings of documented hulks, the craft often appearing far from where they were last encountered. But whenever they appeared, the doctrine for probing a hulk was well established. The first and most essential duty of any Mechanicus expedition was to render all warp engines inert, locking the entire assemblage in place and putting an end to its nomadic, rampaging odyssey.

The crew of the *Peregrinus* was well practised in such undertakings. While the explorator ship's serf decks were replenished periodically – though no more frequently than accepted attrition rates for a void-craft of its class – many of the adepts and acolytes who pursued the sacred Quest for Knowledge from its decks and chambers had done so for decades. *Misery's Daughter* was the third such expedition the *Peregrinus* had undertaken since Sherax's elevation to the role of ductrix.

Xal was aware of the ductrix's impatience as she stalked past him, hard on the heels of the skitarii, who advanced at their rapid, lockstep pace. It was an unquantifiable sensation, but one that he had observed often in the years since the fall.

Impatience, in Xal's unworthy judgement, was a common vice among the honoured acolytes of the Deus Mechanicus. But it had not always been so aboard the *Peregrinus*. Indeed, Xal was aware that prior to the fall of the forge-cradle, Explorator Superior Sherax had received several injunctions from seniors within

the Explorator order to correct what they viewed as an overly deliberate, even unhurried, approach to her holy work.

An example of how thoroughly the ductrix's conduct had changed had arisen less than a day before. Two of the skitarii hunter-clades had penetrated deep into the agglomeration's interior and encountered a slim, needle-like void-craft apparently composed from a form of crystal that did not match any previously encountered material. Their report was rapidly relayed to the expedition's leadership, but Sherax's response had been abrupt.

'That is not our objective.'

<This is not how we once conducted expeditions,> Luren observed afterwards, unheard by Sherax, his words falling into the communion laden with scorn and judgement.

<That is a redundant statement,> Rahn-Bo responded dourly, stilling the exchange, though bleak emotion-signifiers had continued to hover over both adepts.

The ductrix's closest collaborators had grown more reserved in recent years, another change in behaviour Xal had observed. He had been adopted as the explorator superior's lifeward fifty-two Martian years earlier, and had been proximate to her closest colleagues for a similar duration. Their union had once been alive with a vibrant dialogue of data, opinions and analyses, expressed without reservation or misgiving.

Now, they trudged in silence through the bowels of a broken ship.

The vox clicked with a rapid pulse of skit-code from Rho-6-2. 'Obstacle ahead.'

The crawlspace ended abruptly, opening onto what Xal's echolocation indicated was a much broader space. The passage's deck plating and surrounding metal had been sheared off, the warped edges curling out and back on themselves like the unfurled petals of a flower.

Xal ensured that he remained ahead of the ductrix and the adepts as they ventured closer.

Rho-6-2's rangers had already negotiated the razor-sharp end of the passage, and were spread out on a ledge five yards below the crawlspace's surface. They appeared to be perched on the lip of a broken corridor that projected into a scene of devastation.

<Rho-6-2 has a gift for understatement,> Luren noted from the rear of the group, their senses questing beyond Xal's restraining form into the void beyond.

A gulf, a hundred yards across and stretching almost the entire width of the transport ship's superstructure, had been carved from the ship's interior. Xal directed an auspex pulse into the broken mess of structural supports and interior plating. The resulting return gave him a tri-d depiction of a crevasse, extending down towards the core of the vessel.

Xal negotiated the terminus of the passageway, and slowly dropped down to join the skitarii. Above him, three massive sheets of iron, each as thick as his halberd stave was long, formed the outside edge of the cavity. The sheets of armour were layered on top of one another, the space between them created by broad girders set out in a hexagonal pattern. Each honeycomb gap was wide and thick enough for an unaugmented human to stand within it, should they be minded to wedge themselves into such a space.

They had reached the outer edge of the ship's dorsal hull, the first and last barrier between the *Matriovska Hesprilax*'s crew and cargo and the wrath of the void beyond.

It had not been enough. The explorator's party were evidently standing amid the aftermath of a ship-killing explosion. Xal's persistent data files included only cursory analytics on ship-to-ship combat, but it was evident that a macrocannon shell had shrugged aside the transport's paltry armour and detonated within its fragile interior.

Despite the devastation, there was little loose scrap drifting in the null gravity. This was not unusual, in Xal's experience; for reasons beyond his understanding, the unnatural motions and conditions within a hulk tended to pulverise smaller shards of wreckage, reducing them to the faint clouds of dust that occluded detailed visual examination of the impact site.

While the party had been absorbed in their initial analysis, Rho-6-2 and several of their demi-maniple had ventured further round the edge of the chasm, deftly navigating the splintered ends of passageways, power conduits, cabling, and ductwork that projected at varying lengths and thicknesses into the void. They paused on a small platform that Xal estimated to be a remnant of the ship's main dorsal thoroughfare, and the vox crackled into life.

'Protector Xal.' Rho-6-2's sending was in skit-code, a dialect that was entirely unequipped to express anything more than tactical data.

'Report.'

'Objective sighted.'

Sherax received the alpha's message at the same time as Xal. With a single step, the explorator leapt towards the rangers, gliding across the intervening space with a directness only afforded by the lack of gravity.

Xal had been unprepared for her movement, and was not equipped to follow her in the same manner. He set off through the wreckage along the route taken by the rangers, limbs and claws crunching heat-weakened metal in his haste. He sensed the rest of Sherax's company following at a less reckless pace.

Xal reached the platform moments after his ductrix alighted, and found her staring up through a savage tear in the cargo ship's hull. Visible between the cracked metal, almost lost in the murky twilight of the hulk's interior, was a burst of Mechanicus crimson.

The explorator shocked him with a soft exclamation, rare signifiers of pleasure and awe mingled with a single binharic designation.

'The *Almagest*.'

THREE

Edgar Lorristan twisted in his seat. Even after six years – or three Martian years, as his Mechanicus hosts reckoned it – he could not find a position within the Knight Armiger's cockpit that did not leave him bent-backed and cramping.

His auspex pinged. Edgar abandoned his vain attempts at finding comfort, and instead glanced at the read-out. He need not have bothered, as the vox fizzed into life.

'Audex and thermal readings indicate a mass of xenos approaching our position.' Sub-Magos Pagnitz, the tech-priest assigned to this sector of the space hulk's mass, had an augmetic voice box that turned each word into an atonal burr. *'Analysis suggests a ninety-two per cent probability that they are of the orkoid genus.'*

'Thank you, magos.' Major Nastasya Zlata of the Vostroyan 103rd Firstborn stood a few yards from *Vortigern*'s knee-joint. The Armiger's audex-capture relayed her acknowledgement a fraction of a second ahead of the vox transmission back to Pagnitz.

'And if that wasn't enough warning, you can smell them coming from half a mile away,' added one of the troopers near Zlata.

'Shut up, Gennadi.'

'Sir,' the man said, grinning.

Edgar's frown deepened. He missed the camaraderie, the easy wit and jibes of House Cadmus warriors about to take the field. The brotherhood of charging through an enemy's ranks, shoulder to metallic shoulder with friends and rivals for esteem and honour. The retellings that followed the furious release of battle, sweat-soaked and flush with victory.

He looked down at his rear-facing imagifier, which showed the two Dunestalkers and their skitarii escorts that lurked at the back of their position. He would find no such fellowship here.

They were pristine in their Gryphonnen livery. Between the Vostroyans and his Armiger, there was more than sufficient firepower to guard the thoroughfare against any of the minor threats the expedition had encountered within the space hulk. And yet the two multi-legged walkers held station behind them, as though waiting for their all-too-human front line to collapse beneath the strain of battle.

Their silent superiority irked him. His beautiful Knight Castigator, *Bladequeen*, had stood twice their height, and could have dealt with both in a single sweep of her warblade. He could have shown the Mechanicus what a true machine of war could do when bonded with a gifted pilot, rather than their lobotomised servants immersed in their rad-poisoned amniotic cocoons.

What a sight they had been, Edgar and his *Bladequeen*. He permitted himself to lapse into memory, reliving the glorious hunts of his youth through Raisa's mutant-infested wilderness. The grandeur of the tournaments, in which his Castigator's tempest warblade had dominated his peers' lesser machines. The feel of her scarlet honour pennant in his hands, presented by Baron Roland to commemorate his first independent command. Edgar had led three lances into the Angretus Crusade, and *Blade-queen* had taken the head of the renegade abomination in a duel he would remember until the end of his days.

In response to his lapse in focus, the Armiger's machine spirit bucked, its reactor-heart emitting a bright flare of energy. *Vortigern* was a bellicose and jealous beast, seemingly unaware of its own inadequacy. It was Edgar's belief that the Armiger had been alone for too long, without the proper slave-link to a true knight to direct its actions and rein in its impulses.

'Bastard thing,' he muttered as he threw a set of switches into their discharge positions. Piloting a Knight was as much a merging of minds as it was a physical act of cranks and control columns, but despite his experience and noble-born instincts, Edgar struggled to bring *Vortigern* to heel.

The vox crackled once more with Pagnitz's oscillating rasp. *'Query: do you require assistance, Sir Edgar? I am registering fluctuations within* Vortigern*'s power grid.'*

He summoned his reserves of patience. 'No, magos. And, once again, I would thank you to refer to me simply as Edgar, or Master Lorristan.'

'Acknowledgement.' The mechanical tone gave no indication whether the lock-brained oaf would actually heed his request this time.

Humiliation burned anew, tinged with bitterness that he was required to serve as his own tormentor. Edgar had surrendered his honour and his title, and every casual reminder of his lost station cut the wound afresh. Even the ceremony had been a mockery, conducted in exile in a disused storage unit aboard the *Peregrinus* rather than the great hall of Golem Keep, under the judging eyes of his house. He couldn't even subject himself to the proper rituals of defenestration, cut off from Raisa and the few Knights that had escaped the murder of Gryphonne IV.

The carnifex had taken him completely by surprise, thundering into his flank with the force of a freight conveyor. Even so, the beast had died with *Bladequeen*'s warblade in its guts, leaking corrosive bile that ate through the joints of her legs, held pinned beneath its bulk.

Edgar had blacked out at that point, succumbing to phantom pain. Both of his tibias had snapped under the psychostigmatic pressure, his mind's way of making the Knight's agony his own. And there he should have stayed, honoured with a well-earned death alongside his beloved steed.

But the God-Emperor evidently had other plans for him. The Vostroyans had found Edgar during their retreat from the battle's fury, and had pulled him from his throne. The neural shock of that disconnection alone should have been enough to kill him, but Edgar's luck – as Major Zlata had later observed with what had surely been meant as good humour – had held. They had dragged him aboard the coffin ship of the Reaver Titan *Atranis*, huddling beneath the god-machine's hunched, broken form as it escaped the hellscape that the forge world had become.

Edgar did not feel lucky, nor bathed in the God-Emperor's love. He had asked Explorator Sherax, on whose vessel he had found himself when he had awoken, not to relay the fact of his survival to Raisa. Better that his house think him dead alongside his Knight than know that his oaths had been broken. That he had deserted *Bladequeen* in her final moments.

'Prime weapons. Captain Lursa, Lieutenant Syke, your squads to engage their flanks first. Drive them into the centre.' Major Zlata's heavy accent woke Edgar from his melancholy.

'Aye, major.' Both officers acknowledged their commander with terse, professional vox-bursts.

The Vostroyan 103rd, the 'Blackbloods' to give them their preferred name, were good troops, although – like Edgar – reduced to a shadow of their former selves. Four thousand firstborn sons and daughters of Vostroya had answered the Mechanicus' call for reinforcements. Less than a third had escaped Gryphonne IV's fate. Most had taken flight beneath *Atranis'* legs, but in the chaotic year that followed, the regiment had reunited with a few dozen soldiers who had fled with other forces. They had remained aboard the *Peregrinus* not out of any loyalty or gratitude to Explorator Sherax and her magi, but simply because there were no troop transport vessels left among the Gryphonnen diaspora that could be spared to convey them elsewhere.

'*Vortigern*, join your fire with the heavy weapons teams, if you will.' It was to Zlata's credit that she couched her order in the guise of a request, and that she used the Armiger's name in place of his own. It spoke of respect, even if Edgar was ill-deserving of any.

He clicked open his vox-link. 'Gladly, major.'

Not that he would be of much use. The heavy stubber mounted atop the Armiger's carapace was the only weapon at his command, given their environs. His twinned thermal spears would make short work of any ork beast that came close, along with the deck plating, bulkhead, and superstructure behind it. His chainblade would reap a bloody tally if he were released into the midst of the mob, but that would impede the fire of the Vostroyans.

No, aboard this ramshackle agglomeration and in this peasant's steed, he was reduced to the meagre role of a static gunnery position, a task any low-born swine with a week's training could undertake.

'Here they come!'

The orks burst onto the thoroughfare's far end in a predictable wave of noise and violence. They came as a solid wall, fighting one another in their bestial haste. Crude blades and ramshackle firearms were gripped in thick paws, feral rage twisting brute faces. A pack of truly mad creatures leapt into the air with the aid of bulky rockets mounted on their backs, incinerating their neighbours as they soared towards the hall's vaulted roof.

Edgar yearned to charge forward to meet them, to vent his frustration through the letting of xenos blood. If this was to be how he served out his days, at least let him do so to the best of his steed's limited abilities.

Instead, he shifted his position once more in his cockpit, braced his boots in their stirrups, and set his heavy stubber to work.

FOUR

The *Almagest*.

Luren and Rahn-Bo were transfixed by the sight of the vast crimson flank stretching away into darkness. Sherax was certain they were sharing awed expressions of reverence within the communion. Revelling in the synergy of worship. United by the articulation of faith.

Sherax was far from immune to the majesty of such a craft so close at hand, but she kept her veneration to herself. The buoyant optimism that rose within her was not, she told herself, caused by the vessel's grandeur. Rather, it was simply the pleasure of knowing that the object of her search was near at hand.

Though Sherax felt a dull pressure to share her satisfaction with her peers, she restrained the urge. For three years, isolation had been her refuge from the despondency of the times, and her defence against the cloying demands of her crew.

They were not, she knew, unreasonable demands. Leadership.

Direction. Hope, the most ephemeral and essential of human needs. Yet for the longest time, she had had none for herself, let alone any to give to her faltering colleagues.

As had been documented innumerable times in the course of history, after crushing defeat had come bitter rancour. The venerable magi of the Gryphonnen forge-synod had sought to assign blame for the disaster, and fought to set the course of their drifting diaspora. In the first year after the disaster, as the Gryphonnen armada crept from star system to star system – hazarding only brief forays into the roiling immaterium, lest they lose what little they had left – what missives Sherax had received from the diaspora's leaders were sporadic, often contradictory. The refugees of Gryphonne IV had idled, snared by indecision and competing egotism during the most critical period in their history.

Sherax had been no better. She had withdrawn from all contact with her peers and underlings, insofar as the requirements of her station allowed. She had been an infrequent visitor to her command deck, appearing only when required. She had issued orders, and maintained her bond with the *Peregrinus* – itself grieving, in its way. But Sherax had not been present, had not been the animating force that her duty demanded and that her crew had required. She, like the forge-synod, had been absent in their moment of need.

Sherax had lost herself in undirected anger and bitter recrimination. She had spent thousands of hours poring through the data that had been shared between the ships of the fleet, documenting the weeks and months prior to the disaster. Analysing the forge-synod's orders, taking it upon herself to cross-examine their decisions and challenge their actions. Had it been hubris to stand against the oncoming tide, or should an evacuation have begun at the first sign of threat? Were there flaws in the war-doctrines of Arch-Dominus Zane and her strategos that allowed destruction to overtake the mightiest bastion of the Mechanicus save Holy Mars itself?

Sherax could find no flaws, nor did she find hubris in the decision to trust in Gryphonne IV's mighty defences. This had only enflamed her frustrations. Anger turned to anguish as she considered what little had been spared, and how much had been lost. The legacies ended, the works undone. At that time, a comprehensive cataloguing of all that had been saved from the jaws of the leviathan had not been undertaken. The remnant of Gryphonne IV had not known what knowledge had been lost, and what scraps had been saved.

Sherax had taken it upon herself to begin that effort. She had, she knew, been driven by spite, rather than the more noble purpose that ought to have spurred such activity. Sherax had desired to be ready for the synod's call, and scorn them with evidence of her purposeful action.

Arising from her solitude, she had opened the data-stacks brought aboard in the *Peregrinus'* brief, desperate flight through Gryphonne IV's thermosphere and redirected the duties of her crew to examine every record, document every data-shard, and integrate and review it all, assembling an inventory of the few treasures retrieved from the tomb of Gryphonne IV. Sherax knew that it had been make-work – activity best left to the few datamancers and logi they had rescued from xenos jaws. But she had been grasping for purpose in those months, seeing no course ahead.

And yet, it had been that fruitless project that set her on the path to the *Almagest*.

Among the blueprints, essays, schemata, and curios had been a series of texts set down by Magos Nekane Lucanus in the earliest centuries of the last, dark millennium. Lucanus was an archivist and theorist who had spent the majority of his three-hundred-year career as master datamancer of the explorator ship *Almagest*. Like many adepts of the Cult Mechanicus, Sherax included, his fixations had been broad and eclectic, shifting with each new document and artefact he obtained.

One of his secondary interests – almost an idle hobby, in comparison with his greater works – had been the accumulation and interrogation of creation myths.

Genesis. Kumulipo. Enuma Elish. Olodumare. Names given to the oldest of human myths, describing the seeding of life across celestial bodies. Told and retold by countless cultures as they rose and fell across the million worlds of the Imperium.

Lucanus had considered these not for their religious or anthropological significance, although Sherax had retrieved works by several Imperial theologians who subsequently incorporated elements of his work into their imperfect canon of worship; he had collected and deconstructed them in support of a far grander thesis.

He proposed that at the centre of every allegorical narrative lay not the actions of fickle gods and djinn, nor the improbability of spontaneous biological inception, nor even the divine work of the Omnissiah, but a technology. A lost work of humanity's mastery, employed in the first millennia when humanity extended its hand to claim the galaxy for its own.

The knowledge and ability to seed life across barren earth.

Sherax recognised the desperation in her actions, in her singular devotion to a forlorn, implausible hope. It was a behavioural pattern that she had observed in many fellow magi, and ever had she judged them harshly for their monomania, and condemned them for their neglect of wider concerns.

Her judgement, she now knew, arose from a failure of comprehension. She had not known how completely the twin lures

of hope and desperation could overtake a mind. How entirely they could banish all doubts, and render responsibilities as trivialities. She now understood what it was to obsess.

The *Almagest* was the end of an irrational, directionless search, predicated on fervent desire rather than logic and reason. Sherax had committed herself to discovering the fullness of Lucanus' work, the evidence for which he had frustratingly alluded to in a handful of incomplete missives.

She would discover it, or she would not. It was plausible, if not entirely probable, that her search had been for nought, a futile trawl for an eccentric's idle speculation.

Regardless, locating the *Almagest* was an end for her. Her hope was that it would also be a beginning.

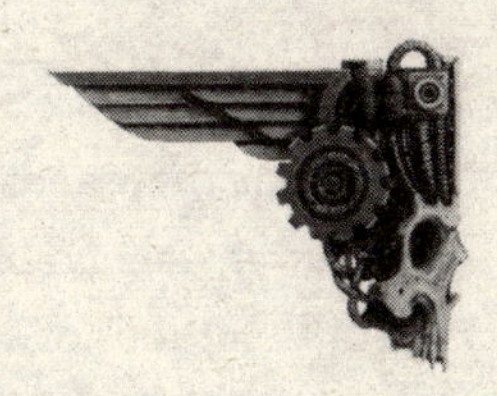

FIVE

The *Almagest* loomed above them.

Xal, along with Rho-6-2 and their rangers, had charted a path up from the shattered interior of the *Matriovska Hesprilax* onto the outer face of the ship's hull. Their vantage point amid the devastated spine of the macro-conveyor placed the explorator's party three hundred and seventy-one yards abeam of the *Almagest*'s port engines, although from Xal's perspective the vessel hung in space directly above him. It was like looking up at a metal cliff face, curving away at both extremities. The rest of the ship's hull, two miles of red iron and cream Gryphonnen trim, extended away to Xal's left, all but filling a vast cavity within the space hulk's interior.

Although Xal was entirely familiar with the specifications of the *Almagest* – Sherax's research had revealed that it had been built to the same Standard Template Construction pattern as the *Peregrinus* – viewing the ship in this manner was deeply unnerving, in a way the lifeward had never experienced.

Humanity's void-craft were cities in space. Even the merest frigate was thousands of yards long, made of millions of tons of sacred metal and blessed components. They were homes to tens of thousands of souls, the majority of whom lived, reproduced, and died without ever setting foot beyond their hulls.

Such vessels were not intended to be observed at such an intimate distance. The fact of them was too great for the mind to comprehend, even for one augmented beyond the capabilities of baseline humanity.

<Give praise to the Omnissiah, and all His wonders,> Erasmus Luren sent, his binharic investing the prayer with all the admiration and worship he could summon. <Great are His works. Blessed are those who witness them.>

<Praise the Omnissiah.> Rahn-Bo added her affirmations.

<Praise Him,> Xal said, incapable of restraining his own declaration. He knelt, head bowed, moved to adopt a pose of religious awe and supplication in the face of such magnificence.

'It appears undamaged.'

Xal was shocked that his ductrix could even speak. She had sought this vessel for years, had bent every resource to its discovery. Would she not take even a brief moment to revel in the majesty of Gryphonnen shipcraft that lay before them?

Duty reasserted itself, and Xal stood. Sherax's analysis, to his uninformed gaze, appeared to be correct, though the *Almagest* was far from pristine. Black scorch marks marred its hull for hundreds of yards, particularly around the nearest of its weapons batteries. Craters and punctures of every calibre scarred its flank, but Xal lacked the capability to assess whether they represented more than cosmetic damage. There did not appear to be any of the dramatic, disabling wounds such as the one above which they stood. The *Almagest* seemed to have been trapped within the space hulk without enduring crippling injury.

Sherax pulled a fist-sized vox-beacon from within the recesses of her robe, and bent to mag-lock it to the *Matriovska Hesprilax*'s hull. 'All parties, converge on this location at best velocity. Objective sighted.'

As a chorus of swift acknowledgements from the other expeditionary clades clicked across the vox, Sherax returned her gaze to the vessel above her.

'We will cross immediately,' she said.

<Reckless.> The judgement exploded from Luren, polluting the communion like an ink drop diffusing in water.

'We will need far more resources to conduct a proper search,' ventured Rahn-Bo, whose own objection had been spoken into the noosphere, albeit with less vehemence.

'They have been summoned,' Sherax replied.

Luren tried next. 'It would be wise to begin an initial foray from a position of consolidated strength, with our logistical route known and secure.'

'I will not delay.'

'Ductrix, I cannot sanction any further progress without an enhanced guard,' Xal said, attempting his own intervention. 'Protocol demands that you be adequately protected.'

Sherax turned to Xal, the bronze and steel of her face incapable of showing any emotion. 'Your protection has always been more than adequate, my guardian,' she voxed, after a pause that Xal deemed longer than strictly necessary to determine her response.

'As you will, explorator superior.' None of them, least of all Xal, was capable of opposing Sherax.

Xal regarded Rho-6-2. 'Secure this position, and await further instruction.' He paused. As part of the skitarii's pressure suits, the demi-maniple wore rebreathers connected to tanks of compressed oxygen, as did the pair of servitors that attended the ductrix. 'We will return before mission-critical resources are expended.'

'Compliance.'

Sherax waited just long enough for her companions to ready themselves, then leapt.

Xal was ready this time and was only a moment behind. Luren and Rahn-Bo followed, though with less zeal.

The four figures drifted up from the macro-conveyor's battered shell, gravity's absence allowing for a directness of approach that conformed to few of Xal's inloaded doctrines. Sherax had chosen a slightly oblique trajectory, aiming further forward along the *Almagest*'s hull, away from the ship's silent engines. The adepts of the Cult Mechanicus coasted through the airless void, each following their own path, spreading out like seeds cast by an inefficient agri worker.

It took them almost a minute to cross the gap between the two ships. Xal's religious awe grew as the distance reduced, but he shunted it aside in favour of more immediate concerns. In the final moments of flight, he made a deft twirl of his halberd, shifting his momentum to send him into a slow somersault and invert his position relative to the *Almagest*'s hull. He now appeared to be falling towards the ship, rather than rising to meet it.

Sherax arrested her approach with sharp puffs of gas from vents in her limbs, alighting with a grace that was rarely found amongst initiates of the Omnissiah. Xal, by way of contrast, landed hard. Both claws cannoned into the hull, sending a soundless wave of resonance rippling through the metal. In the same moment, Xal magnetised his talons to avoid rebounding back off into the void. Rahn-Bo had a similarly ballistic approach, and bent deep on her reverse-jointed legs as she landed.

Techseer Luren had launched himself with a much slower initial velocity, red robes streaming behind him to reveal a gaunt form entirely given over to the machine. For the final moments of flight, he deployed an electro-tether from a socket on his pressure suit's forearm and gently pulled himself onto the surface of the explorator ship.

Xal had assumed that they would need to locate a rift in the hull to gain entry to its interior, but Rahn-Bo had landed within twenty yards of a personnel ingress/egress port, besides the much larger shape of a cargo bay blast door. She approached, and knelt above a control panel.

'The airlock is active and pressurised, explorator superior.'

'Unusual,' said Luren.

'But welcome.' Sherax was already striding towards the port. 'Can you access it?'

No magos, regardless of rank or specialism, enjoyed admitting that a task was beyond them. The cogitatrix's discomfort manifested in the noosphere as a truculent snatch of code. 'The vessel's animus is closed to me.'

'Luren.'

'As you command.' The techseer joined Rahn-Bo at the panel, extending a cluster of mechadendrites from the back of one hand. They coiled in serpentine motion, seeking out various inlets to permit him to commune with the *Almagest*.

While the two adepts worked, Xal looked up along the path they had taken. From his position on the surface of the explorator ship, the damage to the macro-conveyor was even more dramatic. The transport's spine had been broken by a colossal detonation, causing deformation to spread for almost half a mile in either direction along its dorsal plating. It was remarkable that they had been able to approach the impact site without encountering more substantial obstacles.

'Alpha Rho-6-2.'

'Receiving.'

'Monitor this position for any foreign activity.'

'Compliance.'

Luren twitched, emitting the neuroelectric equivalent of a grunt of effort. Stress-signifiers suddenly bled from the techseer.

<Magos?> Xal stepped closer.

The techseer ignored him. 'I have achieved partial synchronicity,' said Luren a few seconds later.

'Partial?' Sherax's interrogative contained no emotive signifiers or expressions of concern.

'The ship's animus is... inconstant.'

Sherax processed this statement, but made no comment. 'Will it permit us entry?'

'I believe so,' Luren replied, though with another delay that spoke of significant effort.

Rahn-Bo appeared unaffected by whatever troubled the techseer. 'Beginning decompression procedure.'

<Witness this function, blessed Omnissiah. Let your grace empower its servos. May your will drive its pumps.> Xal felt Luren intone his prayer, a necessary expression of gratitude and faith to summon the Motive Force that would empower the airlock to function.

The process of evacuating the air from the access port took eighty-nine seconds, and then the outer door ground open on stiff servos.

Sherax led them in.

THE ALMAGEST

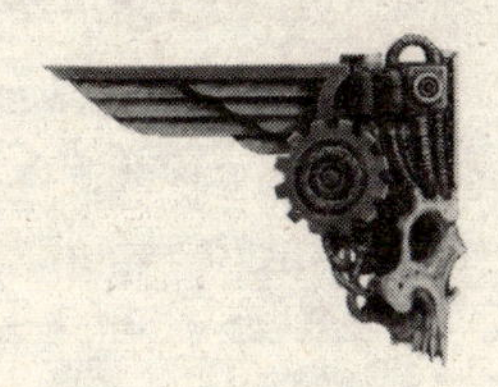

ONE

The *Almagest* was screaming.

Their entry point was a mirror of the *Peregrinus*' own tertiary port cargo receiver, save for the decay and degradation that had taken root. Rust and verdigris had eaten away at every surface, robbing the metal deck and walls of their blessed lustre and sanctified strength. The Cog Mechanicus emblazoned on the far wall was a faded icon, steel and bone denigrated by either abuse or neglect.

Sherax's audex receivers dimmed as soon as the airlock's inner door cycled open, an automatic defence against the nonsense screed of code that popped and burbled from vox-emitters. The ship was crying out at a decibel level that would cause permanent damage to any unaugmented human.

Sherax subjected a fraction of the noise to a penetrative scan, wary of scrapcode assault. Her precautions, however, were unnecessary – it was merely binharic, bellowed from vox-horns mounted in the eaves of the receiving chamber.

The code-shards were overlapping and intermingled, but with effort she was able to discern specific fragments.

'Port thrusters failing. Trajectory deviation minus zero point two-four degrees. Minus zero point two-five degrees.

'Anomalous activity recorded.

'P-port thrusters failing.

'Intruders de-de-detected, all levels.'

She turned on Luren as he and the others exited the airlock and processed the aural assault. 'You stated this vessel's animus was unstable.'

'Confirmation.' Luren's face, dominated by three sensor clusters mounted on rotating stalks, was not equipped to express emotion. Nevertheless, the speed at which the nests of sensors spun was much more rapid than usual.

'That much is clear,' Sherax said dryly.

The squeal of binharic suddenly ceased. Xal stepped protectively ahead of the explorator, assuming that the garbled noise had been deployed as a distraction prior to an ambush.

No such attack materialised. They were alone amid the cavernous receiving deck.

'Primary containment failing. Secondary manifolds unresponsive.

'In-intruders detected, all levels.'

The vox-horns spoke again, hammering snatches of code that reverberated from the chamber's walls, then the ship fell silent once more.

Sherax waited several seconds for any further outbursts, but none appeared forthcoming.

'Diagnosis?' She directed the question at her chief techseer, who had walked past Xal into the centre of the deck in the manner of a beast-herder approaching an unstable mount.

Rahn-Bo spoke for Luren. 'The *Almagest* has lost its mind.'

Sherax considered the datamancer's answer florid, but essentially

correct. Clearly, the vessel's machine spirit was profoundly fractured.

'Prognosis?'

Luren finally spoke. It was unusual for the techseer to show reticence, but evidently the state of the ship had distressed him. 'To heal such degeneration alone is beyond my abilities.'

Sherax was not surprised. Purging and resanctifying a vessel of the *Almagest*'s complexity would be the work of hundreds of techseers and consecrators even under optimal conditions.

'Can you silence it?' she asked.

'Not without the destruction of the vox-emitters.'

'I would prefer to record the vessel's utterances,' Rahn-Bo said quickly. 'Analysis may yield information pertaining to its fate within the macro-agglomeration. And the cause of its corruption.'

Sherax was thankful that her companions could not sense the anxiety that their assessment triggered.

The root of her fear was obvious. She had come in search of answers, of data that would prove that there was a basis of fact and substance to Magos Lucanus' most controversial theory. If the machine spirit of his vessel had suffered irreversible damage, would any connected systems survive? Would data reconstruction be possible, and if so, would anything retrieved be free of the suspicion of corruption or analytical bias?

There was only one way to be sure. As the tenets of the Mechanicus averred, the path to certainty lay through action.

'We will proceed.'

TWO

The *Almagest* was a bleak, unsettling mirror of the *Peregrinus*.

Both vessels were of the same template, and though Explorator Sherax's vessel had been laid down in the illustrious void-yards of Gryphonne IV fourteen hundred years after the *Almagest*, the variations in construction and ornamentation were slight. As Rahn-Bo knew well, the Holy Mechanicus did not tamper with a perfected design.

The datamancer followed the explorator through narrow halls and passages. Sherax took them on an eerily familiar route towards the inner core of the ship, from the port cargo receiving bay in which they had entered into a sorting facility, its conveyors stilled and seized. From there they skirted the rust-rimed outer face of a water silo, driving towards the ship's ventral thoroughfare, which would provide an efficient approach to the forward crew quarters.

Always, Xal led the party, the protector's weapons held ready and senses straining for signs of ambush.

For her part, Rahn-Bo extended her numerous sensors to their

utmost. Beyond the trivial task of searching for signs of life, her augurs took regular soundings of the composition and integrity of the ship's components and superstructure. She obeyed the ductrix's command to avoid interaction with the ship's animus, a precaution that she felt was entirely justified.

It was clear that the stricken ship had suffered minimal internal damage before its interment within the hulk. The corridors through which they walked showed no signs of conflict, no projectile wounds in walls or blade scars through machinery. Despite the ship's continued protestations of intruders rampaging through its decks, there was little evidence of them.

Nevertheless, an insidious enemy had laid the *Almagest* low.

The ravages of entropy had bitten deep into the explorator ship, doing greater – and to an initiate of the Cult Mechanicus, more distressing – damage than any rampaging enemy. Patches of verdigris and oxidised iron coated every surface, and gathered around the base of columns and walls. The air was thick with rust particulates, drifting on inconstant air currents that coughed from ventilation ducts. Cogitator panels that aboard the *Peregrinus* were thrice-blessed daily by Techseer Luren or one of his many acolytes, were here seized, dead things.

The Motive Force was alive within the ship, but it manifested sporadically and with wildly varying strength and potency. Luren had suggested that they attempt to stabilise the *Almagest*'s stuttering power grid, but the ductrix had dismissed the suggestion as a distraction from their goal.

Gravity plating was also active, although subject to the same fluctuations of intensity as the power grid. On several occasions, Rahn-Bo pulsed a warning to the party to divert to an alternate route to avoid a passageway that would drag at their limbs. The gravitic overpressure would not have been damaging – even at triple their maximum magnitude, the ship's grav-plates could

do little more than inhibit the motion of augmetic bodies – but the effect would have been temporarily debilitating.

Their circuitous progress through the bowels of the ship ended abruptly.

They had reached the reactor extraction culvert, a broad avenue running through the centre of the vessel wide enough to allow a pair of Chimera transport vehicles to pass abreast. Or, more accurately, it was sized specifically to accommodate a Zamson load-lifter and its cargo. Once a century, if the proper rites and schemes of maintenance were adhered to, many of the essential elements of the ship's reactor-heart had to be withdrawn and replaced in order to ensure optimal function. A Zamson, along with hundreds of serfs doomed to die from radiation exposure, would carry the spent fuel rods and reactor assemblage through the wide channel, and return with the replacement components. It was a procedure Rahn-Bo had been honoured to witness in her earliest days aboard the *Peregrinus*, shortly after she had been selected to join the crew.

In engineering terms, the culvert represented a structural vulnerability. As such, there were six vast barricades between the reactor cathedral and the ventral cargo hold, which was especially equipped to handle the refuelling procedure.

Sherax and her officers stood at the foot of the sixth and final barrier, located approximately four hundred yards forward of the reactor cathedral. From the cargo hold beyond, they would be able to move freely through the *Almagest*'s interior.

Xal assessed the barricade, which was a full three yards thick at its base. 'I am not equipped to force our way through this barrier, ductrix,' he said.

'Nor would I ask you to.' Sherax placed a claw against the dense adamantine. 'The Motive Force flows through the locking mechanism. We can raise the door.'

Rahn-Bo nodded. 'By your will, ductrix.' She could still sense Luren's reluctance to interface with the *Almagest*, and so headed towards an access port at the foot of the barricade. The terminal was faced with a hinged panel, engraved with commandments to the *Almagest*'s crew against tampering. The panel yielded to her touch, and she began manipulating the dense nest of circuitry beyond.

'Anomalous reading detected.' The burst of binharic barked from a nearby vox-grille, loud enough to momentarily jar Rahn-Bo's nascent connection to the mechanism's controls.

'Ductrix, there is clearly some intelligence directing the ship's outbursts,' Luren said. He was staring up at the vox-grille, which was embedded in the chest of a leering gargoyle. 'It is reacting to our presence.'

'A possibility.'

'A certainty.' Luren pounced on the opportunity to dispute Sherax's statement, as he so often had in recent years. 'The instability of the ship's spirit is driven by a malignance.'

'Anomalous reading detected.' The ship chose that moment to interject, but the words went ignored by the party.

'The *Almagest* has been alone in the void for a long time, Erasmus. Data-gheists thrive in such conditions,' Sherax said.

'Corruption thrives in such conditions.'

Rahn-Bo kept her attention on the workings of the barricade, remaining detached – as far as she could – from the disputes between the explorator and her senior techseer. A final seal yielded to her persistence, and a heavy crunch of metal juddered from the ancient steel. The barrier began to rise, accompanied by a shriek of protesting servos.

'Intruders detected.'

'Good work, Thess.'

Rahn-Bo did not react to Sherax's empty praise.

'Intruders detected.'

A single shot coughed, almost lost beneath another screech of code from the *Almagest*. The shell struck the deck ten yards ahead of the Mechanicus party, its explosive charge bursting into fragments.

They scattered instantly, in accordance with predefined combat protocols. Luren and Rahn-Bo bounded into cover behind one of the culvert's curved reinforcing ribs, while Xal interposed himself between their attackers and the ductrix, covering her with his body as they both lurched out of the line of fire. His physical warding was far from necessary; before the echo of the first shot died, Sherax's form was cloaked within the potent protection of a refractor field.

More shots, staccato and ill-aimed, crashed along the length of the culvert to detonate against the barricade.

<Physical projectiles, heavy calibre.> Xal's analysis was immediate. <Solar-pattern heavy bolters.>

The protector ducked out from behind the concealment of the bulkhead, arc pistol extended. He loosed four shots before the gunfire shifted towards him. Shells crashed into the curve of steel as he stepped back into cover. <Assailants identified. Praetorian servitors.>

Praetorians were vat-grown, their base genomic material taken from ogryn stock for the express purpose of bearing heavy weaponry in combat scenarios. They were a dispensable resource for a ship's secutor or a forge's warden, intended to be the first into contact with an aggressor to fix them in place until more flexible forces could be brought to bear.

Rahn-Bo settled back against the culvert's wall, and extended her internal auspex and other sensors along the channel's length.

A trio of combat servitors advanced in ragged formation. Their legs had been replaced with motorised tracks that rumbled unsteadily along the deck. Two were armed with heavy bolt-weapons that replaced their left arms, with their right ending in thick industrial claws for melee combat. The third bore a multi-laser, which unleashed a torrent of screaming energy that lit up the vast duct in hues of ruby red.

The Praetorians' condition was remarkable. What little flesh remained on them hung from metal bones as stringy lumps. Their tracks were missing links, contributing to their unusually inaccurate fire.

That fire, now it had properly begun, was heavy and continuous. Shells hammered the length of the hallway to detonate against the junction's far wall. Metal and stone shattered under the impacts, throwing splinters and shards in radial bursts that spattered from, or stuck in, Rahn-Bo's armoured suit.

Luren and Xal leant from cover in the same moment, the techseer loosing a searing bolt of phosphorescence, and the protector a blast from his arc pistol. Both pulses of energy cast sharp-edged shadows as they raced the length of the corridor, but both struck a heavy metal plate affixed to the nearest unit's torso, a crude but effective form of armour. The servitor's fire stuttered, but did not stop.

Xal jerked back into cover as the three units converged their fire on his position. 'Cogitatrix, I require three seconds of unimpeded motion,' he called.

Rahn-Bo glanced at Sherax. 'Ductrix?'

'Do it.'

Rahn-Bo went very still. Her eyes, a pair of augmetic spheres that had replaced her organic orbs years before, emitted a faint blue glow as the datamancer sought a noospheric connection with the ship's defenders. It was a risk to open herself to the unstable mind of the *Almagest*, but one that Rahn-Bo took willingly.

Four seconds passed, and then the gunfire suddenly ceased.

Heavy thunks filled the silence, announcing that all three units had begun their reloading cycle simultaneously.

<My thanks, magos.> It was all the opportunity Xal required.

He ducked from behind the bulkhead and leapt, clearing the distance between his position and the closest servitor in two powerful, piston-driven bounds. He landed to one side of the leading unit, his halberd's blade level with the servitor's neck. It slid through without resistance, its vibrating edge unhindered by bone or neural cabling. The servitor's bolter swung towards the floor in the same moment as its head fell away.

Its nearest companion attempted to turn towards the lifeward, but its tracks seized mid-motion and it jerked to a stop with a crunch of distressed gears. Xal sidestepped, and his arc pistol spat another bolt of coruscating energy. The sun-bright burst took the unit in the flank. The servitor spasmed to an arrhythmic death, the grey flesh of its chest flayed raw by the unchained power of the Motive Force.

Rahn-Bo's chronometer had been counting the milliseconds since she triggered the servitors' reloading sequence. As the third servitor rotated to bring its rearmed bolter to bear on the protector, she pulsed a warning, but it proved unnecessary. As the bolter rose to its firing position, Sherax calmly stepped from cover with her archeotech pistol held in one claw. A viridescent line lanced from its barrel, and struck the unit in the centre of its mass. The servitor's pallid flesh and rusted metal withered under the fusillade, and the Praetorian's torso toppled from its tracks.

Xal turned to verify his work, halberd and pistol outstretched. 'Threat neutralised.' The protector briefly examined the skull of the third unit. 'My thanks, ductrix,' he voxed.

Rahn-Bo followed Luren from cover, drawn towards the trio of servitors by their poor condition. What little remained of their organic components had deteriorated past the point of parody. If anything, her initial assessment had been overly generous. That the Praetorians had been moving at all was remarkable.

The foremost drone, the one whom Xal had decapitated, was missing its offside arm. To stabilise its torso against the weight of its implanted heavy bolter, the limb had been hacked away, and a thick spar of metal affixed by pins between the socket and its hip-joint. Its chest was bound to the strut by a reel of thick wire.

'Crude.' Luren's contemptuous judgement was immediate.

'Though moderately effective,' Rahn-Bo said. She was as appalled as her colleague by the primitive repair, but she could not deny that the unit had been kept functioning far beyond its expected lifespan.

'There is a more pertinent factor,' Sherax said as she joined them. 'Who performed this maintenance?'

'Ductrix.' Xal stepped protectively in front of Sherax, gesturing with the tip of his halberd at the arched bulkhead that led into the *Almagest*'s dark interior.

From the shadows beyond the servitors' lifeless forms, mutants peered in curious terror.

THREE

Edgar waited for the Helm Mechanicus to retract its needles from his skull, then roughly tossed it aside. The damned left-leg gimbal had seized up again on the walk back to the staging area, reducing *Vortigern* to an undignified, half-limping gait.

The skirmish – it was too minor an engagement to deserve any greater description – had lasted less than an hour. The orks had charged, and the Vostroyans had killed them. There had been little nuance or cunning in the creatures' attack, just a bestial surge met with calm, overwhelming firepower.

It seemed to Edgar that the hulk was all but depopulated following the xenos' unsuccessful assault on the Vresta System. Their leadership caste, such as it was, had died beneath the guns of Battlefleet Changrit before they could make planetfall, and only the dregs remained aboard *Misery's Daughter* to trouble the Mechanicus expedition.

He scoffed. What an absurdly extravagant epithet.

Through the Armiger's cockpit imagifiers, Edgar looked with

disinterest at the clusters of Mechanicus tech-thralls going about their work. Explorator Sherax had chosen the forward flight deck of an Astartes warship embedded within the outer layer of the space hulk as her bridgehead. Through four days of constant labour, her menials had turned it into a defensible staging post for the expedition.

Carefully ordered pallets of equipment were stacked in rows, delineating alleys and arteries that directed traffic across the width of the flight deck. Servitors moved containers back and forth, while others, laden with flamers, moved methodically around the perimeter of the hangar scorching ork glyphs and other signs of xenos occupation from the steel. Mechanicus bondsmen worked under the direction of their superiors to connect hissing hoses to machines and hoist bundles of cables high into the hangar's ceiling, while robed acolytes wafted smoking braziers over cogitators and crates of construction equipment. Edgar could not begin to fathom the purpose of any of this activity, and so did not make the attempt.

Off to one side, hard up against the starboard wall of the hangar near the arched concourse from which Edgar had entered, the Blackbloods had set up their own encampment. Canvas sheets strung between scaffolding poles marked the border around their territory, which from Edgar's vantage point did not possess the same degree of tightly ordered structure that had been imposed across the rest of the deck. It appeared that the Mechanicus would accept a measure of disorder, so long as it was contained within strictly defined boundaries.

Edgar thumped the cockpit release, and the Armiger's head hinged back, allowing the frigid air of the flight deck to enter. It carried the peculiar odours of the hulk, or at least those of this particular vessel. The familiar reek of machine oil, lubricant, and incense that accompanied every acolyte of the Cult Mechanicus and their contraptions. The tang of promethium from the flamer teams, and the faint fizz of burning ozone that radiated from the atmospheric shield – the distressingly transparent wall between the flight deck's steel and the vacuum of the void beyond. And beneath it all, alarmingly, was the faint aroma of old, dry blood.

Edgar remained in his seat. His leg had cramped during the slow walk back to the bridgehead, thanks to the Helm's psychostigmatic feedback. He made a brief attempt at massaging the muscles around his knee, before giving up in disgust. He'd limp too, like the hamstrung warrior he had become.

He gasped as he started down the rungs of the Armiger's boarding steps. The cold rushed into him with each breath, setting a chill into the centre of his chest. Edgar wore a heavy jacket armoured with lames of steel, and fine quivit-skin gloves – a gift from his father – but the frozen metal rungs still burned like sea ice. He had become all too aware that the worshippers of the Omnissiah paid little heed to creature comforts. Even so, it appalled him that after four days they had yet to set up heaters.

'If you think this is bad, you haven't stood a night-shift on a promethium extractor in a Vostroyan winter.'

Major Nastasya Zlata appeared to be waiting for him. She leant against the wire frame of a storage pallet that formed the wall of the area set aside for Edgar's Armiger to rest. Despite her jest, her grey coat, trimmed at the cuffs and lapels with blood-red fur, was belted tight around her waist.

One of the first things Edgar had learned about the Vostroyans was the source of their moniker, the Blackbloods. Evidently each soldier of the 103rd Firstborn was drawn from a family whose assigned employment was on the planet's deep-water promethium rigs. The Blackbloods took pride in the name, in their heritage. In their service to the God-Emperor, fated by the laws of their world before each of them had even drawn breath.

How he had hated them. It had been one of Zlata's remaining soldiers who had pulled him from the wreckage of *Bladequeen*. Who had robbed him of the death he had deserved at her side. The Blackbloods were a boisterous clan, and his animosity had eased somewhat as the months passed. Nevertheless, his anger had rebuffed their initial attempts to welcome him into their fraternity, and so a tense distance had developed between them.

Edgar descended the final rungs with care, conscious of his stiff knee and fragile dignity. For all that the Vostroyan soldiers were a crude and unkempt tribe, Nastasya Zlata was a handsome woman, tall and broad-shouldered even without her heavy coat and its bronzed joint-guards.

'Major,' he greeted her.

'Our thanks as ever, Master Lorristan.'

Edgar shrugged. He had played little part in the eradication of the orks, though the threat evident in *Vortigern*'s size and armaments had ensured that the majority of the xenos had focused on the Armiger, providing an obligingly dense target for the Vostroyans' guns.

'Ma'am.' He searched for something more. 'Your troops did well. As ever.'

Through the years since Gryphonne IV, Major Zlata had somehow managed to keep her heavy fur hat in one piece, and she swept it off to scrub at her head as she grinned. 'Yes, they're a fine bunch of rogues.' Her blonde hair was shorn down to a finger's width all over, and was as dirty and grease-streaked as her face.

One of Zlata's Guardsmen wandered over, holding a pair of tin mugs filled with a milky grey substance. Chunks of darker grey bobbed on the surface.

'Banner Sergeant Belyev,' Zlata said in greeting.

The man offered one of the cups to the major. 'Sir.'

'My thanks, Gennadi.' She took the noisome broth with apparent

relish, pulling off her thick gloves to warm her hands against the mug's metal sides. 'You're welcome to join us,' she said to Edgar.

The smell that wafted from the cup was a powerful disincentive to accept her invitation.

'I should tend to my steed,' he said.

Major Zlata's smile faded to seriousness. 'Of course.' She handed the mug back to the sergeant, and looked up into the cluster of sensors that formed the Armiger's face. 'My gratitude to you, *Vortigern*.' She made the sign of the cog across her chest with a solemnity that would have heartened any tech-priest who saw it. She nodded to Edgar, then took back the broth and walked away in genial conversation with Banner Sergeant Belyev.

'The people of Vostroya are great ones for paying proper respect to the machine.'

Edgar turned. He had not realised Zlata's unexpected and unexplained visit had lifted his black mood until he saw the face of the man behind him, and it suddenly crashed back into place.

Gregor Ormond was another survivor of the Gryphonnen disaster whose manner of escape had left him stranded amid the Mechanicus refugees. He had become separated from the rest of the House Cadmus entourage when a storm of tyranid spores descended upon their drop-keep, birthing a horde of brood-creatures into their midst. The old man had escaped the massacre that followed, and through sheer good fortune managed to board a Slovo VI orbital conveyor and blast free from the nightmare alongside a dozen maniples of skitarii.

He was a sacristan, one of the many honoured artificers of Raisa whose knowledge and expertise, gained after long years of study among the Gryphonnen magi, maintained House Cadmus' steeds. In the slow process of organisation that followed the exodus from Gryphonne IV, he and Edgar had been brought together aboard the *Peregrinus* along with *Vortigern*, each a stranger to the others.

Edgar guessed that Ormond was at least twice his age; a short grey moustache and thinning hair completed a face that had seen more than its share of years. He was a grim, downtrodden sort of man, much given to bemoaning his state and station.

'A good hunt, sir?' Ormond asked.

'The left-side gimbal seized on me again,' Edgar said brusquely, not bothering to acknowledge the man's obsequious greeting. He loosened the sleeves of his armoured jacket, then turned for Ormond to tug it free.

'My apologies, sir.' The sacristan folded the jerkin, stiff with sweat, over one arm. 'It was overdue for replacement years ago. I have submitted a request to the ship's manufactory decks to assemble such a part, but it has not been forthcoming.'

'I don't care about your excuses. I just want this pile of a scrap to work at the full extent of its capabilities, as limited as they are.'

The old man's face fell at Edgar's casual insult of his machine. Edgar continued regardless. 'I want the gimbal fixed. In fact, rebuild the entire control assemblage, as soon as you can. I may be called to walk again.'

What he had asked would take a team of artificers half a day, and Ormond drew himself up. 'I am only one man, Sir Edgar.'

'You are one man, with one charge – to keep that shit-heap of a machine functioning. And for the last time, I am Master Lorristan. Nothing more.'

Ormond seemed to sag, what little defiance he had been able to summon guttering out in the face of Edgar's temper. 'Aye, master. I'll relubricate the gimbal bearings now.'

Edgar sighed, a short, sharp exhalation that did little to calm his temper. 'No, don't bother. I can do it.' He regretted his anger;

it was not Ormond's fault that they had been thrown together and tethered to a faltering machine. 'Fetch me something to eat, I'm famished. Even that Vostroyan slop will do.'

'Aye, master.' The sacristan hung Edgar's jerkin on the projecting node of *Vortigern*'s right-hand support piston, and set off slowly towards the Blackbloods' Munitorum unit.

Edgar shrugged off his heavy trousers, the armour plating on the thighs clanking as they hit the deck. He shivered, and looked around for the cloak Ormond should have set out in anticipation of his return.

Heavy footsteps on the deck grating announced the sacristan's return after several minutes, but when Edgar turned it was Major Zlata who appeared around *Vortigern*'s right leg. She was holding a steaming bowl of the grey broth, and the earlier friendliness in her eyes had vanished.

'Your servant said you were hungry,' she said.

Edgar was wrong-footed. 'He is my sacristan.'

'It appears that they're the same thing.'

'That isn't quite–'

'I will never see Vostroya again.' Zlata cut him off before he could speak, although he wasn't sure what he had been about to say. 'But this has always been my fate, from the day I was fortunate enough to escape my mother's womb ahead of my sister.'

Edgar was having difficulty keeping up with the conversation. 'You have a sister?' he asked.

'We are twins. Her name is Galina.' A faraway look passed across her face. 'She took up our mother's station on Platform Fifty-Six two weeks before I was called to the founding. To this day, I wonder which of us bears the greater hardship.'

The severity in her eyes returned. 'I will never see Vostroya, and you will not see your home, wherever it is.' She gestured around the deck, at the stacked supplies and the dozens of tech-thralls that moved between them. 'We are all alone, master knight. You. Me. Ormond, my men. We do not belong among the Holy Mechanicus, nor aboard their ship. All we have is each other. The explorator uses us, berths us, feeds us to a standard required by regulations. But that's all. We survive by holding together, by rising above pettiness and vanity. There is no room for ego in this troop. No room for self-pity, either.'

She drew herself up, and for the first time Edgar noticed that Major Zlata was ever so slightly taller than him.

'So the next time you want something to eat,' she went on, 'get it yourself.'

She thrust the bowl of broth into his hands, which half-spilled over his gloves. When Edgar looked up from the sopping mess, she had already spun on her heel and was marching away.

FOUR

'Do not fire.'

The mutants approached in pairs and trios, emerging from dark corners.

They were human, or at least appeared to have devolved from a state akin to baseline humanity. Xal observed fifteen figures shambling from the shadows. They were short, thin-limbed creatures, made smaller by a heavily hunched posture. What flesh they possessed was almost translucent; Xal was able to distinguish every bone and ligament in the closest mutant's torso.

They covered themselves with scraps of fabric that were mouldered past the point of ruin. There seemed to be a hierarchy based on cladding – those that appeared the most healthy, relative to their peers, wore tabards or skirts of red cloth, belted with other tatters. Some were entirely naked, their emaciated bodies displayed without apparent shame.

None, in Xal's estimation, was older than thirteen Martian years. Most were considerably younger.

'Do not fire,' Sherax ordered again.

Xal was surprised to realise he had not even considered it. Each of the creatures was armed, either with a club, a crude blade, or else simply a sharpened length of metal. Two carried more robust weapons: lascarbines, of a pattern that on the *Peregrinus* were held in secondary armoury lockers in case of boarding actions. But they represented no kind of threat to Sherax or her party, neither individually nor collectively.

Nevertheless, they continued to approach. Xal hefted his halberd, and the obvious warning in the gesture halted the mutants' advance.

<What heresy is this?>

As the bravest had ventured closer, horrified curiosity had overcome all of Sherax's companions. The noosphere hummed with tense interrogatives and cautious hypotheses. It took Xal a moment to identify the cause of Magos Luren's fury. And then he saw it.

In addition to their ragged garments, the mutants wore a mockery of Mechanicus purity. Metal plates had been riveted to their flesh, or beaten into shape and held in place with coils of wire. Thin lines of silver ran across their limbs, soldered to their skin in a parody of corpuscarii electoos.

Their mimicry went further. Each abhuman wore a scar or brand somewhere on their bodies, an icon with a vague resemblance to a skull within a wheel carved into their chests, arms or thighs. From the spectropic signature of the scars, Xal could tell they had been blackened by rubbing promethium residue into the wounds.

The largest – one of the two bearing lascarbines – crept closer in its odd, loping gait. It was clearly the leader of the pack. Its body was less emaciated; the vague suggestion of musculature was visible in the lines of the limbs. But more than its

physical condition, what marked it out from their pack was the Cog Mechanicus, corroded but whole, mounted in its torso.

The abhuman must have wrenched the emblem from the plating of the *Almagest* and welded it to the skin of its chest. From the unhealthy swelling and thick pus that leaked around the crimped edges of the metal, the abhuman had adopted the adornment recently.

The placement of the symbol in the mutant's chest exactly mirrored the location of Xal's own icon of the Machine God, a talisman of copper and adamantine presented by Sherax when she had adopted Xal as her lifeward. Even as Xal noticed the similarity, the mutant touched the corroded iron fixed to its flesh with a thin finger, its wide eyes locked on Xal's visor.

<They are servants of the Omnissiah?> Xal's conflicting emotion-spikes made the statement a question. The abhumans' crude echo of his worship of the Deus Mechanicus repulsed him, in a way that his combat-wired mind was ill-equipped to process.

<They are nothing of the kind.> Luren strode forward, one claw withdrawing the magos' phosphor pistol from within his robes.

'Luren, stop.'

The techseer checked immediately. For all that he chafed at Sherax's command, he was bound by it.

'They are the descendants of the *Almagest*'s crew,' Sherax said. She stepped around Xal, taking her almost close enough to touch the creature. It stumbled back, but when it became clear she was not moving to strike, it fled no further.

'This is their ship. We are the interlopers.'

Xal felt Luren's animus flare. 'You cannot be serious.'

'We will not harm these creatures without provocation.'

Sherax had not stepped away from the boldest beast, who

stared back with wide, black eyes. Its gaze roamed over Sherax's augmetics, her robes, the sculpted metal of her face and limbs. Xal's ability to interpret facial gestures was limited, but fearful awe was the obvious emotion that rolled from them, as thick and noxious as their body odours.

Several of the pack began to speak, tentatively sounding out syllables from mouths filled with blackened teeth.

'What are they saying?' Xal asked.

'Gibberish.' Luren was quick to dismiss them.

'You are mistaken,' Sherax said.

Rahn-Bo confirmed the ductrix's insight. 'They are speaking as the ship does.'

With that frame of reference, Xal heard the pattern of their speech. The mutants' clicks and hoots were a crude approximation of binharic, slowed to a pace that a human mouth and vocal cords could produce.

'My audex transcoder lacks the capacity to interpret them,' Xal said.

The rest were taking up the chant, repeating the noises with growing zeal. Many had dropped their weapons, and were lacing their slender hands into what was unmistakably the sign of the cog.

Sherax spoke before Rahn-Bo could. 'They are praying to us.'

The chanting continued for several minutes, during which time Rahn-Bo and Sherax covertly subjected the mutants to a battery of invasive auspex scans. Xal observed them in his own way. He saw that, though bent in supplication, the leading mutant paused between each bow to stare from beneath his heavy brow at Sherax and her party.

'Anomalous reading detected.'

The screech of binharic suddenly hammered from the nearest vox-emitter, and immediately the beasts fell silent.

'Emitter mis-alignment. Manual reset required.

'Fall in for crew inspection.'

As one, the mutants abandoned their supplication, their chant cut short. They clasped their weapons and set off running back the way they had come. The leader trailed the pack, staring back at Sherax. Xal interpreted its insistent grunts as beckoning, and he was entirely unsurprised when the ductrix began to follow.

Sherax allowed herself to be led a short distance. When the pack realised that the Mechanicus adepts were following, they began to hoot and caper once more. Xal quickly took his place between his ductrix and the closest mutant, his halberd levelled and thrumming pistol drawn. The mutants clearly possessed sufficient intelligence to perceive his weapons' threat, and kept their distance.

They rounded a corner, and evidently reached the mutants' destination. It was no site of great importance for the ship – just a bulkhead slightly recessed into the corridor's walls. The recess contained a relief impression of the cog, around which air vents were clustered. Periodic gusts of oxygenated air billowed from the higher vents, while others at the foot of the recess sucked in exhalation for recycling.

What made the site remarkable was not its function, but what the mutants had done to it.

They had constructed a shrine.

Tributes were arrayed beneath the icon. A short length of metal sharpened to a knife's point. Several examples of fungal growth, the significance of which Xal could not determine. Scraps of cloth, stiff with dried blood. The dried residue of phlegm, presumably deposited by those creatures whose low station meant they had nothing greater to offer.

The meagre treasures of a degenerate society.

'Abominations.' Disgust poured from Luren.

'Misguided,' Rahn-Bo corrected. 'They have been aboard this ship for centuries, surrounded by xenos and the spectres of the immaterium. They cleave to the Omnissiah, even if they do not understand what they worship.'

Luren rounded on her. 'Does this not offend you? This is idolatry, not worship. They build nothing, achieve nothing but continuing to exist.'

'Is that not its own achievement in such a place as this?'

'They are wretches who profane the Omnissiah with every gesture.'

'"Sentience is the basest form of intellect."' Rahn-Bo invoked the Fifth Law of the Cult Mechanicus with solemn authority. 'Crude though it is, they show reverence for the machine.'

'"Sentience is the ability to learn the value of knowledge."' Luren replied with the Third Law, no less grave. 'What evidence have you that these creatures are capable of learning? They ape our vestments and imitate our bonding with the machine, making a parody of both.'

'This line of debate is irrelevant,' Sherax said. She had taken no side in their argument, but now silenced them both. 'The existence of remnants of the *Almagest*'s crew is unexpected, but immaterial to our purpose. Purgation would be an unacceptable delay and an unnecessary expenditure of resources. I will not risk further harm to the ship. Accommodating their presence is the most efficient path.'

The two lead mutants beckoned Sherax once more. Pathetic eagerness was written across their distorted features.

Luren was at the ductrix's shoulder. 'Talin, this course leads only to corruption.'

'Incorrect,' she replied. 'This course leads us to our goal.'

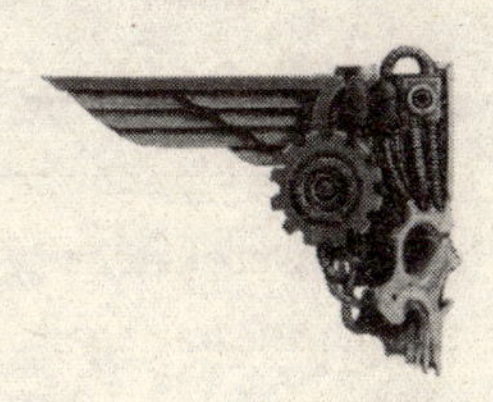

FIVE

Sherax's companions were judging her. In the explorator's estimation, they may have been right to do so.

Their guides led the party through narrow service ducts, taking them deeper into the ship's interior. Even to her own eroded capacity for self-reflection, that she had willingly placed them in the creatures' midst was the gravest sign yet that Sherax had strayed from the path of logic. Their hosts were abhumans, far devolved from *homo sapiens*. Logic dictated that there was nothing to be gained from humouring them. Protocol in this circumstance required but one action: eradication.

Yet despite the requirements of protocol and the demands of logic, Sherax was compelled to follow them. She rationalised her behaviour as pursuing an anthropological curiosity, in full accordance with her explorator's mandate.

The abhumans infested the ship. The pack that had found them was fifteen-strong, but more quickly emerged from unlit corners and rusted conduits. Soon hundreds were following

them in a shambling train. Spavined creatures lurched ahead of the party, announcing their coming in a strange tongue. The sounds were evidently meant in praise of Sherax and her adepts, the manifestations of the Deus Mechanicus that had appeared amongst the beasts. Xal was close beside Sherax, blade twitching at any abhuman whose religious awe overwhelmed its fear.

Their society appeared rudimentary at best. Hierarchy was based on physical strength, and displayed by the disquieting mimicry of Mechanicus augmentation hammered into translucent flesh. Pack behaviour was abundantly evident. Sherax heard a continuous stream of threatening snarls and pops from the trailing column as leader-beasts came into proximity with one another.

In the explorator's estimation, their guides did not rank among the greatest of the mutant populace. Larger, healthier abhumans emerged from side chambers as they passed, but it was clear that the weaker creatures' nearness to the Mechanicus party conveyed a status that superseded their physical inferiority.

The beasts demonstrated the remnants of some human traits. Their guides walked tall and proud before them, and greeted challenges with aggressive barks and gestures that Sherax suspected would not be out of place on the *Peregrinus*' own serf decks.

They passed a hall from which many juvenile or otherwise stunted abhumans bustled, bearing crude containers filled with noxious organic material. A vibrant cocktail of particulates rolled from the hall, feculent and heavy with water vapour. Sherax and her companions halted in the same moment, their attention captured by the violation they observed within.

Aboard the *Peregrinus*, they would have been looking into the secondary agriponics chamber, staffed by honoured serfs

and servitors under the careful supervision of Magos Biologis Lustradin, sub-magistrix for calorific supply.

On the *Almagest*, it was a place for mutants to farm nutrient-rich fungus grown in their own waste.

Mycelial flora covered every surface. The deck plating was entirely lost beneath layers of rotting material, out of which rose dense clumps of fungus in wildly varying strains. Yellow and green streamers of saprophytes climbed iron walls and bronze columns. Red and purple nodules sprouted from milky stalactites that descended from ceiling plates embossed with the Cog Mechanicus. Patches of white balls covered in feathery tendrils were mixed in with the rest, but were avoided by the abhumans that walked barefoot among their foul crop.

Hundreds of mutants were at work across the chamber, squelching to and fro along well-worn lanes, spreading muck or harvesting ripened fungi by hand. Many of the larger, more vital abhumans watched them carefully, wielding lengths of metal or braids of cabling as goads to keep their more wretched kin at their labours.

As Sherax watched, one of the overseer creatures stooped and plucked a grey nodule from a weaker mutant's container. It tossed the calcified mushroom into its mouth, and proceeded to chew with every sign of enjoyment.

It was Rahn-Bo who first found her voice, and spoke the realisation that had arrested the adepts' attention. The chamber held a familiar sight, and it was all the more abhorrent for it.

'These creatures are harvesting fungal spores derived from the orkoid ecosystem.'

The Adeptus Mechanicus classed the ork species as *bestia eradicatus*. It was a plague upon the galaxy due to its enthusiastic aptitude for violence, and its obstinate capacity for endurance and dissemination. Observation of dozens of afflicted worlds had shown that once a planet was occupied by the xenos, its populace would inevitably be required to undertake decades of purgation campaigns, as the spores released from orkoid bodies would take root in almost any condition. Mycelial growth would sustain and, with time, give rise to the semi-sentient variants of the creatures that terrorised Imperial worlds.

The orkoid ecosystem that pervaded the *Misery's Daughter* had taken root within the *Almagest*, and had permitted the survival of the ship's crew beyond any reasonable expectation. What truly appalled Sherax and her colleagues, though, was that it had been cultivated, brought aboard by the degenerate descendants of the *Almagest*'s crew in imitation of the orks' own life cycle.

Such mimicry was not unprecedented. The survivors on Imperial worlds overrun by orkoid invasion had been documented adopting many of the xenos' traits, even going so far as to attempt halting dialogues and commerce with them. But Sherax had not encountered nor heard of such a thorough fusion of xenos and human physiology.

'This undoubtedly accounts for their extreme devolution from baseline humanity,' Rahn-Bo observed.

'Undoubtedly.' Sherax's reply was automatic, unthinking.

'We should acquire samples,' the datamancer continued, her fascination appearing to outweigh her revulsion.

Sherax could not judge her; it was possible that in years past she would have shared her companion's academic perspective on the scene before them. Now, though, all she saw was desecration. The vessel that she had sought for so long had been made a breeding ground for abhumans.

The train of mutants behind them had grown quiet. Their guides were making fearful gestures, urging them on towards whatever destination they intended for Sherax's party.

'Such examination is a secondary concern,' Sherax said. She

compartmentalised her disgust, forcing her thoughts back to their defined course. She and her companions set off once more.

Their followers resumed their chanting, and their coming echoed through the rusting halls.

'We must purify this vessel.' Luren had not offered any contribution while observing the mushroom farm, but now his binharic was heavy with adamant fury. 'Regardless of your objective, ductrix, it is our duty to cleanse the *Almagest* of this taint.'

Sherax did not respond. The rightness of his statement was self-evident. Lucanus' records were what she sought, but her Gryphonnen pride could not overlook the despoiling of his ship.

Eradication had become a valid option.

SIX

The creatures led them away from the abomination they had perpetrated in the ship's agriponics chamber, and towards the *Almagest*'s prow.

They continued to blurt and babble in their distorted approximation of language, but Erasmus Luren paid them no heed. Rahn-Bo, however, was clearly fascinated. Her noospheric aura was in constant flux as the datamancer absorbed more and more information into her formidable and expansive mind.

<The ductrix ordered you not to do that,> he reminded her.

<She ordered *us*, Luren. And I am not violating her instruction. I am merely documenting their language and behaviour, not interacting with them.>

<You find something of interest in these creatures?>

<Do you not?>

<I find them repellent. And your interest unnatural.>

Rahn-Bo did not respond, but her aura clouded with stubborn pique.

Luren ignored the datamancer's continued examination of the mutants. Sherax had been right to prohibit interaction with the creatures. To his mind, the order had been the first indication since they had boarded the ship that the explorator still possessed a modicum of sense.

Luren had struggled to contain his frustration with Sherax's purposeless search for Lucanus' vessel, and his mythic device of ancient lore. It was a dereliction of their duty, a self-indulgent misuse of the resources remaining to the Gryphonnen people. Each vessel, from the largest manufactory ships to the lowliest tender barge, was an irreplaceable asset, yet Sherax had taken the *Peregrinus* on vain hunts that carried it far from the diaspora fleet for three long years. But more than the ship itself, Sherax was wasting its crew. Luren, and the other adepts and acolytes aboard the *Peregrinus*, had more to contribute to their people than merely enabling Sherax's delusional quest.

His judgement had not changed despite the discovery of the *Almagest* within the macro-agglomeration. Indeed, it had sharpened. Whatever Sherax hoped to find within its manifolds would, Luren knew, inevitably be corrupted by the malignance that lay at its heart.

Luren was no stranger to broken machine spirits. As a techseer, he had restored to functionality the anima of countless machines. While the *Peregrinus'* cohort of artificers could patch-weld a holed plate of armour or rethread the crystalline circuitry of a cogitator, Luren repaired their souls. Without his sanctification, the armour would shatter beneath the merest blow; the cogitator would falter when confronted with the simplest inputs. Luren was minister and mechanic. His tools were the unguent, the hammer, and the prayer.

It was in prayer that Luren most excelled. He had attained something of a reputation for the elegance of his fractal psalms,

and the force of his axiomatic declarations. In the days that followed the destruction of Gryphonne IV, the techseer had been selected by the forge-synod to help formulate the hexamantic eulogy for their lost world. He had been one of many authors; more than eighty per cent of the escaping magi had contributed code-shards, exloading their pain and sorrow as an attempt to purge themselves of unwanted emotions. Luren and the rest of the assembled conclave had taken their collective anguish and sculpted it into a song, a hymnal of sublime mathematic poetry to capture the death of an empire.

Luren had set the eulogy to run continuously among his background subroutines – a permanent addition to his psyche. It was the proudest achievement of his long life, but his pride did not temper the agony of the loss that he had memorialised.

After an hour's tortuous passage, the adepts were obliged to climb through a transport shaft between decks. They lost many of their bestial followers there. The narrowness of the shaft's entrance proved too much for the tense truce between the pack-leaders; the sounds of violence and bloodshed accompanied the rhythmic clatter of metal appendages on the rungs of a service ladder. Luren was certain that those that survived would follow them. The mutants' fervour was palpable, a zeal that spoke of either profound fear or deep-seated religious awe.

As Luren emerged from the duct, many decks higher in the ship's superstructure, one of the mutants was standing close beside the open hatch. While the techseer gathered his robes about him, it reached out a withered paw and attempted to caress the crimson fabric.

'Back, beast!' Luren roared, vox-emitter barking a shard of Low Gothic. Whether the creature understood or not, it retreated immediately, cowering before his outrage. The techseer reached for his sidearm, but Sherax caught his claw with her own.

Metal struggled briefly with metal, before Luren recognised the situation and acquiesced.

'There will be a time for that, Erasmus,' Sherax said. 'But not now.'

Luren delayed his reply by several seconds, a petty act of defiance that was as reflexive as his need to strike the encroaching abhuman. 'By your will, ductrix,' he said at last.

The mutant scrabbled further back, disappearing into a knot of its peers who were similarly retreating from him. Luren drew himself up to his full height, projecting austere authority with every movement.

They had reached the level of the *Almagest*'s command deck, and for the first time Luren did not recognise his surroundings. The degradation that had taken root elsewhere in the ship was of a different order of magnitude here. The air was ripe, heavy with water vapour and organic particulates. The deck plating, which on the decks below had been merely sheened with verdigris and rust, had eroded to oxidised powder, thin skins that concealed the disintegrating bones of the ship's superstructure. The *Almagest* was rotting from within, and it appeared that they had reached the epicentre of the contagion.

'Ductrix, I am detecting volatile particles that are beyond my ability to classify.' Rahn-Bo's sending was accompanied by a gust of alarm within the noosphere that swirled about her aura like a cloak.

Warm, humid air sighed from the command deck portal. Luren's own sensors flared as inputs tuned far beyond anything that could be achieved by organic processes detected an array of radiological particles for which he had no reference.

'Harmful?' Sherax asked.

'It is difficult to say.'

'We should withdraw,' Luren said immediately.

'Do not be absurd,' Sherax countermanded him.

'We should withdraw, ductrix, and return with the proper equipment to effect an examination of this ship.' Luren marched up to her side, though he stopped short of physically grasping the ductrix. 'Protocol is clear. We have identified this vessel as the object of your search. We should return in force, cleanse it of the aberrations that infest its decks, and purge whatever corruption has taken route in its spirit. Anything less is reckless.'

The mutants had watched their exchange fearfully, but the boldest were still gesturing, in their degenerate, capering way, towards the open portal.

'I must know,' Sherax said simply.

She led them in. Luren and her companions reluctantly followed.

SEVEN

Rahn-Bo followed her ductrix, torn between fascination and a creeping, disquieting sense of fear.

Like her peers, her suite of sensing apparatus entirely failed to identify the emanations that wafted from the *Almagest*'s command deck. She had as healthy an appreciation for the dangers of radiological exposure as any member of the Adeptus Mechanicus, but unlike Luren, her curiosity and loyalty to Sherax were more than sufficient to carry her over the threshold.

This was not simply a matter of walking the length of the corridor. Rahn-Bo dodged between degraded steel and minor gravitic eddies caused by damaged plating. At one point she unconsciously reached out a hand to steady herself, and the gauntlet of her pressure suit punched through the wafer-thin layer of rust the wall had become.

On the *Peregrinus*, the command deck was entered by one of two portals. Each was guarded by a demi-maniple of skitarii and other, more exotic means of violence. Each was sealed by an

adamantine portcullis that would withstand a volcano cannon's blast.

The entrance to the *Almagest*'s centre was unbarred, and unguarded.

The mutants leading Sherax ceased their braying as they reached the portal, falling into supine poses that left the ductrix towering in their midst. She too had halted, allowing her companions to join her on the threshold. Rahn-Bo was the last to step beneath the raised portcullis. Like the others, she was struck dumb by what greeted her.

To Rahn-Bo's shock, it was Luren whose thoughts first spilled into the communion – an exhalation of pure, unfiltered wonder.

<Sacred Mars... How is this possible?>

A tree dominated the centre of the command deck. Its stout trunk stretched up from the buckled grating, iron roots threading their way between consoles and cogitators. Branches of steel and silver bent and turned among beams and buttresses. Leaves and blossoms budded from the metal limbs, a riot of colour that glittered in the light of wan lumens.

Vegetation was everywhere, an explosion of verdant growth that touched every bolt and rivet of the deck. Steel-fringed moss and silvery coils of ivy covered consoles and cogitators. Grass carpeted the floor plating, ranging in hue from arterial red to copper and bronze. Other arboreous growth – slim saplings and curving vines and thick-leaved fronds – erupted from voids in the walls and hung from the high ceiling.

Rahn-Bo turned to the closest plant, a spine-tipped bush with ochre buds at the junction of each twig. She was reaching out to grasp a spine when her etheric sensor demanded her attention.

The air of the command deck was oxygen-rich, free of toxic taint and the stale markers of overtaxed purifiers. These were not simply sculptures, bizarre artworks that decorated and

dominated the command-and-control centre of the *Almagest*'s enormity. The plants were alive.

Against all the laws of nature, cold metal and stone had been transmuted into the fundamental building blocks of life.

Sensory overload defeated her. Rahn-Bo found it impossible to prioritise which unnatural growth, which contorted impossibility, to examine first. Her savant's mind twitched from peculiarity to monstrosity to oddity, overwhelmed by paradoxical inputs and her need to understand it all. The first insidious tendrils of panic arose from the code-stream of her thoughts.

There was movement at the base of the central tree, and suddenly her attention was fixed on a single point. *Something* was slumped against the grey bark, entangled – or possibly enmeshed – in its roots.

Rahn-Bo, like most adepts of the Holy Mechanicus, understood the human form for what it was – a point of departure, a framework common to all the servants of the Omnissiah, but one that was almost infinitely mutable. She had been privileged to both witness and assist in the creation of augmetic extensions and evolutions that far exceeded the Machine God's template for its servants.

If the thing that squatted beneath the impossible tree had once been human, it had shed all but the most peripheral vestiges of its past existence. A thick body, swollen as though inflated from within, nestled at the base of the metal trunk. It was covered by a carpet of rotting vegetation, concealing whatever it used for locomotion, if it could move at all. Its five arms were many-jointed, erupting at irregular points from its central mass. Heavy mechadendrites – or possibly vines – rose from its carapace, sheened in a promethium-slick substance. Nestled atop its torso was a blackened, misshapen orb, coated in an opaque, viscous fluid.

Visible beneath the verdure was the horrifyingly familiar red of a Martian adept's robe.

From where Sherax found the fortitude to step forward and confront this monstrosity, Rahn-Bo could not say.

'I am Explorator Superior Talin Sherax, of the *Peregrinus*. You are Magos Nekane Lucanus.'

The entity shifted, a slow shuffle of body and limbs, but said nothing. A bark of static crackled from the deck's vox-emitters, but it held no message that Rahn-Bo could discern.

'Archivist Primus to Lord Explorator Traskel. Curator and Sator of the Oblivis Manifold. Author of *A Treatise on the Epistemological Validity of Common Proto-Human Origins*.'

'Yes.' The thing emitted a single wet sound, formed by gummed vocal cords rather than the clarity of a vox-grille. It was more a choking, gargled cough than a word in Low Gothic.

The creature that sat beneath the tree's branches shifted again. It seemed to be animated by a compulsive, involuntary motion. It gave another rattling, hacking breath, and then truly spoke.

'Forgive me... It has been some time since I used my mundane voice. Yes, I was once Lucanus.'

'What are you now?'

The creature said nothing in response. Instead, the lumens inset around the command deck dimmed suddenly, plunging the chamber into twilight. The indicator runes, switches, and flowers that sprouted from the cogitator hedges were pinpricks of light in the gloom.

As one, the mutants surrounding the Mechanicus adepts began a hooting, fearful cry, and pressed themselves harder into the grass-covered deck. The lumens returned to their former strength, and the creature beneath the tree leant back.

'I was once Lucanus. Now, I simply am.'

'I see,' Sherax said finally.

'I thank you for your restraint during your pilgrimage,' Lucanus, or the creature he had become, continued in spite of her hesitance. With each wet rasp of words, a greasy fluid wept from the orb of its skull and its voice became clearer, stronger. 'Lesser minds would have sought to harm my subjects.'

'You claim dominion over these creatures?' Luren spoke before Sherax could respond, gesturing with his axe-staff at the closest abhuman. The techseer's revulsion choked the noosphere, suffocating Rahn-Bo's own cognitive processes. She struggled to focus on the inputs of her senses, without the choleric filter of Luren's disgust.

Lucanus turned its head towards the techseer, a slow, heavy gesture that disturbed a clot of moss and leaves from its shoulders. 'You, however, threatened them.'

Sherax took a short step closer, dragging the creature's attention back to her. 'You instruct the mutants through the vessel's outbursts.'

'I do.'

'You had them bring us here.'

'I did.'

'Why?'

Lucanus did not immediately reply. Instead, it lifted its limbs, gesturing at the impossibility in which it sat. 'What do you think of my domain?'

Sherax again paused for some time. Rahn-Bo ached to know her mind, to have her ductrix within the communion once more so that she might aid her in this moment.

'What is this?' Sherax finally asked.

Lucanus lowered its limbs, allowing them to gently rest upon the iron surface of the tree's roots. 'This is Genesis.'

'I do not comprehend.'

'You know my name. You are evidently familiar with my work. Define "Genesis", as you understand it.'

Rahn-Bo had known Sherax long enough to be certain that she bridled at Lucanus' condescension, but she answered nonetheless.

'Genesis is a device. A tool, to which many pre-Imperial cultures attributed the creation of their worlds.'

'Good. And so I ask you again, what do you think, now that you stand before it?'

'Impossible.' Rahn-Bo spoke without thinking.

The datamancer felt herself become the subject of Lucanus' attention, though it was impossible to say by what means it perceived her.

'In a galaxy so hostile, so inimical to peace and growth, do you not find it unlikely that life could spontaneously erupt from haphazard assemblies of proteins?' it asked. 'The sheer improbability of it requires that a greater will was once at work. Shaping barren rock into worlds that align with human tolerances. Giving birth to complex organisms. Implanting sentience, the seed of ambition so that they might comprehend the worlds around them.'

'The Omnissiah.' Luren breathed the Machine God's name into the noosphere alongside his vox-burst. As Lucanus had spoken, pious awe had swept away his disgust.

'Perhaps,' Lucanus said in a glutinous, indulgent tone. 'You say you are explorators. Your minds must be open to the miraculous. The concept of the divine made manifest. Look about you. Is this not a miracle?'

Rahn-Bo swept her augurs across the altered command deck. The plant life was unlike any flora she had encountered, but it undoubtedly was alive. Thick, porous leaves drew in toxins from the air and exhaled beneficent gases. Capillary action drove nutrients through branches and limbs that burst from steel

consoles and brass-bound cogitators. The grass that covered the deck bent beneath the bare feet of Lucanus' mutant followers.

Miraculous did appear to be the most accurate descriptor.

Sherax's attention had not shifted from the overgrown magos. 'What power caused this transformation?' she asked.

Lucanus said nothing, instead gesturing towards the branches of the tree. At its zenith, embedded within the ferrous trunk, was a blood-red crystal fragment, no longer or thicker than the smallest digit on Rahn-Bo's hand. Its face was smooth, slightly curved, but a sharp edge suggested it had been broken from a larger whole. The fragment glowed faintly, and was clearly the source of the exotic particles that streamed through the chamber.

'This is a shard, the merest fraction of the power that seeded life across the stars,' it said.

'How did you find it?'

'Before the *Almagest* was confined within this prison, I too was an explorator. I crossed the stars, expanding and refining our understanding of the Omnissiah's realm. I saw hints of meaning in the myths and fables of barbarian tribes, once I had parsed their roots through the obscuring haze of Ecclesiarchy propaganda. I began to challenge the orthodoxies of our order. Who can ascribe the evolution of life to chaotic happenstance, we who worship the Omnissiah and seek the relics of His work?

'I was castigated for my theories, but I was undeterred. I delved further. Freed of the strictures of sanction, I sought out proscribed lore, exploring the first legends from the oldest species of the galaxy. All conformed to my theorem. All, ineluctably, led me to Genesis.'

'You did not answer me.'

Even without the communion, Rahn-Bo could sense the tension radiating from her ductrix. Many Mechanicus adepts scorned

the crude interpretation of physical gestures as a form of communication, but Rahn-Bo knew better. The whine of stressed servos in Sherax's clenched claws was perfectly audible to her aural receptors.

'Where did you encounter this power?' Sherax repeated.

'Is it not sufficient to know that it exists? To bask in the glory of pure creation?'

'Where?' Ironclad code-snippets of command enclosed the question.

The thing that had once been Lucanus continued to ignore the ductrix. It coiled in on itself, distended torso rolling towards the protective bulk of its shelter.

'Why did you have your mutants bring us here?' Sherax asked instead.

Lucanus sighed, a profoundly human gesture that Rahn-Bo found deeply disturbing. 'It can be lonely in paradise. Besides,' it added, 'it was you who stole aboard my ship like thieves in the darkness.'

'Do you not understand what this device could do if properly harnessed?' the ductrix said. 'Do you have any understanding of the devastation that unfolds beyond the walls of your prison? You sit here, a lord of wonders and atrocities, and you make no effort to bring the phenomenon to those who need it most.'

'I feared that this would be your reaction.' Something shifted beneath the verdure that coated Lucanus' form. 'I hoped it would be otherwise, but this was my fear.'

Sherax took a step forward, attention no longer on the contorted archivist but on the red glimmer above it. 'This shard must be examined. We must recover the technology in its entirety.'

'I hoped,' Lucanus said softly, a burbled whisper from the depths of its mire.

'Intruders detected.'

The binharic hammered from the deck's vox-emitters. Instantly, a change came over the clutch of abhumans that had escorted them from the lower decks. Prostrate awe was replaced by bestial anger. Xal reacted instantly, placing himself between the ductrix and the closest mutants.

Sherax was undeterred. 'If you will not yield this power, I will take it from you.'

'All hands, repel boarders.'

Lucanus lunged, but Sherax was faster. The explorator's archeotech pistol leapt from its holster into her hand with a pulse of magnetism, and a searing bolt of emerald energy lanced from its muzzle. Lucanus crashed back into his throne, emitting a stuttering cry of broken binharic as the organic matter of his torso burst into oily vapour.

The *Almagest* screamed, and this time it did not stop.

The shriek of enraged binharic poured from the deck's vox-emitters; Rahn-Bo shut down her audex receivers to avoid permanent damage to her sensory inputs.

Mutants clapped hands to the gristle of their ears, howling in sudden pain and panic. Some fell to the floor, rendered insensate. Others cried out, looking to the writhing figure of their god upon his verdant throne. The few that kept their feet clenched tight their blades and cudgels, and leapt at Sherax and her adepts.

Xal killed the first with a halberd thrust that split its chest in two. The protector dropped low and scythed the blade across thighs and shins, dropping half a dozen mutants that approached in a rush.

A blaze of particles scored a sun-bright line past Xal's shoulder, setting a fire in the flesh of a charging abhuman. Luren threw himself into the fight, phosphor pistol whining and cog-bladed Omnissian axe whirling. The techseer vented his pent-up disgust and frustration in a torrent of binharic invective, flooding the noosphere with a battle prayer that set Rahn-Bo's heart pounding.

In moments, a score of mutant bodies lay dead and dismembered before the two adepts of the Machine God. But their malformed brethren simply leapt their corpses, and quickly the pair were mobbed on all sides.

Rahn-Bo retreated from the fighting. Alone among Sherax's closest companions, she was ill-equipped to engage in close-quarters combat. Rahn-Bo had dedicated her considerable augmentation to further her ability to observe, retain, and analyse, but not to fight. Her sole concession to physical protection was a laspistol holstered at her hip, one of billions stamped from the lost forges of Gryphonne IV, issued to her on the first day of her assignment as logi minoris to the explorator ship *Peregrinus*.

Sherax had also refrained from engaging in the struggle. Indeed, she had not turned away from the thrashing body that had once been Magos Lucanus.

'Ductrix?' Rahn-Bo said.

The barrel of Sherax's archeotech pistol emitted a soft wisp of escaping gas. Her arm remained outthrust, still aimed at the dying scholar whom Sherax had crossed a subsector to find.

Rahn-Bo stepped closer. 'Talin, we must act.'

Whatever moment had held the explorator dispelled in an instant, as she burst into motion. 'Thess, aid me.'

She strode into the mess of organic matter and began to pull herself into the lower branches of the ferrous tree. One of Lucanus' flailing mechadendrites caught her claw, and she stumbled. Rahn-Bo leapt forward, grasping for her laspistol, but Sherax casually swung her gun down and fired a second shot. The energised bolt struck the crown of the magos' head. Iron and bone and brain matter burst into steam, and the groping tendril fell away.

From her precarious position amongst the limbs of the tree, Sherax opened a private vox-connection with Rahn-Bo. 'Thess.'

'Instruct me, ductrix.'

'I must know from where Lucanus obtained the artefact.'

'As your command, explorator.'

The cogitatrix strode towards an overgrown console. Nearness to the unnatural flora gave her pause, but she compartmentalised her hesitation and swept a hand through the dense foliage. Beneath a mat of blood-red moss, the console's internal components were encased in a mineral-rich soil, apparently formed from the elements of the cogitator itself. Rahn-Bo sifted the heavy grains aside, probing deeper until her five-jointed fingers closed around the familiar shaft of a data-shunt.

She knew Sherax had sent her order in private to evade the judgement of the others, even while their attention was fixed on the enraged mutants. That did not matter. Rahn-Bo was loyal to her ductrix. But more than loyal, Thess Rahn-Bo was curious. She was a datamancer. She lived to learn, to collate, interrogate, analyse. The inexplicable was a foreign concept to her, an admission of defeat in the face of the grand mystery and essential challenge placed before the Adeptus Mechanicus by a silent, watching Omnissiah.

And this strange artefact to which Sherax had led her was the greatest mystery of her life.

Rahn-Bo extended a slim coil of mechadendrites from her wrist, slid them into the corroded remains of the data-shunt, and went in search of the truth.

EIGHT

Sherax climbed.

Her claws found easy purchase in the ferrous bark of the tree. With each step the *Almagest* emitted another shriek, either of pain or alarm. The extent to which the device had enmeshed itself within the ship was one of thousands of unknown variables that competed for the explorator's attention, but all of them were subordinate to a single impulse. She had to obtain the device.

Beneath her, Sherax's companions battled the degenerate beings that had led them to the command deck. It was a one-sided slaughter, but the welters of thin, pale blood that erupted from mutant bodies did not deter the beasts, who leapt the bodies of their fallen in an effort to reach the Mechanicus adepts. Even as Sherax climbed, questions scrolled across her thoughts. Was the abhumans' devolution the result of genetic decay, the malignant influence of their orkoid diet, or the result of exposure to the Genesis device? What risks was she accepting on behalf of her ship and crew?

Red and silver leaves parted around Sherax's head as she reached the summit. The bulk of her cognition was trapped in a recursive struggle with the readings of her augurs. The tree and the vegetation that had overtaken the deck was alive, and yet they grew from deck plating and the iron superstructure of the ship. None of it was possible, and yet it undeniably existed.

The crystal shard – the Genesis device – had once been contained within a stasis vault. The remnants of the ancient technology were embedded within the tree's core. Sherax presumed that it had been a precaution that Lucanus abandoned during his descent into madness.

She briefly considered how contact with the device would affect her. The explorator's sensors registered no ill effects from the radiation that streamed from the ruby shard, but that did little to calm her doubts.

Nevertheless, discovery required sacrifice.

Sherax clawed at the enclosing matter of the tree. She tore aside brass bark and ebony wood, no less feral than the beasts that were dying below her. The last fibres fell away, and her claws closed around the crystal.

Beneath her, the battle between mutants and Mechanicus had reached its inevitable end. Bodies littered the bronze grass, and sprays of blood painted the moss and ivy. Luren and Xal were unharmed, though abhuman flesh and bone stained their robes and Luren's pressure suit.

'More will be coming,' she voxed. Xal moved immediately to cover the rear of the chamber.

Luren stared up at her, and at the device she held. Without the noosphere to bridge their minds, the techseer's thoughts were unknowable. For the first time in several years, Sherax regretted its lack. She longed to share the triumph and the doubt that coursed through her, to have others join her in the unfamiliar surge of hope that seemed to flow from the red crystal clutched in her claw. Or would Luren's mind be closed, hamstrung by the dogma that ruled him?

Sherax let the impulse pass, and dropped from the tree, crashing through the silver foliage. She was reassured by the dull metallic crunch that echoed as she landed; somewhere beneath the altered deck, the ship was as it once was.

'I have it, ductrix.' Rahn-Bo retrieved her hand from the innards of a console, though particles of mineral-rich soil still clung to her digits. She reeled, unaided as Sherax was by internal gyroscopics.

'Are you functional?' Sherax asked.

The datamancer did not reply immediately. Sherax stepped quickly to steady her, but Rahn-Bo waved away her claw.

'Lucanus lives. Some remnant of what he became, at least.' Behind the armaglass faceplate of her pressure suit, the organic elements of Rahn-Bo's face were contorted. 'He did not make the extraction simple.'

'I am grateful,' Sherax told her. Again, the absence of the noosphere limited her ability to express herself, and once more she felt the temptation to reopen herself to the communion. Once more, she did not act on it.

She addressed her companions. 'We have what we came for.' So much more than she had ever expected. 'We will leave this vessel, and we shall not return.' The explorator broadcast her words on an open vox-frequency. Lucanus, or what was left of the addled archivist, would remain within his tormented ship, with the knowledge the power that he had hoarded had been taken from him.

'We should remain and study the effects of the device within this environment,' Rahn-Bo said, although it was clear that she had little desire to stay aboard the twisted vessel with its corrupted master.

'No. We have uncovered an artefact whose function surpasses our understanding. We require greater resources than we possess aboard the *Peregrinus* to master it.'

Luren contradicted her. 'Protocol forbids bringing an unknown technology aboard our ship. And we must purge this vessel of its taint.'

Study was unimportant. Purgation was unimportant. Sherax would not delay her vindication.

'We will present this device to the synod immediately,' she replied.

INTERLUDE

The putrid stench of arakhia *infected the* mon-keigh *vessel, itself a graceless mass of rotting metal and weak, cloying spirits.*

The warrior picked his way through the wreckage of degenerate humans. Even by their species' standards, these were a brutish, lumpen breed. During his passage through the vessel he had observed several hundred of the broken creatures. Their wounds told not of battle but of slaughter, a casual slaying born of spite. Mere hours had passed since their deaths, their bodies still ripe and steaming in the chill air.

The creatures at his feet had been reduced to gobbets of pallid flesh and brittle bone. The thin blood on his boots sullied the spirit of his armour, but he endured its touch for the sake of the sight before him.

Flora, or a distorted approximation of it, covered the ugly shapes of mon-keigh machines. It sprouted in contorted mimicry of verdancy and life from crude assemblages of metal and crystal. The vast edifice at the chamber's centre, a caricature of arboreal growth, crowned the vision of almost-life: a twisted garden birthed from silver and bronze.

There was no beauty in what the warrior beheld, save in what it promised. No human art created this flawed verdure. This was the work of a power consigned to legend, now found in the heart of a necropolis of broken void-craft.

No, not found.

The seer at his side placed a hand upon his armour. They both felt the power that had resided in this place, felt the weight of its echo in the Sea of Souls. But the source was gone, its lack all too apparent in the cracked and wilting vegetation. Already, the effect conjured by the stolen power was fading with its extraction.

There was no more to be gained from this place. The warrior turned to leave, but an organic burble made him turn, blades bursting into electric life.

The malformed creature at the base of the tree was, improbably, still alive. Foetid steam rose from its torn, twitching bulk, though it was clear nothing sentient remained.

One of the warrior's companions raised their weapon, but he stilled them. Let the creature expire, slowly, in ignominy. Its crimes were manifest. It did not deserve the sympathy of the blade.

The warrior led his host away, following the trail of destruction that had led them to the vegetal chamber. The mon-keigh had cut a visceral path through the dead vessel's occupants, either in the course of their approach or escape. In either case, their spoor was thick in the air and in the warp.

The warrior set out in pursuit.

TOLKHAN

ONE

The forge world of Tolkhan was a wretched orb, trapped within the jealous grasp of an ancient sun. The planet was gravitationally locked with its star, fated to forever present one face to its wrath and the other to the void. Billions of years of radiation bombardment had scoured one half of its surface, while the shadowed hemisphere was a frigid wilderness.

Nature's brutality had rendered Tolkhan bare of life long before humanity reached its barren sands. What reason the Mechanicus' ancient forebears had for delving its desolate crust were lost to the archives. The withering heat and bitter cold had driven those first pioneers to plunge deep into the mantle of the world. Subterranean cities wormed through the rock for thousands of miles, wrapping about the circumference of the planet dozens of times over.

From orbit, the only evidence of humanity's presence were the vast photovoltaic fields that carpeted the world's sunward face, drinking in the star's excoriating energy to power the forges

that lay beneath. Above them, a dense web of void-yards sheltered within the planet's umbra.

In spite of its founders' precautions, the reach of Tolkhan's poisonous star was inescapable. Incidence of mutation among its populace was high, particularly of the kind that gave rise to individuals manifesting psychic potential. What became of such wretches was not disclosed by the Tolkhanite leadership, and had been the subject of some speculation among Gryphonnen adepts for many years. No doubt their fate was linked to the forge world's proficiency with psy-collars and other forms of immaterial restraint, but Sherax had never given sufficient consideration to the question to seek a definitive answer.

The explorator had visited the world seven times over the course of several centuries. That familiarity had bred contempt. Sherax knew that this was an unworthy sentiment for a magos superior to bear towards her fellow adepts, but that understanding was not sufficient to temper her disdain. Tolkhan's people were belligerent and grasping, resentful of their hard-bitten existence and the triumphs of their more prosperous allies. Their forges, in her estimation, produced little of note, and even their greatest minds had contributed only minor achievements to the Quest for Knowledge.

As a refuge, Sherax considered it imperfect, to say the least. But her preferences had not factored into the forge-synod's calculations, and so it had been to Tolkhan that the remnants of Gryphonne IV had fled in the wake of the leviathan's devastation.

'Entering station-keeping, ductrix,' pulsed Isocrates from her cradle.

'Acknowledged,' Sherax responded. 'Submit a request for docking, any available berth.'

The exchange was conducted via vox, as Sherax was far from the *Peregrinus'* command deck. Since leaving the space hulk and its twisted cargo in the care of Battlefleet Changrit, she had isolated herself from her crew. Her rationalisation had been that by hoarding the shard in her quarters, she would minimise the risk it represented. She alone bore the responsibility of studying the so-called Genesis device. It fell to her to unlock its secrets, and harness its potential.

Despite her absence from the command throne, the essential elements of the data stream flowed through her background cognition. The *Peregrinus'* position within the cluttered void was precisely plotted, one more foreign vessel among the gantries, wharves, and maintenance berths that hid in the planet's shadow. Despite five years of torturous passage through the storm-wracked warp and a fractured galaxy, Gryphonnen ships far outnumbered those of their Tolkhanite hosts.

The ident-tags of so many vessels bearing the cream-and-red livery of her lost world still gave rise to unhelpful limbic outbursts that impaired Sherax's higher functions. The collective might of the diaspora did not invoke feelings of strength, but rather tremors of fear. Sherax was too aware that the fleet was merely the beaten fraction of the power Gryphonne IV once possessed.

The *Peregrinus* was a stranger among its brethren. Sherax's pursuit of the *Almagest* had taken the ship and its crew far from Tolkhan and its baleful star. In truth, she had sought out duties that kept them away from the diaspora fleet. The explorator had little patience for the constant squabbles of her peers. Her distaste for politics – and, she had to admit, her lack of skill in that arena – had been a significant factor in her decision to join the Explorator order. Out among the stars, there were fewer opportunities to run afoul of another magos' ambitions and agendas.

Sherax knew that her self-imposed isolation, which had begun long before the fall of the home world, had led to a reputation for haughty indifference that had undoubtedly harmed her standing within the hierarchy of Gryphonnen magi. She had few bonds of fellowship or commonality, even with the fraternity of explorators. Many junior adepts had left the *Peregrinus* after only a decade or two of service, requesting reassignment to other vessels that might present them with greater opportunities to earn the attention of their superiors.

'Berth assigned, ductrix. We will be cleared for approach in twenty-six days.'

In the solitude of her forge, Sherax permitted herself a brief expression of frustration. 'Very well. Rescind our request for a berth. Have us take up position at the outer marker, and prepare a personnel conveyance for my use.'

Though she was disdainful of, and disdained by, so many of her peers, Sherax was not an outcast from her people. There were several adepts who had at points aided her search, and to whom she was required by the iron laws of patronage to first present her discovery.

She reopened the vox-link. 'Magistrix of transmission.'

'Yes, my ductrix?'

'Prepare an encoded communique. Recipients follow.'

'Content?'

'Message reads: "I have met with success. I seek your counsel."'

TWO

Lord Explorator Satavic Yuel occupied the centre of the portside observation passage of Orbital Array 56-B, his attention directed beyond the heavy armaglass portal towards the array's numerous tugs and ancillary craft.

His four locomotive limbs splayed out beneath his considerable mass, presenting a significant obstacle to the scurrying thralls whose duties took them back and forth along the passage. They had grown used to his impediment. Yuel was often to be found at one of the array's observation points, watching the steady procession of ships beyond the armaglass, moving around one another in obedience to the will of the array's executors.

The dance of ships was as close to elegance as anything could be with the Adeptus Mechanicus – tenders, repair scows, and supply vessels drifting to and fro between the immense forms of frigates, cruisers, salvator arks, factorum ships, Titan barques and war-barges. Millions of tons of metal locked in careful choreography, each the product of billions of hours of labour.

A fabricator serf could spend the entire span of their life laying the superstructure of an Ark Mechanicus, and their children's children might not live to see the last weld sealed.

There was honour in that. Yuel was not blind to the conditions under which the labouring masses lived and worked, and he did not expect them to share his perspective on their dangerous, wretched, and often short existence. Nevertheless, their lives were spent in devotion to the Omnissiah.

Which was more than Yuel could say for himself in recent years.

So many ships at anchor, but his was not among them. As the Gryphonnen fleet had limped through its home system, tragedy had been compounded upon tragedy as vessels that had suffered at the claws of the leviathan began to fall behind. The *Kurzgesagt* had been one of them. The damage sustained as Yuel's ship climbed out of the planet's atmosphere had proven too great to contain. Deck by deck, unquenchable bio-plasma had torn the guts from his venerable vessel.

Yuel had remained connected to his ship through every moment of its agony. It had taken a direct order from Arch-Dominus Zane to compel him to abandon it, and join the refugee masses that huddled aboard their saviours' craft.

Those first hours had hinted at the disputes that would define so much of life for the diaspora fleet in the years that followed. Every ship was populated to the limit of its life-support tolerance, if not beyond it. Magi who had commanded entire city-forges were reduced to the status of mere passengers, assigned to berths once occupied by the lowest initiates and thralls.

Acolytes of the Deus Mechanicus were often fractious, contentious souls, who thrived in isolation. Gryphonnen magi whose achievements led them to high rank and prestige had,

almost as a rule, established their own clades and forges rather than continue to work in the shadow of their peers.

But across the void-bound diaspora, solitude and esteem were now scarce commodities, much-prized and fought for.

Bitterness tripped its way through Yuel's cognition. As ever, he indulged the instinct. His vessel was lost. His flotilla had been dispersed, each ship given over to the command of others. He was an explorator in name only – a lord by dint of past achievements.

Yuel's despondency did not rob him of his situational awareness, and beneath the clatter of boots and grinding tracks that echoed from the passage's steel and armaglass, he recognised a pattern of metallic clicks. He did not turn from the observation port, and allowed Sherax to come to him.

It had been Yuel's influence that had ensured Talin Sherax acceded to the role of ductrix of the *Peregrinus* after its previous master expired. She had been his able student for over a century – diligent, dutiful, and thoroughly committed to the Quest. While she had not, before the fall, proven to be especially dynamic as an independent explorator, Yuel had valued her contributions as a member of his flotilla.

She joined him at the viewport. Though Sherax had shaped her physical form towards the upper percentile of mortal height, she was dwarfed by Yuel's insectile bulk.

'Lord.' Sherax invested the title with signifiers of respect, as was appropriate. Though he had fallen far, Yuel was still owed the deference due his rank and accomplishments.

<Talin. I am glad that you have returned.>

Sherax waited, impassive.

'You still scorn the communion?' said Yuel after several seconds, responding on the same vox-frequency by which she had hailed him.

'Scorned is an incorrect explanation. I find I am more efficient in my tasks without noospheric connection to others.'

'More efficient for you, perhaps. But for your crew?'

She did not have a reply to that.

'How sails the *Peregrinus*?' Yuel asked after an instructive period of time had passed.

'The tides of the empyrean remain tempestuous,' Sherax replied, 'but the *Peregrinus* is resilient and swift.'

Yuel noted the pride in her words, and was suddenly glad his former acolyte had not joined her mind with his. Jealousy was an unworthy sentiment for a mentor, but the fact remained that Sherax possessed one of their people's most finite and valued assets, and Yuel did not. She was free to work, to labour and earn repute, and he was not.

'It is well that you have rejoined the fleet, though I suspect you will not be with us for long,' he said, suppressing his resentment. 'The synod rouses from its torpor, and no doubt it will have a task for the *Peregrinus* to undertake.'

Once more, Sherax did not reply. Yuel considered this with some suspicion. Based on his familiarity with her behavioural template, he had expected Sherax to voice a mild but sincere affirmation of her duty to the forge-synod and her people.

'For what purpose do you seek my counsel?' he asked.

'It may be prudent to wait until we are joined by another, lord.'

With uncanny timing, a new pattern of footfalls became discernible within the clatter of traffic. Yuel's carapace was dotted with sensors, and so he had no need to turn in order to scrutinise the new arrival.

'A strange choice of company, Talin,' Yuel said.

'Magos Lyterix rendered invaluable aid to my search, lord.'

Jeremet Lyterix was an augur, one of the strange breed of logis who bent their efforts towards mapping the immaterium.

Such empyric cartographers were rare. The warp frustrated all attempts to comprehend it, to establish a definite framework for analysis or principles of its essential nature. Worse, it was a corruptive force. The danger inherent in peering into the abyss was one of the few things that was truly understood about the warp, and the safeguards required to permit the work of augury were extensive and arcane. Few acolytes of the Cult Mechanicus were willing to accept the derision of their peers for committing themselves to such an inexact field.

Lyterix, however, revelled in it.

The augur had retained an unusually high proportion of his organic components for an adept of his rank. All four of his limbs had been replaced with finely crafted augmetics, but otherwise he displayed few overt modifications to his physical form. Even with a vocaliser embedded in his throat to emit the various dialects of Mechanicus speech, the magos could have passed for a severely repaired Astra Militarum veteran. Silver hair was the only physical marker of Lyterix's age, which Yuel presumed he kept at bay with rejuvenat treatments like some kind of vain hive world noble.

He stopped a few yards short of Yuel and Sherax. Like the junior explorator, Lyterix was less than half Yuel's mass and height. Also like Sherax, he wore his physical inferiority without discomfort.

'Magos Lyterix,' Yuel sent, investing his code with the formal signifiers of an overlord greeting an underling.

'Lord Yuel.' The augur turned, glancing with his still-human eyes through the armaglass towards the activity beyond. 'I understand that you can often be found at this particular observation passage. I can see why – it offers an exceptional view of the fleet.'

Yuel failed to summon a response before Lyterix had moved on.

'Explorator Sherax. I assume from your message that you located the macro-agglomeration?'

'Indeed, magos. Your calculations were accurate to two point four-six astronomic units.'

Yuel was briefly transfixed by the self-satisfied smirk that contorted the augur's sharp, flesh-clad features. Physical expressions of meaning and emotion were vanishingly rare within Yuel's echelon of Mechanicus society; the use of facial gestures was a novelty he had not encountered in some time.

'I hope that Admiral Kroy was suitably grateful,' Lyterix continued, apparently ignorant of Yuel's curiosity.

'Indeed, magos.'

'I require context,' Yuel interjected. It galled the lord explorator to place himself in a position of supplication, but to be excluded from their discussion would be a greater irritant.

'It was Magos Lyterix, lord, who determined the location that the macro-agglomeration *Misery's Daughter* would next emerge from the immaterium.'

Sherax explained that, acting on her own authority, she had passed this dubiously sourced information to the commanders of Battlefleet Changrit, who had acted with commendable speed to greet the threat as it emerged from the warp.

'I see.' Yuel offered no judgement or praise. It seemed probable that Sherax, acting on the dubious wisdom of Lyterix's chicanery, had spared the system from the ravages of orkoid assault. Nevertheless, she had seen fit to act without consultation or sanction from the synod – another deviation from the behavioural template he had recorded over long decades of proximity.

'Can I assume I was summoned to learn the outcome of your expedition?' Lyterix asked.

'You were.' Sherax paused, the same unusual hesitancy in her manner that Yuel had observed before.

She held out a pair of data-reels, offering one to each magos. 'These contain the unredacted records of my exploration of the *Almagest*. I ask that you review them in full before making any determinations.'

Lyterix looked at the data-reel quizzically, then at Sherax, before taking the flat bronze device and connecting it to a data-slate he withdrew from his robes. One of Yuel's primary armatures took his reel and passed it to the many insectile manipulators that ran the length of his torso. The flat oblong disappeared into a cavity in Yuel's body.

Lyterix's thin digits danced across the surface of the data-slate, displaying information for a fraction of a second before moving on. Neither he nor Yuel spoke as they inloaded all that Sherax had chosen to share with them.

Yuel's former pupil waited in silence. To her credit, she allowed them to assess the data without commentary or context.

'You have this object aboard your ship?' Lyterix was the first to break the silence.

'Held within a stasis field.'

'And you have exposed yourself to its properties?' Yuel asked, incredulous. 'With full awareness of its effect on Lucanus and his ship?'

'In the course of study, for a total of sixteen point four seconds over several weeks.'

'And?' Lyterix took up the questioning.

'Do I appear changed?' Sherax snapped.

'Belligerence will not aid you, Talin.' Yuel rose up on his locomotive limbs, physically towering over the junior adept. 'The nature of this artefact is unknown, its effects unprecedented. I am appalled that you would even contemplate examination of this phenomenon without the most rigorous safeguards.'

'My lord, do you not grasp the potential of this device?' Sherax asked, attempting to brush aside his concerns.

'Indeed. Its potential for destruction is remarkable.'

'Not destruction, permutation. The vegetation aboard the *Almagest* is alive, lord. It performs photosynthesis – an entity that sprang immaculate from a navigation console.'

'Fascinating,' Lyterix said.

'Incalculably dangerous,' countered Yuel.

'We can restore the home world!' Sherax finally exploded, an indecorous burst of vox-noise that shrieked across their shared frequency.

Hope – the same fierce, unbridled hope that animated Sherax – had been coursing through the hardened passages of Yuel's cognition from the moment he inloaded Sherax's data. Of course he saw the implications of her discovery. The temptation to abandon caution, to embrace the revolutionary possibilities of the Genesis effect, was intoxicating.

And therein lay the danger. Yuel saw the fervour that had captured his protégé, and he feared it. He feared what news of this phenomenon would do to the fragile spirit of the Gryphonnen people. He feared the chaos that hope would bring.

'We must take this to the synod,' Yuel said after several seconds of contemplation.

'Thank you, lord. I must be permitted to pursue this technology to its source.'

'That was not my meaning. Such a technology must be turned over for quarantine and analysis.'

Sherax actually stepped away from Yuel, as though she feared he would physically restrain her. 'This is my discovery, lord.'

'Ego has no place in a debate of this magnitude, Talin.'

'I will sponsor you, explorator,' Lyterix said suddenly. 'At the next session of the synod, I will sponsor you to present all you

found on the *Almagest*. You will be irrevocably tied to its discovery, and its future study.'

'You have no standing among the synod.' Yuel had entirely dismissed Lyterix from consideration. Indeed, he resented the fact that Sherax had chosen to reveal the Genesis effect to them both. The impudent magos may have played some role in its discovery, but Yuel was – or had been – Sherax's liege lord, her mentor and sponsor. Her debt to him was far greater. Her disregard for fealty only served to harden Yuel's resolve.

'I am confident that a revelation of this magnitude will receive a hearing,' Lyterix said.

That was true. The transparent self-interest of the augur's offer was clear; it was not merely Sherax who wished to tie themselves to her discovery.

'Very well, Talin,' Yuel said. 'I shall submit a request to introduce your findings at the next closed conclave.'

'Good. My thanks, lord.' The combative edge faded, but did not disappear from her stance and demeanour. 'I would request that you not disseminate the data I have shared to any other parties.'

'Naturally.' There was no possibility that Yuel would communicate such incendiary information to others.

She turned to Lyterix. 'Magos?'

The augur smiled. 'I would not seek to steal your thunder, explorator.'

'My thanks, to you both.' Sherax formed the sign of the cog. 'I will return to the *Peregrinus* and prepare.'

Lyterix quickly stepped around Yuel's bulk. 'I will accompany you to your conveyance, explorator.'

'As will I,' said Yuel, just as quickly. 'I wish to examine this object for myself.'

Sherax hesitated, but there was clearly no way to deter either magos. 'My conveyance is berthed on the far side of the array,'

she said. She pulsed the location along with her invitation, and the three magi set off in unison.

'You have not attended the synod since our coming to Tolkhan?' Lyterix asked Sherax as they walked. Though Yuel had had only a peripheral knowledge of the augur before this meeting, he had already come to loathe the snide edge in which all his speech was couched.

'No,' the ductrix said after a pause. Yuel knew Sherax had stood before the forge world's ruling council only twice: to receive their endorsement of her command of the *Peregrinus*, and to receive their censure for her conduct in that office.

Lyterix continued, amusement heavy in his voice. 'I will be curious to hear your views.'

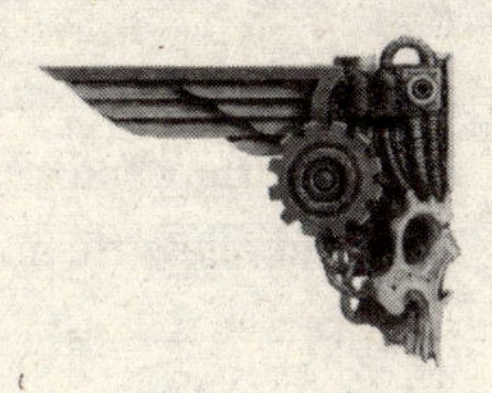

THREE

After three weeks of stewing in his tiny quarters, Edgar had finally had enough.

He dressed in his best dress tunic, or at least in the one with only a single patch on its elbow, and black breeches that concealed most of the grime and stains ground into the fabric. He gathered his resources, and set out.

Once it became apparent that the *Peregrinus'* passengers would be embarked for the long haul, Explorator Sherax had been forced to make arrangements for their accommodation. In Edgar's case, that meant a cramped billet on the starboard side of the explorator ship, close enough to some kind of pump or mechanism that the sound of its operation carried clearly through the metal bulkhead. The tiny room had housed a pair of Sherax's junior acolytes, who no doubt had taken some profound religious joy from the rhythmic chuntering that had stolen more hours of Edgar's sleep than he could count.

The Vostroyans had required more significant concessions.

As with their treatment on the *Misery's Daughter*, the Mechanicus' solution had been to isolate them from the rest of the ship and allow them free rein to remake their space to their requirements.

Edgar made his way through narrow passages, stepping aside stiffly whenever one of the ship's crew hurried past. The mute wretches that haunted the deeper levels of the ship were, he assumed, no different from those that crewed every other Imperial vessel. Edgar had just as little interest in interacting with those of the *Peregrinus* as he had on any other transport ship, and so ignored them whenever their paths crossed.

The Vostroyans' barracks were not far from his quarters, but Edgar had rarely ventured there, and only ever for combat exercises when Zlata felt the need to vary the Blackbloods' routine. He had to backtrack several times when he lost track of the alphanumeric location runes stamped into the plating at each junction. Edgar's knowledge of the ship extended to the route between his quarters and the bay where *Vortigern* was maintained, with occasional visits – always accompanied by one of Sherax's junior adepts – to the command level for his infrequent audiences with the ship's mistress.

After a longer journey than necessary, Edgar finally reached his goal. He had found his way mostly by smell, always turning away from the tang of machine lubricant and towards the ripe fugue of unwashed bodies.

A pair of bored Vostroyans were standing outside a personnel hatch. It was no different to the dozens he had passed by, except that someone had taken the trouble to carefully paint the silhouette of a promethium extraction rig in white paint across its face. The hatch was closed, and it took Edgar a moment to realise that the two Blackbloods were on guard.

'I'm looking for the major,' he told them. Neither soldier had

challenged him, but under their belligerent attention Edgar felt the need to explain his presence. One of the two – a woman with a thick white scar along her jawline – hammered a fist against the steel, and the hatch swung open with a squeal of unlubricated metal. The trooper resumed her idle stare into the middle distance without a word to Edgar.

Sherax had turned over one of the ship's forward cargo holds for the Vostroyans' use, sacrificing valuable capacity in exchange for confining the troopers to a single, contained location. Over the years, the Vostroyan soldiers had colonised the space, segmenting the area into discrete districts with scavenged hoardings and repurposed freight containers. The hold served as barracks, training grounds, armoury, and mess for the remnants of the Vostroyan 103rd.

A harsh skirl of cold air whipped around the hatch as Edgar stepped through, and a thin rime of condensation slicked his hand when he reached out to steady himself. The hold was freezing. The space given over to the Blackbloods was a cavern – the floodlumens that cast a sharp white glare were perhaps a hundred yards above Edgar's head – and he had entered at the lowest point. The icy chill was not unusual for the *Peregrinus*. Throughout the ship, it was either punishingly cold or brutally hot, with no middle ground. As Edgar was profoundly aware, the Mechanicus shipwrights gave little thought to the comfort of their crew and passengers.

Edgar knew that about half of the hold had been set aside for combat training – the click of low-powered lasweapons and the orders of officers and the regiment's sergeants drifted on the air, part of the background noise of the hold. Plastek sheeting was draped between makeshift buildings, some two or three levels tall, trapping the sound and heat of men and women hustling between them.

There were no signs or directions, so Edgar chose to press on in ignorance. He passed domicile halls, hygiene chambers, a tiered pictorium, and a dozen other rooms and buildings within which the Vostroyan soldiers lived and worked. The pale-skinned men and women were everywhere, but most paid Edgar little heed, and the tented passages between the buildings were wide enough for him to not impede them.

At the first junction, he asked a passing trooper for Major Zlata, and was directed along another stretch of flakboard-lined corridor. The sound of raised voices and the clatter of metal mugs led him the rest of the way. A double-width door made from a pair of flakboard sheets stood open, and Edgar let himself into the Vostroyan mess.

It was hot and humid inside, at least compared to the rest of the hold. Close to two hundred troopers were loudly enjoying a rest period, huddled together with mugs filled with either food or alcohol. Most had shed their heavy fur-lined coats, and sat in their undershirts or in further states of undress.

Games of chance were laid out across every kind of surface – repurposed ammunition crates, sheet-metal balanced between more crates, and occasionally an actual table. Edgar suspected that many of the seats drawn up to them had been extracted from Chimera transport vehicles.

A bar-top made of sheets of metal rivetted together ran the length of one wall, although there did not appear to be any stewards or attendants. The bar was bent by the weight of several large plastek containers, which Edgar recognised as fuel canisters. Valves that were sized to deliver promethium to troop transport vehicles instead dispensed a clear liquid, although from the sharp smell of the fumes he wasn't sure there was a significant difference.

At the far end of the room, troopers queued at a hatch that

evidently led to the regimental culina. Men and women not engaged in drinking or gambling sat at long tables with bowls of grey broth.

It was mess hall, drinking den, and gaming hall combined into a single foul-smelling space. All in all, it seemed like the sort of venue Edgar had no business and no interest in frequenting.

He turned to leave, assuming he had been misdirected, when a tall woman emerged from the crowd.

'Master Lorristan. How unexpected.'

Edgar turned back. He had never seen Zlata without her thick overcoat, and the combination of sweat-stained undershirt, black braces, and her remarkable height made for an arresting effect.

'Major.' He'd heard the Vostroyans did not maintain a separate officers' mess. That had seemed deliberately obtuse to Edgar, but evidently it was true. Now that he looked again, he recognised Lieutenant Syke in the thick of a raucous mob of troopers, along with several other officers huddled together over a card game.

'I hadn't expected to find you here,' Edgar said.

'I come by as often as I'm able. In truth, keeping the peace here is one of my most important duties.'

That made more sense. As regimental commander, Zlata was charged with maintaining order among her troops. Given their long periods of idleness, she was evidently required to act as hostess and pit boss as much as a combat leader.

'What brings you to us?' Zlata asked.

Edgar was momentarily lost for words. He had set out to address Zlata's reprimand, delivered on the deck of the space hulk. The major's rebuke had stuck with Edgar for the weeks of their transit back to the Gryphonnen fleet, building to a vague sense of guilt that had gnawed at him.

'I came in search of a diversion,' he said instead. 'The walls of my quarters have lost their appeal.'

Zlata smiled, and gestured at the jumble of tables. 'What is your game?'

'Regicide.' Edgar was familiar with an assortment of recreations, and several of the games of chance played by the serfs of Golem Keep, but he had never taken to them. He had no interest in the fall of dice or the luck of a draw. Regicide was a game of skill, a game of generals and statesmen.

'Of course.'

From the major's tone, Edgar felt that he had failed some sort of test. 'Do you play?' he asked hopefully.

Zlata shook her head. 'No. But I understand that Banner Sergeant Belyev owns a board, and he is always in the mood for a challenge.'

'Banner Sergeant Belyev,' Edgar repeated. He glanced in the direction Zlata had gestured. Belyev was off to the side of the room, amongst a small group of Vostroyans Edgar recognised as belonging to A Company. The remnants of a card game were spread out across the top of an overturned supply crate, along with a substantial quantity of spilt liquor.

'Indeed.'

Edgar considered leaving there and then. He had some pride left. But it was clear that was what Zlata expected, and he had come here with a purpose.

'Very well then. Major.' Edgar touched a hand to his chest as a casual but sincere form of salute, and set off in the direction Zlata had pointed.

The men looked up at his approach. Edgar was surprised to find Gregor Ormond among them. He realised with a start that he had no idea where the sacristan was quartered. It was entirely possible he had been sharing the Vostroyans' billet for years.

'Banner Sergeant Belyev. Sacristan Ormond.' He nodded cordially at the men and women he didn't know.

Ormond dropped his drink in his haste to get to his feet. 'Master Edgar, sir.'

Edgar waved the old man back down. 'I apologise for intruding. I found myself at a loose end, and I hoped I might shed my boredom here.'

The Vostroyans had all remained seated. Belyev had tipped himself back in his chair, and was regarding Edgar as though he were a novel form of ship-louse.

'Major Zlata tells me you play regicide, banner sergeant.'

'I'm familiar with it.' Belyev stuck a filthy finger in his mouth, and made a great display of working at something lodged between his teeth.

Edgar pressed on. 'Can I tempt you to a game?'

The Guardsman's eyes narrowed. 'What d'you have to tempt me with?'

Edgar pulled a pair of carb-bars from his jacket.

Aboard the carrack that had delivered Edgar and the Knights of House Cadmus to Gryphonne IV, he and his brothers had dined like the lords they were. The ship's abattoir had kept their table piled high with grox and verdikine. Its wine casks had seemed bottomless, and the house's sizeable caravan of bakers, pâtissiers, and courtesans had tended to their every concern.

Edgar had known, in an abstract way, that the fare to which he had been accustomed was far removed from the nutriments the lower decks subsisted on. Six years of the Mechanicus' communal protein broth had brought home just how privileged he had been.

The pair of carb-bars were the remnants of an unusually generous ration issued over a year before, circulated to the officer corps of the Vostroyans when the *Peregrinus* had last been berthed around Tolkhan. They were synthetic hunks of sucrose infused with fat and flavouring, and each one was a rich prize in any wager about the explorator ship.

Belyev's stare flicked to Edgar's hands, then back up. A slow smile spread across his face. 'I could be persuaded.'

One of Belyev's men hastily cleared away the scattered pasteboard cards, and a heavy, brass-bound box was put in their place.

'A beautiful set, banner sergeant,' Edgar said after Belyev had laid it out on the scarred metal. He meant it. The board was of shockingly fine quality, made from a cream-coloured wood on which the field had been picked out in thick silver wire. The pieces were artfully carved stone, although one of the black citadels had been replaced by an autocannon shell casing.

'Won it off Colonel Pershing before he died. Second tour of Scarrek.' Belyev drained his mug and tossed it to one of his comrades, then spread his legs wide to either side of the crate to let him lean close to the board. 'Shall we?'

Edgar sat down with more considered grace, and placed one of his carb-bars beside the board. Belyev's wager was a sizeable stack of square-edged currency that Edgar didn't recognise, and had to take on trust was a proper match for his stake.

The prize thus prepared, the older man spun the board with a pale, scarred finger. Edgar came up green, Belyev black. He tried to ignore the cheers and hoots of Belyev's comrades, Zlata's curious stare from across the room, and focus on the game at hand.

Mercifully, it was over in minutes.

Belyev's churl slid across the board, and came to rest beside Edgar's monarch.

'Throne of Terra!' Edgar pushed away from the crate, the metal tips of his seat squealing against the deck. Gales of laughter met his disgust, not least from his opponent, who cheerfully guffawed and accepted the applause of his comrades.

'Well played, banner sergeant.' Edgar managed to force a semblance of good humour into his voice. 'A Vichek Clearance... I

should have been looking for that.' He'd fallen into an elementary trap, one that had relied entirely on him underestimating his opponent.

'On Vostroya, we call it a Catachan Hook,' Belyev said as he began to gather up the pieces. The Guardsman appeared considerably more sober than he had when the game began. Edgar had the distinct impression that he had been conned. He should have been expecting that, too.

'Another game?' Edgar asked. He had another carb-bar, and he'd be damned if he would slink off after just one bout.

Belyev's laughter faded. 'We'd need to play for something richer than this,' he said, as he tucked Edgar's ration inside his filthy overcoat.

Edgar nodded thoughtfully, then looked over his shoulder.

'Gregor.' With Zlata watching, he forced himself to use the sacristan's familiar name. The old man appeared at his shoulder immediately. 'My gloves are in the locker in my quarters. Could I trouble you to fetch them?'

Ormond hastened to obey. All the troopers turned to speak to their comrades, leaving Edgar to silently seethe to himself.

After a few minutes – evidently Ormond knew a much more direct path to Edgar's billet – the sacristan reappeared at his elbow, Edgar's pair of finely stitched quivit-skin gloves held gingerly in one hand.

'Well done on the earlier bout, Master Lorristan,' he said quietly as he handed the gloves over. 'I've observed that taking a loss with grace is well respected by the troopers who frequent this establishment.'

Grace be damned; he was going to flatten Belyev and wipe the smirk from his face. He smiled through his fury, and placed the gloves carefully on the crate. Belyev noticed that the sacristan had returned, and ambled back over to join him.

The crowd were quiet this time. The tension radiating from the two men was palpable, and seemed to spread to the rest of the den. The games of rajet and Blind Quarter had stopped, and even the drinkers at the bar were silent. Men and women in their heavy coats formed a tight cluster around the upturned crate. Edgar was dimly aware that someone was calling the plays to their fellows who couldn't see the board.

After eight minutes of tense manoeuvring, Belyev nudged his citadel to one side, leaving his ecclesiarch unguarded.

He had him. It was a single misstep, but that was all it took.

Edgar saw the flash of panic in Belyev's eyes, and leant back, savouring the moment. It was clear that no one in the crowd recognised the danger their comrade was in.

Edgar's spine clicked audibly as he straightened. As he rolled his shoulders, Edgar noticed Ormond staring at him intently.

It was so rare for the old man to meet his eye that Edgar paused, wondering if the sacristan was about to violate the ancient rules of regicide and offer him advice mid-play. But then he remembered that Ormond had already said all that he intended Edgar to hear.

After a long period of deliberation, Edgar left Belyev's piece unharmed, and instead advanced his citadel.

Twelve minutes later, it was over.

The crowd roared, as loud and proud as if they had just stormed an enemy fortification. Men and women shook Belyev's shoulders, and at least three tin mugs were thrust in front of him for a victor's quaff. The tension evaporated, the mood of the mess returning to the same raucous state in which Edgar had found it.

Edgar hadn't thrown the match; that single opening had been all that Belyev had given him. Nevertheless, the look in the Guardsman's eye told him that Belyev had seen his error, and he knew Edgar had seen it too.

Edgar picked up his gloves and held them out for the Vostroyan. 'Take care of them, banner sergeant, the same way you have cared for that set. I hope I'll have the chance to win them back soon.'

Belyev gave him a single gruff nod, then smiled. 'Aye, I expect you will.' He took the gloves with care, and offered his free hand to Edgar. 'No shame in losing to a Blackblood.'

'No,' Edgar said as they shook. 'But far better to be on the same side as one.' That got a cheer from the Vostroyans, who were already returning to their other entertainments.

'And what about drinking with one?' Zlata emerged from the crowd, holding two tin mugs of the dreadful liquor.

Edgar didn't notice Belyev slip away, leaving him and Zlata standing very close together. He took one of the mugs.

'Why not?'

FOUR

The Basilica Gryphonicus had been a masterpiece of fabrication, as befitted the once-great heart of the Gryphonnen Octad. It had stood at the epicentre of Simurghal, a forge-city purpose-built to be a seat of government, a site untainted by dynastic dispute and rivalry after the bitter strife of the Hermeticon's War. Its cornerstone had been laid over eight thousand years ago, a solid cube of adamantine whose dimensions precisely conformed to the Prime Unitary System. Its walls and columns had been formed of red-veined Martian granite, each massive block the work of decades to cut, transport, and lay in its place. The oculus of its dome had been inscribed with the Hexamantic Constant around its entire circumference, a labour of devotion that had ensured the inscribing magos' name survived through the millennia.

It was the locus of Gryphonne IV and, like everything else on the world, it had been rendered to dust and ash by the tyranids' devastation.

Despite this, Sherax appeared to be standing within its conclave chamber.

Her sensory inputs were a riot of conflicting data. The organs of her physical form – her optical sensors, audex receivers, particulate filters – all reported the truth. Sherax was seated on the *Peregrinus'* command throne, her mechadendrite weave unfurled and pulsing with activity. Her crew were working in efficient silence, though the strike of boot and claw upon the deck and the hum of metriculating engines formed a low, calm murmur of activity. The familiar scent of lubricant rose from a nearby cogitator.

Yet when she closed off her body's reports, Sherax was there, standing beneath the great curve of Nheren's Dome. The tiered levels, sufficient to accommodate ten thousand adherents of the Cult Mechanicus, curved around and about her. The rich perfume of promethium and sacred unguents drifted in heavy streamers. Chill air caressed her augmetics as deftly crafted currents drew excess heat up and away from the assembled magi. The rostrum rose before her, encircled at its base by the plinths for the hundred-strong Shirdal Choir. Servo-skulls, cherubim, and familiars of all description moved in flocks above her, carrying messages too precious or incendiary to be trusted to anything other than physical transfer.

It was an overwhelming feat of noospheric sculpture, beyond anything Sherax had encountered. For three point two seconds, the explorator was entirely overcome.

Her home was restored. The past years of strife and loss were a figment of erroneous code, an apocalyptic hypothetical conjured from the depths of her creative centres. The Gryphonnen people were as they had always been: defiant, unbowed, the Omnissiah's bastion against ignorance and entropy.

Two genetors of the Incunablis order passed her, close enough to touch, and the illusion ended.

Dozens of magi walked, scuttled, and trundled around the tiered levels of the circular chamber. They showed no awe, no wonder at the miracle at work. They appeared entirely at ease, as though the leviathan had never visited absolute devastation upon their home. But Sherax had that knowledge, as must they. As perfect as the construct was, she could not divorce herself from the truth that it was a deception. A hallucination, created to protect the egos of magi too fragile to acknowledge the reality of their circumstances.

The genetors glanced in her direction and let slip a fragment of disapproving code. Her thoughts were polluting the noosphere, spreading like a stain through the weft of the sculpture. With some effort, she raised cognitive firebreaks and safeguards that had gone unused for years. Sherax shaded her thoughts from the prying gaze of others, resentful of the need to do so.

Lord Explorator Yuel was suddenly beside her. He did not walk over, but rather simply appeared, as though he had always been there. Any remaining awe Sherax had for the unplace was banished with that final demonstration of its artifice.

Yuel took up a position on the tier, subtly closer to the central rostrum so as to indicate his superiority over her. Sherax did not resent this; neural pathways of respect and deference to her mentor had been well-worn over decades of service.

She and Yuel were given a wide berth by the magi who were embracing the indulgence, as if apparent proximity had any meaning within the shared fiction.

<Many of them live here,> Yuel sent, by way of greeting.

<What?> Dislocated as Sherax was, the question was all she could summon in response to the lord explorator's statement.

<I have been informed that at least fifty of my peers permanently occupy this delusion. Additional cybertheurgists have been co-opted from their duties to maintain it at all times. I

understand that they have also reconstructed a significant portion of the Attaxic Quarter.>

It took Sherax several seconds to formulate a reply. <That is a gross misuse of resources.>

<Indeed.>

Yuel crouched low on his four legs, his sullen aura bleeding into the noosphere. Despite his scorn, his projected self had been augmented by a cream sash worn across his torso, on which were emblazoned his many accolades and accomplishments. The War-Griffon's Crest, for his service to the Legio during the Yhuripedian Expedition. The chained grimoire of the Keepers of Lexarchy. The star field of the Explorator order. Outside the noospheric fantasy, Sherax's own ordo badge was acid-etched into the metal of her carapace, but when she looked down, she saw that her projection wore it as a scattering of silver stars along one arm of her robe.

Proudest of all was the winged wreath that crowned the griffon-and-cog upon his robe, marking Yuel as a quaestor. Sherax knew that he would likely never rise beyond that rank. Nevertheless, his role as one of the synod's interrogators ensured that he would be heard by the assembled priesthood. It ensured that she, through his patronage, would be accorded her moment.

The chamber was filling quickly. Sherax saw several adepts appear fully formed from the air, their noospheric projections hazing slightly until they aligned themselves with the cybertheurgists' creation. The majority filed in through the many archways that pierced the chamber's circumference. She suspected that it was considered ill-mannered to simply wink into existence in view of others, thereby violating the collective fantasy in which the synod met.

All branches of the Cult Mechanicus were represented. Genetors, logi, artisans, electro-priests. Lexmechanics, skitarii marshals, xenologians, cybersmiths. Reductors, exploratiors, fabricators, acquisitors. The Adeptus Mechanicus subdivided as easily as cellular life forms, and with as much variety and competition. Titles and orders proliferated at will, as each acolyte of the Machine God sought to distinguish themself from their peers by convention and hoarded prestige where they could not do so through achievement and merit.

Sherax chastised herself. Cynicism was not her default state, but such gatherings had always elicited this reaction. She had little patience for vanity and self-adulation. It was unfair to attribute such motivations to all who assembled within the hollow mockery of the basilica, but the judgement was resistant to her efforts to purge it.

A chime rang from concealed vox-casters, a binharic chant that seized the attention of all who received it. Sherax's gaze was drawn to the chamber's doors, tall enough to admit the war-form of a Questor Mechanicus Knight, which were slowly opening.

A train of adepts and acolytes, standard bearers and guardians emerged from the Gyptian Gate, and began to make their way down the processional. At their head were figures whose appearance stole Sherax's cynicism. With solemn pageantry, two of the three tribunes of Gryphonne IV approached the rostrum.

Fabricator General Trantus Kiaron led, in accordance with his station as master of a forge world. Kiaron was a hunched figure, shrouded in a heavy robe that hid much of his form from view. He advanced with a slow, sinuous motion, propelled by six pairs of motive limbs that clicked against the simulacrum of pale stone. Senior tech-priests prepared his route, the censer chimneys installed in their shoulders coughing clouds of incense, purifying the air through which he skittered.

A step behind Kiaron, Arch-Dominus Arcophili Zane was the science of war given form. Her physical augmentations were more subtle than many expected from the war-leader of the most bellicose of forge worlds. Her projection wore a cloak of red-iron chainmail, and one claw held her ceremonial cog-bladed axe of office. But it was her noospheric presence that most emphatically proclaimed her station. Zane's aura glowed with martial calculation. Sherax could sense the war scenarios that constantly buzzed beneath her mind's firebreaks, tempting in their detail and breathtaking in their scope. Sherax imagined that to be connected to her during combat would be overwhelming.

The third member of the synod's ruling triumvirate awaited their peers atop the dais. Supreme Lector Katrovax had abandoned their ambulatory form three centuries ago, and had been considered ancient even before their apotheosis. They were as deeply enmeshed with the machine as any tech-priest Sherax could name, their mind and form given over entirely to the interpretation and didactic expression of the Lex Mechanicus. Their life-support tank had materialised atop the rostrum; in the true basilica, it had taken an industrial load-lifter and a team of servitors to install Gryphonne IV's chief evangelist and magistrate of the Deus Mechanicus upon their station.

Kiaron and Zane reached the dais' summit, and their thralls took up position in the tiers below. Kiaron was at its centre; for this session, evidently the Fabricator General would convene.

He waited for several seconds, limbs raised in benediction. Then he spoke, a desiccated whisper of binharic that carried the immense weight of duty in every line of code.

<We bring this conclave to order.>

FIVE

They talked for hours.

Jeremet Lyterix was no stranger to conclave proceedings. Scorned though he was by the vast majority of Gryphonne IV's more conventional magi, his record of achievements ensured that he was accorded the privilege of synod membership. While this was a distinction that many spent their lives pursuing, for Lyterix such assemblies were tedium, punctuated only occasionally with moments of true importance or scandal.

Noospheric exchange was conducted at the speed of thought. A debate that might last days if the speakers employed binharic, or weeks if they were forced to rely on the imprecise oratory of the spoken word, could be completed in a matter of minutes. Unfortunately, the speed of exchange did little to enliven the substance under discussion.

Protocol demanded that a host of administrative matters be raised and recorded before the true business of the synod could be addressed. While these trivialities were dealt with – mere

seconds of true time, but interminable for those whose minds moved at a rate far beyond such intervals – Lyterix allowed his attention to wander.

In truth, it did not wander so much as it was dragged back to what had occupied his thoughts since Sherax had first passed him the data-reel aboard the orbital array.

Lyterix, more than most adepts of the Machine God, was comfortable dealing with the unfamiliar and the unconventional. Indeed, his vocation as an augur required that he confront the irrational aspects of the universe. To attempt to map the currents and tides of the empyrean was to stare into madness and find meaning. To accept that there was some force or energy that could manipulate inert matter into living organisms did not require a significant intellectual leap on Lyterix's part.

Transmutation was not unprecedented. Indeed, that had been Lyterix's primary concern – the corruptive nature of the warp was extensively recorded, albeit in highly restricted archives. It had taken observing the crystalline shard first-hand to allay his fears. It had remained chained within the arcane cage of its stasis field, but after a thorough interrogation of the data stream offered by Sherax, Lyterix judged that it was not an inherently malign artefact of the immaterium.

Lyterix forced the greater portion of his focus back to the conclave when Fabricator General Kiaron finally brought the housekeeping to an end and called upon Ulysse Rho-4 to speak, grateful for the distraction of substantive, though still mundane, matters.

Rho-4 was a close ally of Arch-Dominus Zane. Their role as magister of astropathy aboard the *Logos* had effectively elevated them to gatekeeper for all astral communication beyond the diaspora fleet. To their credit, Rho-4 did not preen, but instead dryly delivered each message deciphered from the tortured dreams of their psychic thralls.

<At the synod's behest, materiel has been dispatched from Anquaris. The convoy is estimated to complete transit in sixty-eight days.>

Lyterix scanned the appended list of supplies en route to the Gryphonnen fleet. Anquaris was a minor forge world. Like Tolkhan, its magi and its manufactoria had long been subservient to the needs of the Gryphonnen Octad. However, it appeared that the Anquarins no longer felt compelled to maintain that allegiance. The aid they were sending – to call it anything else was a blatant distortion of the truth – was a fraction of what had been demanded. The message was clear. Anquaris was a vassal no longer.

<A missive has been received from Bethod de Couraal, governor of the Shoros Subsector. By their decree, the future tithes extracted from Tygra will be distributed to Imperial holdings.>

This was at once both a lesser and a greater insult than that dealt by Anquaris. Tygra was an agri world whose planetary tithe in processed foodstuffs had supplied half the Octad with sustenance. With the Gryphonnen worlds reduced to a husk, logic dictated that Tygra's exports be diverted to other Adeptus Mechanicus holdings. However, Governor de Couraal had seized the opportunity to redirect its tithe to Imperial worlds. This was not a loss felt by Gryphonne IV directly, but by the Martian Empire at large.

<We have received several urgent sendings from Orymous. Due to the uncertain variables of empyric transmission, they have only now reached us. It is clear that Lord-Militant Salvastari is unaware of our fall.>

Rho-4 presented a raft of requests, demands, then finally pleas from Orymous, one of the worlds governed by the Imperium's Officio Logisticarum. A mustering point for Imperial armies and battlefleets, where newly raised Astra Militarum soldiers were first united with their arms and equipment. It had been the destination of a sizeable portion of Gryphonne IV's output. Without these, claimed the astropathic cries for help, millions of soldiers stood idle while a dozen warfronts faced disaster.

Other, more banal but only marginally less calamitous missives were relayed. Finally, Rho-4 completed their recitation. Kiaron recognised the messages and their bearer with a wave of a manipulating limb.

<Receipt of all communiques is acknowledged, and entered into the record. Responses will be formulated as required.>

Acknowledged and consigned to the archives in the same thought. How appallingly predictable.

Lyterix detected only the slightest thought-murmur of objection pass through the communion in reaction to Kiaron's dismissal of all that the synod had heard. In centuries past, any one of Rho-4's catastrophic reports would have triggered a schism, and begun a bitter power struggle. Now, failures of such magnitude were insignificant compared against the unfolding nightmare through which the remnants of Gryphonne IV were living.

Lyterix considered the impassive figure of Arch-Dominus Zane. Rho-4 had clearly been ordered by Zane to relay these dire messages in open council in an unusually direct attempt to embarrass the Fabricator General, but his fellow tribune's aura remained entirely neutral. Perhaps she had been anticipating greater reaction from the assembly, or perhaps she was simply making a point. The politics of a triumvirate leadership were conducted at a level far beyond Lyterix's capacity for intrigue.

The synod moved on, settling into the more uncontroversial and inconsequential motions of individual members.

They were complaints, in the main. Complaints of inappropriate quarters aboard overcrowded ships. Complaints of inequitable or insufficient resource distribution. Of asset mismanagement or abuse. Of a thousand petty slights and snubs, elevated to the attention of the rulers of a broken empire.

Many bemoaned the progress of negotiations with Tolkhan's Fabricator General, who had been deeply reluctant to allow more than a handful of Gryphonnen magi to make planetfall and escape the squalor of the diaspora fleet.

Lyterix listened to it all, and silently despaired.

Every magos present had worked for decades, often centuries, to draw close to the summit of power, and yet at a stroke that power had been diminished to the merest fraction of its past self. All that had sustained their influence and prestige – their vast armies of serf labour, their carefully curated stables of acolytes and proteges, their forges and laboratoria and archives – everything and everyone beneath them had been swept away. They were lords with no lands, squabbling over the scraps that remained.

Yuel was a prime example. Lyterix regarded his aura, ignoring the falsehoods conjured by the noospheric sculpture. He had been a lord explorator, the commander of a flotilla, a famed prosecutor of the Quest for Knowledge. Yet he had been reduced to nothing. He could call upon no resources, offer no tangible support to those who had once called him patron. Instead, he maintained a parasitic existence, giving nothing while still demanding the deference that was once his due.

Lyterix did not fear that his disrespectful assessment would leak into the noosphere. His mind was guarded to a degree far beyond what was necessary to maintain privacy within the communion.

The conclave considered two hundred and thirty-two motions and petitions before Yuel's request was heard. By Lyterix's internal chronometer, a little over four hours had elapsed since Fabricator General Kiaron initiated the proceedings.

<Tribune Kiaron. Honoured magisters and members of our synod.> Yuel lifted his insectoid form to its greatest height, adopting the bearing of one preparing to pontificate. <I claim my right as quaestor to bring a matter to the attention of the closed conclave.>

Lyterix suppressed a glimmer of wry amusement. For all that Yuel professed to scorn the trappings of this infantilising forum, he obeyed its customs and protocols to the letter. It was disappointing, but hardly surprising.

<We recognise Lord Explorator Satavic Yuel.> There was an awkward absence in Kiaron's acknowledgment. Traditionally, magi were recognised with both their designation and their assigned station: a forge, a facility, a vessel. Yuel, the master of nothing, could not be afforded that honour. Lyterix's amusement grew.

<The matter I bring before you is not mine. I am sponsor, not discoverer.>

Lyterix understood Yuel's caution, even though he was repelled by it. The role of patron was well understood by the members of the synod; Yuel wished to gain credit if their reaction was positive, and skirt the worst of their condemnation if it was not.

<The Quest for Knowledge is the duty of all followers of the Deus Mechanicus. It is the particular duty of the Explorator order to seek what was lost. We probe the shadowed and forgotten corners of the galaxy, reclaiming piece by piece the glories of the past.>

Such rhetoric was the norm, a function of the unplace and its nature. Lyterix braced himself for a precis of Yuel's own discoveries, but instead the old explorator wasted no time.

<One such glory has been returned to us. It is my humble duty to present Explorator Superior Talin Sherax, ductrix of the *Peregrinus*.>

<My lords, I thank you for your indulgence.> Sherax showed

no trepidation as she presented herself for scrutiny. Indeed, she positively burned with the desire to step forward and unveil her discovery. <Many of you will be acquainted with the work of Magos Nekane Lucanus, an archivist of our world active in the early centuries of the last millennium. For those who are not, I share now a summary of the magos' discourse and a selection of his essays.>

Sherax released a slight tome, no more than three thousand collated texts, into the noosphere, and proceeded to recount her journey to the discovery of the *Almagest*. Lyterix was aware of much of it. Sherax had come to him almost a year earlier to humbly beg for his aid. He had agreed primarily to test a new methodology for augury, rather than out of any sincere interest or expectation that Sherax's search would meet with success.

<The macro-agglomeration was halted by the efforts of the Imperial Navy, for which I ask that you commend them. Indeed, though I was embarked upon my search for several years, it was fortune alone that permitted this discovery.>

That, Lyterix thought, was a mistake. Whether the concept of fortune was a measurable phenomenon or simply the manifestation of observer bias was one of the many irrelevant semantic debates that could derail proceedings of the synod for weeks. Furthermore, it minimised Lyterix's own contribution to her expedition.

Sherax pressed on. <With the aid of my crew and adjutant magi, I boarded the *Almagest*. I present now all that took place during that encounter.>

Lyterix had advised Sherax to be cautious with the knowledge she had gained. In his view, Sherax should share only that which would win supporters to her cause. Yuel, however, had counselled her to render up all she knew, reserving none of the horrors she had encountered alongside her miracle.

Sherax's data-burst fell into the noosphere with all the grace and subtlety of a trip-hammer.

The uproar struck Lyterix with a hurricane's force. The aura of every magos that inloaded the information erupted in a storm of disbelief. Every reaction – every emotion – that Lyterix had experienced in the relative isolation of the orbital array raced through the assembled magi, heightened and intensified by the nature of noospheric resonance.

<What blasphemy do you present before this conclave?> Kiaron's will cut across the cacophony of unfiltered shock. <Explorator Superior Sherax, an explanation is demanded.>

So sadly predictable. In this chamber where unwelcome fact died in the face of impassive denial, how else could such incredible, outrageous revelation such as Sherax had discovered be received? For all that the honoured members of the synod professed to be scientists and explorers, they rejected anything that did not conform to their understanding of the universe.

<All that I have presented is the truth. Lucanus' theory was correct. The Genesis device exists. It falls to us to seize it.>

<You present heresy, and claim it is the work of the Omnissiah!>

Sherax was undaunted by Kiaron's reproval. <I claim nothing. Whatever the origin of this device, it undeniably exists. What is more, I know from where Lucanus obtained the shard.>

<Where?>

Sherax, in her anger, dumped one final revelation into the churn – the location of the world from which the *Almagest* had sailed. The world on which the Genesis shard had been found, torn from Lucanus' debased mind by Sherax's chief datamancer.

This set off another storm of protest, and this time even Lyterix was taken by surprise. The destination of Sherax's proposed expedition was the one data point she had not shared with him. It was no wonder she had sought the synod's approval.

The stellar system's common designation was Ikaneos. Within the circles of galactic cartography and stellar classification, it was a question mark, a blank space within a map the adepts of the Omnissiah had spent millennia filling in.

Distant observation, made through the ancient methods of electromagnetic astronomy, confirmed a clutch of worlds circling an unremarkable star. Yet no vessel, no astropathic missive, had ever returned from the system. Lyterix was aware of four separate expeditions mounted in the 36th millennium, each of increasing strength and size, that had been dispatched to probe its depths. All had been swallowed by whatever lay within the system's heliosphere. After the failure of the last mission, the sector conclave of Imperial governors and Mechanicus dominars proscribed any further attempts at exploration.

It was, in short, a mystery, from which the Adeptus Mechanicus had deliberately turned away.

Clearly Yuel had known ahead of time the scale of Sherax's request.

<Lords, I ask that you analyse all that you have inloaded with due detachment,> he implored. <Look beyond the circumstances of its discovery, and see what might be gained.> His attempt at injecting reason into the furore was commendable, but futile. Kiaron was unmoved.

<That system lies under the gravest sanction.>

<That is why Explorator Sherax seeks your leave to pursue this artefact to its apparent source.>

<I seek nothing,> sent Sherax, interrupting with a snarl of thought. <I ask for no sanction. I require no permission. I will find the Genesis device and harness it for our use, whether you permit it or not.>

Lyterix silently marvelled as Sherax continued. The synod

had fallen silent in the face of the explorator's extraordinary defiance.

<Our people are adrift, without aim or purpose. The galaxy burns day by day, assailed on all fronts. How long can humanity endure without this knowledge? How great would be our renewal if we could wield the capability to reform worlds? Or would you have us dwindle, idle and irrelevant, our remaining existence a bleak postscript to the might that once was the Gryphonne Octad?>

Was Lyterix's noospheric sense flawed, or did he discern a number of magi emitting markers of approval for Sherax's rhetoric? He would never know, for all were silenced by the intervention of Supreme Lector Katrovax.

<CEASE.>

It was not a word but a commandment. Katrovax silenced Sherax and the assembled magi by literally stealing away their capacity for expression, obliterating the false reality they shared. The force of his will tore through the noospheric sculpture, shattering the illusion of the Basilica Gryphonicus. Granite columns melted into dust. The marble upon which the magi appeared to stand shattered. In an instant, Lyterix crashed from the perfect simulacrum of his lost home and into the shapeless, formless mindscape of noospheric communion.

<MOTIONS HAVE BEEN HEARD. VERDICTS WILL BE RENDERED,> Katrovax continued, each segment of thought-code bursting into the void like a new-born star, blinding in its strength, irresistible in its gravity.

<THE STELLAR SYSTEM DESIGNATED IKANEOS IS SUBJECT TO *INTERDICTUS ABSOLUTUS*. SO ORDERED BY THE MAGOS MECHANICUS, STANDARD YEAR M37.937.413. SO NAMED THE 'IKANEOS QUARANTINE'.> Katrovax went on to recite the full text of the edict of Fabricator General Tynovaren of Mars. <NO EXEMPTION FROM THIS EDICT IS PERMITTED.

<THE DEVICE DESIGNATED 'GENESIS' IS A NOVEL TECHNOLOGY. FURTHER EXPOSURE TO ITS EFFECTS IS UNSANCTIONED, SAVE BY SYNODIC AUTHORITY.

<APPROPRIATE AGENTS WILL BE APPOINTED TO DETERMINE ITS ORIGIN AND EFFECTS. THE DEVICE WILL BE SURRENDERED. ALL DATA PERTAINING TO ITS ORIGIN AND FUNCTION WILL BE SURRENDERED. ALL CONTAMINATED INDIVIDUALS AND VESSELS WILL SURRENDER FOR EXAMINATION AND PURIFICATION. SO ORDERED BY TRIUMVIRAL DICTAT.>

It was impossible to deny the truth of Katrovax's rulings, to conceive of a reality in which they could be questioned. Lyterix had never felt such directed compulsion, impressing one's will upon another.

<No.> Somehow, through a strength of resolve Lyterix had not previously suspected, Sherax found it within herself to resist the supreme lector's commands.

Fabricator General Kiaron echoed the determination of his fellow tribune, though with far less potency. <You will comply with the will of the synod,> he ordered.

In the shifting unspace of the noosphere, Sherax's aura burned like a candle in the darkness. <I will not.>

With that, the explorator severed her connection to the synod.

SIX

Xal lurched forward the instant his ductrix began to fall.

He reached her in one point four seconds, leaping an ornamental balustrade and stretching out with all three hands to steady her. Sherax pitched from her throne, limbs unbending, making no attempt to arrest her fall. Her neural mechadendrites released moments before they reached their full extension, risking catastrophic damage to both Xal's mistress and the ship had they not.

With preparation, the effects of neural shock could be mitigated, diverted into cranial shunts and baffled partitions. But Sherax had evidently been unprepared.

As Xal lowered her to the deck, fragments of sensory inputs leapt from Sherax's misfiring cortex like sparks from a shorting circuit. They earthed themselves in the minds of her crew, the first noospheric interaction any of them had had with their ductrix in years. Adepts and menials alike cried out, the suddenness of contact exhilarating and bewildering.

<My ductrix,> Xal sent. She did not respond.

'Explorator superior.' He tried the vox. Nothing.

'Talin,' he finally said aloud, appealing to his mistress through every form of input available.

Her incapacitation lasted only seconds. Sherax sagged in his arms, and Xal stepped back quickly, giving his ductrix space to regain control of her physical form.

'Shut down all communication arrays.' The command was a whisper of code, sent while prostrate upon the deck.

'Ductrix?'

'Unpower the primary, secondary, and tertiary communications arrays. Close the ship to all incoming signals. Do it now.'

Obedience was hard-coded into the junior officers of the command deck. All bent to do as she demanded.

'Set course for system departure. Engage primary propulsion as soon as we clear the fleet.'

A skeletal claw reached up, grasping for the edge of her throne. Despite his sudden swiftness, Xal was now hesitant, uncertain whether helping his ductrix to her feet would constitute a violation of protocol.

The node leader for the ship's clade of pilots spoke from her post in the command deck's forecastle. 'Course laid in, ductrix.'

Sherax needed no assistance, though her internal gyroscopics were clearly struggling with the sudden switch of sensory inputs. 'Get us underway,' she commanded.

The thrum of gathering power was felt rather than heard. Xal registered the subtle shift in the constant vibration of the ship's superstructure, and the tempo of activity of the deck's many adepts and thralls. Nothing aboard a void-going vessel happened quickly, and yet the crew responded to their ductrix's urgency.

'Communication arrays shut down, ductrix,' reported an adept after a minute's frantic work.

'I am blind, Talin. I am blind,' Kalida Isocrates voxed from her cradle. Rare panic suffused her code.

'Endure, magistrix.' Sherax's claw was locked in place around the arm of her throne. 'We must endure until we breach the immaterium.'

'Why?' Isocrates asked in a plaintive moan that carried the length of the deck.

That question was foremost in Xal's mind.

The starboard portal to the command deck opened with a growl of servos, admitting the imposing form of Lord Yuel moving at speed.

'Talin, this is madness. You cannot defy the will of the synod.'

'I am doing what I must,' Sherax told him. Another hoarse murmur of binharic, shorn of all but its most essential meaning.

Yuel approached the throne, his heavy scorpion limbs clanking against metal plating. 'I will not allow you to damn me.'

Xal had mag-locked his halberd to his back as he leapt across the deck, and his arc pistol was holstered across his chest. He touched neither weapon, but shifted his stance to ensure swift access to both. Xal had no knowledge of his ductrix's intentions, and nor did he need it. He was an instrument of Sherax's will, and he would act to defend her against any threat.

His vigilance was unnecessary.

'I command the *Peregrinus*, lord,' Sherax said. 'I ask that you aid me in this endeavour, but I require neither your sanction nor your assistance to achieve my goal.' Whatever damage her sudden disconnection had done, it was clear that the iron bars of Sherax's mind were resolutely in place once more.

'Do you understand the magnitude of your transgression?' Yuel asked.

The explorator settled back in her throne, and allowed her

mechadendrites to reconnect her with her ship. 'Success vindicates all crimes, lord.'

Xal could not begin to guess at what variables and scenarios flashed through the lord explorator's mind, but he made no further attempt to hinder the *Peregrinus'* departure. Xal, meanwhile, could only guess as to the meaning of their exchange.

The deck shifted beneath Xal, the vessel heeling as sharply as it was able. Within minutes, it had broken out of the anchor formation held by the rest of the Gryphonnen fleet, thrusting on station-keeping drives to align up and out of the Tolkhan System's ecliptic. In accordance with Sherax's order, the magister of locomotion ignited the ship's main engines the moment the *Peregrinus* was free of its fellows. Unseen by any aboard the exploratory vessel, a vast plume of superheated plasma burst from its stern, heaving its great mass into flight.

Magos Lyterix appeared at the port-side portal to the command deck. Both Yuel and Lyterix had come aboard several days earlier, accompanying the ductrix from her meeting aboard Orbital Array 56-B. In that time, the augur had done little to ingratiate himself with his host crew.

Xal's skitarii crossed their blades to bar his entrance, but with a terse order Sherax bade them stand down. All her focus seemed consumed upon the ship's primary auspex read-out.

'I am impressed, Explorator Sherax.' The augur crossed the deck and stopped beside Sherax's throne, positioning himself to match Lord Yuel's proximity on her other side.

'I do not do this for your praise, magos.'

'Indeed not.'

Hundreds of Gryphonnen vessels were anchored in stages, each flotilla and squadron maintaining careful intervals between one another. The *Peregrinus* had been moored in the outermost arc, far from Tolkhan's gravity well, and so had only a short distance – as such things were measured in the astronomic distances travelled by voidships – before they would be beyond the perimeter of the fleet.

A pair of artillery barques were the closest pickets, part of a wide net of vessels stationed in a diffuse sphere as the first line of defence against aggressors. They were small warships, and unlike most Mechanicus vessels, they were built with a singular purpose. Bombardment cannons and long-range lance batteries studded the flanks of each ship, which turned with ponderous grace to bring every gun to bear upon the *Peregrinus*.

A squeal of clarions erupted from gargoyled mouths, followed by several shocked outbursts from the thralls slaved to the augury cogitators. 'The *Polybian* and the *Kaneda* have established firing solutions!'

'Hold our course. They will not fire.'

'You are unduly confident of that, Sherax,' Xal heard Lyterix say quietly.

Sherax had not ordered the ship's void shields raised. She had not ordered any defensive measures. The *Peregrinus* was entirely at the mercy and forbearance of whoever commanded the barques and their many guns.

Xal opened a private vox-frequency. 'My ductrix, what cause would our own ships have to attack us?'

She did not reply.

'Your will is my command, ductrix. I seek only to comprehend.'

'Later, Xal.' Sherax weaved weary code-shards of gratitude into her sending. Xal closed the frequency, and resumed his allotted position behind her throne.

The ship passed through the firing arcs of the pickets, deaf to whatever protestations the forge-synod hurled after it. True to Sherax's appraisal, neither vessel fired.

The *Peregrinus* sailed on. It was driven as much by its ductrix's

will as its reactor-heart. Plasma burned brighter, the flame of its engines raged from tempest to inferno, and once more the *Peregrinus* departed the company of its peers.

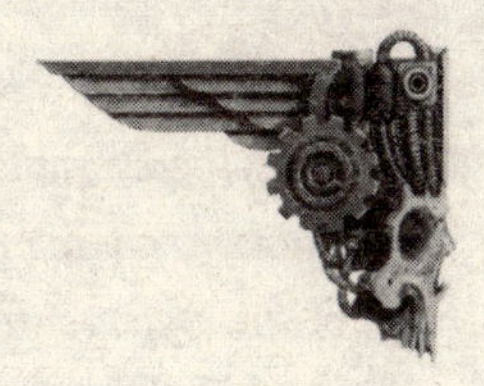

INTERLUDE

The warrior stared into the scrying portal of his ship, grateful that his prey had finally acted.

Thanks to the foresight of the seers and the secret paths of his people, the warrior had arrived at the bale star long before the mon-keigh vessel violated reality and pulled itself from the Sea of Souls. Long days and nights had passed as the Swiftest Nightfall*, cloaked in the protective shimmer of its holo-fields, drifted beyond the sight of the humans and their packs of ungainly craft.*

The mass of mon-keigh vessels were everything he despised: blunt, crude, infested with members of an ignorant species who pretended at mastery of a galaxy. Watching them had been a torment for the warrior; all the belligerent pride of his collective lives demanded that he strike, that he erase their arrogance from his sight.

But he had waited, mind set upon the greater goal. The greatest goal. The prize that would restore all that his people had lost.

And his patience had finally been rewarded.

The human craft he stalked was turning in its ponderous way,

engines roaring into the silence of the void. Slowly, clumsily, it heaved itself into motion, driving towards the outer edge of the stellar system, abandoning its ungainly kin to sear in the infernal blaze of the system's star.

With infinitely more grace, the shadow-clad vessel angled its sails and followed.

IKANEOS

ONE

The door to Sherax's quarters chimed.

The *Peregrinus* had been in the warp for four days. It had been a total of ninety-four hours since she disobeyed the highest authority of her people and set course for a world proscribed by both the Imperial and Martian empires.

She was surprised it had taken her crew so long to approach her.

They had come in person, rather than requesting discourse via vox or noosphere. That too surprised her, though she was certain that their choice of emissary would not.

Luren would be unable to restrain his choler. Akoni and the other magisters had their duties across the ship, and would not seek to be drawn into matters beyond their sphere. The other adepts aboard the *Peregrinus* were too junior to command her respect, and to approach her as a group would have admitted their inferiority. There was only one member of Sherax's inner cadre who could speak for them all.

'Enter.'

Sherax's understanding of her companions was rewarded. The doors trundled back to reveal the fragile form of Thess Rahn-Bo.

'I seek a dialogue, ductrix,' the datamancer said.

'I am occupied.' Sherax weaved impatience and distraction through her answer in an attempt to end the interaction before it could begin.

'Nevertheless.' Rahn-Bo stepped inside. The explorator permitted the door to close behind her, and discarded the data she had been reviewing pertaining to the interdiction imposed on their destination.

Sherax had had few exchanges with her chief datamancer since they departed the *Misery's Daughter*. That was not accidental, and a dim flicker of shame threatened to corrupt her focus. Outwardly, Rahn-Bo was unchanged, but Sherax was aware that she had been impacted by the confrontation with Magos Lucanus. In truth, she had not sought out Rahn-Bo because she had not yet resolved her own unease regarding that encounter.

Sherax's quarters were relatively modest, though they adjoined an expansive personal forge and experimentarium. With only a small rest area and a bay for personal maintenance, there was little room for guests.

The stasis unit containing the shard of Genesis sat beside her in the maintenance bay. Its power unit emitted a soft hum as it restrained the artefact outside the laws of space and time.

Sherax's colleague of almost two centuries walked towards her, her sensing apparatus turned away from the shard. Rahn-Bo's respiration – still the function of organic lungs – was slow and deep, but the particulates she exhaled carried the chemical markers of extreme stress.

'Are you functioning optimally?' Sherax asked.

'Within established norms, ductrix.' Rahn-Bo took an uncharacteristic pause, evidently collating her thoughts. 'I have been elected to–'

'I know what you will say,' Sherax interrupted. There was little purpose to the exchange, and she wished for it to be brief.

'The only way that would be possible, ductrix, is if you returned to the communion.'

Sherax was startled by the accusation in Rahn-Bo's binharic. Rancour was rare for her.

'You know why I do not,' she said.

'No, Talin. I do not.' Sherax had never corrected Rahn-Bo's use of her familiar name, a hold-over from their concurrent time as initiates. 'You have never shared that with me. You no longer share anything with us. You command and we obey, but in ignorance of your motives and objectives. When you severed your connection to the communion, you abdicated your responsibilities as ductrix. As a leader.'

Rahn-Bo threw Sherax's own misgivings at her, as though she had plucked them from the depths of her mind. Sherax found herself unable to summon a defence.

Her old colleague continued. 'Since the fall of the home world, we have done all that you require. We have followed you in your obsession, and now we flee the censure of the synod.'

Sherax finally reacted. 'My *obsession* led us to the greatest discovery of our age.'

'Is it?'

Sherax was incredulous, so much so that she physically gestured towards the shard. 'You saw the power of this fragment first-hand. Can you not imagine what the device entire could achieve?'

She transferred her gaze from the stasis generator to a stellar cartograph fixed to the far wall. It was printed with carbon inks on a cellulose weave – one of the few adornments Sherax valued. The eight systems of the Octad were surrounded by terse runes that described the nature and tithe level of each planet at the time of the map's production. The Gryphonnen star was accorded primacy, a glimmering jewel of silver pigment at the cartograph's centre.

'We have lost so much,' she said. 'How many worlds lay barren in the leviathan's wake? How many died at Kryptman's command?'

Giving voice to that name awoke a torrent of conflicted sentiments. Fidus Kryptman, acting with the absurdly sweeping powers the Imperium granted its Inquisitorial ordos, sought to halt the advance of the tyranid plague through the creation of a galactic cordon. The man's logic had been sound, but his methods surpassingly extreme.

The inquisitor had deployed virus bombs across dozens of worlds, exterminating their inhabitants and rendering each planet a lifeless husk. Billions died, slain in the belief that their murder would spare trillions by denying their biomass to the hungering hive fleet. In so doing, one man orchestrated the largest act of genocide in the Imperium's bloodstained history. Even Sherax, a senior adept of an empire that considered human life to be an infinitely replaceable resource, baulked at such atrocity.

She had learnt, during the diaspora's years of wandering, that Kryptman had approached the forge-synod during his apocalyptic rampage and bade Gryphonne IV join the cordon by pre-emptively obliterating their world. The synod had refused, trusting the might of their defences.

The result, of course, had been the same.

'All could be restored, to say nothing of the wider galaxy,' Sherax said. 'This is the purpose of the Quest made manifest, Thess. How can you deny the potency of Lucanus' discovery?'

'Because I touched his mind, Talin. He no more understood the device than you do, and he had been trapped with it for two centuries. We have no way to know if the changes it wrought upon the *Almagest* were its intended function, or simply a by-product.'

'That is why we must go to Ikaneos. To discover its purpose, discover its origins. Do you not realise that this could be an artefact of the Omnissiah's own creation!'

Even without the communion, Rahn-Bo could clearly sense Sherax's growing agitation. 'We all share the grief, ductrix. We all watched our world die.'

The recursive loop of anguish that was always lurking within the passive processes of Sherax's mind roused itself at Rahn-Bo's address. She clung to her anger as a ward against her sorrow. 'Then why oppose me?' she asked.

'We do not oppose you. We simply ask that you heed the synod's orders, and subject the shard to adequate scrutiny.'

The explorator could not prevent a blurt of exasperated code from escaping her filters. 'Our people take centuries to assess even minor deviations from sanctioned construction templates. This is an entirely unfamiliar technology. We do not have time for hesitant analysis and tortuous debate. We must use it now!'

Rahn-Bo was backing away, but Sherax continued. 'What is it you fear, cogitatrix? What weakness within you would have us turn aside from the Quest? From the restoration of our home?'

Rahn-Bo turned, seeking to depart the chamber, but paused at the threshold. 'It is clear that you have abandoned reason, Talin,' she said. 'You pursue a device of unknown provenance and unclear purpose, on the word of a corrupted mind, to a system declared *interdictus absolutus* by Mars itself.'

This was why Sherax had not sought out her oldest colleague. It was why she had rejected the communion. Rahn-Bo and the rest of her officers would let their people wither and die, if saving them would require testing the boundaries of orthodoxy.

She held the datamancer's gaze. 'I will not turn back, Thess. I must undo what was done. I must save us from what we have become.'

Rahn-Bo triggered the door control. 'You asked of my fears, ductrix. I have only one.' She turned back to Sherax, gesturing at the shard with its stasis field.

'I fear what that device will make of us.'

TWO

Jeremet Lyterix was roaming the ship.

It was rare for any member of the Adeptus Mechanicus to be idle. Even during rest periods, most magi directed their background cognition to continue working on their current preoccupation. This was one of the many ways in which Lyterix differed from his order. He recognised the value in active respite, in purposefully doing nothing. It was in such moments that the mind and animus were rejuvenated, restoring both to the fullness of their power and potential. Too often were such considerations overlooked by his peers, to the detriment of efficient working and intellectual endeavour.

That was the rationale Lyterix would offer to anyone who chose to challenge his aimless wandering through the passages and thoroughfares of the *Peregrinus*.

The more truthful explanation was that he was neither able to work nor rest while within the warp.

It had always been thus. For all the protection afforded by the

ship's Geller field, empyric transit immersed a vessel within the indefinable chaos that existed beneath reality. Lyterix had a deeper understanding than most of the nature of the warp, but that knowledge brought him no comfort. Indeed, it heightened his fears. A single report of the well-documented but ill-explained phenomena that plagued a vessel within the immaterium could prevent Lyterix from obtaining any kind of peace for days on end.

It was in that fitful spirit that Jeremet Lyterix was roaming the decks, and on the upper starboard concourse encountered Erasmus Luren.

Sherax's chief techseer was engaged in his duties, maintaining the sanctity of the ship's systems. He was followed at a procedurally correct distance by a small train of acolytes and thralls, who each bore one of the many tools of Luren's craft – electro-censer, apotropaic totem, crozius mechanicus, runic hammer. The priest himself was unencumbered, as befitted his station.

<Augur.>

<Techseer.>

Their physical proximity triggered a noospheric handshake, aligning the frequency of their thoughts to permit easy communication. Not that Lyterix was minded to indulge in trivial banter. Luren was well known to be one of Supreme Lector Katrovax's creatures, and he wore his contempt for Lyterix openly. Luren, however, halted his procession.

<You are far from your assigned quarters,> Luren observed.

Lyterix, curious as to the motive behind the techseer's instigation of conversation, also paused. <I am exploring the ship.>

Luren's eyestalks rotated, an elegant punctuation for his apparent confusion. <The *Peregrinus* is a Magellenic-class explorator ship. Surely you are familiar with its pattern and layout?>

<I am surprised a seer of your reputation would give such little

heed to the particular characteristics of a vessel's spirit,> Lyterix said. He reached out an iron hand and reverently placed it against the bulkhead beside him. <The *Peregrinus* may be built to a pattern common to thousands of other ships, but nevertheless, it is unique.>

Luren bristled, his aura clouding with indignant anger. Lyterix, for his part, made no attempt to conceal his petty amusement.

He had no respect for Luren and his ilk. Techseers, and the various sub-orders of priests whose function was to sanctify and tend to the machine spirits of vessels and vehicles, were necessary in the same way that a hammer and bellows were necessities for forgecraft. But they did nothing to advance the Quest, to break new ground in the continuing search for clarity and comprehension. Indeed, their dogmatism restrained the Quest by demanding that all discovery conform to their narrow conception of accepted thought. There was no room for inspiration or invention in their world-view, no capacity for the unexpected or unknown.

No role, in short, for Lyterix.

<My congratulations on your role in the eulogy,> Lyterix sent before Luren had summoned a response to his jibe.

The compliment, clothed in sincerity, wrong-footed the techseer. <It... was my honour.>

<*Obligation inherent and destiny manifest, the gift of the Omnissiah through trial and splendour.*>

< *Duty has no end,*> Luren added, completing his own poetic phrase.

<Well said.>

<Is it duty that brought you aboard?> Luren asked, with a directness that created a shiver of discordance within the noosphere.

So, it was for admonishment that the techseer had chosen to stop Lyterix. The augur had to suppress his amusement. <What

could be more dutiful than to pursue a technology of the kind you and your mistress discovered?>

Luren sent nothing.

<Explorator Sherax recounted your experience aboard the *Almagest*,> Lyterix said. <A seer of your robust faith could not fail to be moved by all that you witnessed.>

<It is true that the degenerate creatures that infested the ship were an instructive reminder of the importance of genomic purity.>

<I was referring to the effect of the Genesis device.>

Luren once more did not reply immediately. Lyterix had to pity him. He had initiated their dialogue to scold a perceived subordinate, but was ill-equipped for a true exchange of intellect and wit.

<What outcome do you seek from mockery?> Luren finally asked.

<I do not mock you, tech-priest. But it is curious that you took my statement as such. Is it so far beyond the bounds of reason that your mistress has uncovered a relic of the Omnissiah's own creation? That we sail now to reunite with an artefact from the dawn of humanity's mastery of the stars?>

<We sail towards heresy and damnation. Sherax has let grief blind her, and in her blindness she gropes for miracles.>

<You did not answer my question.>

<You have aided and abetted her in this desperate venture,> Luren said. He had finally stumbled into his stride, and would not be deterred from his denunciation. <You have turned her from the path of logic.>

<Do you believe the explorator is so easily led?> Lyterix countered.

<My only solace is that you will share in our doom.>

<Or in your enlightenment.> The augur would not allow this small-minded creature to have the last word.

His rebuke delivered, Luren set off once more. His thralls followed, in lockstep with their master.

After several moments, Lyterix resumed his meandering progress.

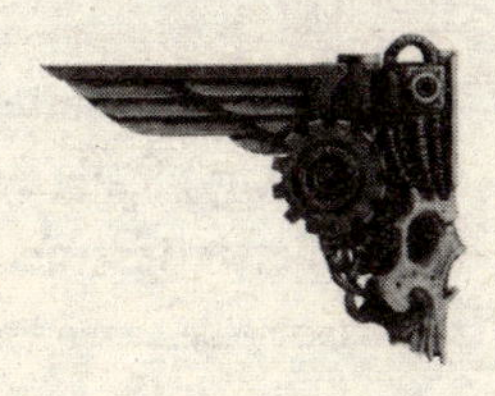

THREE

Twenty-nine days after fleeing the company of its peers, the *Peregrinus* reached its destination. It burst from the empyrean in the manner of a deep-water mammal breaching the surface of a violent sea.

It had been another difficult passage. There were no easy passages in this new, bleak millennium. The *Peregrinus* had fought its way through storm-wracked tides, often struggling to maintain Geller field integrity, much less make headway towards their goal. At the request of their Navigator, Sherax had twice ordered translation back to the void to effect repairs and give the mutant a few hours of respite.

These interludes had been necessary for the entire crew. The ship had been plagued by the warp for the entire voyage, as the membrane that separated the *Peregrinus* from the Inexplicable Realm had frayed. Serfs were struck by waking nightmares, causing continual outbursts of violent despair. Acolytes and adepts found their experiments corrupted by data-gheists.

Tempered iron shattered beneath fabricators' hammer blows. Servitors, typically resilient to empyric ephemera, conjured contradictory instructions from the depths of their lobotomised minds, or else ceased to function altogether.

Such were the trials to be endured by those who sought to travel between the stars.

As the wound in space clenched shut and the ship clothed itself in reality once again, all aboard permitted themselves an expression of relief.

'Void shields to maximum. Prime all weapons.'

Sherax's order rang out across the ship. There could be no pause, no interval in which its labouring thralls could stop and give thanks to the Omnissiah for their survival. Instead, the goads of their overseers bit deep, and scourged flesh hurried to feed more fuel to toiling reactors and rouse gun batteries and lance coils to waking.

The command deck was appropriately silent, though gripped by the same purposeful activity that seized the ship. During the passage Yuel had taken to occupying a position to one side of Sherax's command throne. The throne itself had been empty, though his former protégé had taken her place for the final hours of empyric transit, and sat now in close communion with the ship.

'Proximity threat detection.' Sherax's orders clicked over the vox.

A bent-backed figure reported instantly from the far side of the chamber. 'No readings, ductrix.'

'Long-range auspex.'

A longer delay. 'Nothing, ductrix.'

Yuel sensed a degree of tension ease from the noosphere. The nature of their destination had not been openly stated by Sherax, but the crew had learnt of it nonetheless. *Interdictus*

absolutus was not a prohibition that was applied without cause, nor was it lightly broken. The communion had been a turbulent and fractious mindscape in the past weeks. Disquiet stalked the ship, expressed in a thousand micro-gestures and hesitant actions.

Once again, Yuel reflected on the error Sherax had committed by cutting herself off from her crew.

'Very well,' the ductrix replied. 'Show me the system.'

A hololithic projector hummed into life. The deck was lit by shades of laser blue as the plinth threw a tri-d image of the stellar system into the air below the vox-mistress' cradle. The hololith was an affectation; every command deck officer was augmented with the capacity to interpret the data collected by the ship's auspices directly, without the need for second-hand translation to a visual medium. Despite that, Sherax maintained the aid, as Yuel had done aboard the *Kurzgesagt*, to allow her crew to inload the data visually. There was value in such concessions to the flesh.

The hovering image – and the data-feed Yuel received from the *Peregrinus* – showed four planetary bodies circling a dull red star. Three were ancient gas giants, majestic and entirely superfluous to Sherax's search. The innermost world was a tiny orb, drifting steadily within the system's habitable zone.

From their distance at the edge of the system, it was difficult to make out any details of the planet's surface. Visible-light scans were occluded by an ashen haze. The return of auspex and the ship's other sensing tools were scattered into static.

'Resolve.'

Auspex technicians sought to obey, passing the raw information through cogitators and the slaved minds of mono-tasked servitors. Steadily, the image and the background data sharpened into focus.

Yuel could not contain himself. 'By the Omnissiah...'

Hundreds of Imperial and Mechanicus vessels drifted in sedate motion around the isolated planet. The haze was wreckage – billions upon billions of shards of shattered metal that had accreted into a dense cloud that filled the world's orbit. They varied in size from the microscopic to the titanic. Some were entire void-craft; the *Peregrinus* counted over a hundred and thirteen objects whose profiles either partly or wholly conformed to known STC patterns.

Yuel inloaded the auspex data as quickly as it came. The discovery ranked among the greatest of his career. The mass of the material that could be salvaged from the debris cloud was immense. Obtaining the uncontested claim to mineral wealth of such scale was sufficient to raise the most minor ship's ductor to high rank and prestige.

He was not alone in recognising the magnitude of the find. No one stationed on the command deck paused in their duties, but the noosphere echoed with acclaim and benedictions to the Omnissiah.

'Threat analysis.' Sherax effortlessly punctured the mood.

Yuel chastised himself. His calculations had run away along familiar lines, in ignorance of the nature of their mission and the dangers it posed. Entry to this system had been proscribed for a reason. The bounty that so enticed Yuel was proof of that.

'Zero power signatures or anomalies detected, ductrix. Threat assessment: negative.'

Sherax was motionless in her throne, parsing the reports of her officers from the *Peregrinus'* formidable data stream. It took her several minutes before she was satisfied.

'Astrogation: plot a course for orbital insertion to the inner world. Maintain shields and scan rates.'

* * *

Their entry point to Ikaneos was close to the system's star. The journey from the Mandeville point to a high orbit of the unnamed world took just two days, during which time the *Peregrinus*' sensoria division was heavily occupied. Charting astronomic bodies was the most basic function of an explorator, and both Yuel and Sherax lent their considerable expertise and processing capacities to the task.

Yuel suspected that Sherax found the activity calming. Though she still denied herself the efficiency of the communion, he had registered elevated stress indicators since she had returned to the command throne for translation from the warp. His own connection to the ship, though superficial by comparison, was sufficient to sense the overspill of tension, and her orders to her sub-magisters and auspex technicians remained terse and joyless.

The picture they built of the world, designated Ikaneos-Alpha in accordance with Mechanicus and Imperial convention, was remarkable.

It was not simply orbital space that was choked by wreckage. The planet was carpeted with the detritus of fallen spacefaring vessels. Its atmosphere was wracked by radiation storms, no doubt initiated by the detonation of reactors during their descent. Its primary ocean was a polluted quagmire, exacerbating the atmospheric disturbances. Acidic rain, heavy with toxic minerals that had leached from the shattered starships over the centuries, doused the landmasses, accelerating the process of degradation.

Every data point was fuel for the fire of Yuel's ambition, long banked but far from extinguished. The corrosive chemistry of the planet's air and water could be harvested for a myriad of industrial applications. Some of the fractured hulls that had survived atmospheric entry could be saved; the rest would be harvested of recoverable components and then dismembered for their weight in metal. Salvator scows would sweep the orbiting debris cloud, devouring all they swallowed and refining the minerals for future use.

All analyses pointed to a single, ecstatic conclusion. Ikaneos-A could be the catalyst for the renewal of the Gryphonnen empire.

Mechanicus vessels were as prone to gossip and hearsay as much as any void-going craft, and news of their discovery spread rapidly. For the first time since the fall of Gryphonne IV, the crew of the *Peregrinus* worked with more than just diligent obedience. From the ship's magisters to the lowest deck-serf, triumph could be felt and heard.

'Well done, Talin,' Yuel said finally.

Sherax did not share the ship's high mood. 'I did not come to this place for iron, my lord.'

FOUR

The *Peregrinus* coasted into a wide, elliptical orbit around the world. The density of the debris cloud made drawing any closer a risk; reports of superficial scarring to the ship's prow were already coming in.

It took three full revolutions before a detailed cartographic and spectroscopic assessment of the surface was complete. Sherax scrutinised every update, poring over obscured details and demanding fresh calibrations or filters be applied. She had not been idle during the stormy voyage through the warp. Without aid from her crew – Sherax was still unwilling to expose any other to the Genesis phenomenon – she had developed a detailed understanding of the radiation emanating from the shard recovered from the *Almagest*, and had taught this knowledge to the *Peregrinus*. Its sensoria were primed for any suggestion of a matching signature.

After two shipboard days of continuous scanning, an auspex technician finally spoke from the far side of the command deck. 'Anomalous reading detected on the surface, ductrix.'

'Identify.' Sherax's command was instantaneous.

'I am unable, ductrix. It is extremely weak. Our sensors cannot resolve it.'

Sherax, already still, became entirely immobile as she immersed her consciousness in the ship's data stream.

'The signature is weak because it is masked by a structure,' she said after several minutes. 'Spectroscopic analysis reveals compounds that are otherwise absent from this world, suggesting a foreign edifice.'

She lifted her consciousness sufficiently to deliver this analysis, then dropped back into the flow of information. Moments later, she surfaced once more.

'Show me a visual scan of the area.' The sharpness of her order was sufficient to cause a tremor of feedback through her mechadendrite weave.

An image blinked into being across a dozen pict screens. A wash of static, each speck once a part of a mighty void-forging vessel, was slowly resolved as tech-thralls laboriously scrubbed the feed.

Out of the murk, a shape emerged. A shape made up of sweeping curves and narrow columns. A collection of buildings, fluted and apparently fragile, that followed the contours of the land on which they sat.

Yuel could not contain his disgust. 'Decay and damnation.'

No Imperial building would be so fluid, so organic in form. No Mechanicus structure would deviate so profoundly from established architectural templates.

The data stream stuttered as Sherax struggled to accept what her data-feeds told her. Finally, Yuel said what Sherax could not.

'This was an aeldari world.'

FIVE

Edgar woke to the sound of a fist hammering against steel.

He rolled from the slab on which he had, with much difficulty, learnt to sleep, and staggered the three short steps to the door of his quarters. He worked the crank handle with his eyes barely open, but still winced as the glare of the passage lumens burst in through the open portal.

The hazy outline of a fur-lined helmet greeted him. 'Message for the major, Sir Edgar.'

The outline was holding something for Edgar to take. On the second attempt, he clutched the scrap of vellum, then pushed the hatch closed. He didn't bother to correct the trooper's use of his abdicated title.

Zlata was far more accustomed to being roused in the uncivilised hours of the night. She rolled off the bed and snatched the note Edgar had been given from his unresisting hand.

Their liaisons had begun the night of his first excursion to the Vostroyan mess, and had continued in an infrequent but vigorous

manner. Zlata – her given name was Nastasya, but both she and Edgar preferred that he call her Major Zlata, even during their more intimate moments – had taken to appearing at the door to his quarters in the early hours of the night, stirring him from sleep with demands that Edgar had been more than happy to obey.

While she read the note, Edgar stumbled back towards the slab, but she caught his shoulder before he could drop back onto its meagre comfort.

'Get dressed,' she said.

Edgar blinked. 'What is it?'

'Deployment.'

'Why?'

'It seems the bastard aeldari beat us here.'

That penetrated the fog of fatigue. 'The aeldari?'

Zlata was already shrugging on her uniform tunic. Her heavy greatcoat was back in her billet, and she was ready to leave in moments.

'You're well practised at that,' Edgar said while he pulled on an undershirt with far less vim.

'Usually I sleep with my boots on.'

He had to smile at that.

'I don't see the hurry,' said Edgar. 'I doubt the esteemed explorator will have a great deal for you or me to do.'

Zlata's good humour vanished. She had her back to him, but he could tell from the tightening set of her shoulders that he had said the wrong thing.

'You have to admit,' he said, pressing on in the hope of salvaging the moment. 'We have hardly been well used since we were brought aboard this ship.'

'I go where I'm ordered.'

Edgar's own mood began to sour. 'To fetch and carry? To stand guard like a servitor? Where's the honour in that?'

She turned on him. There was barely enough room for them both to stand together, and Edgar lurched back in response, and ended up sagging onto his bed.

'I'm a soldier,' Zlata said. 'I don't have the luxury to choose where I am sent. I go where my troopers go. We do what we are ordered to do. That is how I serve.' She looked away, and in a softer voice added, 'There is nothing else but service.'

Edgar scoffed. 'Forgive me for aspiring to something more.'

Zlata glared. Edgar was suddenly aware that the Vostroyan commander was, in every way that counted in that moment, a more formidable fighter than him.

'Whenever I think there might be more to you than you pretend, you disappoint me.'

She heaved open the billet's hatch, and left without another word.

SIX

Sherax was moving before the drop-ship's ramparts had lowered.

The howl of engines screamed through the lander's hold, the truest voice of a machine that had fulfilled its function. Cold, acid-tinged air rushed in. Her olfactory sensor tasted the familiar tang of promethium afterburn, the sharp bite of corrosive agents, and the unique melange of bitter organic particulates distinct to the world to which she had come.

Sherax looked out beneath the lander's canopy. The sky was an abused smear of grey cloud, pregnant with alchemicals and the flickering discharge of lightning bursts. The descent from orbit had been brutal. She had been forced to turn the *Peregrinus*' guns on the upper atmosphere, detonating a series of macrocannon shells to punch a hole in the drifting wreckage through which the landers could pass. But that had done nothing to calm the troubled skies of an abused and alien world.

A hiss of pneumatics burst from the lander's pistons. Sherax

walked the length of the boarding ramp, and stood upon earth and rock for the first time in a decade.

She took no extraordinary pleasure from the sensation of storm-force winds breaking against her carapace, or of loose, poisoned soil beneath her claws. Only red, iron-rich sand and the petrochemical reek of working forges would elicit such an emotion.

At her back, rising from their restraints, were three maniples of skitarii, accompanied by a dozen of the eclectic war machines for which the Mechanicus were famed. In a second lander, concealed from her sight by the wash of its engines, were four companies of Vostroyan soldiery, and the compact form of *Vortigern* and its vainglorious pilot.

The *Peregrinus'* orbital scans had revealed no evidence of life. All signs indicated that Sherax had invaded a dead world, but she had come in force. She was familiar with the duplicitous nature of the aeldari.

Though it had been several hours since the scans first pierced the veil around the planet, the ductrix had not yet come to terms with what she had found. She was not ready to face the implications of discovering xenos ruins where she had expected to find the source of the Genesis shard. For a brief moment, a single tick of her thoughts, Sherax's doubts threatened to overwhelm her.

She had not fled the synod's sanction out of selfish greed, or a desire that the glory of discovery be hers alone. She had fled the triumvirate's stricture because she feared their concerns had merit. If that was so, Sherax had forfeited her command of the *Peregrinus*, and likely her life. All who had followed her to the world were condemned by her actions, unless she could lead them to a miracle the like of which had not been encountered in all of recorded history.

With significant effort, Sherax partitioned her unease, chaining it away beneath her higher functions. Her purpose was set. She was an explorator, and she would explore this world and uncover its mysteries.

The landers had struck the earth as close to the aeldari complex as Sherax dared, barely three hundred yards from the outermost of the low, domed buildings that surrounded its central structure. The force of the lander's engines had set sheets of dirt and metal fragments streaming from roofs and along empty alleys.

She sent a command to the drop-ship's flight deck, and a series of metallic thunks echoed from the hold. A flock of servo-skulls detached from the eaves, and raced away on pulsing suspensors to disappear into the narrow streets. Their signals immediately began to degrade in the rad-soaked atmosphere. Clearly more direct forms of reconnaissance would be required.

Sherax was accompanied by more than just warriors. While her skitarii gathered in formation and marched out onto the blasted earth, Rahn-Bo emerged from the armoured compartment above the main hold at the head of a sect of datamancers, logi, and attendant scry-servitors.

The two adepts had not spoken in the weeks since Rahn-Bo's visitation to Sherax's quarters, but it had been unthinkable to undertake an expedition without her. And Rahn-Bo, for all her objections to their mission, would not have allowed herself to be left behind.

Magos Lyterix had also made planetfall. The augur was standing at the boarding ramp's edge, peering from behind a full-faced rebreather and observing the planet's surface with apparent interest. Sherax had not ordered or requested his presence, but nor was she opposed to it. She would take whatever advantage his comfort with the unorthodox might provide.

Sherax had left Yuel in command of the *Peregrinus*. She had been mildly appalled by the eagerness with which the lord explorator had accepted her delegated authority protocols. It was unsettling to leave her soul-bonded vessel in the hands of another, but Sherax had to trust that Yuel would act as steward and no more.

The hum of heavy-lift repulsors filled the drop-ship's hold. Xal stood at the fore of a Skorpius transport, with Rho-6-2 and their demi-maniple already mounted in its personnel bay behind him.

Sherax opened a wide-band vox-frequency as she clanked towards the hovercraft. 'Major Zlata, was your landing optimal?'

The Vostroyan commander answered through a crackle of heavily distorted vox. *'Tolerable, explorator.'*

'Very well. Array your troops to defend this position.'

'Yes, explorator.'

'Marshal Heralin, deploy your cohort. That' – she raised her axe towards the fluted vanes of the central structure, rising over its lesser kin – 'is our destination.'

The commander of the *Peregrinus*' skitarii contingent replied at once. 'Compliance.'

Sherax climbed aboard the Skorpius. With Xal at her side, they set out towards the aeldari complex.

SEVEN

Ikaneos-A was a poisoned world.

Thess Rahn-Bo had spent the vast majority of her life within the confines of Mechanicus constructs. Her home was among the fortresses and factorums of the forge world, or else the narrow warrens of its void-craft. The open sky, storm-wracked and impossibly vast, was a novelty Rahn-Bo found strangely distracting.

She stood in the passenger bay of a Skorpius transport, racing on a cushion of repulsor energy through the streets of an alien township. It had been classified as such from orbit, although it was hard to tell if any life form, aeldari or otherwise, had ever occupied it. The first skitarii infiltrators and servo-skulls to scan the bleached-white structures, which Rahn-Bo took for habitation units, had reported that they were entirely bare of any signs of occupation.

More skitarii loped on either side of the transport, maniples breaking into squads and demi-squads in accordance with Marshal Heralin's instructions. As the outlying buildings had been

discounted as holding little interest for the expedition, the ductrix had swiftly pressed ahead, leading a column of hovercraft and skitarii scouts along the widest path to the centre of the complex.

Their route twisted back and forth in a highly inefficient manner, but it did not take long for the barren road to open onto the only area of significance that had been identified prior to landing. A sizeable expanse of open ground occupied the centre of the township, with a single tower rising from the grey, wind-swept soil.

The nature of the structure and its outworks had been the subject of heavy speculation prior to the expedition's landing. The area had been exposed to every form of scrutiny available from the *Peregrinus*' extensive apparatus, and yet it was only by landing, by bringing themselves to its level, that Rahn-Bo was able to answer that question.

'It is a temple,' Rahn-Bo said as she dismounted the Skorpius. Behind her, the coterie of logi, analytors, and xenologists did the same, and immediately began to spread out through the field following whichever curiosity first caught their interest.

'No,' Sherax corrected. She had reached the field some minutes before, and stood in the shadow of the tower. 'This is not a place of worship. It is a place of mourning.'

Lyterix offered his own contention. 'This is a necropolis.'

The distinction was made apparent by the stelae that surrounded the building. Hundreds of carved pillars were arrayed in no pattern or order that Rahn-Bo could discern. No two the same, varying in height, shape and thickness. Some were thick slabs, others angular columns and pillars. The field stretched for almost a mile in all directions from the fane at its centre.

All were embossed with aeldari runes. Their alien script was clustered on panels, which were subdivided by flowing lines with arrow-like heads, suggesting a linear relationship between the runes. Like Sherax, Rahn-Bo had inloaded all she could on aeldari culture before making planetfall. While this form of stelae were not mentioned in the archives she had accessed, the xenos form of writing was well documented. Each panel was a statement, typically the work of a single scribe. Each rune had a particular symbolism, but the selection and placement of runes within the panel could drastically alter their specific meaning in the context of the whole. It was a maddeningly obtuse form of communication, far removed from the clarity of binharic code or even the arch rhetoric of Imperial Gothic.

A cracked and faded path wound its way between the stelae. It was paved with irregularly shaped slabs of bone, each pitted and scarred by the planet's punishing atmospheric conditions. As there appeared to be no logic to its meandering route, Rahn-Bo assumed that it held some religious significance. In the context of this place, it most resembled the penitent trails found on Imperial worlds. A route through which the sinful and the damned would be driven as punishment for their flaws.

No doubt the curates of the Imperial Ecclesiarchy would be dismayed by the comparison.

A pair of Onager Dunecrawlers clanked along the bone path, grinding slabs to dust beneath their armoured tread. Marshal Heralin had brought the majority of his cohort into the grounds of the necropolis in accordance with standard combat doctrines. Clades of skitarii were garrisoning the low buildings that formed the boundary of the necropolis field, while others pushed outwards to confirm the absence of any hostile entities in the township. Tracked heavy weapon platforms and the stolid presence of the Dunecrawlers offered further reassurance that Rahn-Bo and her peers could conduct their work without fear of interruption.

Before she allowed herself to follow her acolytes and lose herself in study, Rahn-Bo looked across the field to where Sherax stood at the base of the tower – a single broad needle of the same cream substance as the stelae, projecting a hundred yards into the frigid air. It was the only structure of any significant size in the township, and therefore obviously the centre of its purpose, but it was far from impressive. A small balcony projected into the air near its summit, suggesting that its interior was traversable. A pair of thin, fluted arms stood proud of one flank of the tower, curving up to form a flattened oval against its side. The records of Mechanicus xenoarchaeology she had accessed documented this form of sculpture in many aeldari ruins, though their purpose – if they had one – was unclear.

'Ductrix, do you require me?' she asked.

'No, cogitatrix. I will share all that we find inside.' With that, Sherax and Xal disappeared into the darkness.

Thus dismissed, Rahn-Bo turned her attention to the closest stele, a pillar almost twice her height that flared outward at its peak. The sensing wands enclosed within her fingers extended to their fullest, and she waved her hands slowly across the ivory surface.

She had taken the script for carved relief, but closer scrutiny revealed no tool marks, even at the microscopic level. The runes had somehow been extruded from within the material, rather than being chiselled or stamped into it.

<Grown, magos. The aeldari do not extrude, or carve, or hew wraithbone. They *grow* it.>

Rahn-Bo jerked in surprise at the new voice in the communion. Magos Lyterix was on the far side of the temple grounds, apparently wholly absorbed in his own examination of the stelae.

She had not interacted with the augur during the *Peregrinus'* passage through the empyrean. He did not fit into the hierarchy of the ship. His relationship with the ductrix was ill-defined, and his antagonism of Lord Yuel and of Techseer Luren, both of whom the ductrix had left in orbit, seemed needlessly belligerent. All of these factors had combined to mean that Rahn-Bo had, if not actively avoided him, at least not sought his company.

Nevertheless, Lyterix's statement captured her interest. While Rahn-Bo was no xenologist, she had made detailed studies of the orks and the hrud, and in the aftermath of the fall she had undertaken to inload all available data on the tyranid genus. But she had only limited understanding of aeldari technology.

<By what process do they grow this material?> she asked.

<Wraithbone is psychoactive. It responds to the particular psykana of the aeldari species.>

<That is not an answer.>

<In their terms, they sing their structures into being.>

Rahn-Bo frowned. <Perversity is the hallmark of the alien.>

<Indeed.> Lyterix's response appeared sincere, but Rahn-Bo found his aura uniquely difficult to read.

<Are you familiar with aeldari lexicography?> she asked.

<I have some experience.>

<Will you assist me in translation?>

<Gladly.>

Lyterix abandoned his stele, and wandered through the field of pillars to Rahn-Bo's side. He showed no sign of discomfort at walking on an alien world, nor observing the icons of their religion. The augur squatted with a soft growl of actuators, and considered a section of wraithbone Rahn-Bo indicated.

<I believe that this collection of runes relates to grief and loss,> she sent. <Given the proximity to this glyph, the context is not merely loss of life, but loss of hope.>

<The aeldari are a florid race.>

They examined other panels, pulsing conjecture and analysis

back and forth in easy collaboration. Several minutes went by, then Lyterix interrupted the flow of data.

<It was you who retrieved the knowledge of this world from Magos Lucanus?>

It took Rahn-Bo some time before she responded. <It was.>

<I commend you. To touch such a mind is no easy thing.>

<It brought us here,> Rahn-Bo sent after another long pause.

<A further reason that praise is due.>

Rahn-Bo looked up, across the field towards the xenos temple Sherax had entered. <I am not so sure.>

She returned to tracing her hand over the surface of the column.

THE FANE

ONE

Xal took each step through the xenos temple with care, his weapons raised and auspex pulsing at its maximum frequency.

The protector had encountered the aeldari three times, but each battle had taken place on Imperial worlds, against villainously fast attack craft and their cruel but fragile riders. He had no frame of reference for the aliens' architecture and construction methods, besides the disturbingly fluid lines and bladed vanes of the raiding vehicles.

The fane was *alien,* in a way Xal had never before encountered. The gallery through which he led Sherax was lit by ruby-red gemstones, though he could discern no power source or circuitry to support them. The strange, osseous walls were deeply curved, and seemed to reflect light in a diffuse, unnatural glow. Yielding to an unfamiliar sense of curiosity, he unpowered his halberd and touched the tip of its blade against the wall. The metal bit and gouged through its surface, leaving a powdery trail, though it offered greater resistance than he had expected.

'Xal.' There was no censure in Sherax's vox-pulse, but nevertheless he withdrew his blade and resumed their steady progress through the tunnel.

The tunnel curved up and around, leading them higher through the tower's interior. The gallery was broken at intervals by shallow alcoves in which the scarlet illumination crystals sat.

After a dozen rotations of gradual ascension, the gallery opened onto what appeared to be the fane's only chamber. A single wall, circular at its base and studded with more glowing gems, stretched towards the tower's apex. The chamber was not large, barely a dozen yards across at its base. The far side was open to the elements, the narrow balcony they had seen from the ground permitting a panoramic, if unspectacular, view of the township.

A phalanx of piston-limbed infiltrators had already secured the chamber, and now stood at intervals around its perimeter. Their domed heads permitted constant vigilance of their surroundings, and their power swords and flechette weapons promised a swift end to any threat.

Xal exchanged a brief status upload with the scouts' alpha with a click of skit-code, and advanced into the chamber. It was an austere space, its floor unmarked except for drifts of grey dust that had accumulated at its edge. A narrow plinth rose from the chamber's epicentre to the height of his chestplate. Its dished surface was conspicuously empty.

'Ductrix,' he said, pointing.

Sherax glanced at the spot to which Xal gestured. 'Indeed. Clearly, this is the site from which Lucanus took the shard.'

The explorator placed one claw protectively over the stasis field generator at her waist. Though she had brought the shard back to its former resting place, it was clear she had no intention of restoring it.

Sherax's attention had already moved on. Six tall, narrow alcoves were recessed into the wall. Each contained a panel of aeldari script, reminiscent of the standing pillars that surrounded the fane, but also bore sharply detailed pictograms that reached up into the tower's dome.

Sherax opened the vox. 'Magos Lyterix.'

'Yes, explorator.'

'I require your analysis.'

'I will join you immediately.'

Xal scanned each image. In the circular room, it was not apparent if the scenes were intended to be viewed linearly, but the first he examined showed the orb of a planet lit by the rays of a gentle sun. Secondary images, showing arboreal growth and ocean depths, surrounded the world. Insofar as he could tell, the other tableaus represented scenes of aeldari life. Long-limbed aliens engaged in farming, fabrication, martial poses with swords and other exotic weaponry. Runes that Xal had no means of deciphering were inset around each image.

As Xal finished his own limited examination of the scenes, Sherax had moved to stand before the panel on the left of the opening to the balcony. It showed a world – presumably the same world as in the first panel Xal had examined. But where that stood in sunlight, the final tableau showed the planet in darkness. A scattering of stars was all the ornamentation this panel received.

The strike of footsteps on the osseous floor echoed from the gallery tunnel, and though Xal could sense Magos Lyterix's approach through the noosphere, he nevertheless turned to cover his approach.

The augur stepped into the chamber with little ceremony, and immediately crossed to the same relief that had caught Sherax's attention. 'Fascinating.'

'Do you see the pattern, magos?' asked Sherax. Xal detected an urgency within his ductrix's message that was deeply disconcerting.

'Indeed. This... is interesting.' The augur had become motionless, directing the whole of his focus towards the panel.

'Is this sufficient to reconstruct an astral locus?'

Lyterix's reply was interrupted by the crack of displacing air, accompanied by a dramatic drop in ambient temperature. Xal's auspex briefly registered a host of impossible, incompatible inputs, and then the aggressive timpani of an unfamiliar heartbeat.

Xal spun, arc pistol a blur of electric motion. Standing on the far side of the chamber was an aeldari warrior.

TWO

Every weapon turned towards the intruder. In less time than it took for Lyterix's heart to beat, two dozen radium carbines, arc pistols, and plasma calivers were fixed on the figure. It was testament to the rigid discipline of the skitarii that they had not opened fire the moment the alien appeared.

It was alone, or so it appeared. Lyterix could sense no other bodies in the vicinity, but nor had he detected the aeldari's presence before it manifested before them. He opened a sub-vocal vox-link with Sherax.

'Explorator, I have encountered these creatures before. Where there is one, there are surely others.'

Sherax did not acknowledge his sending, but instead cast a wide-band message of her own to her people and the soldiers beyond: 'The aeldari are here. One has appeared within the fane. Be on guard. Take no provocative action.'

The xenos was clearly a warrior. Blood-red armour clothed its long limbs, shaped in echo of its musculature but far heavier and broader than other examples Lyterix had seen. A pair of static arms ending in the wide muzzles of energy weapons projected from either side of its torso, in strange mimicry of arachnid anatomy. Its ivory helm was flanked by bladed mandibles, and a long, curved razor was fixed to each of its forearms. Its armour revealed nothing of gender, nor of its intent.

'I am Idranvel of Biel-tan. I am Idranvel of the Shrouded Blade.' The creature's voice emerged from its helm as a deep, sibilant whisper, unclouded by vox distortion. Its Gothic was fluent, but invested with disdain. Each word seemed to sully its speaker.

'Know that this is a sanctum of my people,' it continued. 'You trespass on ground sung into being long before your species gained sentience.'

Alone of all the Mechanicus personnel, Sherax had not drawn her weapon. She was unmoving, one claw still raised towards the scene upon the temple wall. Slowly, she turned to face the aeldari.

'I am Explorator Superior Sherax, of the *Peregrinus* and Gryphonne IV. We intend no insult by our presence.'

'You profane all you touch, mon-keigh. Your existence is an insult. And yet, it is one I must endure.'

The aeldari paused for a long moment, seemingly inviting Sherax to reply. But she said nothing.

'I know why you have come,' it said after some time. 'I know what you seek.'

The warrior that called himself Idranvel began to pace, taking slow steps back and forth across the length of the plinth. There was a languid, unnatural grace to his movements, in spite of his heavy armour. The broad plates accentuated his slow, shoulder-rolling gait. Lyterix recorded all that he saw and sensed for later analysis.

As the alien paced, Xal matched his movements, never allowing a direct line to open between the xenos and Sherax. The protector was unwavering, never closing the gap nor allowing it to grow. His halberd was outthrust in two of his arms, while the third trained an arc pistol on the warrior's helm.

'Do you know what this world was, before your people came? It was a paradise, as even your backward race would understand it. It was a garden. Verdant, unsullied. The home of millions, at peace with themselves and with a hostile galaxy.'

The aeldari gestured towards the fane's arched entrance. 'Look what you have made of it.'

Lyterix was unmoved. Humanity was eminently adaptable; environmental adversity was a by-product of resource extraction and exploitation, to be mitigated but hardly lamented. Compared to some worlds on which he had walked, Ikaneos-A was far from ruined.

Sherax was similarly uninterested in the alien's rancour. 'Your kind has no monopoly on enmity. How many worlds have been robbed of valued serf stock by your slavers? How many worlds starved and warfronts lost due to aeldari piracy against Imperial convoys? How many times have aeldari warships emerged from the void professing peace, only to abandon those foolish enough to trust them in the midst of combat?'

The warrior was impassive, the insectile features of his helm giving no indication of whether he was affected by Sherax's charges.

'Is there a purpose to your presence?' she asked. 'Or do you merely seek to carp and caper in your jester's attire?'

The alien ceased its pacing and turned to face Sherax squarely. 'I came to enlighten you. You mon-keigh who bind yourselves to metal and machines so often profess your desire for knowledge, even if you show nothing but ignorance by your actions.'

He gestured at the shard chained to Sherax's waist. 'Do you wish to know what that is?'

'Yes.' The single word was dragged from Sherax, but there could only be one answer. For all the corruption she invited by treating with the alien, she had come in search of knowledge.

'It is *Turellea Dandramensha*. In your mongrel tongue, it would be called Dominion Genesis. It is the gift of Vaul the Maker.'

'I have no interest in your heathen mythology.'

Though the warrior's face was hidden beneath his helm, Lyterix felt the furious stare he directed at Sherax.

'In the ancient past, while your species still languished in primordial slime, the gods created my people.' His hand swept across the pictographs. 'The gods favoured us. They saw our works, our spirit. They foresaw our rise, and in their wisdom gave us the means to bring forth life.' The aeldari paused once again.

'Countless worlds owe their existence to the labour of countless aeldari generations. Dominion Genesis was our tool, god-given, and we used it to make a garden of the galaxy.'

He gestured at the panel that Sherax and Lyterix had been examining when he made his entrance. 'Do you know where you stand?'

Sherax did not answer immediately, evidently weighing whether to continue to humour the xenos. At last she said, 'This world was the last to be conceived by the Genesis device. This place is a monument to its loss.'

The white helm dipped slightly. 'Indeed.' Idranvel ran a blood-red gauntlet softly over the wraithbone relief. 'We have lost so much. More than your brute empire could ever know.'

'Your failings are your own, aeldari.'

Idranvel turned, whip-fast. Lyterix again marvelled that none of the skitarii fired as a reflex response.

'Your Imperium sits upon worlds birthed by my people. You are colonisers, polluting all you touch. Squatting in the filth that rises around you.'

'And your race fades into obscurity.' Sherax took a step towards the warrior, emerging from Xal's protection. 'Whatever achievements you once claimed are nothing but dust and myth. Now answer me. For what purpose did you come here?'

'I wished to face you. To meet you as honour requires, though you are far from deserving of it.' Idranvel crossed his forearms in front of his body. Ruby light glinted from the edges of his blades. 'And because you have something that I need.'

As Sherax's pistol leapt into her claw, the other protectively grasped for the shard at her waist, the alien stepped back into the shadows and vanished.

Then he reappeared, his blades reaching for Sherax's body.

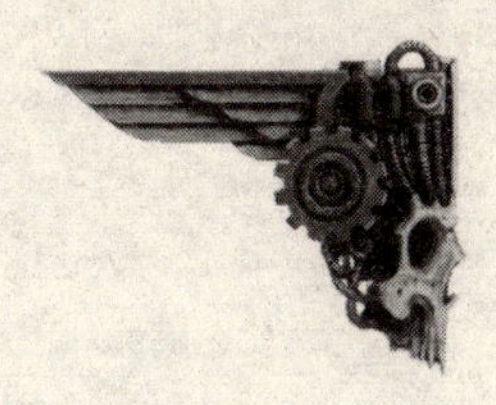

THREE

Xal was at Sherax's side, and that was what saved her life.

The aeldari lunged with both blades, one high, aimed at the place where her mortal heart once sat, and the other low, and both pierced the armour of her carapace. She felt the bite of alien steel through internal systems, and for a fleeting second the difference engine that was her brain calculated a single inescapable outcome.

Xal moved in a blur. His halberd struck the more lethal of Idranvel's blades, forcing it up and out of Sherax's torso before it could plunge into her cardiac pump. As the xenos pulled back into a duelling stance, his lower blade tore through the systems installed in her abdomen. Warning signals surged from Sherax's body, drowning out all other thought.

Xal and Idranvel fell into a blistering duel. Bolts of energy flashed between the two warriors, and both danced aside. Xal had the advantage of his halberd's reach, but the aeldari moved like smoke.

As Sherax fell, her motive functions suddenly impaired, other xenos burst from nothingness. Three of the skitarii died instantly, destroyed in a way she had never before encountered. The crimson assassins levelled heavy, wide-mouthed weapons that spat clouds of whispering death. The infiltrators disintegrated, their metal bodies riven into shards.

Her remaining warriors leapt at their assailants. The chamber rang with the clash of blade against blade, and glowed with arcs of unchained electro-force and the reflected brilliance of the gems that studded the xenos' armour. Sherax was dimly aware of urgent reports blaring across the vox, but she could spare little cognition for them.

Xal was outmatched. Sherax's combat protocols were at least as detailed as her protector's, and it was clear that the xenos commander was a peerless fighter. Bolts of power flashed from Xal's arc pistol as he gave ground, but there was too little ground for him to give.

Sherax reached for her archeotech pistol, but her synapses were a jumble of misfiring signals and she fumbled the weapon.

Xal parried one blow, another, and then Idranvel struck. One flawless blade sheared through the haft of the protector's halberd, and the other hacked through the claw that held his sidearm. Both weapons clattered away. The xenos lashed out with a heavy boot, and Xal followed his weapons to the ground.

Idranvel turned on Sherax with rapid, inhuman grace. The weapons mounted to either side of his torso flashed, but her refractor field erupted into shimmering life. The bolts of arcane energy burst against the shield, and the triumph in Idranvel's stance faded.

He advanced on her, still prone upon the chamber floor. A pulse of magnetism finally pulled Sherax's weapon to her hand as the alien leant over her.

The tip of his wristblade hooked around the chain locked about her waist, which parted like silk. The aeldari's hand was waiting, and closed on the stasis field generator as it fell free from her body.

Sherax's pistol was in her hand, and her enemy was inches from her faceplate. She fired.

The xenos was gone.

He teleported by whatever bewitched xenos craft had allowed him and his warriors to materialise in their midst. Idranvel of Biel-tan leapt away, bearing the only relic of a technology that he would have Sherax believe gave birth to the galaxy.

FOUR

The drop-ship rocked as something struck its hull. *Vortigern*'s audex capture relayed every wail and cry of the lander's clarions as it sensed its destruction.

Edgar threw a brace of switches, raising *Vortigern*'s reactor to full power. The Armiger responded immediately. It had been galling to both their spirits to sit in the dark, waiting, their strength held in abeyance, for the ambush that Zlata had feared would come.

The Blackbloods had arrayed themselves in the xenos hab-units, laslocks thrust through loopholes hacked in the strange, bone-like material of their walls. Heavy weapons teams occupied the roofs and streets, watching in all directions.

Nevertheless, the first whickering volley of xenos munitions had taken them all by surprise.

'Sergeant Jzyinsky, drop smoke and pull back – A Company will cover you. Captain Lursa, concentrate fire on the constructs!'

The vox relayed a constant stream of orders as Zlata put her force in order.

'*Vortigern*, get out of the lander, it's about to go up!'

Edgar didn't need to be told twice. 'By your will, major.'

He gripped the control columns, and *Vortigern* rose to its full height within the tight confines of the lander's hold. Another impact sent a tremor through the deck, and the Armiger staggered.

When he stabilised the Knight, he saw a wall of flames and debris. The entire forward portion of the drop-ship had collapsed under the enemy's fire, blocking the boarding ramp.

Edgar turned. There was no exit, except for one that he made for himself.

Vortigern took a single step forward, and released a blade from its thermal spears. The lander's inner hull shuddered as the gout of superheated air struck. Fuel lines exploded, metal burst into vapour, and *Vortigern* charged. Edgar ran towards the flames, shards of hull plating shrieking as they gave way to the Armiger's mass. He leapt the final step, an ungainly manoeuvre that the Knight was ill-equipped to make.

The hull shattered before the Armiger's weight, and Edgar's stomach lurched as *Vortigern* dropped twenty feet to the ground.

He braced, hydraulics ready. The impact kicked through the Armiger's frame. He felt a tooth crack as his jaw struck the edge of his cradle, but through the sudden pain he rolled the control columns. The Knight leant into the drop, legs bent almost double, then set off at a dead run.

The Vostroyans were heavily engaged. They had formed a front half a mile across, guarding the two drop-ships from the cover of the aeldari dwellings. But the xenos had struck from within the tangle of low buildings, and it was bitter hab-to-hab fighting across the Imperial line.

Two alien walkers, three times the height of the lithe warriors that darted from cover to cover at their feet, were advancing along the wide street closest to the Vostroyans' ruined drop-ship, shrugging off all the fire Zlata's troopers directed at them. They returned the Guardsmen's attention with a glittering array of xenos weaponry, allowing groups of aliens to advance on either side without fear of Zlata's sharpshooters.

The closest aeldari construct was directly in his path. It stood no chance at all.

Edgar didn't even bother to make a cut with his chainblade. Instead he bent low, couched the Armiger's stubby head beneath its armoured carapace, and charged.

Vortigern struck the construct with the centre of its mass. Imperial steel met xenos bone, and the aeldari walker was thrown from its feet. It struck the earth a shattered wreck, its bulbous head pulverised to dust.

Edgar's head slammed into the padded rest of his cradle, but he kept *Vortigern* moving, running on through the Blackbloods' defensive line. The second construct was firing at him, both unnaturally dextrous hands bent into fists and loosing a hail of tiny, razor-sharp discs. *Vortigern*'s hull plinked as the projectiles bit into its armour. An alarm wailed as one dug deep and cut something important. Edgar arrested his pace, clawed feet throwing up a drift of dirt and grass. He was straining against the maximum tolerance of *Vortigern*'s chassis, but for the first time Edgar felt that he was using his machine's full capacity and capability.

He twisted, rotating the Armiger on its narrow waist, and loosed a blast from the thermal spears. The construct was caught in the epicentre of the shockwave. Overpressure blew it apart, shards of baked bone blasting in all directions.

The Blackbloods cheered, and Edgar heard them.

This was what it was to be a warrior. A Knight of the Imperium. Man and machine, fighting in perfect synchronicity. *Vortigern*'s movements were smooth and fluid; Edgar's will was clear. How could he have ever doubted the spirit of such a steed?

A bolt of purple energy roared past *Vortigern*'s sensor cluster, so close that its picters fuzzed into static. Edgar staggered back, blind, turning sharply in the direction of the threat. His pict feeds returned in moments, in time to show a third construct racing towards him from a parallel street. It had taken the deaths of its fellows to heart.

The alien pilot of the construct had chosen to bring the fight close. That suited Edgar.

Heavy stubber rounds ricocheted from the construct's torso, blasting free ivory chips in a steady stream. In reply, another bolt of plasma flashed across the closing distance, and struck *Vortigern*'s left leg.

The armour cracked apart, and fresh alarms wailed. Edgar felt the blow as a burst of heat across his thigh, burning through muscle and bone. He growled through the pain, too lost in the zeal of battle to truly notice.

The aeldari stepped in close, long blade raised. Edgar surged forward, chainblade roaring defiance. The adamantine teeth struck, bit, churned. Powdered bone burst from the growing wound, coating *Vortigern*'s sensors, but Edgar did not need to see his enemy to kill it. He pushed harder, forcing another effort from the Armiger's overtaxed servos, burying the chainblade up to its hilt in the construct's chest.

The xenos emitted a moan as it died, a mournful cry that *Vortigern* met with a triumphant blast from its clarion. It toppled back, almost dragging the Armiger down with it, but with a final whirl of teeth Edgar wrenched his blade free.

He held his blade aloft, the flourish of the victor. He was restored, a lord of war once more, with broken adversaries at his feet. His audex capture relayed the cheers of the Vostroyans kneeling in the bone buildings. He let *Vortigern*'s clarion sound again, acknowledging their praise. Even as he did, he turned the Armiger on its axis and let its heavy stubber turn a clutch of xenos warriors to a red mist.

An atonal burr of metallic sound growled across the vox. Marshal Heralin's vox-caster was clearly damaged. *'Subject:* Vortigern. *Instruction: Redeployment, all haste. Destination: Central complex.'*

Edgar glanced at his port-side imagifier. Beyond the domed tops of the hab-units came the flash of discharging heavy weapons. The tower at the centre of the township was lit with lurid colour every few moments.

'Marshal, we are heavily engaged,' Zlata replied before Edgar could key his vox. *'With* Vortigern*'s aid we can cleanse this position and link up with you.'*

'Countermandment: Vostroyan One-Zero-Three Regiment to remain at present location. Clarification: All Mechanicus units to rendezvous at original position, following disengagement. Vortigern*: Deployment order restated.'*

That seemed perfectly clear to Edgar. 'By your will, marshal.'

He set off at a laboured run towards the flash of particle weapons.

FIVE

'Sherax, we must go.'

It was Lyterix who roused her, his intrusive touch triggering a reset of Sherax's cognitive faculties. A thin, bone-deep cut showed along the line of the augur's skull, but there was strength in the hand that gripped Sherax's claw, and an unfamiliar sternness to his unaugmented face. She allowed him to pull her to her feet.

The other xenos had vanished with their master. All but three of Sherax's skitarii were dead. A pang of regret made her unsteady thoughts stutter. Each warrior had been the product of agonising labour and martial artifice. No alien bodies lay with theirs, but when Sherax unspooled the last few moments from her memory coils she saw several fall to Mechanicus weapons.

Xal lived. His chestplate was a buckled ruin, and the third arm that emerged from his waist was a sparking, truncated length of steel. But he rose when Lyterix and Sherax approached, grasping a radium carbine taken from one of his deceased comrades.

Sherax crossed to the balcony, though Xal swiftly stepped out ahead of her.

Beneath them, all was chaos. Aeldari warriors in green and white were everywhere, unleashing a hailstorm of razor-edged discs from spindly weapons. Her adepts cowered behind the scant cover of stelae, though many already lay dead. Skitarii squads were spread throughout the memorial field, exchanging rad-soaked hard rounds with lithe xenos figures and relentless war-constructs. The heady mix of lubricating oil and alien blood rose on the air, and the vox was alive with the click of skit-code and insistent pleas for aid.

As Sherax watched, an Onager Dunecrawler turned on its heavy legs and loosed a searing beam of energy. The air rippled as exotic particles eradicated all they encountered. A handful of xenos were caught in its expanding radius, rendering them to ash. The beam lanced onward to core through the wraithbone buildings that lay behind the aliens, in a display of gratuitous and glorious overkill. The Onager's hardwired crew turned the walker, one leg casually pulverising a stele to dust as it sought new targets.

Sherax's trauma-scrambled mind had finally recovered sufficiently to partition her focus between her immediate surroundings and the various inputs that demanded her attention. She rapidly replayed the transmissions that had been broadcast since Idranvel's attack, then opened her vox.

'Marshal, report.'

'Status: heavy engagement. Opposing force disposition: light infantry with heavy weapon support. War-constructs, unclassified. Threat assessment: severe.'

'We should pull back to the drop-ships immediately.'

'Concordance.'

She switched frequencies, and in the same moment the bow

wave of an immense explosion crashed through the complex. A fountain of flame and shrapnel rose from the outskirts of the township.

'Major Zlata?'

'We are under heavy attack, explorator.' The Vostroyan commander's voice was calm, though the punch of an autocannon's staccato fire punctuated each word. *'The xenos appeared without warning.'*

'The landing craft?'

'Gone, explorator. Xenos infiltration units have destroyed them and now assault my position from the rear.'

The xenos had noticed their appearance at the fane's balcony entrance. A brace of razor-edged discs struck Sherax's refractor field, and each flashed into nothingness. She turned her pistol on them, and the aliens died screaming.

With the landing craft destroyed, a fighting retreat was impossible. Only one course remained: purgation.

As she summoned the full extent of her battle stratagems, the vox crackled once more.

'Talin.'

The frequency was so degraded by atmospheric turmoil, it took her several attempts to decode the data packet.

'My lord Yuel.'

'Aeldari warships– ...under sustained and overwhelming assault.'

The xenos were striking from land and from the void.

A rhythmic pattern of breaking porcelain announced the approach of *Vortigern*, scattering a knot of aeldari from its path. From their vantage point, Xal loosed irradiated rounds with lethal precision at any aeldari that showed itself. Across the stelae field, augmented warriors were finding their lost cohesion, and traded shot for shot with the green-clad xenos attackers.

The Mechanicus warriors were rallying, but the battle's outcome was clearly balanced in favour of the xenos.

A discordant thrum of gathering energy suddenly began to resonate from beneath her claws. The tower itself was trembling, energised by some arcane means. The explorator's auspex registered the same atmospheric disturbances that had heralded Idranvel's arrival.

'Back, ductrix.' Xal pulled her off the balcony into the tower's chamber, and so she did not see the portal open between the fluted vanes that climbed the tower's face.

A war-construct emerged, a thing of fluid musculature and bleak, daunting presence. Where Idranvel's ambushers had worn blood red, and the infantry that swarmed the stelae field were armoured in green and white, the tall walker was ink black, the colour of the dark spaces between the stars. Sherax did not possess a knowledge of the significance of colouration among the aeldari race, but she needed none. Its arrival heralded their destruction.

The lone Onager left in the field rotated on its axis, swinging its eradication cannon to bear. The aeldari walker took a single step towards it, and with an idle swing scythed an enormous blade through the war machine. The Onager was carved in two, spilling radiation-infused amniotic fluid in a great gout across the ground.

Sherax's thoughts of battle tactics and a hard-fought reversal died. Idranvel had orchestrated a masterful ambush. There could be no victory for the Mechanicus now.

She diverted all her discretionary energy reserves into her vox-emitter for a final, desperate cry towards the void. 'Run, lord. Take the *Peregrinus* and all we have seen, and run. The synod must know what is here.'

Even in the midst of impending destruction, she could not escape her own vanity.

'My lord?' Yuel had not replied. '*Peregrinus*, respond.'

A starburst winked into existence far above her. The briefest

flash of light, barely visible through the haze of clouds. A burr of vox-frequencies, suddenly emptied of their carrier signals.

A detonation in high orbit.

A scream erupted from Sherax's vox-grille, a wordless screech of agonising grief. Her thoughts fled into static, her mind emptied of all but horror and loss.

Sherax's home world had been destroyed. Her acolytes traded blows with aliens. Her ship had died, and with it her soul.

What more was there for her to lose?

SIX

The construct that stepped through the portal was an order apart from its lesser kin. Where they had been thin, spindle-limbed things that barely matched Edgar's Armiger in height, this was powerful, muscular, exuding threat and dominance. The blade it held in one strong, nimble hand was as long as *Vortigern* stood tall. This was an aeldari Knight, black-clad and deadly.

Edgar charged. It was instinctive, a charge born of a lifetime at war. His only chance was to overwhelm it, to savage the construct before it could stamp its authority upon the battle.

He tried not to focus on how and from where it had appeared. The void behind it, the hole that had opened in reality, was dark, a blank space in the world. Pale mist coiled from its edges, into which aeldari warriors ran in retreat.

Wraithbone slabs shattered beneath *Vortigern*'s heavy tread. He loosed a blast from his clarion and a bolt from his spears, but the tempest of heat was repelled by some kind of void shielding. The air ignited around the Wraithknight, forming a wreath of

flames through which it took an unhurried step. It moved with a disturbingly fluid grace, as though there were true muscles and bones driving it. Four vents or chimneys rose from its shoulders, accentuating its rolling, swaggering motion.

The vox suddenly crackled into life. '*Vortigern, cut left.*'

Edgar obeyed immediately, jerking the Armiger's lumbering charge to one side. A projectile raced past him, a smoky trail marking its passage. The missile exploded against the construct's shield, then another, then the eye-searing blast of a lascannon. It was brave of Zlata to redirect her heavy weapons teams; he did not want to think what those shots would cost her. Edgar continued the Armiger's lateral motion, expanding the arc of the threats it faced.

'My thanks, major.'

Zlata's voice was tight and grim. '*We can distract it, but you have to kill it.*'

'A task much easier said than achieved.'

'*The Emperor protects, Edgar.*'

He reversed his charge as sharply as he dared, hoping to catch the Wraithknight unaware. But it turned with its distressingly organic motion, and met him head-on.

He raised *Vortigern*'s chainblade, but the construct moved like the wind, forcing Edgar to turn his slash into a desperate parry. Blade met blade, and the aeldari sword sheared a dozen teeth from *Vortigern*'s roaring weapon. The xenos blade whipped through the air above the Armiger's carapace, streamers of violet energy flitting in its wake.

Edgar loosed a pair of melta blasts, praying that proximity would defeat the Wraithknight's defences. The bone stelae around the construct's feet shattered into dust under the sudden heat and pressure, but the alien's shield still held.

Warnings blared, and his hand throbbed. The thermal spears

could only fire for so long before the heat of their use rendered them inoperable. Vents cracked open along their length, flash-boiling the foggy air to steam.

Edgar back-pedalled, wrenching the control columns furiously. The construct turned to follow. It was fast, so damned fast. Two more missiles smashed into its shield, to no effect. It kicked out, an almost casual gesture that struck *Vortigern*'s hull like a hammer blow. The Armiger crashed back, crunching a brace of pillars to powder beneath its drunken recoil.

The wail of alarms reached a new tempo, matching the feedback Edgar felt throughout his body. His Helm Mechanicus translated every impact and wound to his mind. Pilot and war machine suffered together – the price to be paid for the purity of action a Knight could harness.

The construct stepped closer, and Edgar lunged. It was a feeble effort, hampered by the Armiger's range of motion. The xenos war machine batted the chainblade aside then back-swung, as casual as an agri worker threshing crops. The blade hooked inside Edgar's guard and sheared through the chainsword's mounting. The entire arm flew away, its roaring teeth churning a bloody path through a melee of Vostroyans and green-armoured aeldari.

Edgar reeled back, pain-blind. He pulled the severed mounting close against *Vortigern*'s carapace, shielding the arm from further harm. The Armiger's left leg, weakened by the lesser construct's earlier shot, finally gave out, and he fell to one knee.

How he would have loved to test *Bladequeen* against this foe. Her warblade against its broadsword. Her bolt cannon against its infernal shielding. That would have been a battle for the ages. A test of skill against skill, not the execution this had been from the start.

The Armiger bucked, its wounded spirit incensed by Edgar's disrespect. Its reactor flared, beating to an inferno's heat. Edgar's heart hammered to match. Both knew they had little time to live, and both raged at being outmatched by an enemy.

The Wraithknight stepped close, its sword levelled to deliver the killing blow.

If this was to be Edgar's end, then he would earn it.

'Die!' He roared the single word as *Vortigern* poured all of its energy into a last, almighty thrust, hurling itself onto the blade of its enemy.

Metal shrieked and tore.

'Die!' Edgar screamed through the piercing pain that lanced into his chest. The Armiger was impaled, and agony tore through his body to match the wound that would kill *Vortigern*.

The Wraithknight staggered back, but could not dislodge the Armiger from its blade.

'Die!' Edgar roared again, bellowing the curse from *Vortigern*'s vox-caster, heaving with all his strength at the control columns.

Slowly, inch by inch, the twin muzzles forced their way through the faltering shield. Metal sparked and tore as arcane energies ripped and fizzed and raged. Finally, the xenos void shield burst with a plate-glass shriek of undirected power.

Edgar leant forward in his throne, blood on his lips. 'Die, now.'

The thermal spears sang one last time. An inferno barked out, and the construct broke like sundered pottery.

The Wraithknight's torso was shattered, a charred and smoking ruin. Burnt bone poured as ash from the wound, a black cloud that seemed to Edgar to bear away the soul of the xenos construct. It moaned, a low, inhuman sound that eclipsed the wail of sirens and alarms within the Armiger's cockpit.

The construct lurched away. Its blade fell from its grip, releasing *Vortigern* with it. Slowly, impossibly, the Wraithknight fell.

Around him, xenos warriors fled from the impossibility of his victory. They ran for the portal in the tower's flank, chased by

las-bolts and arcs of energy into the darkness from which their beaten champion had stepped. Imperial soldiers and Mechanicus thralls cheered Edgar's victory, cheered their vengeance.

Vortigern staggered, drunk, broken. Dying, Edgar knew. The Armiger had given all it ever would, against an enemy that outmatched it in every way.

The war machine slumped to its knees. Edgar fell with it, the cockpit restraints holding him in place as the world pitched forward.

His head struck a console, and everything went dark.

SEVEN

The two war machines, Imperial and xenos, died together.

Rahn-Bo flung herself against the stele as the Knight Armiger finally crashed to the ground. The runes and panels that had absorbed her interest were now painted with the blood and hydraulic fluid of a skitarius who had taken cover behind it. His body lay at her feet, augmetics twitching with short-circuit discharge.

The xenos were running. They fought as they ran, covered by a hailstorm of their wicked discs to mask their retreat, but they were abandoning the fight.

It was their victory, however. For all that the Knight's sacrifice had destroyed their construct, the aeldari had slaughtered Sherax's expedition. The bodies of a dozen of Rahn-Bo's acolytes lay slumped against the pillars they had been studying. Hundreds more skitarii were broken beside them. They had spent their lives in defence of their learned masters.

She watched the last of the aeldari disappear into the mist-wreathed portal. They fired a final brace of shuriken. One clicked into the wraithbone pillar, barely inches from her head.

<Remain in cover, cogitatrix, until Marshal Heralin deems the battle over.>

Rahn-Bo looked up. Lyterix was on the far side of the field, at the ductrix's side, tantalisingly close to the portal and its eldritch darkness.

<That technology is unknown to me.>

<The opportunity for study has passed us by, I think.>

It was only then that Rahn-Bo considered Lyterix's condition. A blade or shuriken had cut a deep wound along the augur's head, coating one side of his face with gore.

<You are damaged,> she sent.

<We are all damaged, cogitatrix.>

Rahn-Bo stood from behind the pillar, and reached out with her mind. The noosphere was a desolate wilderness, emptied of so many of the voices that had given it shape and meaning.

Grief threatened to overwhelm her.

<The *Peregrinus*?> she asked instead.

Lyterix sent nothing.

<What now?>

The silence in the noosphere was deafening.

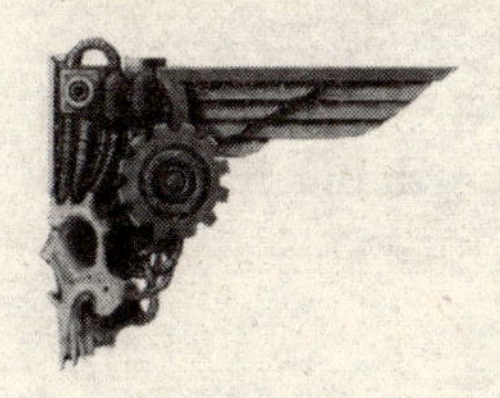
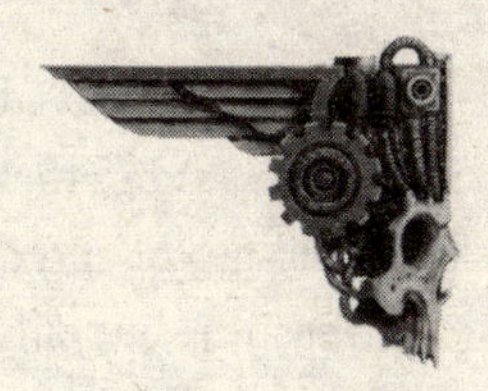

EIGHT

Something was on fire. The acrid stink of fused electronics filled the Armiger's cockpit. Edgar tried to reach behind his cradle for the fire-suppressant canister, but a dagger of pain shot its way up his arm instead. Dazed, he looked down.

His left arm was broken at the elbow, snapped in the same place that the Wraithknight had shorn *Vortigern*'s chainblade from its mounting. His right arm was no better. It was whole, apparently unharmed, but when he tried to lift it, fire flashed along every nerve ending. The pain tore into his flesh, into his bones. His shoulder was a knot of agony. It felt as though the limb were trying to amputate itself, mirroring the eviscerating pain he had forced *Vortigern* to endure to achieve that final, victorious blast.

Edgar screamed. He thrashed, torso writhing from side to side, which only served to heighten his agony as his broken and immobile arms were jerked about.

A good death. He'd truly earnt it this time. Let him pass now, and go to stand before the God-Emperor's judgement in victory.

But the pain stayed with him, kept him conscious for each agonising second that ticked by. His strength finally deserted him, and he collapsed back in his cradle. That at least brought some respite, but only some.

He was still conscious when Banner Sergeant Belyev prised open the carapace of the dying Knight. Edgar sucked in a breath of cold air. It tasted of metal, but that could have been the blood on his lips.

Belyev passed a length of broken metal to someone outside Edgar's view, then reached into the cockpit to release him from the cradle. 'This is the second time I've had to pull you out of one of these things, Sir Edgar.'

The humour of the moment was lost on Edgar. He tried to wave the man away, but both his arms still refused to move. 'Just... Edgar.'

Belyev looked into Edgar's eyes as he got the first clasp free. 'No, sir. I think you've earned it.'

THE WASTES

ONE

Night had fallen. It had been a swift transition, the pale, storm-wracked sky giving way suddenly to an oppressive, starless darkness.

Sherax had paid little heed to external stimuli in the past hours. She was aware of the passage of time and the change in atmospheric conditions only as a function of passive input. Her eyes saw and her sensors recorded ambient temperature and pressure, but she gave them no thought. Such things held little meaning for her now.

The survivors of the expedition had gathered at the outskirts of the aeldari settlement. They had been drawn to the flames that rose from the wreckage of the drop-ships, a ward against the rapidly dropping temperature.

The craft that had carried the Mechanicus expedition from orbit were in ruins. One was emphatically destroyed; the detonation of its fuel reserves had spread engine components and shards of hull plating across hundreds of yards. The other was

whole but irrecoverably broken, one more shell of a void-craft to litter the surface of the world.

All that remained of Sherax's skitarii were arrayed as a heavy cordon around the huddled adepts and Vostroyan soldiers. Barely enough units remained operative to form one maniple, out of the four Sherax had led to the surface.

The Vostroyan troops had suffered just as grievously. Hundreds were dead, and dozens lay wounded on the wind-swept earth. The bloody cuts torn by aeldari shuriken were staunched only by the thick fabric of their greatcoats; the ancillary resources to treat injuries had been lost with the drop-ships.

The skitarii guarded them, but it seemed improbable that Idranvel would return. Sherax knew that Ikaneos would finish what he had begun.

'We should set out now.' It was Lyterix addressing her. Some time ago, Xal had guided Sherax to the interior of an aeldari habitation unit where Rahn-Bo and several others had gathered. The senior adepts and officers of all that remained of the expedition sat or stood in the cloister of what had once been an alien's home.

'The closest intact wreckage is one hundred and twelve miles east of this position,' the augur continued.

The scans of the surface were within Sherax's memory coils. What Lyterix said was accurate, but she could see no value in his observation.

'We can reach it in four days.'

'Why?'

Lyterix looked at her, his still-human face unreadable. 'We cannot survive here.'

Survival. What an absurd notion.

As Sherax was unresponsive, he instead turned to Xal, Rahn-Bo, Heralin and Zlata. All bore damage of one kind or another.

Marshal Heralin, in particular, appeared to persist in defiance of the injuries he had sustained. The left side of his body had been ripped away by the blast of an energy weapon, and the metal of what remained of his exoskeleton drooped in beads of steel.

'We will strip the wrecks of all that can be salvaged, then set out for the hulk,' Lyterix said, vocalising his statement for the Vostroyan commander's benefit.

'To what end?' Sherax asked from her slumped position.

Lyterix turned back to her. 'It may be possible to repair the vessel. Or find some other means of returning to orbit.'

'To what end?' she asked again.

'To survive, explorator.' He spoke each word slowly, as though to an infant or an addled servitor.

'False hope is a corruption of logic.'

'And it is a corruption of our purpose to surrender to adverse circumstances.'

Sherax was incapable of expressing amusement, even at the best of times. 'You have a gift for understatement, magos.'

'Where is your hatred?' There was an unfamiliar inflection in the augur's voice. It took her some moments to recognise it as contempt. 'Where is your fury? Are you content to remain in this xenos hovel until we all expire?'

Grief dragged at her thoughts, and she resorted to the rote teachings of the Cult Mechanicus. 'Hatred is irrational.'

'Look around, explorator. The xenos have murdered your followers. They have disabled or destroyed your vessel. They race now to claim the relic that you pursue. Nothing could be more rational than hatred.'

Rahn-Bo and her peers were silent, impassive, but Zlata nodded in approval.

'Consider all we have experienced since the fall,' Lyterix pressed on. 'Consider what assails our species. Hatred is purity. It is clarity of thought and purpose. It is the will, explorator, to endure so that you might repay in kind the hurt that has been inflicted upon you.'

She felt it. Lyterix kindled the loathing in her. His words gave licence to all that she had chained away, that she had partitioned deep within the vault of her psyche since the death of Gryphonne IV. Rage was not a source of shame, but a source of strength. Contempt was the fire that stoked the engine of action.

'Is a trek through the wasteland of this world the wisest course?' Rahn-Bo asked. Among them, she was the least damaged, showing only incidental lacerations beneath her cloak. 'If the *Peregrinus* lives, Lord Yuel will look for us here.'

'The *Peregrinus* is dead. We can expect no aid except that which we find for ourselves.' The admission tore at the wound in Sherax's mind and soul, but the truth had to be faced.

She rose, setting off a wave of warnings from her damaged internal systems. It was questionable whether she would endure a forced march through the hostile wilderness of the world, but that was true for hundreds of others.

'Catalogue what resources remain to us, and recover all that we can,' she ordered. 'We shall set out at daybreak.'

TWO

Out of all the agonies that beset him, it was the strange, prickling pain in his ankles that woke Edgar.

Awareness returned by degrees, slowed by the remorseless torment that struck at every part of his body. He dimly sensed the light of the risen sun, but there was no warmth in it. When he was finally able to open his eyes, a static grey sky greeted him.

Something was wrapped tight around his chest. He tried to reach up, but his arms refused to obey. Pushing through the pain, he looked down and around to see what had been done to him.

He was bound to a sheet of metal. There were several straps of synthweave looped around his torso, beneath his arms, and up through a mounting bracket, holding him against the panel. Tilting his head back as far as he could, Edgar saw the backs of two skitarii. The straps ran up, stiff with tension, to disappear over their shoulders.

That was why his feet hurt. He had been bound to a makeshift stretcher, and his boots were wearing through as they were dragged over the dirt. Fragments of stone caught and scraped at his heels, each one a tiny knife that jabbed at the soft flesh.

'Stop.' The word came out as a dry rasp, inaudible even to him. 'Stop.'

A Vostroyan Edgar didn't recognise was near at hand and noticed his attempts at speech.

'Major!' The Guardsman cupped his hands to shout over Edgar's head in the direction the skitarii were pulling him. 'Hold up,' he said to the two units pulling Edgar along.

Slow minutes passed, as did more skitarii. Most had lost their cream cloaks, leaving bare metal limbs exposed to the elements. Edgar watched them, still drunk with pain. They appeared to glance back at him, if he was reading the tilt of their heads and whirring of visors and optical scanners correctly. Most bore their own scars of battle – sharp-edged lacerations across armour panels, and jagged burrs and foreshortened spars where metal limbs had been shorn away.

Zlata appeared, her heavy fur hat almost blending in against the dark clouds above. She was upside down relative to him. He tried to tilt his head around, but that set off another starburst of pain in his neck.

'So, you're alive.' Exhaustion showed in every line of her face, and it was impossible to tell whether she spoke in jest.

Edgar tried to reply, but the words emerged as a crackle over dry lips.

As Zlata smiled down at him, the merest hint of sunlight slipped between the clouds. 'Good.'

'There is something galling about being thirsty while soaked to the skin,' Edgar said.

Banner Sergeant Belyev snorted, then spat a gobbet of bloody mucus onto the wet earth. 'You're not wrong.'

By nightfall on the first day's march, Edgar had recovered sufficiently to be able to walk on his own. His arms were still useless knots of pain. He was just about able to close his right hand into a fist, but the neural feedback of *Vortigern*'s death-wounds had left their mark on him. Each time the party paused for respite, one of Zlata's troopers had to hold a canteen to his lips and trickle a bitter stream of poisonous water past his lips.

While Edgar was being cut from his stretcher, a monstrous peal of thunder had split the sky, and acid rain had started to fall. By what had passed for noon, every member of the column was pockmarked by the splash of caustic spray. The Vostroyans were more fortunate than the Mechanicus contingent; the weight of their sodden fur-trimmed greatcoats was immense, but the garments kept the bite of the rain at bay. Edgar had been given the coat of a fallen trooper, and he was grateful for it.

Far worse than the stinging deluge was the harsh, acrid burn of that same water passing his lips. The expedition's provisions had been destroyed along with their landers, and the Vostroyan troopers' canteens had quickly emptied. The pouring rain had offered a means to refill them, but purification was impossible on the march. Edgar, like the rest of the survivors, choked down only what he absolutely needed, swallowing blood as much as water.

The Vostroyans, with whom Edgar walked, did not complain. Neither did Edgar, but he took little pride in that. He took pride in nothing. He simply walked, one foot in front of the other, over rocky scree and brown, brittle grass. Zlata occasionally walked beside him, and when she was called away by the demands of duty, Belyev or others of his squad took her place. Their pity drove him further into himself, into thoughts of failed duty and machines whom he had loved as dearly as any man or woman.

The column walked in silence. Or, at least, the Vostroyans rarely spoke; if the Mechanicus contingent had anything to say to one another, they presumably did so over the vox, or whatever kind of arcane communications they shared.

There was little enough to say. The ground passed beneath them at a trudge, as bleak and uniform as the bitter sky above. Hope was a punchline. It was inertia that kept Edgar moving – inertia and a weary determination not to impede his companions any further than he already had.

As the days passed, each member of Sherax's expedition slept, marched, and wondered how Ikaneos would kill them.

On the third night of the march, they learned that they were not alone on the poisoned world.

In the previous two days, they had climbed from the plains and up into the passes of a flint-faced range of hills. There were no paths to follow, since nothing lived to carve them – or so they had thought. The expedition climbed over sharp-edged stone and tufts of ashen grass, turning from their course only when larger outcrops of rock demanded it.

The night was something conjured from Edgar's deepest terrors. No moons or stars pierced the wasted sky, leaving only a stygian darkness in which the lumen indicators and glowing visors of the Mechanicus adepts stuck out as brilliant pinpricks and bars of claret and jade. A precious few lumen-packs, either attached to the Vostroyans' laslocks or mounted to the carapaces of individual skitarii, provided the only means of true illumination.

There was no sound, no warning. Just a blur of movement, a scream, and then Trooper Greshen was face down in the dirt.

Las-bolts lit the darkness, striking nothing. Edgar was pushed aside as Greshen's comrades rushed to his side. He swore as the passing Blackbloods jostled him; the feeling in his arms was returning, but it was still agony to lift a hand to his face.

Greshen was still screaming, fighting against the two Vostroyans who were trying to tie off his wound. The stump of his thigh was a ragged flap of flesh and bone, but the rest of his leg was nowhere to be seen.

'What did that?' someone asked.

'It was a grox,' said a sergeant named Ashyeli.

'What?'

'It was a grox,' Ashyeli repeated, blood hot on his hands.

The rumour ran through the column in minutes, and as the night wore on it was confirmed. Again and again and again.

They struck without warning. Reptilian beasts, individually or in pairs, would dart towards the head or rear of the column, and were met by the snap of arc rifles and the crackle of laslocks. If the Imperial soldiers were fortunate, their fire drove the beasts off. If the grox were lucky, three or four men fell beneath their weight and jaws.

Sherax's datamancer, Rahn-Bo, was the one to offer an explanation. She hypothesised that the grox were the descendants of creatures that had been on the ships that survived the fall from the void. That made sense to Edgar. Every Imperial ship he had ever set foot on had been lousy with vermin, and most kept a livestock pen to feed the appetites of the officers.

Centuries, or possibly millennia, of scarcity had made them solitary, wary hunters, but with such rich prey entering their midst, the beasts had remembered or relearnt the way of the pack.

None were the size of domesticated grox – the fattened, alchemically docile herd beasts that fed the Imperium's insatiable demand for protein. These were lean, vicious creatures, and each was more than capable of killing a man in moments. If it couldn't carry the body away, it would drag it, all the while the screams and shots chasing soldier and beast into the rocks.

The screams of their stolen comrades were mercifully brief.

Their hides were thick, overlapping scales that could absorb a horrifying volume of las-fire. They were all but proof against the skitarii's arc rifles as well; it was only in close quarters that the Mechanicus troops could reliably bring them down.

The grox learnt that the column was dangerous. If they were too slow in ambush, if their charges took them across open ground, they were met by a torrent of fire that was enough to turn them back, if not kill them outright.

Edgar joined these fusillades when he could. He was regaining more sensation in his right hand with each day. He had reached the point where he could draw his laspistol from its holster on his thigh and fire more or less without fumbling the grip. What good he did was debatable, but it gave Edgar the first flicker of pride since he had awoken on the march. He was still a warrior, fighting shoulder to shoulder with other warriors.

There was one benefit that arose from their persistent stalking: the column had a source of food.

The grox meat was beyond foul. It had a sharp, metallic tang that made Edgar want to spit after every mouthful. He assumed that it was loaded with poisons, the same as everything on the accursed world. But he choked it down, trying to ignore the burning pain each swallow set off in his belly.

Edgar was sitting so close to the fire that his boots were almost in the flames, but its warmth barely reached him. The Vostroyans had resorted to burning any combustible material that could be spared. He'd even seen one man tear the fur covering from his helmet and hurl it into a fire. And though his comrades had sharply jeered his insult to their heritage, they had all crowded closer to the invigorated flames.

Edgar tucked his feet underneath him as Belyev made a slow circuit of the burning detritus. One by one, he encircled the fire with the charge cells of the Vostroyans' laslocks. Edgar had no idea what he was doing, but none of the troopers challenged the banner sergeant, so neither did he.

One of Sherax's adepts chose that moment to walk past their huddle, and caught sight of the cooking las-packs. The adept emitted a loud blurt of alarmed code, and rushed towards the fire. Belyev was quickest, and caught the man before his gloved hands could reach into the flames.

'No! Stop! Metal degradation. Cell endurance! Material decay!' the adept screeched.

Belyev held him firmly. 'It's an old soldier's trick. Old as the Imperium, I reckon.'

'It is unsanctioned!'

'Maybe, but it works.' Belyev let the man go, but still barred his path. He plucked a cell from a pouch on his belt, the exterior catching the light with the same blue-black sheen as those in the fire. He loaded it, and held the breech of his laslock towards the adept, who stopped struggling long enough to look at the charge indicator.

'See? I emptied it this afternoon, but now it's got three shots in it. Four, if the Emperor smiles upon me.'

'But it is unsanctioned!'

Belyev took the adept by one arm. 'One of these shots could be the one to save your life.' Belyev let him go, firmly but not roughly pushing the man away. 'This is not the time for lectures about Mechanicus doctrine.'

The adept tugged his fraying robe into place around his thin shoulders. 'I shall inform the ductrix.'

'Yes, you do that,' Belyev muttered as the man retreated quickly into the darkness.

The skitarii began to fall.

Each unit was augmented well beyond the template of baseline humanity. Indeed, in most cases Edgar found it hard to believe there was even a person inside the metal shell, so completely did their augmetics cover them.

But even machines had limits.

After six days of ceaseless marching by day and constant vigilance by night, the skitarii started to falter. Some seized up, others stumbled and fell. In every case, their comrades marched on, paying their fallen brethren little heed.

That night, Zlata found the explorator while they rested.

'You wish to speak with me,' Sherax said. Her vox-caster had picked up a defect in the past few days, leaving her spoken voice an atonal, static-edged burr.

'We must slow down.' Zlata wasted no time; the march had stripped them all of the niceties that would be expected in any other situation.

'If we slow, we will die in a matter of days.'

'If we do not, we'll die much sooner than that,' Zlata countered. 'We cannot march all day and fight all night. Even your skitarii can't maintain this pace.'

Sherax said nothing. The silver and bronze of her face revealed nothing.

'And we cannot carry the wounded, fend off the grox, and keep up this pace.'

Sherax panned her gaze across the sleeping Vostroyans. The hum and bite of seizing servos was clearly audible.

'Abandon your weapons. Their weight is a burden – my skitarii will protect you.'

Zlata's eyes were red-rimmed and chapped from the bite of airborne toxins. The fur of her coat was soaked with acidic rain and the blood of her troopers. Edgar was certain she had not slept since they had made planetfall.

She unslung her weapon, and held it in both hands for Sherax to inspect. Like the other officers' weapons, a broad axe-blade was mounted to the underside of its stock. 'This laslock has been carried by fourteen generations of the Zlata clan. If I die, my men will pick it up and leave my body for the grox. While I live, I carry it.'

Edgar believed her. Zlata had occasionally spoken about her weapon, about its heritage and the hands that had carried it before her. The thin layer of lacquered wood that enclosed its stock was new, and she had had to replace its barrel and firing mechanism after the Blackbloods' first deployment. But even to Edgar's eye, it was clear that the spirit of the weapon was as old as Zlata had claimed.

Sherax held the rifle for several seconds, then returned the weapon to its bearer. Zlata did not snatch it back, but nevertheless held it tightly, its axe-blade flat against her body.

'I comprehend,' the explorator said. 'Very well. We will moderate our pace.'

The column marched during the day, pausing twice between the first ghost of light and when the clouds shaded from grey to black. At night, both skitarii and Vostroyans formed a tight perimeter around their meagre camp. The wounded still died, but nothing Zlata or Sherax could say or do could stop that.

Three days later, they reached the ship.

THE OBDURATE

ONE

They found it on the seventh day of the march.

It was named the *Obdurate*, and it wore the heraldry of the Imperial Fists Chapter of the Adeptus Astartes, where the planet's corrosive atmosphere had not stripped back its hull to the bare metal.

It was a Gladius-class frigate, a template well known to the Mechanicus adepts. The ship had evidently been under power when it crashed, its engines defying gravity's pull to the last. Its blunt adamantine prow had carved a furrow twenty miles long through thin soil and soft bedrock, and the two vanes that projected from either side of its stern had gouged matching trails on either side. Those enormous plates had kept the vessel upright, ensuring a stately, dignified posture even in death.

The *Obdurate* was remarkably intact considering all it had endured, but it would never again take to the void. No craft of its size was ever intended to descend into a planet's atmosphere; even if it had been whole and undamaged, the frigate did not possess the strength to raise its ponderous mass from its grave.

Rahn-Bo feared that the ship, like the *Almagest*, would be infested with the degenerate descendants of its crew. But no challenge was issued as Xal led a squad of skitarii closer to the hull, nor when they used magnetic clamps to scale its flank and enter through a rent in its outer hull.

Sherax led the rest of the column forward, towards the ship's prow, where a rise in the terrain permitted almost level access into the *Obdurate*'s starboard decks. This was fortunate, as many of the survivors of the march were barely clinging to life. For every able-bodied Vostroyan trooper and skitarii unit, another was injured or damaged. Even the slightest hazard to entering the safety of the frigate's interior would have doomed them.

Rahn-Bo's fears were unfounded, as the expedition discovered in the first hesitant hours of exploration. It was clear that there had been many survivors of the initial crash, since the expedition's initial search revealed not a scrap of sustenance. A cursory examination of several skeletons revealed a loss of mineral density consistent with acute starvation, a conclusion that did little for the morale of the remaining Vostroyans.

Nor, for that matter, did it help Rahn-Bo's state of mind. Though she had replaced the majority of her digestive tract with a more efficient form of metabolism almost a century before, her organic elements still required regular sustenance in order to remain operable. She had compartmentalised the warnings her internal sensors had been sending for several days, but their frequency and volume were becoming difficult to ignore.

All attempts to rouse the *Obdurate*'s machine spirit failed; it was clear that the Motive Force had deserted the vessel. They dared not approach the rearmost quarter of the ship, as the radiological sensors of all Mechanicus personnel began to pulse warnings whenever their search took them towards the stern.

Sherax spread the expedition throughout the areas of the ship deemed untainted by radiation, hunting for any and all resources that might prolong their endurance. Rahn-Bo was among them. Hope, as the ductrix had said, was a corruption of logic, but nevertheless the datamancer worked her way through crew quarters, storage holds, and arming chambers with the single-minded determination she applied to any endeavour. It was either that or surrender to the malaise that had set in amongst her colleagues over the course of the march.

As the seventh day of their exile upon Ikaneos-A drew to a close, Rahn-Bo was struggling to deny the reality of their situation. Then the vox clicked into life.

'My ductrix, come to the forward flight deck. We have a positive development.'

TWO

'Is that an angel?'

The question echoed along the passageway at the same moment that Xal reached the junction. He and a brace of Rho-6-2's skitarii had been exploring the starboard flank of the *Obdurate*, searching for any trace of supplies or materials that might prolong the party's endurance.

A quartet of Vostroyans had evidently been foraging the same corner of the ship, but had stopped in their tracks. Ahead of them, the body of an Astartes warrior lay slumped against the bulkhead.

The warrior – a squad leader, assuming the Imperial Fists used the standard designations for leadership as defined by the Codex Astartes – wore armour the colour of a sunburst. Xal was rarely given to expressions of poetic licence, but in this case the ochre ceramite, streaked with garnet splashes of dried blood, precisely matched the hues of a dawn-break he had witnessed during the Thalosian Purge. Red eye-lenses, set deep within the helm, stared at them sightlessly, unpowered and dull. One lens was cracked.

The hilt of a combat knife, the kind issued as a weapon of last resort to the Chapter's armsmen, protruded from the weaker, flexible material at the warrior's neck. Others – thirteen in total – were stuck fast in the joints of his arms and legs. Bones, presumably those of his attackers, carpeted the deck. Their bodies had decayed and intermingled far beyond the point where individual identification was possible.

All four Vostroyans jerked around at the sound of Xal's approach, laslocks leaping to their shoulders. They dropped them once their muzzle-bound stablights caught him in their glare, but they remained highly agitated.

'Protector. We... we found it like this.'

Xal assessed the man's statement. His vocal pattern suggested guilt. There were any number of sins he could have committed, but it seemed most likely that he feared Xal would somehow hold him responsible for the death of one of the Omnissiah's vaunted Angels of Death.

The irrationality of unaugmented humans was a ceaseless mystery to Xal.

'This warrior has been dead for approximately three centuries.' Xal's vox-emitter had been steadily degraded during the march; his statement was almost lost within a snarl of electronic noise.

This fact, or his tone, did not appear to bring any comfort to the men. 'What happened?' the squad's leader asked.

Xal had perforce analysed the scene as he approached, and delivered his assessment without regard for the troopers' emotional state. 'The crew lost hope, and turned on their lords. Many of them – I would estimate between eighty and one hundred of the ship's serf-caste – ambushed this warrior. He was the last of the ship's Astartes company to die.'

The man's face, which in Xal's estimation had been displaying confused curiosity, now registered profound horror. 'Is that possible?'

'Which element of my analysis seems implausible?'

'That the angels' servants could betray them!'

Xal felt, insofar as he was able to experience it, a degree of sympathy for the soldier. He was upending a lifetime of religious indoctrination and faithful conviction.

'Yes,' Xal said simply.

'How do you know?'

He gestured at the scene. 'It is apparent.'

Xal saw it all. The torn stubs of femurs and forearms, roughly severed by a chainblade. The random scatter of fallen ribs and fragments of skull, blasted the length of the hallway by the explosive force of bolt shells. The way the remains of the crew were piled upon one another, lying in mounds where they had fallen at the Astartes' feet.

They had been desperate, past caring about their own fate, giving their lives so that their brethren could stand atop their corpses and lash at their former master with broken blades. Others had worked their way to the warrior's rear and hamstrung him. An effective tactic, as evidenced by the ceramite shell that sat slumped before Xal.

The squad's leader seemed compelled to ask for further information, even though he did not appear to desire it. 'How do you know that he… that this angel was the last to die?'

'His fellow warriors would not have left him like this. His weapons would have been gathered. His body would have been harvested for its genetic material. If time allowed, they would have removed his armour and entombed him within the ship's sepulchre.'

The troopers had no further questions, or if they did, they did not ask them.

'Continue your assigned function.'

The soldiers tarried, unwilling to move on in spite of his order. Xal understood their hesitation. The Imperium's masses were indoctrinated from birth with images of the Astartes, the vengeful angels of the Omnissiah – their God-Emperor – whose bolters and blades stood watch over humanity. To see one alive would have been the greatest honour of their lives. To see one fallen was a very different experience.

'This was an Astartes vessel. You may observe others in similar condition during your search. Master yourselves, and proceed with your assigned function.'

This time they obeyed, but not before each soldier, without acknowledging the act, stooped to retrieve a fallen shell casing or a broken tooth from the warrior's blade. Such relics were highly prized by the Imperial Ecclesiarchy, though Xal doubted that these would ever be traded away by their new owners.

Xal returned his attention to the dead Astartes as the men's footsteps receded along the corridor. Despite what he had told the Vostroyans, he had no knowledge of the Imperial Fists' traditions or practices to honour their dead. His description applied to any number of martial societies. This warrior's brethren could have cannibalised his remains, for all Xal knew of Astartes rituals.

Without that knowledge, Xal considered himself free to obey his immediate directive – to salvage useful items and equipment from the *Obdurate*.

The warrior's bolt weapon was gone, presumably taken as a trophy by the traitors who finally killed him, but his chainsword lay clenched within his armoured grip. The blade was a heavy, brutal implement. The work of Chapter armourers, not true artificers, turned out in their hundreds to feed the demands of Astartes warfare. Nevertheless, it was an effective weapon, and Xal was intimately familiar with its use.

He knelt and prised each finger of the warrior's gauntlet from the chainsword's handle. Or, rather, he attempted to. He reached out with his third arm, reduced by the xenos warrior to nothing more than a truncated spar and a set of stuttering actuators. He emitted a blurt of frustrated code, a rare expression of his inner cognition, and folded the damaged limb back against his body and grasped the weapon with his two remaining claws.

With moderate effort, Xal lifted the blade. To his surprise, he felt the spark of life within its engine cowling, the subtle hum of the Motive Force caged within its engine. He shifted his grip, and triggered the chainsword.

The engine seized, stuttered, then caught, setting the rusted teeth into a blur of motion. The bellicose growl of its machine spirit was fractured by time and neglect, but nevertheless sang out, echoing away through the darkened corridors of the *Obdurate*.

Xal had no means of outwardly expressing the satisfaction he took from the sensation of the weapon bucking and snarling, alive in his grip. He stilled the chainblade's spirit and magnetically locked its hilt between his shoulders.

The protector signalled his skitarii to continue. A moment later, the expedition-wide vox-frequency crackled open.

'My ductrix, come to the forward flight deck. We have a positive development.'

THREE

The Thunderhawk's designation, according to the chipped and acid-worn paint beneath its pilot's canopy, was *Dagger of Inwit*. Lyterix looked up at its hull, silently praising the resilience of its construction template.

Despite his prayer, not all of the *Dagger*'s peers had displayed the same strength of spirit. The hulks of two other Thunderhawk gunships, and one of the heavy-lift variants designed to transport Astartes war machines, littered the flight deck. They were all canted over, rocked from their resting positions by the *Obdurate*'s impact with the ground. Their projecting wings and struts were splintered, their engines crumpled into useless hunks of shattered machinery. Miraculously, *Dagger of Inwit* had survived where its brethren had not, its landing claws enduring the violence of its parent vessel's impact with Ikaneos' barren earth.

'Will it fly?'

Sherax was above Lyterix, having emerged from an approach passage onto a rusted gantry that overlooked one side of the

deck. She had acquired a profound limp in the past four days, and the drag-clatter of her malfunctioning limb echoed around the iron hangar. Below, a brace of adepts swarmed the gunship, their various sensing apparatus extended to their utmost. Several were operating a manual pump to lower its boarding ramp, though the mechanism was resisting their efforts.

'Will it fly?' There was a desperate hope in Sherax's repetition, one that Lyterix shared but to which he would not give voice.

'It appears to be intact,' he sent back instead. 'There are no breaches in its outer hull, and the thruster assemblies appear undamaged.'

Sherax gripped the gantry's railing for support, placing what Lyterix felt was an undue level of trust in the corroded metal. 'The Omnissiah blesses us.'

'Indeed, explorator.'

'To work, then.'

The Vostroyans quickly attempted to rename the gunship *Last Resort*, but were strongly rebuffed by the Mechanicus contingent. If they were to live, it would be due solely to the grace of the *Dagger*'s machine spirit, and no insult would be borne.

A full inspection revealed that the Thunderhawk was remarkably undamaged. Its interior had remained sealed against the corrosion of Ikaneos-A's atmosphere, although at some point it had been ransacked for its consumables. However, all the support mechanisms of the frigate's flight deck were in dire disrepair.

While the Vostroyans scoured the *Obdurate* for sustenance, Sherax and Lyterix directed the work of their adepts. Few were particularly skilled or familiar with the equipment – Sherax had brought logi and analytors, not fabricators and enginseers – but all of them, down to their metal bones, were acolytes of the Deus

Mechanicus, and they bent their minds and bodies to the task of preparing *Dagger of Inwit* for flight.

A major obstacle was fuelling the craft. With the deck's equipment in ruins, the transfer of any material was an exercise in brute strength. But while replacement battery packs could, with difficulty, be manhandled into place, fluid dynamics were not so straightforward. In the end, Sherax was forced to construct a crude manual pump from the components of four separate machines. While it conformed to no template or pattern of construction, extreme circumstances necessitated unsanctioned solutions. Shifts of six skitarii worked for eighteen hours to siphon thick, glutinous promethium from the flight deck's only uncracked reservoir into the gunship's tanks.

An Adeptus Astartes Thunderhawk was as aerodynamic as a thrown brick. Its purpose was to deliver the Omnissiah's chosen warriors into the heart of battle, and cleanse any enemies that threatened their mission. The short wings that projected from the rear of its fuselage were attachment points for armaments, not airfoils that could lift over a hundred tons of titanium and ceramite into the air. It was directed thrust alone that allowed the craft to fly.

As such, all that could be removed was tossed aside. The interior became a hollow metal box, shorn of seats, storage units, even handholds. The massive cannon mounted on its dorsal hull was cut free, though it took a heavily rusted crane assembly and the combined strength of every member of the expedition still capable of standing to haul aside. Had it been possible to strip away the outer layers of ablative armour, Sherax would have done so.

Each pound of mass that did not contribute to the gunship's lift capability, navigation, or void-seals was ejected in order to ensure that every member of the expedition could be extracted

from the surface of this accursed world. After all that they had endured together, Sherax could not countenance leaving any one of them behind.

As the last members of Sherax's expedition worked, they weakened. The *Obdurate* had been picked clean of any sustenance long before they reached her. Stagnant pools of water were crudely filtered to leach away the worst of their toxins, but the Vostroyans and Mechanicus adepts who still ingested liquid orally all bore chemical burns around their mouths, and hacked bloody coughs as they worked.

Major Zlata volunteered to lead a party out of the ship to hunt more of the predatory grox, but Sherax would not sanction it. *Dagger of Inwit* would be made ready before starvation could kill them. If it could not, then there was little point in delaying the inevitable.

It took three days of continuous effort, and the lives of four more of Sherax's followers. But, as a pale dawn broke on the fourth day, the gunship was ready.

FOUR

Sherax stared up at *Dagger of Inwit*'s ochre hull from where she lay upon the deck. Several hours earlier, the actuators in her left leg had finally seized, stressed and corroded beyond their limit. She had directed the final preparations while propped against an emptied munitions container, alongside two dozen Vostroyans and other Mechanicus adepts whose strength or pneumatics had given out.

The runes had been struck, and the gunship's somnolent machine spirit praised. There could be no testing, no careful and sequential examination of the thousands of components that were necessary for its operation. Either the *Dagger* would fly, or all that remained of her expedition would die.

'We give ourselves to you, machine. We commend our souls to your strength. We place our bodies in your care.'

For the first time since the death of her home world, Sherax prayed. She prayed with all the fervency of a neophyte faced with the overwhelming wonder and terror of the void. She

prayed for herself, for her crew. For the ship she had lost, and the future she had dared to imagine.

A shadow fell across her. Xal loomed, indefatigable.

'All is prepared, ductrix.'

Sherax ceased her prayer. 'Then let us leave this benighted world.'

The protector carried her, cradled in his arms, up the *Dagger*'s assault ramp and into the cockpit. He laid her in the void that had held the co-pilot's throne, propped against the bulkhead, then settled into the pilot's seat. The sight was vaguely absurd. The throne was sized for an Astartes' armoured frame, and Xal could barely see beyond the cockpit's console. He began to flip switches while murmuring praise to the gunship's machine spirit.

Below them, the rest of the expedition hauled weary limbs up the short incline and into the passenger bay. Most lay or fell the moment they reached a bare span of metal, exhausted of their last reserves of energy. Sherax's skitarii, whose inhuman endurance had saved the lives of all who came to Ikaneos, were the last to step aboard.

It was to their eternal fortune that the Thunderhawk was oriented in the direction of the flight deck's opening. Had it drifted from its position, had its magnetic lock to the *Obdurate*'s deck failed, there would have been no hope of escaping the broken vessel.

An analytor named Astinas had assumed responsibility for connecting every power pack that could be found into a single volatile assemblage that ran through fraying cables to the Thunderhawk's primary batteries. She had volunteered to be the one to discharge them, but, like Sherax, her motive functions had failed hours earlier. Jeremet Lyterix, insulated by multiple layers of scavenged plastek sheeting, stood beside the makeshift generatoria that would kick the gunship's systems into life.

He opened the vox. 'I am ready, explorator.'

'Xal?'

The protector gave one final pass of the wide console, then gripped the control columns. 'Yes, ductrix.'

'Very well. Thess.'

Rahn-Bo sat at the fore of the passenger deck. Out of Sherax's senior acolytes, she was the most human, and she had suffered most because of it. One of her ocular implants had failed soon after the expedition had reached the *Obdurate*, and the poisonous water was fouling her internal organs. Nevertheless, half-blind and with blood upon her chapped lips, she began the invocation.

'We call upon the Master of All Knowledge.'

'Ave Mechanicus!' The devotees of the Machine God answered Rahn-Bo in a chorus of broken voices.

'We beg you confer your powers upon this machine.'

'Ave Mechanicus!' The Vostroyans joined the cry. Those who could not speak stamped their boots against the deck.

'We beg you to invest this device with your holy charge.'

'Ave Mechanicus!'

'Grace us in our hour of need,' Sherax added softly, unheard as Rahn-Bo began the prayer once more. She reactivated her vox. 'Now, magos.'

Lyterix threw the switch.

The Motive Force crackled and sparked. In a fraction of a second, the battery packs discharged in a single surge of power. The Thunderhawk's engines coughed, caught, then released a thunderous blast of soot and debris that painted the walls of the flight deck black. The choking reek of unburnt promethium immediately flooded the gunship's personnel bay, but the engines were alive.

A weak cheer erupted from the Vostroyans, while the chant

of the Mechanicus chorus reached its crescendo. The bark of three RX-92-00 Mars-pattern turbofans bursting into life was the sweetest sound Sherax had ever heard.

The engines' stuttering cough became the high-pitched whine of restrained propulsion in the same moment that Lyterix leapt through the starboard boarding hatch. A Vostroyan trooper slammed the hatch closed, and one word was passed along the length of the hold.

'Go!'

Xal released the primer cables, pushed the throttles forward, and the world began to scream.

The Thunderhawk's landing claws dug runnels through the deck plating, ceramite shrieking against steel. Reactive ducts along the length of the hull came alive, and inch by inch *Dagger of Inwit* pulled itself into flight.

The gunship rushed towards a flint-grey sky. It burst free of the hold trailing oily smoke, barely keeping itself level. Sherax and her expedition left the *Obdurate* in its grave, their saviour in death.

Xal immediately lifted the gunship's nose, and opened the shipwide vox. 'Brace for rocket ignition.'

The main engine fired a bare second after Xal delivered his warning, kicking Sherax in the spine with the force of a bomb's detonation. Acceleration pressed her against the bulkhead. Cries of complaint and pain from the passenger hold were barely audible over the deafening roar of rocketry, but they were inconsequential. All that mattered was that the gunship climbed.

On a pillar of fire and smoke, *Dagger of Inwit* heaved its way skyward.

In the final seconds before the Thunderhawk was swallowed by storm-clouds, Sherax glanced out of the armaglass viewportal at the barren grey earth. She had landed at the xenos fane with almost two thousand skitarii, Vostroyan Firstborn, and attendant acolytes and thralls.

As *Dagger of Inwit* wheezed its way from the surface of Ikaneos-A, she left with ninety-seven souls.

THE VOID

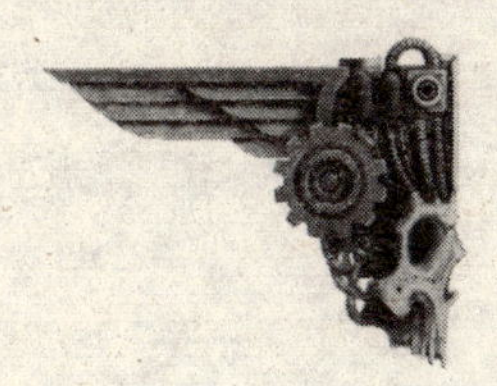

ONE

It was either fortune or the warding hand of the Omnissiah that allowed them to escape the planetary debris field. For six long minutes, *Dagger of Inwit*'s hull had shaken and rattled with the constant percussion of minor impacts. Any one could have been the strike that broke the gunship's armoured skin and tossed them all into the void, but they had made it through.

After the first euphoric moments of take-off, the passenger bay had fallen silent. Some of Sherax's junior acolytes continued to chant in praise of their saviour-craft, but the rest said and sent nothing.

The Thunderhawk's engines faded from a continuous bellow to a mere background roar as Xal throttled back. 'We have attained a high orbital trajectory, ductrix. As far as I am able to ascertain.'

'We have,' confirmed Lyterix. He stood in front of Sherax, still wearing the plastek sheets that had insulated him from the potency of the Motive Force. He had taken the co-pilot's

position, assuming authority over the craft. In her condition, Sherax was ill-equipped to prevent him.

The augur's metal hands moved over the consoles many controls. 'Initiating broad-spectrum scan.'

This was the moment of greatest risk, though Sherax knew it was farcical to think in terms of a hierarchy of danger. The void was the most hostile environment to human life yet discovered, save the aberrant dimension of the empyrean. Escaping Ikaneos did not make them safe. She had merely traded the certainty of a slow, lingering death on the surface for a host of more immediately lethal factors.

The Thunderhawk's auspex array was impossibly crude compared with the majesty of the augur apparatus that festooned the *Peregrinus*. Nevertheless, *Dagger of Inwit* reached out with its meagre senses, searching for whatever lay before them.

If the aeldari had remained in orbit, if they had left even a single vessel to wait in ambush, then they were all about to die. The gunship possessed no countermeasures or defences they might take. It was unlikely they would even be aware of their deaths. A bolt of alien energy would simply reach out across the void and extinguish their forlorn attempt to prolong their lives.

The seconds dragged on. Old instincts made Sherax yearn to stand in Lyterix's place, as though by watching the auspex screen she might make the data return faster. Instead, she was forced to lie in futile impatience.

'Ductrix!' Xal's exclamation burst across the communal vox.

Sherax's command was no less urgent. 'Report.'

Lyterix was faster than the protector. 'There is a significant ferromagnetic return within two hundred miles of the *Peregrinus*' last known trajectory.'

She had to see it for herself. 'Aid me.'

Lyterix and Xal lifted her between them, and held Sherax in

place until she could lock her working claw to the deck. Balanced, with Xal's support, she leant over the gunship's console.

Magos Lyterix awoke the picter mounted to the Thunderhawk's forward fuselage. The chain of heavy bolters it was linked to had been abandoned with the *Obdurate*, but the gunsight picter itself had been deemed an unnecessary effort to extract. For the first time in her life, Sherax gave thanks for the sin of lethargy.

The imagifier mounted in the gunship's console flickered into life. The grain of static became the wash of distant stars as Xal deftly adjusted their heading. After agonising moments, the stars fixed in place once more.

At the centre of the screen was an object, slab-sided and glorious.

Sherax did not breathe. 'Magnify.'

The image fuzzed once more, then resolved to show the light from the Ikaneos star gleaming from a crimson hull.

'By the cog...' Lyterix breathed.

'Praise the Omnissiah,' said Sherax. She spoke the words with all the conviction she had once known, and now felt suffuse her being after so many years of absence.

It was a miracle. Her ship had died, yet there it lay.

'Vox.' The command was almost lost in the jumble of confused, elated code that poured from her mind.

They waited for the pulse of electronic noise to reach across the distance.

'No response, ductrix,' Xal reported.

Lyterix pointed at the imagifier. 'The primary communications array has been destroyed.'

He was right. Though they were still tens of thousands of miles away, the magnification provided by the gunsight picter was sufficient to understand the devastation that had been visited upon Sherax's ship.

It was a ruin. The *Peregrinus'* starboard flank had been laid open to the void. Its engines were silent, cold for the first time in centuries. Wreckage tumbled in its wake.

Their elation stalled, stillborn. There were many ways for a void-craft to die, and most were agonisingly slow. The spectacular detonation of reactor cores and warp engines were the rarest of fates for ships lost in battle, as the ring of broken hulls that circled Ikaneos attested.

'There could be survivors,' Rahn-Bo said. She had appeared from the passenger bay, standing on unsteady legs. When Sherax turned she saw many more bodies crowding the approach to the cockpit.

'The vox?' Sherax asked Xal again.

'Nothing, ductrix. No answer to our hails. No electromagnetic emanations.'

'The noosphere.' Once more, it was Lyterix who prevented her from plunging into despair. 'The *Peregrinus'* noospheric emitter is not a part of the primary communications array. It may be intact.'

The volume of data shared by noospheric transmission was far too vast for anything more than close-range communication. They would have to get closer.

'Xal, take us in,' Sherax ordered.

Over the next four hours, the distance closed at an achingly slow pace. Sherax's ocular sensors remained locked on her ship as it grew from one pinprick of light among many to the indomitable silhouette she knew and loved.

As they closed to within one hundred miles, Xal feathered the gunship's thrusters, wary of a sudden systems failure that would paint the Thunderhawk across the ship's hull. Sherax took a final moment to prepare herself, then reached out with unfamiliar senses.

Sherax laid herself completely open, her firebreaks and mental defences entirely lowered in the hope of making any kind of noospheric connection. Immediately, she was bombarded by the thoughts of the adepts in the passenger bay. Their shock, their hope. Above all, their soul-deep exhaustion.

It was only now that she comprehended how far she had driven her crew. The intimacy of the communion allowed for no dissembling, no carefully chosen words or dutiful reserve to conceal their pain from their ignorant ductrix. She had driven her crew past the point of breaking, and she felt their pain far keener than her own.

Sherax struggled to filter out the agony of the minds around her, while straining with disused subroutines towards her ship and home.

Nothingness greeted her. There was only a void where she had hoped, against all probability, to sense the waiting presence of her crew.

Then, impossibly, she felt the alignment of noospheric frequencies. A subtle tick, a shift in her perceptions, as her consciousness bridged the distance and joined with another.

<Talin.> The familiar neural patterns of Satavic Yuel greeted her with all the austere warmth she had thought lost to the abyss.

Sherax was unable to weep, and she could not cheer. But she was equipped to thank a god that had answered her prayers.

The *Peregrinus* lived.

TWO

Dagger of Inwit struck the flight deck with little grace. An anvil's song rang through the gunship's passenger bay long after Xal had shut down the Thunderhawk's engines.

Lyterix, and all who had survived the trial of Ikaneos, waited for nine minutes as the flight deck's void doors were steadily closed, and air pumped back into the chamber. Ordinarily, a permeable pressure field would keep a tolerable atmosphere within the deck, but whichever logistics executor was in command was wise to take a more thorough precaution.

In short order, the atmosphere within *Dagger of Inwit* had grown ripe with corruption – debris-clogged oils, weeping wounds, and the fecund particulates of bodies worked beyond their endurance. Finally, the gunship's assault ramp hissed open, permitting the first lungful of shipboard air Lyterix had tasted in ten days.

It tasted of smoke and ruin.

The flight deck's blast doors shuddered open, permitting work

crews and medicae thralls to emerge from their armoured bunkers and attend to the Thunderhawk's abused frame and its broken occupants. Lyterix, metal arms pressed in mute exhaustion against the pilot's console, looked through the cockpit's fogged armaglass at the ship serfs and their crew bosses. They seemed as beaten and worn through as those aboard the *Dagger*.

Those who could stand assisted those who could not. After so long without nutrition or potable water, and the blunt force assault of atmospheric escape, barely any of the Vostroyan soldiers were conscious, much less capable of walking off the Thunderhawk. Medicaes and biologians waited at the foot of the assault ramp with wheeled gurneys and life-sustenance pods for those who required them.

Xal and Lyterix carried Sherax down from the cockpit, and out onto the patterned steel of the flight deck. Yuel's ponderous form was waiting for them, a crab-legged obstacle around which the serfs, servitors, and adepts flowed.

Sherax raised a claw in weary greeting. <My lord.>

They had exchanged only the most essential information during their approach; the ship's noospheric transmission array had fluctuated too wildly to permit anything greater.

<Talin.> Yuel linked each pair of the small manipulator claws that lined his carapace together, forming a quartet of cogs. <I give praise to the Omnissiah for your deliverance.>

<As do I, lord.>

Xal lowered Sherax into an ambulant, one of several insectile prostheses that were waiting on the deck. The ambulant would provide her with independent mobility until she could be repaired, though by necessity they robbed her of any physical expression of poise or command. Yuel, already close to twice Sherax's height and mass, loomed over the recumbent explorator.

Sherax paused as mechadendrites encircled her limbs, while beneath her, six pairs of slim motive legs skittered as the ambulant took her weight. Then she stared up at Yuel.

<What happened to my ship?>

The lord explorator relayed all that taken place. With surprising tact, he shared only a stripped-back retelling, rather than simply exloading his recorded experience of the aeldari ambush. Lyterix suspected that he was sparing Sherax the trauma of reliving the ruination of her ship, though she would nevertheless confront it once she connected with the *Peregrinus'* data stream.

The aeldari had melted from the void in the same way that Idranvel had appeared in the midst of the fane. They were broad-winged craft, as though they had been built for atmospheric flight instead of the emptiness of the void.

They struck immediately, five slight but vicious vessels targeting the *Peregrinus'* void shield emitters. They overwhelmed the explorator ship's defences immediately, dancing around its primary firing arcs and lancing precise blasts into the vessel's critical infrastructure. That they knew exactly where to strike spoke of a hunter's patience, which accorded with Lyterix's brief impression of their enemy.

The blast the expedition had seen and sensed from the surface had been caused by a particularly devastating laser strike. With savage ill-fortune, one of the ship's macrocannons had been midway through its reloading sequence when alien energy had ripped through its embrasure. The shell ignited before it could be manoeuvred into the open breech, and a chain reaction ripped along the *Peregrinus'* starboard flank, detonating charged energy coils and magazines in an explosion that came close to breaking the ship in two.

In the wake of the catastrophe, Yuel had ordered the ship's heart to be silenced, a sudden cessation of all fusion reaction that killed thousands of serfs in the resulting rad-cascade. The sudden termination of the Motive Force left the ship adrift, apparently disabled, entirely at the mercy of the xenos attackers.

<By the grace of the Omnissiah, the xenos accepted the deception, and did not attempt a final blow. Once the aeldari departed, we waited for two days before attempting reactor ignition. A full catalogue of damage sustained and personnel lost can wait. Suffice to say that it is extensive.>

Sherax absorbed the data in silence. Yuel's summary had only taken a fraction of a second to transmit, but she took far longer to process the information he had shared.

<Thank you, lord,> she said finally. <Your actions saved my ship.>

<The arrogance of the aeldari spared it,> Lyterix sent. It was a foolish, impulsive act, born of savage exhaustion and long-held rancour.

Yuel reared up, his four motive limbs lifting him to tower over the augur. <It was a calculated risk.>

<And one I would have made myself, my lord,> Sherax sent.

Lyterix subsided. There was little purpose to seeking an argument with Yuel, at least at that moment.

<How did you know there were survivors from the expedition?> Sherax asked.

<We watched your passage through the wastes. What the planet permitted us to see, of course. I dared not light our auspex, but optical scans occasionally revealed your progress.>

Lyterix assumed that Yuel was attempting to be heartening, but the knowledge that the once-lord explorator had been observing as he slew grox and subsisted on acid rain was not comforting.

All three magi turned as their proximity sensors detected an approaching figure. Banner Sergeant Belyev stood on unsteady legs waiting for their attention.

'With your permission, explorator,' Belyev said.

Behind him was Major Zlata, borne aloft by a quartet of Blackbloods. The Vostroyans' commander had lapsed into unconsciousness after the news of the *Peregrinus* had been delivered to the passenger bay, finally able to rest once she knew her troops would survive without her.

The soldiers carried their leader past Belyev towards the care of waiting medicae staff. The pale, scarred soldier's attention wavered between Sherax and his stricken officer.

Sherax acknowledged him immediately. 'Speak, banner sergeant.'

He looked around the flight deck. 'Where's the rest of the regiment?'

Yuel and Sherax hesitated. The deck was bustling with hundreds of ship's thralls and other crew, but no fur-clad bodies had come to greet their comrades.

'The detonation of the starboard gun decks caused significant damage to the surrounding decks,' said Yuel finally.

'Throne of Terra...' The oath emerged as a whisper of horror from Belyev's scarred and bloody lips.

Sherax had learnt of the Vostroyans' fate in Yuel's transmission. 'I am sorry, banner sergeant. The cargo hold in which the One Hundred and Third was billeted was exposed to the void.'

Belyev nodded – a single terse jerk of his head. 'Survivors?'

Yuel took over. 'Sixteen of your comrades were in the ship's sanitorum, or otherwise elsewhere during the ambush. They, and you, are all that remain.'

Neither Sherax nor Yuel had much understanding of the conventions of mortal interaction, but both were deeply acquainted with mourning. They turned away as aqueous fluid gathered in the soldier's eyes.

THREE

Edgar awoke in stages, pulled from slumber by the tang of counterseptic and the brutal ache that sunk into his bones.

'Lie back, sir.' A worn, familiar voice commanded him, and a gentle but firm hand pressed against his shoulder.

'Help me up,' Edgar said, fighting the weariness that dragged at his thoughts.

After a moment's hesitation, the hand moved to under his arm, and with shocking ease lifted Edgar upright. A sharp stab of pain accompanied the movement, and Edgar's eyes opened to admit the harsh, bright glare of lumen-bars.

He was in one of the *Peregrinus'* infirmaries. A bleary twist of his head revealed dozens of figures – mostly the Vostroyans who had made it off Ikaneos – laid out on articulated slabs, with medicae servitors and white-robed biologians walking between them. Thickets of cables and articulated metal arms hung from mobile arrays mounted to the infirmary's ceiling, looking more like implements of torture than healing.

Zlata lay on the bed opposite him, flanked by a pair of Blackbloods. She was unconscious, her head wrapped in bandages and a nest of plastek tubing connected to her veins.

One of the two troopers guarding their commander was Belyev, who nodded a greeting. The banner sergeant was gripping the barrel of his laslock with both hands, with its stock planted heavily on the deck. Edgar reckoned that he was only standing with its aid.

A rustle of fabric beside him made Edgar turn his head. Ormond was beside his gurney; it had been he who had helped Edgar up. He looked as worn through as Edgar felt. The sacristan's overalls were torn and ragged, stained with both blood and promethium. Whatever the *Peregrinus* had been through, the old man had evidently not been idle in setting it right.

'I lost her, Gregor.' He spoke without thinking, the confession bursting from his lips.

'I know, sir.'

There were tears in Ormond's eyes. There were tears in Edgar's, but he blinked them away.

'She fought well. Throne, but you should have seen her fight. The xenos thing that killed her...' Edgar's voice cracked, but he persevered. Ormond deserved to hear of *Vortigern*'s heroism. 'She disembowelled it. Twice her size, clad in that bastard shield. A blade bigger than she was. But it died with her spears in its guts.'

The sacristan started weeping, tears rolling freely down the old man's cheeks. 'I'd have liked to see that, sir.'

'To think of all the times I cursed her. Scorned her for a peasant's steed. If I had but known...' Edgar's voice finally failed him. The sight of Ormond's stoic pride, the enormity of his shame, robbed Edgar of the last of his reserve.

The humiliation of defeat. The loss of another Knight, as

worthy of reverence and remembrance as his *Bladequeen*. The shame of burdening the Blackbloods on the march to the *Obdurate*, of lying helpless while men and women hungered and died around him. It was too much.

Ormond suddenly lunged forward, gripping Edgar by his shoulders hard enough to make his joints ache. 'Don't give in. You coddled bastard, you can't give in. I've watched you wallow in your wounded pride for six years, but no more.'

Edgar was too far lost to his misery to acknowledge the transgression of what was happening. He simply lay on his bed, peering up at his old servant, who was roused to a potent fury.

'You're dishonoured? You're ashamed?' Ormond said. 'Then live with it. Wear it like a brand. Live to pay it back, to find whoever humbled you and make them choke on their victory. To prove that you were ever worthy of being called a knight of the Imperium.'

'I'm not a knight, Ormond. Not any more.' Even Ormond's scolding was not enough to break through his anguish. 'Two steeds dead, yet still I live.'

The sacristan's gnarled hands loosened their grip. 'You don't need a steed to be a knight, sir.'

FOUR

Sherax was dimly aware of the howl of cutting discs and the shriek of severed metal. Fabricators were addressing the most urgent of her body's wounds, hacking away her corroded body plating and rerouting functions around damaged components. Every few moments a fresh warning burst into her awareness, demanding her attention, but she shunted each of these alarms to her archive for later review. Sherax's immediate concern was for her ship, not herself.

The *Peregrinus* was on the verge of ruin. Even ten days after the xenos attack, the explorator ship's fate was balanced on a knife edge. Where its starboard weapons batteries had once been was now a chasm, a gaping horror of torn metal. Beneath, its superstructure had been opened to the void. Secondary detonations and the horror of explosive decompression had laid waste to its innards. The ship's fabricarium was a gutted hollow of shattered tools. Its deepest munitions bunkers had,

miraculously, weathered the storm, but stores of nutriments, consumables, and potable water silos had been cracked apart.

Every wound the ship had taken had left its mark, both physically and metaphysically. The *Peregrinus*' animus was gripped by the maddened, frantic anguish of a wounded beast. The absence of so much of itself had become a recursive nightmare. Each unanswered signal that pulsed along severed cables, a million or more every second, was like a goad pressed into the mind of the machine spirit.

Sherax worked to seal off each of these open connections with a single-mindedness born of desperation. There was no entity in the galaxy with which she had a greater bond. The *Peregrinus*' suffering was hers, greater in every way than the trivial injuries of her own form.

It had almost been a relief, when she first retook her command throne, to abandon her body's needs and diffuse her cognition through the ship's animus. But that had been ninety-six hours ago. In that time she had fought a dozen concurrent battles to realign fractured systems, and coax the *Peregrinus* into accepting the hurried patches its crew applied.

As Sherax worked in the ship's data stream, her crew laboured on its decks. From stern to stem, along every corridor and through every shaft, rang the song of industry, as tech-priests and serfs strove to save their stricken ship. They sealed cracked ducts immersed in caustic coolant. They suppressed raging fires, and patched chambers that lay open to the void. They rethreaded mile after mile of cable-veins, and cut away ton after ton of ruined metal. Luren and his cadre of techseers reconsecrated damaged cogitators and power conduits. Magister Akoni condemned two thousand enginarium labourers to a rad-soaked death to reawaken the ship's reactor-heart, forcing through blood and torment the majesty of fusion.

Everywhere there was labour, and the unity born of desperate purpose. The *Peregrinus'* crew saw how close they were to their end, in the vacuum-sealed bulkheads and depleted work parties, and they rose to the challenge. It was not merely a case of repairing what was broken, but rebuilding what had been lost.

From within the data stream, Sherax saw and felt it all, and was riven between pride and shame.

The pride was in her crew. Every one, from her closest adepts to the lowest menial, bent to the task of restoring their vessel and home. Despite all that they had endured, they were not broken.

She ached to let her pride show, to lower her resurrected noospheric barriers and broadcast her admiration for all they did. But to do so would also share her guilt, a fatal erosion of what authority she had left. Let her crew see their ductrix, austere and distant as ever. Let them resent her, curse her, and be spared the knowledge that their scorn could never match the contempt she held for herself.

She had brought this upon them. Because she could not endure the torpor that gripped her people, she had instead committed her ship and crew to a trial that was beyond them. She had driven them past the point of endurance. And yet the greatest shame was that her quest might have been in error from the beginning.

Through every step of the march across Ikaneos, Sherax had been plagued by the doubts that the alien Idranvel had awoken, and what they meant for her quest. The pursuit of ancient archeotech, the relics of humanity's great past, was the mission of all explorators and adherents of the Cult Mechanicus. The acquisition of xenos devices, however, was the gravest heresy. Could she continue on her search when her prize might be an artefact of a fallen, degenerate species?

The answer was inescapable. Of course, she would not turn back.

Too late, Sherax became aware that her fervent thoughts were slipping past her mind's firebreaks. Immediately, she felt the prickling of noospheric contact, not unlike the gathering of atmospheric pressure that preceded a storm.

<Akoni and his adepts report that the warp engines have been restored to stability, and we will soon be able to depart this place,> Lord Yuel sent. <What course will you give to the magister of navigation?>

Yuel was on the far side of the command deck, coordinating the reconnection of the ship's operations centre with its extremities. The noosphere's bridge conveyed the full force of the lord explorator's sarcasm.

Sherax lifted a fraction of her consciousness from the ship's data stream. <We go on, my lord.>

<You sacrifice all that we have left.> Yuel's sending was blunt and direct, full of exhausted anger. <Look around you. You waste their labour on the altar of your pride.>

<It is not pride that drives me, lord.>

<No? Then is it fear of punishment? The synod would accept you back, Talin. Not without sanction – you would surely lose the *Peregrinus*. But in the calculus of survival, we must look beyond individual concerns and consider the needs of the whole. This ship, broken though it is, is a resource that should not be wasted in the name of vanity.>

Sherax elected to ignore her old mentor's naked ambition.

<And then what?> she asked. <To what role would the *Peregrinus* be put? Certainly not as an explorator. At best, it would be a messenger, carrying missives and pleas to those who once begged us for aid.> When Yuel did not interrupt her invective, she went on. <Stagnation and decay grip the synod, you said

as much yourself. Since the loss of the home world, we have drifted, idle and unused. I would have us reach for more. I *need* more, my lord.>

<And as the object of your desire you have chosen a xenos relic?>

The noosphere was a far more perfect conduit for communication than any encoded language could hope to achieve, and Yuel's derision struck like a scalpel.

Sherax clung to the facts that she had seen, and the dogmatic certainty that the words of the alien were the lies of the corrupt and iniquitous. <The Genesis device, whatever its provenance, can reawaken us. It can animate our people, unite our efforts, perhaps more than ever before. We could *rebuild worlds,* my lord.>

<A grand dream, Talin, but no more than that.>

<We are the Adeptus Mechanicus, lord. We only thrive when given a task worthy of our nature.>

Sherax stopped suddenly. Such thoughts had been far from her mind in recent years. Indeed, she could not recall when she had last expressed positive terms about any member of her order.

<Look about you,> she sent, sharing with Yuel the extent of her pride. <The crew works with that goal in mind.>

<They labour, Talin, because this ship is their home, and it is gravely wounded.> There was a patronising undercurrent to Yuel's sending that soured Sherax's pleasure. <You are their ductrix. If you order it, the ship will fly in pursuit of the xenos and their fable. But do not mistake their exertions for complicity or enthusiasm for your mission.>

<Granted,> sent Sherax, hardening herself once again to the lord explorator's connection. <But as you say, I am ductrix of the *Peregrinus*, and it will go where I require.>

As Sherax submerged her consciousness fully within the data stream, Yuel tried one final appeal. <After all that the *Peregrinus* has endured, how long do you calculate that the ship will survive in a second encounter with the aeldari?>

<We are going on, my lord. There is no other course.>

THE EMPYREAN

ONE

It galled Rahn-Bo to play no part in the repair of the *Peregrinus*.

She had attempted, from the ship's sanitorum, to support the restoration of the ship's data stream, but even that had been too much for her overtaxed body. Ataraxics and pain suppressants had robbed her of the necessary cognitive focus to meaningfully contribute to any task, leading to several sharp debates with the magos biologis responsible for her treatment.

As the days had passed and her frustrations grew, Rahn-Bo's thoughts had dwelt on her options for further bodily augmentation. She was, by the standards of her rank, modestly modified from the human baseline, and the majority of her augmetics were confined to cerebral enhancements in support of her function. Unlike so many of her peers, the weakness of flesh had never been a serious concern for Rahn-Bo. But the trial of Ikaneos had forced her to reconsider that opinion.

She had been confined to an ambulant's embrace upon finally leaving the ship's sanitorum, though one of the tertiary medicae

fabricators had altered its form to permit her to stand upright, rather than lie recumbent. The machine had a sinuous, arthropodic gait that Rahn-Bo found gratifying, adding further fuel to her thoughts of augmentation.

It was due to these idle musings, so unprecedented for the monotropic datamancer, that she directed her prosthesis to take her to the chamber that Magos Lyterix had been given for his use. Though she was restricted, by Sherax's direct order, from taking on any task that would inhibit her recovery, she hoped that she might at least find employment in support of his activities.

<Enter.> Lyterix acknowledged her presence at his door with an unusually distracted pulse of thought.

As the door trundled into its recess, Rahn-Bo was struck by a susurration of overlapping voices, each one tense with pain, fear and suffering.

The chamber was brightly illuminated by the brace of lumenstrips that lined its vaulted ceiling. Beneath, their forms cast in stark white light, were twenty people of varying ages, genders, and body types. All were dressed in sterile medicae gowns, though they were clearly all members of the *Peregrinus'* crew. Each was strapped to a metal gurney, connected by hoses and cables to a brass-bound medicae cogitator suspended in the centre of the room. Autoscribe servitors stood between the beds, metal fingers recording the murmur of pained words that were being spoken by all twenty figures.

It could have been a minor wing of one of the ship's infirmaries, but in place of biologis magi there was Magos Lyterix, and an atmosphere of harm rather than healing.

<Cogitatrix,> Lyterix sent in greeting. He did not cease in his movement. He appeared to be in a state of continuous activity, walking swiftly from bay to bay with a data-slate clutched in one

hand. Most of the individuals were still, save for the uninterrupted motion of their lips, but every few moments one of Lyterix's patients twitched a limb, summoning the augur to their side. He would briefly interact with a control mechanism through which several of the plastek cables ran, which appeared to end their mild convulsions.

Confusion was a state anathema to Rahn-Bo's nature. <I seek clarification,> she managed, after two seconds of impeded function.

<The explorator superior asked me to guide us to the source of Genesis.>

<Is that not the role of our Navigator?>

<Quite so.> Lyterix straightened from performing some adjustment to the regulator panel fixed to a bound man's chest. <But our vessel is compromised. Thus, I seek the tranquil paths of the immaterium, the placid currents upon which we might be carried, rather than the violent tides upon which we would surely be broken.>

Rahn-Bo struggled to parse Lyterix's meaning. Such artful phrases had little place in the lexicon of the Cult Mechanicus. <And this… apparatus,> she sent. <It is–>

<Necessary, cogitatrix. It is necessary, to achieve the task Sherax set me.> He finally paused and turned to regard Rahn-Bo, still standing just inside the chamber's threshold.

<Many of our fellow adepts believe that the vagaries of the warp are immeasurable, unknowable. And it is true that most instruments are perplexed by the immaterium. Even something as simple as a mechanical chronometer can be baffled when immersed in the stuff of the warp. That is because they are tools for determining certainty, for parsing reality through their lens to arrive at an essential truth. But the empyrean is, by its nature, uncertain. Untrustworthy. Therefore, the tools we use must be equally changeable.>

Rahn-Bo grasped his meaning immediately. <The mind.>

<Indeed. Nothing is as inconstant as the human mind. Most minds, in any case.> Evidently Lyterix considered himself an exception to his judgement; Rahn-Bo wondered how many others were afforded that honour.

<Every utterance of the warp-touched speaks of the currents of the unreal to which their souls are connected,> the augur continued. <Under the proper conditions, that connection can be directed towards a useful end.>

<What end?>

Lyterix smiled. Facial expression was a supremely rare form of communication among the Adeptus Mechanicus, so much so that Rahn-Bo had trouble interpreting its meaning. <The augur's craft is not easily explained to the uninitiated.>

For the briefest moment, Rahn-Bo hated the flare of curiosity that Lyterix's enigmatic statement provoked.

Several of Lyterix's wards had begun twitching once more. <They appear to be in a state of discomfort,> she sent.

The augur had already turned to respond to his charges' apparent needs. <I assure you, cogitatrix, this is no worse than they experience in the course of their daily labours. You are simply seeing it for the first time.>

For a moment Rahn-Bo sensed a sharp edge beneath Lyterix's sending, but the augur masked his thoughts before Rahn-Bo could probe it.

<The *Peregrinus* carries a complement of six astropaths,> she sent instead. <None have been reported missing.>

<I am gratified to hear it.>

Rahn-Bo felt her choler rising, a rare lapse for one who was ordinarily so measured in her thoughts. <Who are they?>

<Individuals with a latent or otherwise hidden sensitivity to the warp.>

She paused, surprised that there were so many undiscovered psykers aboard the ship. <How did you find them?>

<There are methods of detection.> Lyterix gestured towards a series of arcane devices, unfamiliar to Rahn-Bo, that sat upon a nearby storage unit. <Should we survive our present voyage, I would be happy to explain their function.>

Rahn-Bo was about to interrogate Lyterix's use of the modal verb to describe their passage through the warp, when another voice joined the miserable chorus that echoed around the chamber. This one was fuzzed by vox distortion, but also louder and more coherent.

'Falling, always falling. Dropping through fire, through agony and ecstasy. Dear God-Emperor, shield me from your trials.'

Lyterix continued to work beside a slight young woman, ignoring the plaintive moans that rang from the vox.

<Is that Kian?> Rahn-Bo asked.

<Indeed,> said the augur. <I have been impressed by your Navigator, cogitatrix. In the bleak days since the Cicatrix Maledictum reaved the galaxy, to be immersed in the empyrean for a voyage such as ours requires immense strength. He is a stalwart example of his kind.>

'Thunder from the depths. Claws and thunder, and the laughter of maddened faces torn and boiling. Oh, Merciful Throne, why have you deserted me?'

It did not sound as though the Navigator was bearing the strain that Lyterix so casually discussed.

<Should we be concerned?> asked Rahn-Bo.

Again, a moment of hesitation. <No. I am monitoring him closely, as is the ship's magister of astrogation. Though he has been speaking in that manner for the past twelve days, he remains responsive to course corrections, and his biorhythm remains within acceptable limits. As I said, he is resilient.>

Rahn-Bo's curiosity was piqued. <What has he been saying?>

Lyterix idly dumped a transcript and audex recording into the noosphere. Rahn-Bo, true to her nature, did not hesitate to examine it.

Kian had, as Lyterix had described, begun babbling over the vox almost continuously on the fifth day after their flight from Ikaneos, seemingly speaking every thought and impulse without filter. Sometimes he had wept, as he described the tormented images that rose and fell in the matter of the warp. He had whispered snippets of Navigator lore, of the fate of ships and souls that had foundered beyond the sight of the Astronomican. His most frequent topic appeared to be the moral shortcomings of Sherax and Lyterix. Kian regularly spouted foul tirades against them both, decrying their maniacal obsession that would doom them all.

<I see.> Assimilating the Navigator's words had not alleviated her curiosity. In fact, it had only sharpened it; as with anything she did not understand, Rahn-Bo's savantic nature yearned to comprehend what meaning Lyterix could glean from such ravings.

<For what purpose did you seek me, cogitatrix?>

<I came,> Rahn-Bo sent after a moment's pause, <to offer my aid to whatever project you had been assigned.>

The noosphere made both her curiosity and her hesitation readily apparent. <My apparatus makes you uncomfortable. I understand.> Lyterix's mental walls were far too stout to reveal any emotion to accompany his sending. <Be assured that the methods of augury I employ are all thoroughly documented, and have been sanctioned by successive Fabricators General. Though not always, it must be admitted, without difficulty.>

Rahn-Bo did not doubt Lyterix's word. <And is the ductrix aware of your... methods?> she asked.

<Explorator Sherax presides over graver deeds than this,

cogitatrix, I assure you,> Lyterix said, neglecting, she noticed, to answer her question. <The Imperium of Man and the Martian Empire are built on suffering. Every servant of the Omnissiah is a tool. Consider the agonies of those who labour at this moment to ensure the *Peregrinus* continues to function. Hundreds have died in the days since we returned to this vessel, and countless thousands, if not millions, have breathed their last aboard its decks since it first set out into the void. Yet every drop of blood and pang of suffering has been in service to the ship, and to the quest to which it is pledged.>

He gestured at the figures restrained on the gurneys. <These creatures are no different. I have taken them from their meagre roles, in which they were replaceable and unremarkable, and elevated them to the most essential of tools. Without them, and without my work, the ship will founder on the tempests of the immaterium, and we shall fail in our task. A task which, I assure you, is the most vital the *Peregrinus* has ever embarked upon.>

Rahn-Bo took precisely two point six seconds before responding to Lyterix's impassioned speech. She did not share his belief in the Genesis device; the xenos attack on Ikaneos had only sharpened her conviction that Sherax led them all towards heresy and destruction. But it would be hypocrisy to deny the truth in his words, and foolish to not recognise that the augur's work was, as he said, necessary for the ship's continued passage through the empyrean.

<If you will permit me,> she sent finally. <I renew my offer of aid.>

Gratification, seemingly sincere, arose within Lyterix's aura. <You are most welcome, cogitatrix. Please, attend me.>

With its Navigator's cries echoing from the bulkheads of his armoured chamber, the *Peregrinus* flew on through the hellscape of the warp.

TWO

Erasmus Luren did not rest for the entirety of their time in the warp. Once every three days he was forced to pause his efforts for two hours while his circulatory system was flushed of the toxic build-up of alchemical stimulants, but otherwise Luren was constantly at work. He and his coterie of techseers crossed and recrossed the ship in the continual work of spiritual dedication.

They reconsecrated damaged cogitators, and blessed power conduits. They ceremonially disposed of the dead in the ship's furnaces. Above all, they chanted a binharic song of worship to the vessel that carried them. Luren transliterated the hymn into skit-code, lingua technis, and even Low Gothic, so that all elements of the crew could give praise to the steadfast spirit of the *Peregrinus*.

This was as vital a task as patching coolant ducts and rethreading cable-veins. If the ship's animus faltered, disaster would befall them all. The Geller field generators would fail. Its warp engines would sputter and fade, leaving them aimless in a hellish sea from which they would be unable to escape. The atmospheric regulators would shut down, and steadily the crew would be poisoned to death by their own exhalations.

To be a passenger of a void-craft was to place one's life entirely within its care. To offer a prayer of thanks was the duty of all who laboured along and between the *Peregrinus'* decks. Luren had no faith in Sherax or her mission, but he worked until his augmentations seized to ensure her ship would not fail.

It was during one of the mandated interruptions to his duties that Luren felt the unusual touch of a mind addressing his. A mind that had, at one time, been familiar to him, though never more than that.

<Magos Luren.>

<Ductrix. It is gratifying to sense your return to the communion.>

He was sincere. Though Luren appreciated the importance of oral communication, not least for the purposes of praise and veneration, the clarity of noospheric interaction had been the techseer's preferred method of exchange since he had first been blessed with the required augmentations.

<I seek your counsel, Luren.>

<Then I am at your disposal, explorator.>

Immediately, the entrance to Luren's quarters ground aside, revealing Sherax silhouetted against the lumens of the passageway.

<I have always considered one of the chief benefits of noospheric exchange to be the defeat of physical distance,> sent Luren.

<True. However, my absence from the communion has instilled a preference for physical proximity during discussions of vital matters.> Sherax stepped forward, and allowed the door to close behind her, immersing the room in darkness.

Luren's quarters were as limited as any other personnel space aboard the *Peregrinus*, though more richly furnished. In addition to the many tools of a techseer's vocation, each held securely in racks and trestles, were objects of widely varying quality and provenance. Luren's only vice, as he saw it, was his habit of hoarding articles that he felt bore value or meaning within the Cult Mechanicus. Technical implements, transcribed hymnals and hexamantic music, occasionally weapons and organic trophies. Objects obtained over the course of a life spent in devotion to the Machine God.

No light source illuminated his collection, but that was immaterial for both Luren and Sherax. Their sensory instruments were capable of perceiving a far broader range of spectra.

The techseer stood in a shallow alcove on the far side of the chamber from its entrance, plastek tubes connecting sockets upon his body to a filtration system that emitted a rhythmic chunter as it worked. Luren's robe had been set aside, with due care, revealing the full extent of his patchwork body. Bronze sheets and iron plates studded with runic displays and indicator lumens stood out from white, pallid flesh. The techseer's skull – an armoured augmetic vessel that for forty years had served solely as a container for his organic brain – connected with his narrow shoulders by a complex collection of struts and pistons.

Luren's trio of eyestalks whirled. <On what vital matter do you require my counsel, ductrix?>

<I believe you already know.>

The techseer considered Sherax's defensiveness, and elected to ignore it. <You seek to atone for your loss of faith, and the errors of logic and judgement stemming from it.>

Sherax's animus bristled, as Luren had expected, but beneath her reflex response there was a complex nest of restrained emotions.

<Atonement is an incorrect paradigm,> sent Sherax, evidently as the preamble to a prepared confession.

<That surprises me,> Luren replied swiftly, cutting off Sherax's rehearsed exculpation before it began. He had no interest in coddling the explorator. Truth was often harsh. <Had I erred so far from the path of the Omnissiah, I would prostrate myself in the hope of undeserved salvation.>

<And what about my forgiveness?> Sherax's anger burned across the communion with the sudden intensity of an arc welder. <What will the Omnissiah do to earn my pardon? In our hour of need, He abandoned us.>

The techseer concealed his satisfaction. The dam that he had sensed within the explorator had burst with only the slightest pressure.

<A god cannot fail its followers, explorator.>

<Luren, the home world is nothing but ash and rock.>

<The Omnissiah did not fail us. Those who broke their faith failed Him.> Luren was relentless. This scourging was long overdue. <Those who lacked the fortitude to endure when tested. Who demanded aid when strength was already theirs. They failed Him. *You* failed Him.>

Sherax's capacity for his scorn had evidently been reached. <And what of those who turned inward, seeking solace in maudlin prayer and recrimination? I can hear the eulogy repeating over and over in your thoughts, as self-aggrandising as it is mawkish. You are quick to identify my shortcomings, techseer, but say nothing of your own.>

Luren did not respond.

<I have acted where others would not. I lead. You may not agree with my direction, but I have set one. I have acted.>

<Out of fear, not wisdom. You strike out blindly, desperately, seeking something that might replace your abandoned faith. And in your foolishness and vanity, you have chosen the work of aliens.>

<Do you trust the words of xenos now, Erasmus?>

He ignored her attempted denial. Both Sherax and Luren understood that, at her core, the explorator knew what waited for them at the end of their passage.

<Had your faith held,> he sent, <we would not be on a course that surely ends in apostasy. We would be among our people, where we belong.>

<Instead, we stand upon the cusp of revelation.>

<Or damnation.>

Sherax turned suddenly, her patience with his interrogation run through. <It was clearly an error to seek your input on these matters. You have never had the breadth of mind to fully grasp the nature of the Quest. You have never been able to suspend your judgement long enough to see beyond orthodoxy.>

<You sought me out for my judgement, explorator. You know that you have erred, and you seek absolution for your sins. But I have none to give you, Sherax. The Omnissiah judges us all. My only hope is that we survive so that you fully grasp the extent of your failure.>

<Continue your duty, techseer, as soon as you are capable of it.> The explorator withdrew from Luren's mind and quarters, leaving him with the rhythmic thump of the biofilters cleansing his blood.

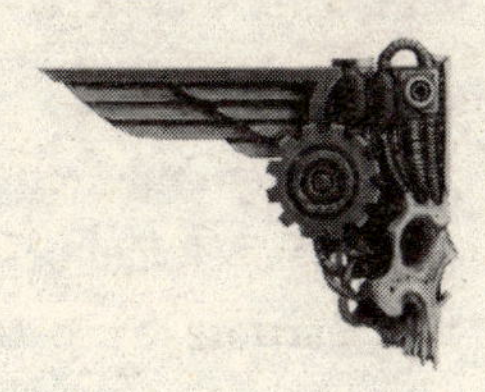

THREE

'Second Squad, step forward!' The tramp of twenty pairs of boots felt uncomfortably loud to Edgar. He took a single pace forward to the firing line, a white smear of paint dragged unevenly across the deck plating.

'Take aim!' Captain Lursa's order, like the scuff of boots on the deck, was too loud. He was used to pitching his voice above the din of hundreds of troopers engaged in combat drills. The close confines of the emptied storage unit threw his words back at his Guardsmen.

Lursa heard it as well. His voice dropped to a weary monotone. 'In your own time, commence firing.'

While the rest of the ship fought to keep the *Peregrinus* alive, the Vostroyans trained. They could play no role in saving the ship, and so they prepared to avenge its wounds.

The kick of Edgar's laslock set off a dull pulse of pain through his shoulder, but he had learnt to revel in it, to lean into the

discomfort. It was a reminder of all he had been through, and all that he would return upon the aeldari.

The laslock had belonged to Trooper Egor Vespesian, and he was learning to use it. Through the long, sad days of their warp passage, Edgar drilled with the weapon, carried it, and slept with it beside his bunk. The model of an Astra Militarum cadet.

He had joined the Blackbloods in their new barracks – his quarters had been lost in the devastation that had claimed the Vostroyans' cargo hold. The 103rd had been billeted to a skitarii arming chamber, occupying the berths and bays of the maniples that had fallen on Ikaneos. The long, low-ceilinged hall was far too large for the subdued Guardsmen, who had only raised token objections to the pervading odours of promethium distillate, unwashed flesh, and the nutrient gruel the skitarii were fed – although in truth, the gruel was little different from the bricks of slab that the Blackbloods themselves subsisted on.

Edgar squeezed off six las-bolts in quick succession, each striking close to the centre ring of the target. He had always been a good shot – hunting with ornately decorated fusils was a common recreation among the knights of House Cadmus. But now he learnt to fight as a Guardsman. He marched, he ran, and he fought alongside all that remained of the Vostroyan 103rd Regiment.

Seventy-six souls. Four thousand men and women had marched from Vostroya following the God-Emperor's banner. One thousand had escaped the hell of Gryphonne IV. Now, less than a hundred remained.

Major Zlata walked behind the firing line, arms folded tight across her chest. The thick fabric of her coat was acid-eaten and threadbare, and beneath her bearskin her head was thickly bandaged, but every day, without fail, Zlata was beside what remained of her command.

In front of her troops Zlata was stoic, pragmatic. It was the fate of all firstborn Vostroyans to die for the Emperor, far from the icy chill of their home. Just two days after they had returned to the *Peregrinus*, she summarily discharged herself from the ship's medicae facilities in order to lead the prayers for the dead. The moment the last name had been commended to the God-Emperor's grace, she had passed out the assignments for reorganised squads. Those who had been fit to do so had run close-quarters combat drills that same day.

Edgar and Zlata had not renewed their entanglement. Without words being spoken, they both knew that that brief period of their lives had passed, and was buried in the grit of Ikaneos. Neither of them had time or energy for anything but revenge.

Her reserve had broken only once. The night after the ceremony for her lost troops, she had found Edgar. Once they had wept their tears, Zlata had wiped her eyes, straightened her acid-stained bearskin, and led Edgar back to the Blackbloods' barracks. The following morning, he had been back in platoon formation, hammering shot after shot down the regiment's firing range.

Each target was cut from sheet metal in the shape of an aeldari warrior.

DOMINION GENESIS

ONE

Moving between the empyrean and the void was never an ordered, sedate affair. Even the most routine of passages, if there ever had been such a thing, was an act of supreme violence.

Despite her station as ductrix of a voidship and inductee of the Explorator order, Sherax had only a peripheral understanding of how her ship entered and exited the immaterium. She knew that the arcane devices that formed a craft's warp engines drew on immense power, and directed that astounding force to slice apart the membrane between realities. But even that crude description was wholly flawed – a metaphor, to aid the uninitiated in comprehending the ineffable.

'Navigator?' Sherax sent across the vox. The command deck around her was silent, tensed for what was to come.

'Our destination approaches. Its shadow grows like the maw that swallows hope.' Kian's voice was a hoarse whisper, worn ragged by a month of continuous raving.

Over many decades, Sherax had become familiar with parsing

the florid imagery employed by the Navis Nobilite. Even so, there was a febrile, fragile edge to Kian's statement.

'Acknowledged.' Sherax opened herself to the noosphere. <All stations, prepare for empyric translation.>

Across the *Peregrinus*, hatches were locked, and prayers spoken. Non-critical work parties set down their duties and adopted the watchful poses known to all travellers of the void. Demi-squads of skitarii advanced to staging posts across the ship, a precaution against any intrusive empyric phenomena that might arise at the boundary between the real and unreal.

Within the cavernous chambers of the ship's enginarium, Magister Akoni and his attendants began their work. Chains were hauled, rites were intoned, and a thousand voices were uplifted in praise of the Motive Force. Vast capacitors, each the size of a hive world hab-block, began to thrum with gathering power.

Akoni, himself enthroned amidst the enginarium's galvanised workings, answered Sherax's clipped command. <Translation systems priming, ductrix.>

The noosphere had cleared of all but the most essential exchanges. The month's passage had reacquainted Sherax with the sensation of minds working in unison, the resonant hum of shared expression and calculation. Yuel had been right; it had been foolish of her to retreat from the communion.

She felt the weight of expectation from the coalesced consciousnesses. Yuel, Lyterix, Luren, Rahn-Bo. The collective minds of her crew, whom she had driven to the point of breaking.

Sherax had prepared for this moment. No doubts could cloud her focus, no philosophical misgivings could impede her judgement. Whatever awaited them could not be changed, only faced.

Finally, Akoni pulsed readiness from the bowels of the ship. <Empyric engines charged, ductrix.>

Sherax returned his signal, then opened the vox. 'Navigator, translate the ship.'

'A tomb for us all, cold and deep. A welcome end to a life of sin.'

Concern flickered across the communion, emitted unbidden by all who were party to the vox-channel.

'Navigator Kian, translate the ship,' Sherax repeated.

'I weep, and all about me slumber.'

'Kian?'

There was a scream, then a series of dull thuds emerged from the vox. Across the command deck, a subaltern raised their head. <Reports of gunfire within the Navigator's chambers.>

Concern became alarm. <Praetorians, enter the chamber and attend to the Navigator,> Sherax sent.

In the halls of the enginarium, the restrained thrum of the Motive Force reached its apex. Akoni reached out, alarm alive within his sending. <Ductrix, we cannot sustain a transitional charge for long.>

Akoni's warning was unnecessary; the data stream sang its distress into Sherax's mind, competing with the trepidation of a familiar task suddenly upended.

'Kian.' Sherax's vox-grille was incapable of investing her tone with any pacifying qualities. 'You must translate the ship.'

The vox opened once again, but only to permit the screams of the Navigator's victims to echo around the command deck.

<Magister, begin shutdown procedures.>

<Impossible, ductrix.> Akoni's alarm had been upgraded to sheer panic. <A cascade is already underway.>

<All hands, brace for turbulence!>

Sherax pulsed the briefest warning, and then the ship erupted into chaos.

In the enginarium, arcs of Motive Force leapt from capacitor contacts, immolating the servants dedicated to their maintenance.

Arcane force, meant to be summoned and held only briefly, burst free of its restraints, seeking any outlet. The warp engines released that force in a single apocalyptic expulsion, blasting a torus of energy that surrounded and engulfed the explorator ship.

Every crew member not physically connected to their station was cast to the deck. Even Sherax was hurled from her throne, her mechadendrite weave detaching in the final instant before her body was slammed against the iron. She flung out a claw to arrest her slide, metal fingers scrabbling for purchase on iron plates embossed with the cog and skull of the Deus Mechanicus.

A nightmare of sound and violence overtook her. A thunder rose from the reforged bones of her vessel as they were strained anew, an agonising creak of overstressed metal that travelled the full length of her stricken ship. Power surges burned out cogitators, and sundered the slaved minds of the servitors connected to them. The command deck's gravity plating failed, subjecting Sherax and her officers to the unrestrained force of inertial drift. Armaglass cracked. Bronze icons buckled.

And beneath it all, for the merest fraction of a second, Sherax heard the shriek of brass claws against iron skin.

Beyond the ship's hull, the maddened sea in which it had been immersed broke and burst, splitting apart like an overripe fruit. From the centre of the rift came the *Peregrinus*, tumbling from the warp. Two miles of iron and adamantine pitched end over end, out into the emptiness of the void.

Which was not empty at all.

TWO

The explorator ship hurtled into the void. Weld seams and freshly patched ductwork shattered under the sudden, unforeseen assault. Its crew were tossed from their feet, bodies breaking against pipes and levers. The work of weeks to repair and rebuild was undone in moments.

<Damage control parties, attend to all decks.> Sherax pulsed her order while lying prone across the deck. <Astrogation, bring us under control.>

The noosphere was alive with the twin disorders of panic and dread. The *Peregrinus* was home to forty thousand sentient souls, and every one equipped to do so had cried out in mortal terror at the instant of translation. For all the layers of stoic detachment and cerebral partitioning the servants of the Omnissiah had clothed themselves in, an unrestrained empyric cascade had revealed the terrified, barely evolved mammal at their core.

The command deck echoed with the riot of clarions that

screamed their warnings. And yet, somehow, the *Peregrinus* was able to awaken more.

'Proximity alert. Xenos vessels detected.' The monotone announcement was delivered by a servitor whose body was wired into its station. It was bent double, spine shattered, yet it continued to perform its function.

Sherax dug her claws into the metal beneath her. <Tactical display.>

The gravity plating took another sixteen seconds to compensate for the *Peregrinus'* headlong fall. The instant she was able, Sherax clamped her claws to the deck and levered herself upright, in time to be bathed in cobalt light by the hololithic projector.

Not one but two creeds of vessel danced in the vacuum of space, most perilously close to the uncontrolled explorator ship. The prismatic blaze of weapons fire leapt between them.

At the battle's centre were thirteen aeldari ships. They flew in a broken shoal, the strange sails of their vessels angled to catch the light of the system's unnamed star. The *Peregrinus* recognised many of the craft as those that had ambushed it above Ikaneos. Angry designation runes appeared beneath the tri-d representation of each of these vessels, listing their observed weapons arrays and manoeuvring capabilities. The rest of the aeldari ships were denoted with only estimates of their potential, based on mass, power signatures, and similarities to their kindred craft.

The others moved in a swarm, dozens of relatively slight craft that raced through the void without visible means of propulsion. They were of a design entirely unknown to Sherax, and to the *Peregrinus'* extensive manifolds. The largest was of a size with the smallest aeldari vessel, a crescent of dark, sinister metal crowned by a pyramidic superstructure. Most were even

smaller, akin to ship-launched bombers and attack craft carried by many Imperial vessels.

The *Peregrinus'* arrival had bred anarchy through the complex dance of xenos ships. The warp rift that had birthed the explorator ship appeared to have swallowed a clutch of the unknown craft, judging by the way their formations had scattered. Most of the aeldari fleet had been at a remove from the rift's aperture and so had escaped immediate destruction. Nevertheless, as Sherax watched, one of the largest aeldari vessels was struck by a tendril of immaterial force that curled like a whip. It burst apart, scythed in two by forces not of its reality.

Worse still, the warp rift was not closing behind the *Peregrinus*. The ragged shear lashed the space around it for thousands of miles, the unchained force of the spiteful domain coiled in tongues of shifting colour.

Chief among the manifold gifts of the Omnissiah was calm. Sherax unceremoniously severed the connections to her amygdala, ending the panic that had threatened to overtake her.

<Astrogation, stabilise our trajectory by whatever means necessary. Magistrix of warding, light our void shields. Weapons batteries, prepare for close engagement.>

The deck lurched in time with the blasts of the ship's manoeuvring rockets. Halting the momentum of millions of tons of metal was a task of brute strength and deft precision, but with the application of both, the *Peregrinus'* ungainly tumble was slowly corrected.

Sherax staggered back to her throne, but did not rejoin the data stream. For a brief moment, she required the respite of detachment from so much information.

<The status of the rift?> she called out over the noosphere.

<Closing, ductrix.>

Slowly, agonisingly slowly, the kaleidoscopic puncture was

withdrawing upon itself. The pressure of reality was too great for even the diabolic energies of the warp to overcome.

The xenos adapted quickly. Both breeds of craft were viciously agile. From the spread of runes across the hololithic display, it seemed that they had more interest in continuing the fight with each other than in avenging themselves against the *Peregrinus*. Nevertheless, incidental fire began to strike the ship's unstable void shields, painting the interface with a promethium sheen.

Torresh Ventarin, the centuris overseer of the *Peregrinus*' weapons arrays, lifted her thoughts from the clamour of the noosphere. <Should we return fire, ductrix?> Her belligerence was echoed in the communion. Her crew sought retribution for the wounds suffered above Ikaneos, and the exculpatory outlet of violence to banish their recent sin of fear.

<Negative.> As much as Sherax felt the desire to indulge that same impulse, there was nothing to be gained by becoming caught in a void battle that would surely destroy them. <Let them obliterate one another.>

It was Rahn-Bo who asked the vital question. <What are they fighting over?>

The mystery resolved itself soon enough. As the *Peregrinus* forced its way clear of the embattled xenos, it reached out with its sensoria to survey the battleground. When the long-range auspex began to return results, the object of their conflict became clear.

Three planets turned around the unnamed star. One was a vaporous giant, a swollen orb of highly compressed gases. Another was a distant, barren rock, barely held by its sun's strength. The third turned with sedate grace, its skies a swirl of cloud, its land a riot of green growth.

In the void above the third world was a construct unlike

anything Sherax had seen. An object pulled from myth, alien and unreal.

Need, urgent and angry, abolished all other impulses in Sherax's mind.

<Locomotion: void engines to full power. Astrogation, new directive. Take me to it.>

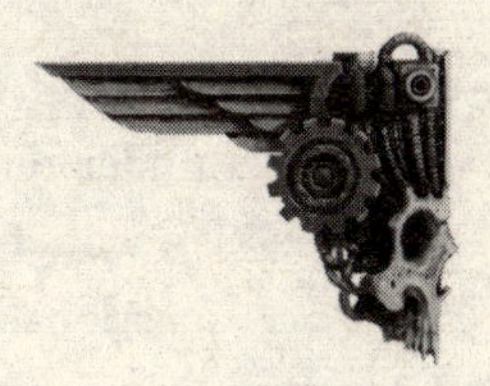

THREE

The ship's astropaths were dead, slain in the first instant of the titanic expulsion of warp energy that had driven the explorator ship from the empyrean. For all that the *Peregrinus*' Geller field had warded the physical matter of the ship from harm, the minds of the psychically touched were far too attuned to the immaterium to be spared under such an assault.

Reports from across the ship told of hundreds of others gripped by seizures and aneurisms, or spontaneously combusting into human candles of witch-fire, or shedding arcs of lightning that welded their bodies to the deck. Much of the ship's remaining skitarii had been deployed to suppress the worst of the rioting and panic that had followed. The *Peregrinus* flew on, but with many of her decks overrun by a crew that had been pushed beyond what their minds had been made to endure.

Navigator Kian was alive, though he had been forcibly placed in a catatonic state by his praetorian guards and the few body-slaves that had survived his madness. Yuel had inloaded the

report that spoke of the horror the mutant had unleashed as he buckled under the psychic strain, failing at the very last. Whether Kian would retain his sanity sufficient to mourn his crime was questionable at best.

But these tragedies and crises went unremarked by all on the command deck. Their attention was elsewhere.

Ahead of them, a half-made world turned within the sharp blue light of the system's star.

Yuel had witnessed many wonders in his six centuries as an explorator, but never had he observed a sight so strange as the contradictory orb that hung in space before him.

In purely geologic terms, the planet was unremarkable. It sat at the inner edge of the system's habitable zone. Its dimensions and rotational velocity were approximate to that of Terra. Its mass gave it a surface gravity that sat precisely within the median for settled Imperial worlds, and its ferrous core provided a strong and stable electromagnetic field to shield it from the star's radiation. As a stellar body, it was no different from a hundred thousand other worlds that humanity claimed as its own.

Yet in every other way that mattered, it was unique. Singular. Utterly without peer or precedent in the comprehensive annals of the Adeptus Mechanicus.

One hemisphere of the planet was a tumult of seismic upheaval. Vulcanism continuously hurled ejecta high into its poisoned atmosphere, fuelling dark skeins of shadowy storms that raced across its face. Chasms that delved for tens of miles hatched its three broken continents, veining the land with countless rivers of lava. It was a world of fire and brimstone, the crust of the planet laid bare and roiling.

None of this was what made the planet unusual. Seismic instability was common on telluric worlds. What made it strange was the pristine, verdant growth that covered its far side.

The other half of the planet was a vision stolen from human myths of paradise and Elysium. Azure-blue seas filled the deep valleys, and rich, fertile soil hugged their shores. Green plains cloaked the slopes of peaceful mountains, and dense forests and jungles lined sinuous rivers. The toxic clouds that crowded in from the far side of the world dissipated into mist at the fringes of the idyllic range. A heavy curtain of metal-rich rain encircled the patchwork continent of seas and fields, drawing a boundary around this vision of Edyn that was visible from the void.

For all the unnamed world's astonishing incongruity, it was not what held Yuel's attention. The cause of the planet's extraordinary disparity hung in the void, no more than a thousand miles above its ionosphere.

In the crudest terms, the Genesis vessel resembled a fat-bellied, many-limbed arachnid. Its centre was a vast disc, studded with domes and etched with valleys. From this central body, equal in scale to a continental shelf of the world below, dozens of ivory arms projected for thousands of miles. Between each limb were stretched gossamer-thin sails that reflected the starlight in a glittering fan of golden threads. The underside of each limb emanated a scarlet light, evidently breathing the transmuting Genesis phenomena down onto the planet below. The arms of the massive craft curled inwards, as though holding the half-made world in an unseen grip.

The command deck had fallen into idleness as officers and thralls stared in wonder.

<Magnificent,> breathed Lyterix.

<Impossible,> sent Yuel in turn.

<Believe the evidence of your ocular inputs, lord,> said Sherax. <It appears we must reframe the bounds of the impossible.>

The exhausted satisfaction that rolled from Sherax's aura was monumental. She was right. All she had said, all she had promised, was true. The power to reshape planets, to birth and sustain life in defiance of all natural laws.

And it stemmed from the occult witchcraft of the aeldari.

<It would seem that the xenos warrior you encountered spoke the truth,> sent Yuel. <This is no artefact of human craft.>

Sherax's pleasure faded in the manner of an eclipse, swallowed by the bleak truth of Yuel's statement. <Indeed.>

<Does it matter?> Lyterix's presence in the communion was an irritant, forever contradicting and gainsaying Yuel's counsel, but there was little he could do to shut the augur out. <The fact of its existence reframes the entire orthodoxy of galactic history. How many worlds owe their origins to this device? Are there others? For how long has this world been sustained in this wholly unnatural, bilateral state?>

Lyterix's rhetorical questions, which were at the forefront of Yuel's own thoughts, were rendered into their proper priority by a broadcast from the far side of the command deck.

<Xenos craft have adopted a pursuit vector, ductrix.>

The vision of the planet and its cradle disappeared from the hololithic display, replaced by tactical data. Three aeldari ships, small dart-like vessels, had detached themselves from their ferocious void battle with the crescent-shaped craft, and were turning to follow the *Peregrinus*' course. Though slight, in her crippled condition they would be more than a match for the explorator ship.

<Time to intercept?> Sherax asked. There was no question that the swift xenos vessels would overtake the *Peregrinus*.

<Four hours, ductrix.> Urgency had a different meaning in void war. Even moving at monumental speeds, the distances to be crossed made any battle among the stars a ponderous affair.

<They cannot catch us before we reach the Genesis vessel,> sent Lyterix. Yuel could sense the augur moving through the

ship, heading for the command deck, as though physical proximity would lend weight to his argument.

Rahn-Bo approached Sherax's side. <We must flee. We can take all we have seen back to the synod. They would bring the full might of the fleet to bear. For this, Mars itself would rouse its legions.>

<It is too late for that,> replied Sherax. <Xenos already battle for control of this vessel. We cannot allow this power to fall into the possession of the alien. If it exists, it must be in human hands.>

Yuel granted that the explorator's logic was undeniable, but it was also incomplete. Humanity was the rightful master of the galaxy, and the xenos races were aberrations. Nothing that empowered them could be allowed to persist. But that did not mean that the Mechanicus should lay claim to their works.

<But we cannot defeat them, Talin,> Rahn-Bo persisted. <Even if we outpace their pursuit craft, even if we board this... thing. The *Peregrinus* will not survive a protracted battle. Our skitarii are decimated. There is no possibility that we can claim this device for our own.>

<Your datamancer is correct, Talin,> Yuel sent. <This vessel must be destroyed.>

<Vandal. Desecrator. Despoiler.> Lyterix's animus erupted in outrage, casting furious code-shards at Yuel with all the venom of a striking serpent. <You behold the miraculous and think only to tear it from the heavens.>

<And you are an apostate.> Yuel matched the augur in his acrimony. <Your familiarity with the unnatural has made you prey for its temptations.>

<Enough.> Sherax summoned her will, and stilled the roiling communion. <We are adherents of the Cult Mechanicus. While we may agree on little else, let us at least recognise that that truth holds for us all.>

Softly, Yuel felt Rahn-Bo make a final attempt. <Talin, we do not need this thing.>

Sherax's reply admitted a fraction of the doubt Yuel knew churned within her. <I do.>

The explorator mounted her throne, though she did not renew her physical connection to her ship.

<I will lead an expedition, with as much haste as can be mustered,> she sent. <We will learn what we can, and find a way to deny the vessel's use to the enemies of humanity.>

<How?> asked Rahn-Bo. If the *Peregrinus* were to slow in order to make any kind of boarding action, it would be eviscerated by the pursuing aeldari.

Sherax had already calculated her answer. <Prime the teleportation array.>

FOUR

Edgar shifted the weight of the laslock in his arms. It was odd to prepare for a battle without the cramped cockpit of a Knight around him. Without the invasive pressure of a Helm Mechanicus upon his skull, and the promise of immense weight and strength in his limbs.

It was strangely invigorating. He was merely one amongst many, a body whose purpose was to aim and fire a laslock, and nothing more.

Preparing for battle as a line trooper was not the only novelty Edgar was uncomfortable with. The strange apparatus of the *Peregrinus'* primary teleportation array loomed above him, a nightmare of clawed metal struts and impossibly complex pipework.

The centre of the array was a broad circular platform, large enough for several hundred men and women to stand upon and be shunted through space. The platform's base was level with Edgar's eyeline, revealing the nest of ribbed cables and coiled

wires beneath. A lambent blue light pulsed within, or possibly along, many of the ducts and machines, while a brace of robed attendants fussed with their workings.

As with the operation of any Mechanicus implement, a chorus of incense-wielding techseers cast their thuribles over the cogitators and other devices. For once, Edgar did not resent their presence, or their pious odour. If it would ensure that the array would not scatter his body to the winds, then he would gladly swing a brazier of his own.

Explorator Sherax swept into the chamber at the head of a phalanx of skitarii and heavily armed combat servitors, followed by two other magi, Lyterix and Rahn-Bo. All were armed and armoured for war. Sherax carried a cog-bladed axe, and the golden emblem of her refractor field generator glistened from its place in the centre of her chest. Beneath the heavy fabric of her Gryphonnen robe, Edgar could see that the explorator had donned a cuirass of interlocking metal lames, hanging down to the struts of her legs.

Sherax halted, letting the skitarii march past and up onto the platform. She turned her metallic face to the Blackbloods, drawn up by squads to one side of the chamber's entrance. Zlata, Lursa, and Belyev stood ahead of their troopers, the last of the Vostroyan 103rd.

'Do you understand what I am asking of you?' she asked Major Zlata without preamble.

'Yes, explorator.'

The order to mobilise had come while the regiment had been collecting itself from the violence of the *Peregrinus'* arrival in-system. Edgar himself had been tossed across the arming chamber, fortunate that a pile of ration sacks had arrested his fall rather than anything more lethal. Four troopers had sustained disabling injuries, and all four had strained the rigours of discipline when Zlata had ordered them to report to the ship's infirmary rather than don their flak armour.

Even Ormond had tried to join them, after Zlata had relayed their destination and their mission. Edgar had firmly ordered the old man to stand down, though he had promised to carry the sacristan's avenging anger with him to the colossal xenos world-craft. Disabling such a vessel would be a fitting retribution against the aliens that had killed *Vortigern*, and left him stranded to walk Ikaneos' wastes.

Sherax hesitated before Zlata. 'I am grateful for your service, major, and that of your regiment in the years since the fall of the forge-cradle,' she said finally.

With tight formality, Major Zlata placed her laslock's axe-bladed stock against the deck and rested its barrel against her chest. With her hands free, she laced them across her chest in the sign of the cog. 'Praise the Omnissiah, explorator.'

Neither Sherax's steel-and-bronze face nor her vox-emitter was capable of expressing emotion. Nevertheless, it seemed to Edgar as though the ductrix tried to invest her reply with sincerity. 'The God-Emperor protects, major. Please, have your troops take their places.'

Zlata nodded, then half turned her head. 'By squads, form up!'

Edgar jogged in lockstep with his fellows up the teleportation array's steps, heartbeat rising to match the pulse of the machine. By chance, he found himself standing beside Xal, the explorator's bodyguard. 'Protector.'

The skitarius – it was hard to think of the protector as a man, born to the same baseline as Edgar, when not an inch of flesh was visible – was occupied with inspecting his weapons. He held his enormous chainsword in two metal claws, and briefly revved its horrendously sharp teeth. 'Master Lorristan.'

Edgar tried not to flinch. 'Trooper Lorristan, now.'

Xal did not acknowledge his correction.

Sherax had not joined her party on the teleportation platform. Edgar could see her standing in front of the leader of the techseers, holding the stiff, motionless stance that he had come to associate with tense conversation between Mechanicus adepts. Whatever passed between them was silent, and over in moments. Sherax turned abruptly and marched up the array's steps, claws clattering against the grated metal.

At an inaudible signal, the adepts clustered around a bank of control consoles began to interact with their machines with greater urgency. Beneath Edgar's feet, the platform started to emit a hum, and the cobalt glow took on a greater intensity.

As the gathering power shifted, a new fear entered Edgar's mind. 'I've never been teleported before,' he said.

Xal did not pause his inspection of his weapons. 'The experience is... singular.'

'That's not very reassuring, protector.'

The skitarii warrior lifted his chainsword and clamped it to his back. 'I did not intend it to be.'

The growing thrum of electric force precluded further conversation. Edgar gripped and regripped his laslock, nervous as a squire approaching his first steed. There appeared to be a cyclical movement to both the sound and the radiant light, chasing one another around the platform beneath his boots. The hum rose to a scream, chained power spinning faster and faster until it seemed to Edgar that the world would shatter from the sound.

Beneath the scream of eldritch energies, Edgar just barely heard Xal emit a whisper of vocalised prayer.

'In the name of the Omnissiah, let this be the end of it.'

The world disappeared in a burst of blinding light, and then Edgar was falling.

FIVE

Discordant data assailed Rahn-Bo. For a fraction of a second, her senses told her that she was both falling and rising. Compressed, yet something tugged at her limbs. Desperate cries in a language she did not understand drowned out all sound. A sibilant whisper, promising knowledge and the end of strife, slid across the deepest reaches of her cognition.

And then reality asserted itself. The physical laws of the universe were once more as they had always been.

The glow of teleportation faded swiftly. Rahn-Bo was familiar enough with the confounding sensation of translocation to shrug off the worst of its disorienting effects, but most of Sherax's hastily assembled expedition was not. Several of the Vostroyans were on their hands and knees vomiting, or weeping blood from their eyes and ears.

The two hundred soldiers and skitarii were standing on grass, emerald green and yielding to the touch. The sensation was so astonishingly alien that Rahn-Bo, entirely without consideration

of her wider surroundings, bent down to run a hand through the individual blades. It was not the false, metallic growth she had encountered on the *Almagest*. This was true vegetation, sprouting in a dense layer from thick, black soil.

<Alphas, disperse.>

Sherax's order to her troops broke Rahn-Bo's fascination, and she straightened.

They had emerged in one of the many domes that studded the Genesis vessel's back. It was a vast cavern, its far edge lost in mist. The stars were visible through the transparent crystal roof, hundreds of yards above them.

The dome appeared to have no purpose. There were no structures or works of artifice nearby, besides a scattering of pure white trees. Rahn-Bo had no frame of reference for aeldari craft, beyond the fluid and grotesque architecture of the Ikaneos enclave. This vision of verdant peace might have been unique to the Genesis vessel, or perhaps all aeldari used their resources so inefficiently. Perhaps all their warships had gardens.

As the skitarii broke into their units and spread from their entry point, radium carbines and arc rifles raised, Rahn-Bo sensed Sherax reach out across the noosphere.

<We appear to still be in contact.>

Lord Yuel answered. <For now. Aeldari craft continue to pursue us, and we will be out of range shortly.>

<Preserve the ship, my lord. That is paramount.>

Yuel's sending held no emotive signifiers, nothing to inspire confidence or cause doubt. <I shall alert you to our return.>

Rahn-Bo felt her ductrix's fears. She could do nothing to influence the fate of her ship. She had abdicated that ability, her responsibility to her crew, for the chance to explore the Genesis vessel. Yuel would take the *Peregrinus* in a wide, rapid circuit of the half-made world, evading the wrath of the aeldari as it ran. Sherax's expedition had until the explorator ship returned to learn all they could, or else they would be left to wander its domes and passages for evermore.

'Major Zlata?'

'Explorator?' The Vostroyan commander was standing beside one of her stricken troopers. She appeared to have been unaffected by translocation disorder.

'My skitarii will form the vanguard. Deploy your troops to protect our flanks as we advance.'

'As you say, explorator.' Zlata appeared to take no slight from Sherax's order, and none was intended. They had emerged at the heart of an unknown structure. Whatever threats they would face could appear from any quarter.

Sherax's plan, as far as she had shared one with Rahn-Bo, was simple. They would locate a command-and-control node for the operation of the Genesis vessel, and learn all they could of its function. If possible, they would acquire further samples of the crystal that had worked its changes on the *Almagest*. If sabotage was an option, Sherax had committed to disabling the vessel, though Rahn-Bo could sense the conflict within her ductrix.

It was, she knew, ludicrously optimistic. It was doubtful the *Peregrinus* could weather even a cursory assault from its pursuers. The Genesis vessel was the size of a continent, to say nothing of whatever guardians might dwell within its domes and whatever else that might hinder their search. They had passed beyond desperation, and were trusting now to the capricious whims of fortune alone.

As the first skitarii squads fanned out, claws biting deep into alien soil, Rahn-Bo watched Sherax take her first tentative steps through the object she had sought for so long. She moved to stand beside a pair of servitors, burdened by a casket-sized auspex held between them. The heavy scanning unit had a single function – to seek the unique signature of the Genesis shard Sherax had documented, and that had led them to the Ikaneos fane.

With a pulse of thought, the explorator slaved the auspex feed to her own senses. There was a fractional hesitation as Sherax inloaded all that the device told her, then she turned on her heel and set off towards the dome's far side.

<Let us proceed.>

SIX

They first passed through gardens and parks. Or, at least, that was what Xal had taken them to be. The dome into which the expedition had teleported was divided into discrete spaces by low walls, made of the same resilient bone that the aeldari appeared to use for all their constructs. Statues and sculptures, in abstract and alien shapes, adorned low plinths. Tessellated paths roamed between trees that were lit from within, their branches glowing with the strength of lumen-bars. The true purpose these spaces held for the aeldari, Xal could not say, and had no desire to learn.

It took fourteen minutes for the expedition to reach the dome's edge at a rapid pace. There was a continuous murmur within the noosphere as the ductrix conversed with Rahn-Bo and Magos Lyterix, debating the nature and substance of the grass, the dome, the bone walls they passed. It was a familiar, reassuring texture to the communion, and one Xal had no difficulty in ignoring. His purpose was, and had always been, to

safeguard Sherax and her adepts from harm while they pursued their questions, each of them serving the Omnissiah in the way that matched their form and function.

The auspex had identified several openings within the dome's edge as the expedition approached, undifferentiated from one another as far as Xal could tell. But Sherax's order had been clear; evidently the casket had yielded a signal to be pursued. <Down.>

Rho-6-2's rangers led the way, descending through a curving tunnel into the body of the vessel. The tunnel's walls were lit from within by witch-light, sourceless and diffuse. Shadows were banished within the confined space, an effect that evidently had an unnerving effect on the Vostroyan soldiery.

The shaft levelled out, joining what swiftly became apparent was a network of passages veining the interior of the Genesis craft. Many of these opened onto halls and chambers of varying size and function. In some, jewel-studded consoles curved up from the floor, or hung beneath mirrored surfaces. They did not encounter a single aeldari, or any sign of occupation.

Xal's internal auspex was baffled by the bone corridors, but evidently the servitor-borne unit was providing greater returns. As the expedition reached each junction of the network, Sherax would direct them onwards, leading them ever deeper into the warren.

<Hold.> Sherax pulsed the command suddenly, before repeating the order over the vox for the benefit of the Vostroyans. As one, the skitarii halted, their rifles and carbines levelled along the length of the tunnel. The brace of combat servitors that accompanied them were slower to respond, and continued to scan left and right from atop their tracked locomotive units.

Xal detected nothing, but knew he could not trust the readings of his own sensors. <Ductrix?>

<There are anomalous objects ahead.>

<Aeldari?> asked Lyterix, whose own weapons were drawn and raised.

<No,> Sherax answered. <This is something else.>

The expedition advanced with caution, the explorator's warning paramount. Xal led, claws clicking on the bone floor. After a hundred yards the passage opened suddenly, its ceiling curling up and away to become the lowest point of a high, asymmetric dome. But where so many similar chambers had stood empty, this one was not.

And it was there they found the soulless machines.

'Do not touch them. Do not approach them.'

The chamber was lined with great slabs of ebony metal. Each block, in places as thick as Xal's arm span and three times his height, was cut through with geometric bars of emerald light. The metal seemed to have been grafted onto the bone walls of the aeldari craft, rather than merging with or emerging from them. They clearly were fundamentally incompatible; the sweeping fluidity of the aeldari jarred violently with the flat planes and sharp edges of whatever xenos species had created the metal entities.

Both were anathema to the edicts of the Mechanicus. Xal knew, in his soul, the purity of human-forged steel was superior to both the osseous growth and whatever perverse alloy had invaded the Genesis vessel.

Attached at intervals along the walls were coffins, set upright and taller than any unaugmented human would require. The caskets were of the same metal as the slabs they sat upon, and emitted the same jade light from hexagonal patterns etched into their surfaces. Whether anything was contained within - indeed, whether they were in fact containers and not simply blocky outcrops of the same, apparently purposeless plinths – was a mystery.

But it was not the slabs of metal and the sinister caskets mounted upon them that captured Xal's gaze, but the creatures that stalked and scuttled across them.

'Do not approach them.'

The ductrix's order was entirely redundant. Xal had thought himself incapable of the majority of human emotions, but it appeared that revulsion remained within his grasp.

Dozens of constructs skittered across the alien metal. They were small, most no larger than a human child's skull. Their design – it was instantly apparent that each was an artificial creation – was insectile, with most skittering along on multiple wickedly sharp limbs. Xal swiftly classified several basic subtypes: arachnid, scarabic, and more infrequently, pterygotan, propelling themselves through the air by means that Xal could not identify. There did not appear to be significant subdivision or specialisation; indeed, they seemed to have been forged or stamped out of identical templates.

These creatures were clearly built by the same xenos that fought the aeldari in the void. There was no mistaking their kinship with the crescent-shaped vessels.

Their function, as far as Xal could discern, was to tend to the caskets. Swarms of the creatures clicked and clattered over each obelisk, adhering to the alloy despite their needle-like appendages. The same emerald light burned from what Xal assumed were their ocular sensors, and around the joints of their carapaces.

They were wholly, utterly repellent.

The most apposite, and yet the most odious, comparator Xal could make was that the caretaker constructs were analogous to Mechanicus servo-skulls. But while it appeared they were both monotasked servants, created with the intention of serving higher beings, a servo-skull adhered to the tenets of the Omnissiah. They were a fusion of the organic and the machine. These constructs were a perversion of the sanctity of metal. They were empty, soulless automata, the antithesis of every tenet of the Adeptus Mechanicus.

A hiss of sudden depressurisation made Xal lift his sidearm, appalled that he had allowed his attention to drift from his core function.

<Hold fire.> Sherax broadcast her command; the carbines and laslocks of every member of the expedition had trained on a pair of the dark metal caskets, which had opened down their centres without warning. The two coffins emitted a blaze of jade light, casting a sickly glow against the bone walls of the chamber.

If Xal had been repelled by the sight of the lifeless constructs, what emerged from the caskets chilled him to the core of his being.

A skeletal figure emerged from each box, a grotesque mockery of the human form. They were identical, tall and spindle-limbed, made of the same alien metal as the rest of their aberrant technology. Angular craniums narrowed to sharp, pointed faces, in which shone the lambent green light of whatever power animated these creatures. Articulated hands that were clearly made to grasp weapons were empty.

The scarabs and spiders did not react to the emergence of their grander peers. Neither did the figures appear to take note of Sherax and her expedition; soundlessly, they turned and marched away towards the far end of the chamber. What had activated them, and what purpose they were embarked upon, was entirely unclear.

The sight of the creatures in motion was the greatest profanity yet, and Xal felt the rare compulsion to override his ductrix's command and open fire on their unseeing backs. They were a facsimile of life, a crime against which Xal's entire being rebelled.

The holy synthesis of flesh and steel was the foundation of the Cult Mechanicus. It was the central tenet of Xal's faith – the divine spark of the human soul, conjoined with the purity and inviolate strength of metal. One without the other – cold metal somehow imbued with an abstraction of life – was anathema to all Xal knew to be true.

<Do not fire,> Sherax repeated. <We must not provoke an engagement.>

<Do you know these creatures, ductrix?> Rahn-Bo asked. Xal detected the murmur of recognition, and fear, within the noosphere as the datamancer spoke.

<No,> Sherax replied. <But I have heard rumours of such things. Anecdotal tales of malign intelligences inhabiting bodies of corrupted metal. Highly resilient, and eminently dangerous.>

<They are not a part of this craft,> Lyterix sent, strangely declarative. <They are evidently parasitic. They do not appear to play a role in the Genesis vessel's operation, nor do they inhibit it. They need not concern us.>

<These entities cannot be dismissed so casually.> Sherax's noospheric aura, which had been betraying the ductrix's gathering concern at their fruitless hunt through the Genesis vessel, was now clouded with the same loathing that dominated Xal's mind. <This will not be an isolated enclave. Whatever their origin, this species claims this craft, and evidently defends it in the void. They introduce a host of uncertain variables.>

<Explorator, they are not relevant to our goal,> Lyterix implored, his own desperation slipping around his mental firebreaks. <We are here for Genesis.>

On the scale of an augmented mind, Sherax took an age to make her decision.

'Advance with caution,' she ordered aloud. 'Avoid proximity with them, if you can.'

Xal crept between the silent constructs, balancing swiftness with surety of position as he led the way through the thicket of lifeless metal. He kept his carbine lowered but gripped tight, not wishing to make any provocative gesture, although how and whether the constructs could perceive the expedition was yet another unknown to contend with.

Sherax had been correct; there were hundreds more of the metal creatures, infesting the corridors of the vessel. The skeletal figures continued to pay them no heed – indeed, despite their profusion through the craft they seemed to be entirely purposeless – but their numbers and choice of gathering points brought the explorator's party unsettlingly close to their lifeless, unseeing forms.

They congregated at junctions, where more protrusions of their artifice had been established. At each crossroads the explorator would point their way, always seeking the source of the transmuting Genesis radiation. Invariably, their route would take them through a cluster of the inanimate constructs.

It was a constant struggle for Xal to hold his wrath at bay. The very sight of one of the soulless machines set off a chain of unfamiliar error codes through the protector's thoughts, corrupting his focus. It was not merely hatred – the artificers who had wired Xal's synapses had understood the value of loathing for a skitarius' targets – but the far more insidious spectre of fear. Fear should have been an impossibility for him, and yet proximity to even the merest of the constructs was sufficient to make Xal's claw tense around his chainsword.

The expedition's caution, and Xal's forbearance, proved unnecessary. It was not the metal creatures who broke the fragile peace.

The faint crump of displaced air was the only warning they received. Halfway along a tunnel, no different from any of the others they had delved, a xenos warrior in red armour erupted into being, its vast wide-mouthed cannon silently levelled at Sherax.

<Enemy contact!>

One of Rho-6-2's rangers stepped in front of the warrior, loyal to its protocols, and received the full force of its blast. The xenos' arcane weapon coughed soundlessly, and the ranger was destroyed, riven into shards of flesh and steel by a grey mist.

As Sherax's refractor field burst into life and every warrior around her turned on their attacker, it vanished, swallowed by the same eruption of strange energies. The Vostroyan officers bellowed orders, matching the buzz of skit-code that set the skitarii into a defensive pattern, but their actions were all too late.

<The aeldari are among us,> Lyterix sent.

Sherax, encased in the shimmering protection of her refractor field, cast a soft snatch of code. <It was only a matter of time.>

They bled, but the aeldari bled as well. Between the reactions of Sherax's skitarii and the ferociously fast talons of the soulless machines, four of the ambushing xenos died, though at a cost of thirty Vostroyans and skitarii.

They advanced at a crawl, in a tight, almost circular formation. At every turn, a brace of laslocks and arc rifles were aimed at every corner and open space. Aeldari flickered into existence, to be met by a volley of energy if the expedition was fortunate, or else to claim a life if they were not. The gravest single tally was taken by an aeldari who teleported into the centre of their formation, a heavy falchion in its grip. Nine Vostroyans fell beneath its blade before a round from Sherax's archeotech pistol burst the xenos to greasy mist.

The constructs aided the expedition, in a fashion. After the first attacks, a signal appeared to have passed through the somnolent creatures, rousing them into directionless action. The next aeldari to appear in ambush was taken by surprise, and was snared by the sharp forelimbs of an arachnid construct as it levelled its cannon. After that, the xenos were more cautious, which granted the Mechanicus forces precious seconds to react to their sudden appearance.

It galled Xal – another emotional reaction the protector had been surprised to uncover within himself – to passively accept the assistance of the heretical xenos. It was clear that they would fight the aeldari with single-minded determination wherever they encountered them, but the urge to simply purge all the alien life they encountered was palpable. It was only his tactical algorithms, and the edict of his ductrix, that kept him from enacting that urge. To engage the numerous metal constructs whilst also watching for aeldari ambush would commit them to an unwinnable battle.

Xal kept an eidetic record of their route through the Genesis vessel. By his calculation they had descended over three hundred vertical yards through the core of the craft, and yet they continued to follow curving passages that took them ever downwards, with no discernible change in architecture. They would occasionally encounter discrete chambers housing curving consoles and shimmering screens, but Sherax directed them past these points. The auspex casket – which had been picked up by a pair of skitarii after its servitor bearers had been cut down – was clearly drawing them onward.

<We have not been attacked for over sixteen minutes,> Rahn-Bo sent as they reached the end of another tunnel. <This is the longest interval so far.>

Xal's chronometer had been keeping his own measure of

the time between attempts at ambush, which tallied with the datamancer's.

<Indeed,> replied Sherax. She pulsed the return of the auspex into the noosphere. <I believe we are close to our objective.>

SEVEN

The enemy was waiting for them.

Sherax had relayed what they were to expect, but forewarning had not prepared Edgar for the sight that greeted him as the expedition finally emerged from the endless tunnels into a vast domed chamber.

The crystal floor was transparent, stretching away from the arched entrance for at least a mile. Edgar stepped out, tentative at first, not wishing to trust the alien material with his weight. Then all concerns disappeared, as the sight beneath the crystal surface took his breath away.

Hundreds of miles below Edgar's feet, the half-made world turned, a jewel of colour and life against the endless darkness of the galaxy.

Edgar had been privileged to see eight worlds from the void, but nothing had prepared him for the sight. The green of vegetation reminded him of Raisa's deep forests, but they were a different hue in his memories. The oceans and seas were a vibrant cerulean, studded with white clouds.

'Enemy front,' snarled Zlata. Edgar had, he saw with guilty relief, not been the only one to lose focus. With an effort, he tore his gaze from the world below, and concentrated on the warrior who had made his stand above it.

One of the aeldari stood at the centre of the chamber. It was clear that whatever path he had taken to find them within the Genesis ship's vastness, he had not taken it unscathed. His armour was cracked and torn, stripped of its crimson colour in places by razor talons. Two wide arms, each evidently ending in some manner of weapon, gave him the appearance of a tall, bulbous arachnid. He stood defiant but broken, apparently alone.

'Be vigilant.' Xal spoke the warning aloud, though after the past few hours it was wholly unnecessary.

Edgar lifted his laslock. Its charge pack was almost depleted, but it would have to do.

'Is it not a wonder?' the warrior said as greeting. The distortion of Gothic repelled Edgar, but, listening closely, there was a wetness to his intonation of the words. Something deep within the alien was damaged.

'It is,' replied Explorator Sherax. She appeared to be as distracted as Edgar had become.

'And you would take it for yourselves,' the alien said.

'We will,' she said.

'I cannot permit that.'

'It need not be like this, Idranvel of Biel-tan.' To Edgar's surprise, Lyterix took a step forward, his hands empty as a gesture of peaceful intent. 'It is clear your people value this craft. Its power is self-evident. Let us learn its secrets together. This craft could be the cradle of a new understanding between our empires.'

The warrior tossed his helmeted head in derision. 'Pitiful, mon-keigh. The *Turellea Dandramensha* is the gift of the gods to my people. It cannot be portioned out, nor shared with those unworthy of gracing its halls.'

Xal boldly stepped past the augur, a champion approaching a rival. His enormous chainsword came to life in his hands, its engine growling through the reverent silence. 'I tire of your whining, xenos. If you intend to stop us, do so.'

Idranvel bowed his insectoid head. 'As you wish.'

The aeldari winked out of existence. An instant later, crimson-armoured warriors emerged from the empty air.

'To me, Blackbloods! To me!'

The last of the Vostroyan 103rd rallied to Zlata's cry, or made the attempt. There was no shape to the battle, just a swirling melee of dying troopers and red-armoured murderers.

In ambush, the spider-like aeldari had been lethal. As a collective, they were a horror. In one moment they would erupt in the midst of a squad of skitarii and immolate them with their strange weapons. In the next they would vanish, and a brace of their kin would strike at the unseeing backs of Blackbloods. But they could be killed.

Edgar jammed his laslock between the joints of a spider warrior's back plate while it was entangled with three members of his squad. He pulled the trigger, again and again and again, emptying all that was left of the weapon's charge into the aeldari's spine. It dropped its weapon, arching away from his shots. Its arms clawed at its back, before pitching forward to land atop the bodies of fallen Vostroyans.

'Form up!' Belyev cried, but his order was impossible to obey. The aeldari danced among the expedition, dropping more Mechanicus and Militarum soldiers with each passing second.

Edgar turned, gripping his laslock like a club, looking for Zlata. He spotted her in a crowd of skitarii, lit by white arcs of crackling power. Between them they were bludgeoning a spider warrior to death, hacking with short, brutal strokes at its projecting limbs.

He grinned, gripped by a vicious, bitter glee. In any second he would be killed, cut down without warning. It was a better death than he could have wished for.

'Major Zlata!' Sherax strode through the combat, encased in her shimmering armour and torn robe. She slashed the cog-bladed axe into mid-air, and met the body of a xenos as it winked into existence. The warrior fell, bisected.

'Major Zlata!' The explorator forged on, ignoring Edgar, who fell into her wake. 'Form up your troops. They will not stand against a united front.'

'Explorator!' Zlata ignored her order, and instead pointed towards the duelling figures of Xal, and the xenos commander. Sherax turned to follow her sign, as did Edgar. Xal was giving ground, clearly outmatched.

In concert, the three began to push their way through the scrum of bodies towards the embattled protector.

Xal's stolen weapon had been well chosen. Every clash of blades jerked the xenos warrior off balance, as the chainsword's racing teeth gripped and pulled at the blades at his wrists. Xal was relentless, pressing close after each swing and parry.

He fought methodically, clinically, slashing blow after blow against Idranvel's arms. The alien's wrist-blades were not made for this kind of combat. They were made for murder, for the dance of a duel, not to fend off the heavy strokes of an Astartes blade.

But he was losing. The aeldari adapted, shifted, dancing around Xal's sword to jab cruel thrusts that parted the protector's armour

like smoke. Xal was weakening rapidly, servos in his limbs failing. His core systems were bleeding critical fluids into his carapace.

'You have lost, xenos.' Xal spat the challenge, attempting any tactic that might achieve a second's hesitation. 'Look about you. Your warriors fall. You fight only to prolong your misery.'

Idranvel responded by darting forward once more. His wrist-blade slid around Xal's guard, and the alien steel cut through both of the skitarius' primary wrists.

Xal reeled back, the chainsword still bucking as it fell. Idranvel kicked out, casting Xal to the transparent floor just as he had in the Ikaneos fane. This time, he stepped closer for a final impaling thrust.

Three figures burst from the maelstrom - Sherax, Zlata and Lorristan, united in fury and hatred for the alien warrior that loomed above Xal. A las-bolt struck Idranvel's shoulder guard, and an axe-bladed laslock swung for his head. A golden cog, wreathed in energy, swept towards Idranvel's midriff.

The xenos employed his witchcraft, and vanished, leaving Sherax and Zlata to stumble through the space he had occupied.

The warrior reappeared an instant later behind Xal's rescuers. With ruthless speed, he punched both wristblades through Major Zlata's back.

A scream of denial erupted from the closest Vostroyans, and a torrent of las-fire struck the xenos warlord.

Xal demanded one last effort from his failing body. He lunged, chainsword outstretched in his remaining claw. Its tip passed the dying Zlata's head, and its whirring teeth found Idranvel's face.

The xenos reeled away, both hands clutched to the ruin of his skull. The Vostroyan commander fell from his blades. The soldiers that saw her die gave up a bestial roar, and threw themselves on their remaining enemies.

He had taken Idranvel's sight. Gore dripped between the alien's gauntlets as he staggered back. He made no sound as he collapsed to his knees.

Xal fell, mimicking his beaten enemy, his internal systems finally failing. He looked around, the light of his visor flickering as vital fluids poured from his many wounds.

<My ductrix.>

He spoke one final time into the noosphere, a single pulse of loyalty and devotion, and then the protector crashed to the crystal floor.

The moans of the wounded and dying were appallingly loud in the massive chamber, which had only moments before rung with the screams and cries of battle.

Edgar knelt beside Zlata's body, borrowed laslock still clutched in both hands.

He had known, in that last charge through the melee, that he would die. The thought had struck him, with a clarity and force that had only lent strength to his limbs. And yet it was Zlata, not he, who lay dead by alien blades.

'It was my time. Finally, it was meant to be my time.' There were no tears in his eyes. Confusion, more than sorrow, was what gripped him. There was also, shockingly, no pain in his body. Somehow, impossibly, he had come through the battle unscathed.

There was no justice in the galaxy. None at all.

Banner Sergeant Belyev put a bloody hand on his shoulder. 'She wanted this as much as you, Lorristan. Believe me.'

The last of the Vostroyan 103rd had gathered around. They were the very last; no more than two dozen Blackbloods remained on their feet.

Edgar knew Belyev was right. Zlata had been broken by the loss

of her troopers, just as he had mourned the death of *Vortigern*. But there had been no respite for her, no novelty of learning a new way of making war to let her reforge some piece of herself. This was the peace owed to her, just as it was owed to every warrior who took up arms in the God-Emperor's wars.

'Help the wounded.' Belyev's order was a cracked rasp.

Edgar gave Zlata's body a final glance, then pushed himself to his feet. His peace was yet to come.

EIGHT

Lyterix loomed above the dying alien. The barrel of his phosphor pistol emitted a wisp of irradiated smoke, and alien blood painted his tunic.

'The metal constructs we encountered. They are not of aeldari making.'

The alien did not reply. His head rocked back and forth, as though seeking to triangulate the location of his interrogator. One arm stretched out hesitantly, bloody blade wavering in the air. Lyterix knocked it aside. 'Answer.'

'No,' Idranvel said finally, in spite of the ruin of his face.

'What are they?'

'They… are the ancient enemy. Their race and ours… have fought since the beginning of time. Soldiers, in a battle between gods.'

At any other time, with any other interlocutor, Sherax's curiosity would have driven her to press for more. But she felt nothing but the potent, human urge to raise her axe and end the xenos' existence.

'How did they come to infest this vessel?' Lyterix continued.

'I knew nothing… until we encountered them in the darkness. They… lie dormant, as guardians… I hoped the *Turellea Dandramensha* would be free of their taint.'

While Lyterix and the alien spoke, Sherax stood from Xal's body, leaning heavily on her axe's stave. She said nothing for some time, regarding the beaten warrior. Lyterix stepped back as she levelled the axe at Idranvel's throat.

'How did we come to pursue this place together? It is no coincidence that you awaited me on Ikaneos.'

'No.' A sharp smile showed through a mask of blood. The warrior's capacity to endure pain was incredible. 'Know this, Sherax of Gryphonne. It was I who set you on the path of discovery. You have been my implement, the tool of prophecy. It was you who led me here.'

'How?'

'It was I who lured the leviathan to prey upon you. I brought about the death of your world, to lead to the resurrection of my own.' Idranvel's smile was a bloodstained crescent. 'I did it gladly.'

Every warrior still standing levelled their weapon at the beaten aeldari.

'Wait.' Sherax was locked in place, servos whining in complaint. 'A swift death is too merciful.'

She loomed over the alien, her shadow cast across his unseeing features.

'Were I able, I would exact the same punishment you brought upon us,' she told him. 'I would raze your world of Biel-tan to ashes. I would irradiate your fields and slay your serfs. I would tear down every monument your species ever placed in the sky. And even then, it would not be enough.'

Idranvel's bloody lips curled in animal hatred.

'Instead, I must be content that you will die knowing that your quest was in vain. That you came so close to all you desire, yet your actions have caused its destruction.'

Finally, true horror penetrated the warrior's stoicism. 'No.'

'Yes, aeldari. You shall die, and this place will die with you.'

'No!' The xenos lapsed into his own heathen tongue, no doubt desperate pleas or impotent threats.

Lyterix stepped closer. <Sherax, you cannot be serious.>

<I am.>

<You mourn your protector's loss, and feel the power of the alien's mockery. I understand. But if it is revenge you seek, what could be more sublime than to take this power for ourselves?>

Sherax lifted her axe from Idranvel's throat, her true threat delivered. <Yuel was right, magos. We do not need this place and its unnatural power. It would pervert us. No facet of this vessel shall return to the *Peregrinus*.>

Successive waves of emotion boiled in Lyterix's aura, changing so quickly that Sherax could barely keep up. <We have come this far, and now you falter,> the augur said.

<It is alien, magos. Look around you. Nothing built on such foundations can stand.>

<It is everything you have pursued. Every grand vision you have imagined. The restoration of the home world. We cannot survive without this power.>

<I was wrong.> Sherax seemed to grow in certainty with every moment that passed. <Either we endure and rebuild as ourselves, as servants of the Omnissiah and true to His law, or we fade away. Another empire to fail in the face of a hostile galaxy.>

<You make this choice for every soul in the Imperium.> Lyterix's vehemence grew in turn, his aura shifting from outrage to fury.

Sherax matched his choler. <And you would corrupt the species itself.>

<Do you think the dead care about purity? Do the living, and those who might live? You cannot turn away now!>

<We must.>

Lyterix raised his phosphor pistol. <You have faltered at the last, explorator.>

NINE

Rahn-Bo froze as Lyterix raised his weapon towards her ductrix. Unregarded between them, Idranvel continued to plead in his barbaric attempt at the Imperial tongue.

<You are so invested in your status as martyr, you are blind to the truth,> spat Lyterix. <It is I, not you, who has driven us ever onward. I lifted you from the dirt of Ikaneos. I led us through the wastes. It was I who kept you true to our course.>

<Magos, lower your weapon,> Rahn-Bo sent as an attempt to intercede. Her own emotions, usually restrained beneath layers of logic and savantic abstraction, were as wildly fluctuating as Lyterix's. Sherax's decision had released a burst of relief so intense that it had reduced Rahn-Bo's higher functions to error codes. Yet fierce resentment burned within that relief, a deep-seated anger that it had taken so much loss, so much sacrifice, for Sherax to see the wisdom the datamancer had counselled for weeks. Nothing less than coming to the precipice of heresy had been sufficient for the explorator, her oldest peer and companion.

<Look around you, Lyterix,> sent Sherax, who had not moved. Neither she nor the augur had acknowledged Rahn-Bo. <Is this the image in which you would rebuild the home world?>

<Power is power, Sherax. Taming it would no more corrupt us than does harnessing the Motive Force.>

<Your logic is flawed. The Motive Force is an aspect of the Omnissiah. This> – Sherax gestured with her axe at the alien domain around them – <this would make monsters of us all.>

Lyterix lifted his head with a deeply human flourish. <If that is what it takes to save our people, I accept it gladly.>

<But I do not,> sent Thess Rahn-Bo. For all the conflict within her, she knew that Lyterix would not be moved from the rightness of his stance. She lifted her laspistol and fired.

Her las-bolt struck Lyterix's phosphor pistol, and the charge pack burst into flames. Lyterix's hand was instantly engulfed in a pillar of incandescent, unquenchable fire.

Sherax's axe whirled in a golden arc, and struck the augur in the centre of his chest. Lyterix fell to the crystal floor in a heap of augmetic limbs.

The explorator watched Lyterix's burning body for some time, then wrenched the cog-blade free.

'I have failed you,' Sherax said to the soldiers around her, but her mind was turned towards Rahn-Bo. 'You followed me when no others would. But I was wrong. I led you from the tenets of our order in pursuit of hope, of strength. Yet I was ignorant of the strength we still have.'

None of her expedition responded. There was nothing to be said. They had come by her order, and now that her will had changed, they would follow her on its new course.

'We will leave this place and render it to ash,' Sherax went on. 'If we return to the surface now, it may yet be possible for the *Peregrinus* to retrieve us.'

One of the Vostroyans nodded. His face was plastered with sweat and blood. 'As you say, explorator.' The troopers hefted their depleted weapons and headed back towards the passage that had brought them to the chamber. Sherax's remaining skitarii, as impassive as ever, set off at their usual insensate pace, leaving Rahn-Bo and the explorator together.

Lyterix was still alive. The wound in his torso was grievous, but pain and outrage flooded the noosphere. Beside him, within reach of the augur's immolated hand, was Idranvel.

<What about them?> Rahn-Bo asked.

Sherax looked down at them both. <Let this place they coveted be their tomb.>

They left Lyterix and Idranvel together, one blind, the other broken. Both railed at Sherax as she and the last of her followers limped away.

'You cannot destroy Genesis!'

<You have betrayed us all!>

The expedition climbed, following the path that had led them down. They ran in silence, at as quick a pace as they could manage. Every one was damaged or wounded in some way, and yet the remaining Vostroyans carried the body of Major Zlata with them. Edgar, the fallen knight, led them, bearing both his laslock and the commander's.

The metallic xenos had vanished, leaving no trace at all of their presence within the vessel. Rahn-Bo had no cognitive power left to devote to that mystery, and instead simply gave thanks that they had not turned against the expedition.

As they emerged into the clearing from which they had first descended, a single snippet of code slipped across the communion.

<Sherax?>

The return of contact with the *Peregrinus* was a balm upon Rahn-Bo's soul.

The explorator's response was immediate. <Kill this craft, lord. It cannot be allowed to endure.>

If Yuel was surprised by Sherax's new position, it did not carry across their connection. <We are in no position to destroy anything, Talin, let alone a construct of such mass.>

Sherax did not hesitate. <I know what can be done.> She dumped a short string of instructions into the noosphere.

Yuel digested her plan. <A grave solution, Talin, but effective. Transmit your location, we are reaching the limit of teleportation capability.>

Rahn-Bo sensed it. Sherax's final moment of egotism. For a fraction of a second, the explorator considered letting the *Peregrinus* fly on without them. The shame that engulfed her led her to contemplate the oblivious peace found in death.

With an immense effort, the datamancer put aside her anger. <We should go home, Talin.>

Sherax hesitated, then pulsed a soft acknowledgement. Her claw found a depression in the axe's stave, and a lumen at its head winked into life.

<Stand by for translocation,> Yuel sent.

Rahn-Bo, Edgar, and those few skitarii and Vostroyan Blackbloods who had not given their lives crowded about their tormentor. The teleportation beacon hummed with the promise of salvation.

In the final moment before rays of arcane energy claimed her, Rahn-Bo felt the last, faintest touch of Lyterix's mind, still railing at Sherax's perfidy, and her betrayal.

TEN

The glow of teleportation had not faded before Sherax sent her order.

<Now, lord.>

Magister Akoni had been primed by Yuel. The ship's reactor-heart had been strained to its limits to keep itself ahead of its pursuers, and then it had been forced to prime the warp engines. If the *Peregrinus* survived Sherax's desperate manoeuvre, it would face a slow, limping journey back to Tolkhan.

Translation control had been removed from the Navigator's chambers. In the time that Sherax had led her futile expedition to the Genesis vessel, Kian had been roused from his sedation, confronted with his deeds, and found to be sane enough for remorse. Now, with a pair of praetorians stationed within the Navigator's sanctum and his limbs bound to his controls, he would guide the ship back into the warp, and pray that penance could erase his shame.

<Now, lord.>

<Brace for translation.> The command was passed to a bone-weary crew, too exhausted to question what new trial was about to beset them.

The mechanisms by which vessels passed into the warp were the guarded secrets of their keepers, but the hazards of their use were known to every void-craft captain in the Imperium. Chief among them was the act of entering the immaterium within a gravity well, which would invariably unleash untold ruination.

As space around the *Peregrinus* was rent apart, and the explorator ship made its escape from the unnamed system, the warp rift grew. A cavity in reality, thousands of miles across, roared its might across the soundless depths of vacuum and crashed against the Genesis vessel's hull.

Within its chambers and gardens, empyric phenomena melted into existence, enraged and elated to be within a dimension that despised them. Their reign was short-lived, as arcane lightning sundered the ancient wraithbone. The energies that sustained the verdant life across the planet beneath it comingled with that of the warp, birthing horrors that bent and buckled reality with the strength of their atrocity.

Broken beyond recovery, the Genesis vessel began to slowly fall towards the half-made world.

THE VOID

The command deck's chapel sings, even though my ship is fractured near to ruin. Despite all that the Peregrinus *has endured, despite the hubris and heresy of its ductrix, its engines are still lit. Its reactor still beats. Its servants still labour.*

I listen to the hymn of fabrication, standing at the chapel's centre. I will not undertake any performative supplication. I know of humbled tech-priests who seek repentance through the electro-scourge, who perform penance through the repeated ruination and repair of their physical forms. Others set themselves herculean tasks of creation or achievement, breaking themselves upon the anvil of action in order to escape their shame.

I have no need of such primitive excoriation, nor will I attempt futile expiation. I carry my torment in my mind.

I stand before the icon of my god, unworthy of the Omnissiah's gaze. The magnitude of my failings is immense. I have forsaken every bond of allegiance. I pursued xenos technology, fully aware of its nature. I succumbed to hubris, believing that I alone had the will and ability to save my people. That I knew better than the greatest minds that remain to us.

It is not merely my own remorse I live with; always, the condemnation of my companions is with me.

I have remained a part of the communion. This is my penance. I am laid bare before my peers; I cannot conceal my shame, nor they their judgement. Rahn-Bo is conflicted, torn between sympathy and revulsion. Luren's contempt is a vigilant blade, ever ready to remind me of how close I came to apostasy. He is my confessor, and a fierce and zealous chastener he will be in the years to come.

Yet despite all that I have done, despite the catastrophe I almost brought about, I have found clarity. Perhaps it is because I came so close to dooming myself that I have gained this new-found awareness.

The salvation of my people will not arrive in the form of long-lost archeotech. It will not come through the rediscovery of mythic devices and miraculous forces. Such things exist – it would be absurd to deny it, since by my hand one of the wonders of the universe was destroyed – but they will not save us. They will not restore what was truly lost when the leviathan consumed our world.

We must rediscover our purpose. The dispossessed of Gryphonne IV must reforge our sense of self, our will to achieve, and strike back against encroaching anarchy. We must shed our torpor and rise once more as the bastion of the Omnissiah against a spiteful galaxy, full of horrors and temptations.

My new certainty may be hubris, just as before. Another manifestation of my need to act in order to reckon with the ever-deepening crisis that grips humanity's empires. Surely it is folly to believe that a lone individual, no matter how driven, can save a species.

Nevertheless, I know this to be true. At our centre, we who worship the Omnissiah are not explorers, nor scientists, priests, archivists or warriors.

We are builders.

We can rebuild.

ABOUT THE AUTHOR

Jonathan D Beer is a science fiction and alternative history writer. Equally obsessed with the 19th century and the 41st millennium, he lives with his wife and assorted cats in the untamed wilderness of Edinburgh, Scotland. He is the author of the Warhammer 40,000 novel *Dominion Genesis,* and has also written the Warhammer Crime stories 'Old Instincts', 'Service' and 'Chains', as well as the novel *The King of the Spoil.*

YOUR NEXT READ

THE LION: SON OF THE FOREST
by Mike Brooks

The Lion. Son of the Emperor, brother of demigods and primarch of the Dark Angels. Awakened. Returned. And yet… lost.